# CHARLES H. LNUOO

was born in Sheffield and spent his early years without much direction. With a misspent youth playing video games and tabletop RPGs he somehow fell into a career as an Engineer. After a brief sojourn in Barnsley, Charles and wife Jo moved to a quiet village in Nottinghamshire. Here, they hope to turn their love of writing into a full-time career. The Butcher in the Night is Charles' second published novel and he hopes to release many more.

# ACKNOWLEDGMENTS

There are many people who have helped me with the process of writing this book, those that follow are key amongst them.

A massive thank you to my Beta readers: Newton Webb and Thea Marler for being endlessly encouraging, Anna Flack for being a font of knowledge, Lauren Henshaw for taking the time despite other commitments, and all the others for their valued contributions!

I also wanted to thank the members of my writers' group for helping me to hone my skills, and for keeping me motivated to write.

Finally, I'd like to thank Jo for her editing skills and endless patience.

*For Paula!*

*Hope you enjoy it!*

# THE BUTCHER IN THE NIGHT

*Charles Cross*

## CHARLES K. CROSS

www.charlesxcross.com

This paperback edition 2021

Copyright © Charles X. Cross 2021

A catalogue record of this book is available
from the British Library
ISBN: 978-1-8380101-2-6

The right of Charles X. Cross to be
identified as the Author of the Work has
been asserted in accordance with the
Copyright, Designs and Patents Act 1988

Printed and bound by Amazon KDP

For Tinker.

Who says you can't dedicate a book to
a cat?

Also by Charles X. Cross:

Crooked Empires: Vol. 1
The Man-Butcher Prize

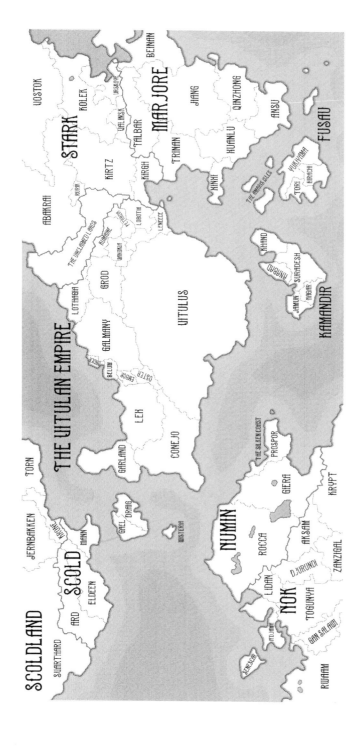

# THE STORY SO FAR

The **Butcher in the Night** is a direct sequel to **The Man-Butcher Prize** and it is **strongly** recommended that you have read the first book in the **William of Fairshore Trilogy** before proceeding.

For those who have read the first instalment in the series, I have included this refresher of the main events. Needless to say, the following contains **spoilers** for **The Man-Butcher Prize**.

As a child, William fell from a bridge and was lost at sea. He was pulled out of the water by a fishing boat. There, he met a slave with only half a head, who the slavers referred to as Lamebrain. Having been "rescued" and sold into slavery himself, William was subsequently rescued again by the renowned assassin, Ojo Azul.

Ojo wasn't particularly kind to William, and while he was still young, forced him to kill a child of a similar age. Then, when money became tight and Ojo could no longer support an apprentice, he abandoned William to compete in the Man-Butcher Prize. He subsequently won, gaining the funds to solve his problems, but before he could return for William, he was killed.

Stranded at an Assassins' Guild Outpost, William met Cathal, a kindly assassin with only one lung. Cathal taught him how to shoot. For a short time he was a good mentor for William, but died through a combination of injuries and advanced years. After Cathal's death, William set out on his own.

After a career of varying success, William was contracted by a woman known as The Daughter to kill a judge in Fairshore. Unfortunately, he made the very public mistake of killing the wrong man: Fairshore's mayor. As a result, he was blacklisted from the Guild. With nowhere else to turn, and knowing no other way of life, he decided to follow in Ojo's footsteps and enter the Man-Butcher Prize – his only chance for redemption.

Upon arriving in Blackbile, William met Goldin, a lovable rogue, and Dr Barber, a surgeon who claimed to be able to bring the dead back to life. While travelling through the streets, William learned that Ojo was still alive and was competing again in this year's Prize. He also learned that each entrant in the Man-Butcher Prize required a sponsor – someone who would stake their life for him and work as his partner.

After attempting to ally with a cult known as the Sacrificial Lambs, William decided instead to take Vesta, a young woman dead set on revenge, as his sponsor. She agreed to join him if he helped her to kill the leader of the cult – her brother. William also learned that the slave known as Lamebrain, was being a rival assassin's sponsor.

When the fighting began, William and Vesta were chased by her brother's cult into a clock tower. Lamebrain and Dr Barber were holed up in there, along with Lord Beechworth and his sponsor – his grandmother.

Lord Beechworth was a former winner of the original Man-Butcher Prize. He bested the Prize's inventor, Terrowin the Man-Butcher, but his victory was achieved with underhanded tactics.

In an assault by the Sacrificial Lambs on the clock tower, William made a rolling bomb out of Beechworth's grandmother, a crate of brass bullets, and Dr Barber's wheelchair. In doing this, he managed to fight off the cult, but Lord Beechworth felt betrayed by the sacrifice of his grandmother. It didn't matter to him that she had been willing to martyr herself for the safety of the others.

Beechworth turned on William, and just as he was about to kill him, Lamebrain revealed himself to be the half-failed reanimation of Terrowin the Man-Butcher. He recognised Beechworth in a moment of clarity and fought with him before dragging him over the edge of the tower steps. They both fell to their deaths.

With Beechworth defeated and the Sacrificial Lambs decimated, William went on to confront and kill Ojo, his mentor.

While fighting Vesta's brother, the leader of the Lambs, Vesta was shot from behind by the callous assassin, Genevieve Cholmondeley. While Vesta lay dying, her brother rushed to her and she managed to kill him before her last breath.

Devastated by Vesta's death, William took revenge upon Genevieve and killed her. As the last assassin left standing, he won the Prize. His moment of glory was short lived, however, as Genevieve's sponsor, presumed dead after a building had collapsed on him, was found barely alive. William had unwittingly broken the rules, and was subsequently disqualified. Genevieve's sponsor – her son, William Cholmondeley – was made the new man-butcher by default.

William was disgraced, alone again, until Goldin sought him out in search of a travelling companion.

Before leaving the town, the pair were approached for a contract by a crooked old man and a bug-eyed boy. Having had his fill of mayhem and death, William turned the job down. Together, he and Goldin decided instead upon a nice holiday, and to put the sorry events of the Prize behind them.

William was happy to finally have a friend and ally.

# PROLOGUE

## 1682
## WALTER PERRIN

A bullet skewered the crooked face of a pumpkin. Seeds and stringy membrane were ejected, patterning muddy ground that was more accustomed to blood and viscera. The scarecrow-target slumped from the force and a kid-skin glove fell from the broom handle that served as outstretched arms.

'Excellent shot.' Mayor Perrin champed around a wad of steak pie. 'Do another one.'

'Another one?' William Cholmondeley screwed his narrow face into a petulant scowl.

'Yes, another one.' The mayor affected a stern tone, pushed his shoulders back, and frowned reproachfully at his new ward's questioning. 'Practice, practice, practice. I can't have my man-butcher missing a shot now, can I?'

William blew air through pursed lips, rolled his eyes overtly, and broke the rifle. Even the simple task of reloading another brass-clad bullet was slapdash and arrogant.

Walter's tongue worked inside his mouth, seeking the last vestiges of pie; he swallowed. He hadn't married because he had never desired children, preferring instead the simple pleasure of a mistress or two, but he had ended up with this foul boy nonetheless.

Unruly, argumentative, simultaneously lazy and restless, the boy was impossible! As far as Walter was concerned, once William Cholmondeley was competent enough to contract, he would be out there working. The sooner he was earning coin and keeping his sullen outlook away from the mayoral chambers, the better.

The boy scalped another scarecrow, orange chunks scattering over the square. A whole line of beheaded targets had been hemmed in by repurposed velvet ropes to stop the townsfolk interfering, and a few guild clerks walked the perimeter. One man held up a red flag to indicate the training ground was being reset, and four more clerks hurried to replace the ruined gourds.

Glad for the brief pause, Walter left his post at the window in favour of his desk, where the remains of the steak pie still steamed from atop a stack of ledgers. It would have been preferable to sit and enjoy his lunch, but alas, the man-butcher had commandeered his red leather chair. It had been dragged to the window and the boy was knelt on it to more comfortably shoot into the square. Worse, the sight of the paperwork made his stomach gurgle. He was so far behind with his clerical duties, he wasn't even sure if the Guild was in the red or black, all because of his duty of care to a man-butcher too young to murder alone. He calmed his rumbling guts with gravy-sodden beef and pastry.

'Do you think I'm as good as Lord Beechworth?' The young man-butcher reloaded, a breeze ruffling messy brown hair and dusting ash flakes over his tweed trousers. There was a scab still healing on his cheek and a red scar marred his weak chin. Without the bandages that had wrapped his head and torso for weeks, or the splint that had fused his leg, he looked scrawny with too-large ears and knobbly knees.

Walter chewed for a moment as he thought on his answer. At first, he had been determined to be endlessly encouraging with the boy, as his own mentor had been with him. He would have been an even tempered tutor and a role model worthy of respect, but the sod's cheek had fixed him in a sour mood. Besides, if he was truthful, it was only a technicality that had seen the boy win the Prize anyway. Walter swallowed his mouthful and simply said, 'No.'

William was visibly disappointed, perhaps even upset by the pointed retort; an encouraging sight for a weary mayor at the end of his wits. He decided to twist the barb a little. 'Claude was an artist with a rifle. A man of good Garlish stock, trained by the best. You're just a boy, and though you have a fancy title, you still need to earn the reputation that comes with it.'

William scoffed and aimed out of the window. His rifle clapped and clicked rapidly, targets splattering in quick succession. The final shot was punctuated by an anguished scream that was loud even at the elevation of the office window.

'Oh dear.' William looked over his shoulder with a pantomime approximation of remorse. 'It seems you're right, Walter. I'm no Beechworth, just a boy making silly mistakes. Still, there's plenty more where he came from.'

Walter spat pastry flakes over his unfinished paperwork, marking them with grease and gravy. He could feel his face flushing red. Not for the needless loss of life, he had gotten used to that shortly after Terrowin had been and gone. It was the increased cost that irked him, hazard pay that would be demanded by his clerks for the danger of the prepubescent killer the Guild had lumbered itself with.

Gods, did he wish he had stuck with his gut feeling and kept his first winning William. Had it not been for the shock of losing Beechworth, Walter was certain he would have stood his ground against the committee and had the injured little darling put back under the rubble where he'd been found. Things would have been so much easier for everyone if the new man-butcher had been William *of Fairshore* rather than William *Cholmondeley*.

'You can't just kill my men.' Walter pounded his fist on the table, appalled by the ungrateful wretch. Strings of over-done ox ground between clenched teeth. 'I know you do it on purpose, and I know you're angry about your mother, but my clerks had nothing to do with her demise. I let your indiscriminate shots slide before, but this guild is built on rules.'

Young William's eyes drifted away in an infuriating show of indifference.

'Listen to me, you…' Walter trailed off, realising that his churlish butcher was, in fact, focused on something or someone behind him. He rounded to find the cause of the boy's distraction.

'Forgive me for interrupting.' Klava Ilyina had entered silently and was pouring herself a generous helping of the mayor's finest whiskey from the bookshelf bar.

A lean woman of sharp angles and savage cheekbones, she wore her habitual charcoal dress and her hair scraped into a severe bun, wrapped in linen. It was a combination often sported at Stark burial ceremonies. Today however, she had a small gold band on her little finger, adorned with a pin-prick of glittering ruby. It was an extravagant decoration on a woman whose entire being tended for dreariness; she was surely here to impress.

'We were just training, weren't we?' Walter replied brightly, a smile pulling his fleshy cheeks too wide. He tugged his jacket closed around his girth, trying to fasten the single button over the gravy spots on his shirt, but somewhere in the last few weeks he'd lost some inches of fabric. Or gained some inches of flesh, he reasoned; perfectly understandable with the pressures he had been under of late. He would ask his assistant to have a discreet word with the tailor.

The young man-butcher only grunted, which Walter was grateful for.

'You can go,' he instructed the boy. 'It seems Klava and I need to talk.'

William rolled his eyes and shouldered his rifle. He didn't bother with any goodbyes or even acknowledge the committee member before leaving, which she seemed to appreciate. Walter wasn't the only one in the Guild with a distaste for children.

'Would you like one?' Klava held up a pair of filled glasses and took the lightest sip from one. Her ring winked in the bleak daylight.

Walter could just imagine the sensation of the warming liquor washing over his tongue and wanted nothing more than to accept, but he had learned not to take offerings of food or drink from the Guild's chief poisoner. Untimely bouts of sickness and diarrhoea could not always be traced to a morsel of undercooked chicken or souring milk.

'No, thank you. I had a little snifter with my luncheon, if I have any more I might not be fit to tackle these papers.' He slapped a tower of parchments, generating a dusty thud.

Klava sashayed around an antique globe, deposited one of the crystal tumblers on his desk, and claimed his expansive leather chair. She crossed one leg over the other and rested a slender hand on her knee. 'I will be curt.'

'Excellent.' Walter took the far smaller and less comfortable chair that he usually reserved for visitors. He didn't want to appear perturbed by the attempt to subvert the dynamic between them, but he most certainly was.

'We on the committee know you're struggling without Lord Beechworth: falling behind with your duties, failing to capitalise on our new man-butcher. Do you have any idea how many high-paying contracts we have sat gathering dust? Everyone wants the man-butcher, and you have him cooped up in here.'

Klava's dark eyes flicked to the glass she had set down for the mayor. She wasn't going to let him forget it.

'I can't likely let him loose now, can I? What if he dies? We'll lose our best asset. I thought we'd agreed this last month.' Walter moved a hand to stroke the stubble burgeoning on his chin and found he was now sporting the beginnings of a beard. Looking after the boy had taken too much of his time; even his grooming regimens had suffered.

'I know you're a busy man, but you know what a fickle bunch the committee can be. I've even heard whispers of dissent.' Klava's thin lips curled to a sly smile as she took another sip. 'There are many who think you're weak, unable to lead without your noble prop.'

She set down her liquor and reached for a document. As her hand passed over Walter's unfinished lunch to pick up a ledger, his stomach knotted. He could envision some unseen powder tipping from her palm to dust his roasted vegetables.

Perhaps, for once, a committee member had been straight with him. They may have decided him a poor figurehead without the strength of Beechworth at his side, and she had come here to finish him and take his position of prominence. Even if it wasn't her plan, now the thought had been seeded, he couldn't be confident in the loyalty of a single assassin. He reached for liquor as an instinct, but remembered not to drink and simply cradled the glass in thick fingers.

'I want to help you,' Klava continued, 'and as your new right hand woman, we could form a mutually beneficial alliance. What do you think?'

She smiled – the first broad and full smile that Walter had ever seen on her. It was a crooked expression that exposed one pointed canine and looked entirely unnatural on her usually placid features. 'There is no need for us to be enemies, is there?'

'No, of course not.' Walter shuffled on his seat and fussed with his necktie. While an ally was exactly what he needed, he didn't want to risk offending anyone on the committee by playing favourites. That was a jar of worms that was better left closed, and he wasn't entirely convinced that she wouldn't kill him anyway. 'I appreciate the offer, I really do.'

'We should drink to it then.' She raised her glass. 'To a deal well done.'

'I'm really not that thirsty.' He looked down at the pool of brown glossy liquid. The surface was quivering ever so slightly in his grip.

'Oh, come now, Walter. You don't think I would poison you?' She shook her raised glass with some immediacy, sloshing a single drop onto the desk. 'We should drink… to our continued friendship. We can discuss this alliance later.'

Walter grimaced. Calling out the tension between them was a dirty trick. They both knew as well as each other that she was incredibly likely to poison him, but now his choice was clear. Drink and possibly die, or decline and offend, which would most certainly increase the chance of a more subtle poisoning in the future.

'Cheers.' He toasted the glass and quickly knocked back the drink. He couldn't be sure if there was a spike of sour venom as, to him, it tasted like instant regret. He slammed the glass down and stood in a hurry, feeling anxiety churning with the liquor in his gut.

'Well… Klava, I'm glad you came to see me,' he spluttered out, 'but I really am a very busy man. I–'

Klava stood as if he had instructed her to go.

'No, please, sit and finish your drink.' He made a move for the door, his mind already racing over the foul concoction she could have slipped into his drink. He could have hours or minutes to live, or perhaps merely an embarrassing bout of sickness, or even nothing at all. He couldn't be sure, but he couldn't take a chance. 'Make yourself comfortable, but... I... have to go. Business needs and all that.'

He strode from his office and made his way down the hall. He could feel sweat beading on his forehead, and his heart was pounding in his ears. Claude would have told him it was a symptom of his anxieties, but in his nervous state it was further evidence of foul play. His shoes buffeted on a fine Kamandi rug as he quickened his pace, and when he reached the stairs to the foyer he was practically running.

'Send for a coach,' he called to his blousy assistant behind the reception desk. 'I'm headed to Barber's down the Eastway, I've no time to wait. The horseman can find me on route.'

'Yes, Mr Perrin,' she called after him as he burst out of the town hall. He squinted against the sun through the haze of light cloud and almost crashed headlong into Tobias Lietner, the guild's weaponsmith and inventor.

'Walter, you need to be careful.' Tobias appraised him through half-moon, wire-frame glasses perched on the end of a port-hued nose. He clapped him about both shoulders amiably with the strong hands of a smith. 'Gods, you look just like Prior! I dare say that prickle on your chin suits you, are you growing it out?'

'No, just haven't gotten around to shaving these past few days...' Walter lingered on the memory of his father, the great Prior Perrin. He suspected he did look a little like him, though with a touch darker hair and far lengthier belt. He dismissed the thought, returning to the worry of his potential poisoning. Only then did he realise it was poor form to offend another committee member. Hurriedly, he added, 'Thank you, Tobias. I'd love to stay and talk, but I have pressing business.'

He tried to pull out of the weaponsmith's grip, but wasn't released so easily.

'Ah, business. We're all too busy these days, aren't we?' The weaponsmith's eyes crinkled into merry crescents, and with a final bruising pat, he freed Walter. 'Before you go, speaking of business, I have a few new weapons to show you. A personal demonstration would be superb.'

Walter swallowed. It was possible that Tobias was amongst the assassins spreading dissent. He dreaded to think of what a personal weapons demonstration might entail.

Behind the weaponsmith, desperate doctors were failing to save the clerk in the paddock of scarecrow-targets. Their proximity would be a blessing if he had ingested anything other than Klava's toxin, but only Barber would have the antidotes he needed.

'I'd love a demonstration. I'm just a little busy at the moment. Ah, look.' Walter felt an immense sense of relief at the sight of his carriage rolling into the square, although he had hoped to be a quarter of the way to Barber's by now. His stomach gurgled ominously at the prospect of his own impending doom. 'My coach is here. Pop in to see my assistant, she'll set up a meeting.'

He dashed for the carriage, feeling his pie and gravy straining against his waistband. There was another bout of indigestion coming on, or perhaps a heart flutter, it was hard to know what one's body was doing for certain in the midst of a panic. He thundered to the carriage, ripped the door open so that the whorled silver handle clattered against black lacquered woodwork, and lumbered inside. The sprung iron squealed under the sudden addition of his weight and sagged as he leant out and thumped the side of the cab.

'Get to Barber's compound. I need to be there five minutes ago!' He slumped back inside, his breath heavy and wet; phlegm caught in his gullet. As the carriage surged into motion, he briefly met the gaze of the confused weaponsmith, still watching from the town hall steps. Then he was away down the street.

# PART 5

## 1683
## WILLIAM OF FAIRSHORE

Goldin wrestled with the map, bunching it into a great crumpled ball. At its fullest extent, it stretched to easily one and a half times his arm span, which was only half the problem. He scowled and grumbled, turning it this way and that as he sucked thoughtfully on his cleft lip. The single protruding tooth poked upwards through the gap in his flesh.

'I think you've got it the wrong way up,' William mentioned in a wry attempt to stoke the fire of Goldin's frustration. He hadn't been paying attention enough to know whether the map was right side up or not, but his companion's distress was the best source of amusement for miles. 'Are you sure you don't want me to read it?'

'Look, I might not be the best reader, but I am a damned good navigator. I know where we're going. Well, I don't know where we're *going, going,* but I know what direction we're headed.'

'That's a relief.' William smirked, not entirely believing the little man, and not all that worried about their destination either. After the shambles of the Man-Butcher Prize and being stripped of his title, William was glad of the simple joy of travelling with a friend. He didn't mind that they had been stood in the middle of a dusty road for at least half an hour; idyllic farmland and lush coppices of merrily tweeting birds stretched as far as the eye could see.

'We're here.' Goldin jabbed the map with a stubby finger. 'Not too far from the border – that's that dotted line – and in a few days we should arrive in… um. Well, from the shape, it looks like the place is called Darrow.'

The little man looked up at William for confirmation. His eyes squinted against the sun, high in the cloudless sky.

'It's D'Arnao, but you were close. Did you really think there'd be a Darrow in Vitulus?'

'I got the gist of it.' Goldin withdrew the map and peered closely at the dots and squiggles. 'To *Darno* then… I just need to figure out the exact route. Shall I navigate us by a few taverns on the way?'

William nodded silently and licked his lips. Pleasant as the current vista was, it had been a long time since they'd had a proper meal. While they were both consummate hunters of men, rabbits and sparrows proved to be far more elusive.

Shortly after leaving Blackbile, William had stolen a horse and put plenty of miles between the Assassins' Guild and himself. Goldin had grumbled the whole way, unable to overcome his distaste for horses, and finally convinced William to sell "the beast" after three days. It meant William had a bulging coin purse; it also made the journey considerably slower. Granted, his coins were copper and not gold, but they would buy a hearty meal or two and enough ale to negate the necessity for a good bed. All they needed to do was find the next roadhouse, which required Goldin's map reading to prove competent.

'I've been thinking…' William began.

'That's dangerous, but go on,' Goldin replied, frowning at a compass.

'I'm not so sure about, well, anything, and… I don't think I want to be an assassin anymore.' William set his gaze on Goldin, expecting some over the top reaction, but the little man kept himself to his map. He was either not listening or refusing to countenance such a silly notion. William decided to clarify. 'I don't want to be a farm hand or anything like that. Maybe I could be a thief. It might mean less killing.'

'Really?' Goldin grimaced. 'A thief?'

'Yes, a thief.' William stretched his back, fidgeting under his companion's scrutiny. 'I can't see myself working for a living, so it's the next best thing. I don't want to keep killing all the time.'

'A thief...' Goldin worried his protruding tooth while he cogitated. 'But you're a really good killer; it seems daft to throw it all away. You were trained by the great Ojo Azul, a man-butcher! And you're nigh on a man-butcher yourself.'

'Throwing all what away? I have nothing, everyone hates me, and I'm a well renowned liar *and* a cheat, *apparently.*' He counted off the points on his fingers. 'Yes, I'm a good killer, but I don't really want to be, and I'm *not* a man-butcher. Ojo wasn't that great, anyway. He was... never mind.'

'We'll see what happens in *Darno.*' Goldin shrugged. 'There might be some good contracts there, something to get you back into the swing of things. And you're not half as disgraced as you think; that lanky creep and his mad-eyed son wanted to hire you, didn't they?'

William considered the spindly man who had propositioned him after the Prize was done. He hadn't had the stomach for hearing the details of a contract after so much loss and death. Since then, his enthusiasm lessened dramatically. He grimaced at the thought of returning to that hollow lifestyle.

'Why don't we focus on this holiday first?' Goldin changed the course of the conversation, still sceptical of the career change. 'I can ask in *Darno* about that beach.'

The little man had set their destination on day one: some resort on the southern coast of Vitulus which he couldn't quite remember the name of. He did know the region had the best vineyards and classiest whores. He had called them *mignotta,* women who needed paying twice before the deed could be done, once in gold and second with an evening at one of the regions finest eateries or prestigious play houses.

William wasn't particularly interested in whoring, but high class prostitutes meant wealthy clientele, and the contents of their pockets was something he found himself thinking about more and more. The Man-Butcher Prize had really dampened his enthusiasm for killing, and while he knew he would never give up his flintlock, thieving seemed an obvious career move. He would have to shoot or stab the odd person if he was caught in the act, but it was survival, not death as a transaction.

He decided not to mention his plans to Goldin again.

A woodpecker landed in a tree that split the roadway and started to tap at a half-formed hollow. From the rusted nails that protruded from the bark, it seemed there had once been a sign affixed there, a sign that might have saved Goldin the agonising map study. William wondered whether the bird had pecked the sign from the tree to get to fresher wood, or whether the worms or mites the bird sought had originated from the sign. Either way, there was no trace of a board with any directions now.

'A-ha!' Goldin snapped his fingers and tossed the map aside with a flamboyant sweep. In one awkward motion he whipped around in a full circle, chasing the blunderbuss tied to his backpack with string. Pots and pans, that were similarly affixed, clanked and clicked. When he eventually caught the firearm, he spun about, planted his feet, and raised it at the woodpecker with a sneer. 'Hand me your silver!'

He looked across at William with a cocked eyebrow, still keeping his blunderbuss trained on the woodpecker. 'Is that right?'

'I think it's: *stand and deliver.*' William blinked.

'Ah, right.' The little assassin shuffled his feet in the dirt, let go of his blunderbuss so that it swung merrily behind his back, and retrieved the road-dusted map. 'Stand *and* deliver? They're a funny sort them thieving types, eh? Reckon I'd make a good one. We could be a pair of highwaymen gents.'

'Can't say I picture you being very gentlemanly, but a partner in crime is appreciated.'

'Here we are!' Goldin exclaimed as he straightened out the map, ripping it slightly down one of its many creases. He pointed down the first of the two paths. It appeared to William to curl to the left so far that it might turn them back towards Blackbile. 'All we have to do is follow this road for… hmm… give me a moment.'

The little man turned the map over in search of the scale.

William pulled his pistol from his belt and took his turn aiming at the bird. If he shot it, they could eat tonight, even if they didn't make it to another tavern, which with Goldin's map reading skills was looking more likely by the second. He checked the cartridges in his pocket: only five spares left. Perhaps it was better to keep hold of them for now. A gentleman thief needed protection as much as an assassin did, and he could put the shot to better use if he came across any affluent travellers.

He pondered for a moment on what his new name might be in the tabloids if he became a renowned highwayman. Whatever it was it would surely be better than the Masquerade Killer, not that it had a bad ring to it, just a bad connotation.

'Ah…' Goldin nodded and winked as if he had finally achieved orienteering enlightenment. 'It's that way.'

He pointed to the road that forked on the opposite side of the tree. This one, William could agree, looked far more promising. It dipped into a valley, wound through a stand of trees, and continued over a grassy hill at the far side. From the position of the sun and time of day, this road seemed to be heading south, towards warmer climes, which was exactly where they wanted to go. William had settled on this option himself as soon as they had come to a standstill, but Goldin was the navigator.

The way William saw it, if they kept heading roughly south, they would reach the coast eventually. If they couldn't find the resort Goldin was looking for there would be plenty of others, which was lucky because the little man couldn't remember anything about the resort other than wine, women, and white sands. The name of the beach was a blank, local landmarks long forgotten. Even after looking at the map, the name of the region couldn't be remembered. Goldin blamed the forgetfulness on his age, but William suspected the lapse to be the result of whatever drugs and alcohol had been imbibed on the little man's last visit.

'Come on then, time's wasting.' Goldin screwed the map into a ball too large to fit into the rucksack pocket it inhabited previously. A few failed attempts to cram it in frayed and ripped it a little more before it was stowed under a strap and fastened tight. 'The next tavern's only a few miles over that hill. We'll get there by nightfall, but we need to get a wriggle on.'

William set off at a brisk pace. The tavern was calling to him, and if the coppers in his money pouch got any hotter they might burn through his trousers.

The sun had set, and the last of the light was fading. Goldin had led them south, through the small wood and over the brow of the following hill, only to find a far larger and more foreboding forest. The way was barely wide enough to walk side by side and there would be no hope of carriages passing in opposing directions. It was clear that not many outside the Guild travelled this way. After all, it was one of many forgotten roads between the Empire's seat of power and the unclaimed lands.

The most common way in or out of Grod was usually through Galmany or Vanokia. The route Goldin had selected was far quicker, but more remote. After the next tavern, that he assured William would be coming into view at any moment, they would have to cross the border. That meant a stretch of three days on foot without any sign of civilisation.

'Not much longer now.' Goldin whistled heavy breath.

He was clearly struggling with the journey. Picking his legs over gnarled tree roots must have been all the more difficult given his stature, and his pack was almost twice as heavily stuffed as William's, though pride kept him from sharing the load. His baggage clattered as he rocked over the next root, and a few steps later he braced against his knees to catch his breath. As he leant forward, his blunderbuss swung around the side of his pack on loose strings and the stock cracked him in the ribs.

'Bloody thing!'

'Why don't we stop here?' William looked to the edge of the road. It appeared almost comfortable with the covering of loam and bracken. He'd certainly slept on worse, and the comfortable tavern bed would still be waiting for them tomorrow, though he wished he hadn't spared that woodpecker. His stomach was grumbling awfully and he had been hoping for roast boar and a flagon of ale. It would pain him to go foraging again. Goldin could only identify mushrooms with certain ill-effects and any other vegetation was a gamble.

'No, it's ok. Give me a minute and we'll carry on.' Goldin opened his water canteen and took a disappointing draught of air from it. 'Empty.'

'You're sure there's a tavern near here?' William peered down the darkened road. It was hard to see far as it undulated around jagged boulders and tightly huddled trees.

'Sure as I am handsome.' Goldin winked again, sealing his empty canteen. 'And I'm not roughing it. It's too late to hunt, and I've worked up a terrible thirst. Let's crack on, and I'm sure there'll be a big pot of stew waiting on the hearth when we get there.'

William gave the last of his water to Goldin and offered that they swap packs for the remainder of the journey. The little man accepted the water, but refused to give up even an iron pan. They set off, slower than before, but were determined to reach their destination before the full dark of night swallowed them. William wished they still had that horse, they would have been at the tavern a day ago. Slowing to keep pace with Goldin, he voiced his thoughts. 'If we find this tavern, what would you say to stealing another horse?'

'No bloody way.' Goldin shuddered. 'You know how I feel about those creatures. That last one kept flicking me with its tail, and did you see that thing between its legs? You probably didn't, but a man of my stature has to watch out for these things. If it had swiped me across the back of the head… It could knock me out just by turning around!'

The little man slapped the back of one hand into the palm of the other, producing a loud crack that startled a few birds to flight.

'What if we stole one with a cart?' William pushed, grimacing as he tramped through a sloshy puddle. 'I'd drive and you could just relax in the back, well away from the horse. I doubt any tavern goers would follow us, not across the border.'

'It does seem the sort of thing a pair of dandy robbers would do…' Goldin pondered, warming to the idea now that he'd had his fill of walking. 'I'll sleep on it.'

William imagined that, to Goldin, becoming a thief automatically made him some Conejan bandido-come-sex-god from a bawdy novel. He wasn't sure quite how the little man might have learned the contents of a book, but it was clear that Goldin fancied the idea of becoming a famous thief, loved and admired by all. He had plenty of fans already, but they were all the sort William would dismiss as creeps and weirdos: death-tourists obsessed with only the most gruesome kills. So it was surely a good thing Goldin was throwing himself so wholeheartedly in this new direction, even if it meant wearing a little black mask around his eyes and affecting the cadence of William's deceased mentor.

Night closed in rapidly, the overcast sky soon turning to the blackest pitch through the dense canopy. It didn't help that due to their poor travel preparations, and the subsequent excitement of fleeing with a stolen horse, they had only acquired the one lantern.

'You might just have to sleep on it here.' William stopped near a soft looking hummock beside granite boulders. He lifted the lamp, throwing ghastly shadows into the branches. They were alone. 'We can have another look at the map and find this tavern tomorrow.'

'Look!' Goldin squinted down the road. 'Is that light?'

William blinked. Now that his lantern was pointed away, he could make out something. A distant glow blushed the gathering night from far down the roadway.

'You shouldn't have doubted me.' Goldin chortled and trotted ahead, then without warning, set off at a brisk jog. 'I knew there was a tavern down this road!'

William pursued the little man, who was now thundering down the road with renewed vigour. Excitement spreading quickly, he called out, 'Get me a whiskey and orange.'

'Hurry up. You've got the money!'

William couldn't help but grin. He gained speed, stomping past Goldin. He could almost taste the sweet orange and feel the warmth of liquor in the back of his throat.

'Wait for me,' Goldin panted as William raced ahead.

It only spurred him on, and he doubled his efforts. Ideally, he would make it to the tavern so far ahead of Goldin that he would have ordered a drink and be reclined in a booth by the time he arrived. Then, he could say something sarcastic and terribly funny that would probably come to him in the moment.

A distant caw echoed through the woodland, but the jaunty see-saw was like no owl or nocturnal bird William had heard before. Over his heaving breaths he realised it was the sound of an accordion, bringing to mind a riotous party that would carry deep into the night. Hastening through a pair of shallow bends, he followed the beacon of tavern light. He could hear the patrons laughing and singing along to a bawdy drinking song. Then, he rounded the last corner.

What he found wasn't exactly what was expected, but it wasn't entirely unwanted either. A carriage – almost as wide as the roadway itself – had pulled to the edge on a heap of moss and underbrush. The passengers had taken up camp just a short way beyond, singing around a fire and toasting bread on sticks.

William's hand fell onto the handle of his flintlock. It was a natural precaution if the travellers were hostile, but they hadn't seen him yet and it was perhaps better to approach affably. These folks might just be the welcoming sort, and William would much rather join their cookout than die in a shootout at this hour.

He forced his hand off his flintlock and approached cautiously, studying the scene so he would be ready should things turn sour. The horses had been removed from the carriage and tied to a tree a short way into the forest; they whickered softly as he passed. It would be possible to steal them now, but far easier after the travellers were asleep, and Goldin wouldn't stand them without the carriage. If the travellers were friendly, he and Goldin would be invited to eat, drink, and rest. Then, they could alight with the carriage in the early hours.

'Hello there!' William waved his hand so the silhouettes at the campfire could spot him more easily in the gloom. The accordion stopped with an atonal honk.

He continued towards the camp. There were three people he could see, but possibly more in the trees. Logs had been arranged by the fire for seating and two remained empty. His instincts were telling him to return his hand to his pistol and ready himself for a fight, but those were the instincts of an assassin. There was no need to be so paranoid outside of guild circles. A thief had to remain calm in order to carry out their entirely more subtle plans.

'May I join you?' He gestured vaguely over the camp.

'No,' was the only reply. The man was a Gael from the sound of it, but his accent lacked any of the bouncing affability of William's old friend, Cathal. 'You'd do yourself a favour by heading back where you came from. We don't want no trouble, just our privacy.'

The man had a messily chopped bowl cut and from the glints across his pupils William could tell he was walleyed; a boon if things did devolve into a shootout. He set the accordion aside in an attempt to hide a small bottle of ether that William had already spotted. It was an expensive commodity that a thief might like to steal and sell, but also a potent drug that could be used to knock out a man in seconds. More often than not, however, it was peddled as a relaxant on the black markets, offering a fleeting high if huffed in the correct quantities.

'I don't mean to intrude...'

'Don't then.' Another of the three craned around. The voice was feminine, but husky from tobacco and hard liquor. She was thin and her back was hunched; each vertebrae poked out awkwardly giving her the silhouette of a southern marsh lizard. William thought he caught the gleam of black iron across her lap as she shifted, perhaps a rifle or scattergun.

Goldin was conspicuously absent. There was the chance he'd sensed danger early and taken an advantageous position, but it was equally likely he had tripped on a root and knocked himself senseless. Without him, William felt exposed under the travellers' scrutiny. The atmosphere was as sour as any he had tasted before and there were only two options: make his apologies and leave, or take the first shot. There was only one real choice.

'I think I'll be on my way.' William the Thief spoke before William the Assassin could act. He could backtrack to Goldin, then come back later and rob the carriage once the strange travellers had succumbed to their ether. 'Sorry for bothering you.'

'Wait,' someone called from behind William. For a moment he thought it might have been Goldin, the voice was gravelly enough, but the timbre was more akin to the slack-jaws around the fire. 'Turn around, let's get a look at you.'

William slowly pivoted, his fingers aching for his pistol, but he wouldn't snatch for it just yet.

'Doesn't look like much, does he?' The two doors on the rear of the carriage hung open and an old woman inside stooped over a twin-barrelled scattergun. A yellow horn lantern guttered, casting deep shadows in her weathered face. 'Don't look like no man-butcher to me.'

'He's the False Butcher, ma.' The woman by the fire hocked and spat. 'Liar and a cheat, I heard. Looks like just that type of worm to me.'

'False Butcher, eh? That makes more sense.' The old woman appraised him with a cocked eyebrow then lazily raised her aim. 'Off with you then. Carry on down that road and don't stop till you're over that border. We don't want to kill you if we don't have to.'

William was pleased that these travellers shared the same desire to keep the peace as he did, even if they weren't as accommodating as he'd hoped. He took the opportunity to mutter a quiet thank you and goodbye, and turned away. Before he had the chance to take a step, the sound of a branch snapping, or perhaps a weapon being cocked, echoed from the dark of the forest. As footsteps thumped closer between the trees, a pall of dread settled over William's shoulders.

'Stand and deliver!' Goldin roared, bursting into the light.

Gunpowder barked and smoke spewed from the mouth of his blunderbuss. The shot peppered the carriage and sent the old woman reeling over, her legs kicking into the air. Pain tensed her own trigger finger, punching two holes through the carriage roof. Splinters erupted into the night and suddenly everyone was in a flurry of desperate activity. The woman at the fireside grabbed her scattergun and the two men thrust to their feet. One had a pistol. The other wielded a whiskey bottle like a glowing club, backlit by the fire.

Goldin dove behind a tree root and began rapidly reloading his blunderbuss. It bore a similar mechanism to William's flintlock, hinging in the middle so that one might thumb another cartridge into the breech. He wouldn't be out of action for long, but if William didn't do something, one or both of them would surely be shot.

He snatched the flintlock from his belt and levelled it at the pistol-toting traveller. Before he could pull the trigger, the traveller fired at Goldin. There was an echoing ping as the bullet ricocheted off a pan on the little man's backpack and was sent crackling away through the trees. William shifted his aim to the woman with the scattergun, who was now the biggest threat, and fired as she pivoted to face him. Her body jolted from the hit, and like the old woman, the shock squeezed a shot from her firearm. The scattering pellets knocked off the head of the whiskey wielder and sent his body into spasms.

The last of the travellers – the one with two wild eyes and an empty flintlock – dropped a cartridge in a failed attempt to reload.

'Drop it.' Goldin staggered upright, shedding leaf litter, and readied his blunderbuss. 'Your money or your life.'

'Fuck you! You killed my sister.' The traveller pulled another cartridge from his pocket and attempted to charge his pistol. He didn't make much progress as a blast from Goldin's blunderbuss knocked him off his feet and onto the campfire. His screams could probably be heard from a mile away, but they were short-lived. An evening spent huffing ether – one of the most volatile substances in the known world – had made his body a powder keg. His chest and stomach erupted outwards in a ball of flames, illuminating the roadway in glorious lilac and spattering everything with gore.

William looked around, from the yawning ribcage to the headless man and crumpled woman, then out into the dark trees, ready for more assailants as he reloaded. Nobody came.

Goldin dropped the blunderbuss and clapped powder residue from his hands.

'That went as well as could be expected.' He scraped flecks of offal from his brow with a grubby handkerchief. 'Think I might take to this thieving life after all.'

'You can't just parrot the catchphrases and call yourself a thief.' William cast his eyes across the blood-splattered earth. A sight, he was ashamed to say, that didn't evoke any disgust at all. What it did evoke, however, was that ever so familiar feeling of regret. Four more lives had been lost through his actions; he couldn't even remember the total anymore. 'We have to be more, I don't know, subtle.'

'Subtle, yes.' Goldin shrugged and moved to the fireside, the man's corpse still smouldering atop it. 'But what do you expect? While I'm a trained assassin, I'm only a novice thief, and I'm supposed to be on holiday. This all has the tinge of hard graft to it.'

'Maybe we should have taken the carriage and left these people with their lives?' William closed his pistol with a cartridge in the chamber and tucked it under his belt. 'They didn't want to hurt us. They knew who I was.'

'Water under the bridge.' Goldin dismissed William's concerns and grabbed hold of the burning man's legs. 'Help me, *oof*, get this bugger off the fire. Now they're dead we've a ready-made camp, so their sacrifice wasn't for nought.'

Goldin made his usual light-hearted grin, but it didn't have its usual effect at the centre of such swiftly dealt carnage. William followed to the fireside, the smell of the burning corpse prickling at his nostrils like freshly roasted pork.

'I'm sorry, Will. I tried. "Your money or your life" and all that... but I suppose I can make a bit more effort. It's your holiday as much as it is mine, and if you say no killing, I'll give this thievery thing another whirl.' He tugged a boot off the corpse as if taking it was an act of noble theft, then balked as the leg twisted off what substance remained of the torso. He tossed it into the ferns. 'Just help me clean this mess up and we'll start fresh in the morning. I bet they've got some bread we can blacken on the fire, and maybe other supplies in that carriage.'

'I...' William smacked his lips and tried not to admonish himself for where his stomach had taken him. 'I wouldn't mind some bacon.'

'Great stuff!'

# 1644
## CLAUDE BEECHWORTH

'Nanny?' Claude's voice wavered nervously.

He hoped his grandmother might respond with something profound to disperse his anxieties, but she was slow to reply. As he waited, he fidgeted with his cravat and ran a finger around his starched white collar. His tailored suit felt too tight all of a sudden, the charcoal-grey too hot for Vitulus.

She traced lines of an article in a financial broadsheet, rocked gently by the motion of the carriage. Under her narrow chin, the thick ribbon of her bonnet swayed in time with her. Wrapped in her finest bombazine dress, with an elaborate muslin shawl twinkling with speck-like onyx, Nanny was both elegant and formidable. Though she made no move to answer him, Claude knew better than to ask again; she had heard him.

Swallowing, he peered out of the window in an attempt to gauge the distance to the city centre. Grand buildings loomed on either side, each structure like a cathedral to a particularly competitive god. White stone gleamed in the sunshine, festooned with statues, stained glass, and gilded iron railings. All signs pointed him towards a simple conclusion: they were very close to their destination, a fact that did little to allay his trepidation.

'He's your father.' She finally lowered her paper and peered at him through precariously balanced spectacles. 'Not some bandit or thief.'

He knew what she was saying: that it was pointless to waste so much energy worrying over someone who meant no harm. A few days prior, he had used his rifle to fend off a band of ruffians on the road and had kept a level head throughout. But this was different, he didn't care for the opinions of any thug or cutpurse. His father, he was seeing, the glint shifted and a small puff of smoke exploded out. Moments after the strange sight, the distinctive sound of a rifle firing brought him to an immediate and disturbing conclusion.

His grandmother shrieked. The butler lay on the white slabs before her in a fan of his own blood.

Claude's first instinct was to protect his grandmother, but his father had other ideas. One large arm swept him onto his tip toes and crushed him against the senator's solid chest.

'Find the gunman!' his father roared.

'He's on the forum roof!' Claude cried, fighting to keep his footing even as his father dragged him bodily towards the cathedral.

The rifle clapped again and one of the senator's personal guards slumped, gurgling a final breath through his ruined throat. Other guards readied and fired their flintlocks, but at such a range they had no hope. Panic spread through the crowds in the square, who hurried for shelter and cried in alarm.

'Send for more guards. Get riflemen out here, and get some men up there!' Senator Beechworth ploughed through a group of screaming archivists.

Bumped and jostled, Claude wrenched himself free and sprang away in another direction.

'There's a rifle,' he panted, 'in the carriage.'

The gunman shot again and a noble lady in a warm yellow tunic slumped to the ground, her head exploding in a shower of pulped flesh and bone fragments. Somebody shouted in a distant language. Claude thought his grandmother screamed, but it could have been anyone. Guards barked orders all around and kept firing their hopeless shots at the lone gunman.

A bullet struck a stone slab paces from Claude, sending rock chips and dust into the air. It spurred him onwards. Before he had the chance to realise the stupidity of what he was doing, he thundered into the carriage and collapsed onto the seat. Breathless, he fumbled with the case of his hunting rifle. Seconds later, his father leapt inside, almost filling the close space with his bulk.

'Here, it's loaded.' Claude thrust the rifle into his father's hands.

'No.' The senator touched below where his monocle would normally rest. 'I can't hit a target without it, not anymore.'

'Then we'll take it to the guardsmen.' Claude tried to take the gun back, but his father wouldn't let go.

'No, I'm not having you going out there. I'll take it to them.' Senator Beechworth made a move to leave, but this time it was Claude who wouldn't release the rifle. He'd only just got his father back and he wasn't about to lose him to some mad gunman.

'I'll do it. I'll shoot the gunner.' Claude bit his lip, barely believing the words that were coming out of his mouth. He had only ever killed animals before and now he was offering to end a man's life. He had gone into law to avoid this sort of violence. 'Through the lace curtain. He won't see it coming.'

His father nodded and relinquished his hold.

Claude rolled onto his belly along the length of the seat. He slid the barrel under the curtain, resting it on the sill to steady his aim. Something reminded him of his first ever shoot and he focused on it to still his nerve. Nanny had taken him out to cull the herd; some of the sheep had been plague stricken and needed killing from a distance. He had been reluctant at first, but she had convinced him that, in killing the sickened lambs, he was saving countless more. This was just like that: killing one to save many, and in thinking so, he felt little apprehension.

As he peered through the scope, he could see the golden statue atop the forum, an effigy of Harm – Pity's twin. A Scoldland flag had been tied to his staff. Claude searched for the gunman nearby and caught a glint of the killer's scope looking straight for him. He couldn't know if his own gunsight had been spotted through the curtain, or if the rifleman had seen the pair go so purposefully inside. It didn't matter much, but it meant he had to act quickly.

The rifleman fired first, thumping a hole in the carriage roof. Claude felt cold for a moment, fear convincing him he had been hit, but sense prevailed and he took his aim.

A mess of orange hair made it hard to determine exactly where the scalp of the rifleman was while he reloaded, but as he settled to take another shot for the carriage, his scope betrayed another wink of sun, sealing his fate. Claude twitched the bead in the rifle scope over the shimmering glass, then adjusted for range and wind without thinking. He pulled the trigger.

There was no return shot, no spray of blood confirming the kill. The wind-whipped ginger thatch didn't noticeably slump. Then he saw the rifle winking as it spiralled through the air, clattering on the forum steps.

'I got the bastard.' He exhaled, releasing his fingers ever-so delicately from the rifle. It was a strange feeling – to know he was a killer. He felt powerful, or was that just the waning shock? He turned away and slumped on the seat, panting with relief.

His father was reclining on the other bench, a look of proud contentment on his face. He could have been asleep had his eyes not been open.

Claude couldn't quite process what he was seeing. There was a lot more red on his father's robes than he had previously noted, and it seemed to be growing, some of it dripping onto the carriage floor. His father opened his mouth as if to speak, but no words came out. It was muscles falling slack.

Claude leant against the great marble block that served occasionally as a stage. It was said, that before the war with the southern continent, the emperor had stood atop and orated one of history's most compelling speeches. Afterwards, immense gold braziers had been erected at the corners to commemorate the victory, the precious metal plundered from Gieran temples. Being a great admirer of anything exquisite and expensive, Claude had wanted to get a closer look, but as he neared the plinth the relics pulled out of view. The block was so large – about the size of a townhouse – that one had to be halfway across the square before the angle was sufficient enough to see the Kadiri Lanterns.

He was here to meet a senator, and to fulfil an obligation he would have rather reneged upon. He looked across the empty square, frustrated by his long wait, but still duty-bound to remain. There was hardly anyone crossing the expansive stone-slab plain. Since the shooting, it seemed any that weren't required to be here had chosen to stay far away, lest another shooter make an attempt on the capital.

'Ah, Senator Beechworth. Please, come up,' a Vitulan drawl carried from overhead.

Claude jerked his head up. Peering over the edge of the block, a dark silhouette was drawn against the blue sky. He squinted to make the Vitulan out, but could only discern vague curls of hair.

'Come around, we're ready for you,' the Vitulan reiterated.

Claude pushed himself upright from his slouch, made his way to the edge of the plinth, and followed up one of two marble staircases that ran along the sides. He gained the top step and turned onto the plinth, passing by one of the intricately decorated braziers — there was no time to stop and admire them now.

As his father's heir, it had fallen to him to complete the term as senator. Today would be his first meeting since the funeral. Nervousness clenched his guts as he passed beneath the imposing columns supporting the forum roof.

He acknowledged the Vitulan, who didn't look exactly as Claude had imagined a senator might. His hair was an oily shock of swaying curls, and his chin sported a covering of dark stubble. His robes too were loose about his shoulders, like some kind of bath-house gown, baring black chest hair for anyone to see.

'So glad you could make it,' the senator, who held himself with a particularly lazy dignity, greeted Claude with open arms in a way that suggested he might swaddle him in a greasy, silk-laden embrace. At the last moment, his hand swung forward to clasp Claude's and he shook it like a Garlishman. 'I'm D'Elia, senator primo for Vitulus.'

'An honour to meet you.' Claude felt instantly becalmed by the customs of his homeland. Spotting an aide of some kind behind the senator, he added, 'And to you.'

The young lady, in a smart brocaded dress of green and white, bobbed a curtsey. She could do little else, as both arms were wrapped around an enormous bundle of parchments, papers, and ribbon-bound scrolls. She seemed to be struggling with her load, but D'Elia paid her little mind.

'Do you have no robes?' D'Elia looked Claude up and down, appraising the three piece suit he had brought himself in.

Claude hesitated a moment before opting to lie. 'I've been measured, but the tailor is still at work.'

He adjusted his jacket, momentarily self-conscious. His robes had arrived the previous morning, but when he donned them, his slender frame, pallid complexion, and bald chest made him look exceptionally boyish. He couldn't imagine any of the southern imperials taking him seriously like that.

'The extra time will be a measure of their quality.' D'Elia shrugged and sauntered off, his expensive fabrics trailing in his wake. 'Walk with me.'

Claude didn't feel ready for any of this. His father had been in the ground only a week and his grief was still keen. He wanted nothing more than to make his excuses and return to his grandmother. Even so, he fell into a slow step with the senator.

They passed between columns, entering an airy foyer with archway lined walls. At either side of every arch two guards had been stationed, dressed in the most ridiculous outfits. Muscle embossed chest plates, leather skirts, and brush-topped helmets made these men look as though they belonged between the pages of a history book. The only things that set them apart from their ancient frescoed brethren were the rifles and guns awkwardly strapped to their belts where knives and swords should have been. The uniform looked all at once impractical, uncomfortable, and defenceless. Claude couldn't quite believe the Vitulans had managed to spread their empire so far.

'He was a good man, your father.' D'Elia led them through an archway into a narrow corridor, inlaid with rose coloured marble and carved depictions of cardinal laws. 'I would have liked to have been at the funeral, but things have been hectic since the attack. I trust my assistant got flowers to you and your grandmother?'

Claude had no idea whether D'Elia's flowers were among the countless bunches and wreaths he had received, but he nodded anyway and offered his thanks.

'The meeting should be fairly brief, most of the motions are as good as decided already.' D'Elia bowed to a pair of blushing women in similarly archaic robes as they passed in the opposite direction. Claude reached up to doff his hat, but he wasn't wearing one so it just looked out of place, especially as hats weren't the status symbols here that they were back home.

'I'll introduce you to the senators, a few motions will pass, and then you can return home. This should be fairly easy. However, you will have to act as senator primo for Garland. Your father's companion took ill last month and left us merely days before your father. We have selected a new senator already; when he arrives you will be his secondo. Until then, you will have to step up. It might help keep your thoughts occupied, no? There's no use wallowing, I know the feeling well enough myself.'

Claude agreed, despite finding the senator more than a little indelicate.

D'Elia perhaps sensed this as he stopped, pivoted towards him, and continued more kindly. 'It will be good to have a Garland voice again. Your father and I didn't exactly see eye to eye on a lot of things, but I always respected his opinions, and he mine. Good man.'

D'Elia took a moment to stare into Claude's eyes. 'You look nervous. You shouldn't be.'

Claude was taken aback by the blunt statement, and felt a pang of pain most keenly in his ego.

'I'm about to enter a forum with the emperor.' He sought to defend himself. 'Who wouldn't be tense in my place?'

'*The emperor,*' D'Elia scoffed. 'I wouldn't worry about him. Between you and me – and you'll know soon enough anyway – the man has the wits of an olive. He fell off a horse in Mann, a pitiful display. His head lost a battle with a sharp rock and our empire won the war without him. Now come, the senate will be waiting.'

Claude hid his surprise poorly, but D'Elia didn't seem to notice as he had already sashayed ahead.

The corridor opened into a wider chamber, studded with bright and fragrant honeysuckle that had been trained to grow up the columns. It reached for spears of natural light emanating from cleverly designed hatches in the roof. There was also a bubbling of water, crisp and clear from a fountain in the centre; a young man filled swan-necked pitchers from its base. At the far end of the chamber was a large wooden door sided with two more-practically outfitted guards.

D'Elia paused as he laid a hand on the bronze-studded portal. 'Obviously, don't mention such details outside our walls.'

He was referring to the revelation about the emperor. Such information would be highly sought by any of the news-sheets, and it was a wonder the senate had managed to keep the emperor's ailment a secret for so long. Claude supposed it was a testament to their power, or perhaps the ferocity with which they treated their enemies. He nodded and followed D'Elia into the next room.

Inside was expansive, a circular hall rimmed with tiers of desks and chairs, all arranged in concentric circles around a central point. There were two senators present for every nation in the Empire, numbering almost forty between them, and each had their own collection of clerks and assistants. D'Elia led him down to the lowest, most central ring of tables and directed him to sit.

The Garlish desk, decorated with swags of blue and yellow to imitate their flag, was the only one unattended. Claude sat at one of many empty chairs, feeling particularly exposed without his senator primo, and lacking any clerks. D'Elia continued with his assistant to the next table and sat amongst a group of his countrymen.

As Claude waited for proceedings to begin, he couldn't stop himself from sneaking a glance at the emperor. The great man was reclined in a throne so tall it obscured the three nations positioned immediately behind it. "Reclined" was perhaps too generous a term; his body lolled to one side as if his spine hadn't the strength to hold him up, and his head rested on one of the throne's leather wings. He didn't look particularly old, maybe in his late fifties, but his hair was greying and unruly as straw. A servant had attempted to tame it under a platinum circlet, but it was swallowed in the thatch. His feet were bare and dirty-soled, propped up on a velvet cushion on a marble block.

Claude found himself dwelling on the sorry figure, and was suddenly worried he would be rebuked for gawking. He forced his gaze away and tried to occupy himself with the workings of his new-found contemporaries.

The leading nations' representatives fidgeted behind vast desks – papers, ink-charged dip pens, and carafes of wine at the ready. Vitulus, Galmany, Conejo, Garland, and Lex were represented at the innermost ring, with two sizeable gaps separating them from the emperor's throne and retinue. As each tier rippled outwards, the influence of the represented countries depleted. Not least because when it came to vying for the lectern at the centre of the room – positioned as such for each speaker to address the vacant emperor directly – they were simply further away. As such, getting their opinions heard would be all the more difficult.

The emperor's head lurched to one side as he watched one of the Conejan senators approach. A streak of pure white through his hair was revealed as his head sagged downwards; it led to a crude ravine of flesh where an ear once sat. Accompanied with the man's childish expression of curiosity, the sight of it turned Claude's stomach. The man's body still lived, but it seemed his mind was gone. As the senator took to the speaker's lectern, an assistant laid a hand on the back of the emperor and his head raised a fraction.

'First item of business,' the emperor slurred on a trail of drool. The weak announcement shocked Claude and he averted his eyes as if he had been caught ogling some sordid freak show specimen. Then the emperor repeated his statement again, his eyes wandering, wide and confused. 'First item…'

The assistant retreated from the emperor, and another swept in to administer him with a small cup of wine. Claude came to realise that the man was more than a shell; a fate somehow worse, as there was a possibility that he knew of his own state. There was certainly enough awareness in him for them to train him like a dog. It was an obvious cruelty, but even Claude knew that the death of an heirless emperor would wreak havoc given the tensions with Scoldland.

The Conejan senator aligned a small stack of papers on the lectern. She wore her robes of state with aplomb, a graceful woman in her late forties with a fashionable crescent of blonde ringlets over her brow. With a subtle cough to clear her throat, she began, 'The Scoldlandic emissaries have been questioned again, most thoroughly. They denied their involvement in the killing of our good senator right to the end, but our chief interrogation officer is convinced that these were the men responsible. I am inclined to agree. However, the failure to obtain a suitable confession is a considerable blow and the interrogators will be disciplined.'

'What of the man who pulled the trigger? Has anyone found him yet?' one of the back benchers interjected out of turn and was instantly silenced by the clap of a gavel from amongst the emperor's retinue.

'I shot the killer,' Claude blurted.

'It was a valiant attempt.' The Conejan primo turned to address Claude directly. 'The gunner dropped his rifle. There was a lot of blood, but by the time our guards got to his position, he had fled.'

A chill gripped Claude. The assumption the assassin was dead had been the only thing letting him sleep at night. Now, it seemed that wasn't the case.

'We might never find him,' the primo continued, 'but we can punish the regime that sponsored your father's killing.'

Claude sneered to himself and clenched his fists. To know the murderer might still be out there, celebrating his victory and laughing, made him feel positively ill. He didn't care for political motivations, or for the despicable creatures who ordered the termination of a senator. He wanted the one who pulled the trigger to suffer.

'How can we be sure these Scoldlandics are the men responsible?' One of the Galman senators stood. 'If they had secrets to spill, surely our esteemed friends in the Conejan Interrogation would have succeeded?'

The Galman was corpulent with a hairless, sweat-sheened head, and was tightly swaddled in generously proportioned robes. Claude's initial reaction might have been to assume the man was an oaf, but he made a fairly cogent argument.

The Conejan pursed her lips. 'Their silence is precisely the reason the chief interrogator deems them guilty. It takes a highly trained man to keep his mouth sealed under the rigorous scrutiny of a hot poker. An innocent would have spilled any number of lies. These emissaries said nothing, not a single thing.'

'I concur with Senator Primo Velásquez,' D'Elia proclaimed. 'The Scoldlandics are savages. If it wasn't these emissaries, it was most certainly their kin. The flag raised by the killer confirms it, and when we resume our campaign in the northern continent, we will make them pay.'

'Hold on a moment,' the Lex secondo, a matron with a severe chignon bun, interrupted before pausing to confer quietly with her fellows.

'It has not yet been decided that our campaign will continue,' the white haired Lex primo concluded, sipping daintily at his wine.

'With a senator's death, surely that decision is all but made.' The Vitulan secondo, who looked so similar to D'Elia that he might have been his younger brother, puffed out his chest in an attempt to look imposing.

'Senator Beechworth was a military man,' D'Elia continued the thought. 'It is fairly obvious what he would want of us.'

'But you can't be certain,' Claude said. Maybe it was the fact that D'Elia was using his father's death to justify his own personal means, or that two possibly innocent emissaries had been killed, but he couldn't stay out of the debate. 'The man who killed my father is still out there, Scold or no.'

'Well said, Acting Senator Primo. We cannot rush into a continuation of this war, it has taken too many resources as it is.' The Lex secondo tried to turn Claude's interjection into fuel for her own fire.

Ignoring the interruption, and hoping to keep the conversation on the topic of justice, Claude continued, 'We can't just go to war and call it revenge. We need to know who did it; who it was specifically. There are surely people who know something. Can't we get the guard to investigate?'

D'Elia's assistant, the one who had been carrying the huge stack of papers, dropped a pile of them from the edge of the Vitulans' table. Sheaves fluttered all over and she looked about, embarrassed as the outer rings of representatives jeered.

'War is expensive business.' D'Elia sprung into a counterpoint. 'But the more ground we take the more taxes we can accrue. This war will pay for itself in time. We all know how it goes. War, rebellion, acceptance, assimilation, *tax!*'

'War!' the emperor repeated, the notion seeming to rouse something in him. He looked about, gritting his long, yellow teeth. His wide eyes bulged in their purpling, sunken pits. 'Expansion!'

'Yes!' D'Elia thrust a fist of papers upwards, getting carried away with himself. 'This is the greatest empire in the known world, and we are built on war and expansion. We should follow the example of our great conqueror; we should not back down.'

There was a round of cheers and jeers from the outer representatives.

The emperor thumped a fist on the arm of his throne, shaking away his long sleeve. The skin underneath was pale and liver spotted, and looked aged well beyond his years. Bracing his arms on both sides of the throne, he pushed himself upright on trembling legs. To Claude, his actions seemed more an ape of D'Elia than a genuine contribution. He was like a child caught up in excitement for something he couldn't comprehend.

'And what?' Senator Velásquez barked from the lectern. 'What happens when we overextend our forces? What happens if the southerners mobilise against us? Are we to follow our glorious leader's example right to our very undoing? I'm not sure what the imperial equivalent of staving in one's head is, but I'm sure it's not pretty.'

The room fell to silence. The emperor looked at D'Elia, confused and excited, his fists clutching bunches in his robes.

D'Elia took a step forwards, and pointed a finger at the Conejan primo, rage plain across his face. 'How dare you…'

The emperor took a step too, but his legs hadn't the strength to keep him upright. He tumbled forwards. His head cracked on the corner of his marble foot stool, missing the safety of the velvet cushion by degrees. Blood spurted across the floor. His neck twisted and his body crumpled. Even in the immediate there was no doubting it. The emperor was dead.

In a moment of stunned silence, the senators looked warily to one another. The Conejan primo shuffled her papers into order, lowered her head, and sloped back to her desk.

'Someone get a surgeon in here.' D'Elia clapped his hands twice, then sat. He stared off into the distance for some time as the silence drew out, then added, 'And someone else bring the sommelier while they're at it, we might not be leaving this room for a good while.'

Claude fidgeted with the cuff of his jacket. It was blatantly apparent that his father's death had become a non-issue in one missed step. Not one member of the senate would be focused on justice anymore, not when there was an empire to inherit.

He would have to find the killer himself.

# 1683
## WILLIAM OF FAIRSHORE

The last tavern before the border was nothing more than a heap of blackened wood and ash. William was disappointed, but couldn't say he was surprised. It was just his luck. This road was so seldom used, he found it hard to believe any kind of business could survive here anyway. What did surprise him, however, was that the ashes were warm to the touch and still glowing in places. The building had only recently burned.

'Where is everyone?' He kicked through a mound of debris in search of anything that might have survived the fire, perhaps a purse of coins that had coagulated into one golden lump in the heat.

'I haven't the foggiest idea.' Goldin toed through a pile of ash, looked hopeful as he uncovered something, and then kicked it away. It was just another charred and useless remnant. 'It must have burned while we were in the forest. We'd have seen the smoke otherwise. I'm surprised the landlord gave up searching the ruins so quickly. It was a wise decision mind, I can't find bugger all.'

'Maybe it was derelict before the fire.' William tramped back to the road.

'You could be right. There was that storm a few days back, maybe it was struck.' The little man shrugged. 'Strange though.'

William returned to their stolen carriage. It wasn't nearly so ominous in full sunshine without its entourage of slack-jawed substance abusers, and it was a vast improvement to walking. Against the light smog that clung to the roadside and made everything else grey, it looked positively luminous. Red carriage wheels and boldly painted tulips on yellow sidings made William's road weary eyes ache at the sight.

He climbed two steps to the chintzy interior and assessed what supplies they had left. A small store cupboard yielded a few stale loaves, half a sack of dried beans, and a short string of dried apple slices. Convinced there would be a place to restock, Goldin had devoured most of the food and several bottles of alcohol with abandon. He wasn't entirely to blame for the meagre amount that remained, as William had followed his lead, but it was most certainly Goldin's lead. There wasn't much reason to be bitter; they would have enough food to get them to D'Arnao, but it would be difficult.

'We'll have to ration what we have,' he concluded.

Goldin grimaced in the doorway and stroked stubble that would soon be a scruffy beard. 'I had a hard time of it when I first joined the Guild, was living hand to mouth for most of it. I can do it again.'

'I'm surprised.' William hefted the sack of beans back onto the shelf, then opened another cabinet. This one was filled with all manner of wines and spirits; at least they had plenty of supplies in that regard. 'You don't have much problem pulling a trigger now. You're too keen if anything.'

'It wasn't that.' Goldin paused to smile at the sly dig. 'I was good at killing, but nobody *knew* I was good at killing. I had no idea how I was supposed to find any custom and I was competing with hundreds of other assassins. All the high-profile jobs went to known names – like that bloody Beechworth – even when their skills weren't right for the contract.'

William had just fallen into the job, and hadn't even wanted to be an assassin. It was thrust upon him and had seemed like his only option for a long time. The idea that someone would have to struggle to make a living at it was entirely unknown to him.

'How did you make it then? Everyone knows you now.'

'I had to work at it, longer and harder than I worked on anything in my life. Contracts eventually started picking up, just as I was thinking of leaving the Guild. Glad I didn't though.' Goldin looked at William and something in his expression changed. 'It's the same way for most, you know? Not everyone gets to be the apprentice of *the great Ojo Azul*. We didn't all get the easy life.'

William scowled at the accusation and decided to set things straight.

'Ojo was...' He struggled for a way to describe it. 'Not the best teacher. He was a good killer, but he didn't know how to teach killing. I think, the way he was, what he believed, it made him see death as mundane. He hadn't a single qualm with taking a man's life, and he couldn't understand that I did.'

'Well, you need to kill if you want to be an assassin. If he hadn't forced you to do it then you might not have made it.'

'He didn't really care about me.' William grimaced. 'He wanted to use me to earn more money, to increase his own killing potential. When I was ten, he had me kill a boy about the same age. That was my first real contract, and it would have made him a lot of money if I hadn't messed it up. There was a fire; the boy burned. I still wake up sometimes, hearing his screams.'

William's tone had an air of finality, one that clearly meant this would never be spoken of again. His palms began to itch, remembering how it had felt to clamp an ether-soaked rag on the child's sleeping face. He slammed the cabinet door. It helped to dispel a little of the unwelcome recollection, and without further comment he left for the driver's seat.

The day trundled on as steadily as the carriage was drawn by tired horses; the barren plains that bordered Grod offered few places to properly rest and water them. Dismal scrubland and tumbled rock formations stretched for miles, scattered with spiny grasses that hissed in the wind.

Goldin stayed inside for a time to give William some space, but emerged in the late afternoon. He clambered out of the shot-blasted hole in the roof and almost fell back in when a cartwheel thumped over a jutting rock. Unwilling to relinquish his hold on a bottle of liquor, it took him a little longer than expected, but he was soon settled beside William.

'What say we have a good time tonight, there's no need to ration the spirits is there?' Goldin sloshed the brown liquid.

William transferred the reins to one hand and took the bottle. He inspected the label. It was some eastern variety, its name in a script with unfamiliar letters.

'Just the one?' He frowned, pulled the cork out with his teeth, and spat it to the road. 'Are you not having any?'

Goldin's eyes brightened and he practically threw himself back inside to collect three more bottles.

The journey went well enough after that, the passage of four days lubricated by the constant flow of warming spirits. In the mornings, they would drag themselves up, feast on a miniature portion of their supplies and then get straight back to drinking – there was little else to do on the yawning blandness of the plains. In the afternoon, Goldin would sing travelling songs, and at night the pair would share stories of their triumphs and defeats. William had the lion's share of the defeats and Goldin's triumphs were dubious in their validity, but it was entertaining nonetheless.

Goldin stowed his blunderbuss in exchange for the stolen scattergun, reasoning that he should move with the times. Once they found the dead travellers' store of cartridges, they alleviated the worst of the boredom by taking it in turns to toss and shoot earthenware.

William quite enjoyed himself. Yes, they were hungry, but their bellies were full enough with alcohol, and the occasional drink from a stream was enough to stave off death. He didn't have to worry about being recognised, or branded a cheat, or attacked for being a guild embarrassment. He almost didn't want to arrive in D'Arnao. Civilisation brought with it a whole host of worries.

Goldin burst into another verse of song that seemed to be made up on the spot. *'She had thick rippling thighs, as pale as the moon. Her sister was buxom, and her mother was too.'*

William set his sights on the horizon, trying his best to soak up the warmth of the sun and appreciate the gradual approach of verdant greenery. Most of the continent was this way, but after the barren plains it was something he didn't want to take for granted. He hummed along with the melody, which was the same for any of Goldin's songs, and did his best to avoid hearing the lyrics. They all tended to stray rather quickly into self-worship, thrilling murder, risqué fantasy, or all three at once.

*'They served me my luncheon, and I was well fed.'*

Goldin was far from an accomplished minstrel. The complex ditties sung by even the lowliest tavern bard were lost on him. Usually, he tended to pick a single word and rhyme with it for the entire duration of the song, so William was quite pleased he was mixing things up a little this time.

*'Then I checked my pockets, no coin for my bread... I asked them if there was a way... No... They demanded...*

'Give me a moment, I'm just trying to *remember* the next bit.' Goldin had set the bar too high too early and couldn't keep up with his own lyrical prowess. 'I'll see if it comes back to me later. What now, shall I get the scattergun out?'

'How many cartridges do we have?' William was thankful in the least that the singing had stopped, but would have preferred it if the little man had fully tired himself out with a whole song. It was about this time in the afternoon Goldin usually dropped through the hole in the roof and went for an afternoon nap. The little man had a different word for it, something Conejan to go with his newly assumed bandido persona, but it meant "nap" all the same. It was just a blessing he'd gotten tired of doing the accent.

'About three dozen, I'd say.' Goldin rummaged in a pouch between his legs. He was sat beside William on the driver's bench, very brave to be so close to the horses, and not one to keep quiet about it either. He kept grumbling and muttering under his breath about their smell.

'We'd better leave it then.' William spotted a solitary tree over the brow of the next hill. The end of the plains would be a blessing, but another darkened forest with a mess of awkward roots would not. 'We might need them.'

'I thought you didn't want to kill anyone, and now you want to keep hold of enough cartridges to kill thirty?' Goldin chuckled through his façade of shock.

'It's better to have them and not want them, than want them and not have them.' William liked that saying. He wasn't sure if he'd made it up himself, but couldn't exactly remember where he had acquired it. It might have been one of those ubiquitous Garlish phrases, he supposed.

Goldin harrumphed, then leant back in his chair and closed his eyes. 'It's a hard life being a thief.'

By the time they crested the rise, Goldin was asleep.

There were more trees here, and hopefully some animals to hunt, but there was also a black trail of smoke streaking from the horizon. Half of William told him it was the accumulated smoke from the hearths of the nearest settlement, but that was the naive thief in him. The other half – the untrusting, suspicious assassin – told him it would be the smouldering remains of a second tavern. He didn't know why he instantly leapt to that conclusion, perhaps because it was the worst he could imagine.

He didn't bother to wake Goldin, but continued more cautiously, keeping his wits about him and studying the shadow of every tree. He stopped the carriage momentarily to retrieve the scattergun from within and laid it across his lap, then continued down the road with the horses at a trot.

In a way, it was a relief to roll up to the burned carcass of a second roadhouse. It meant he wasn't going entirely mad with paranoia. Being the False Butcher could do that to a man, he supposed. To his knowledge, nobody had ever been so publically shamed before. On the other hand, it did also mean that somebody was travelling this road with arson in mind, and the few scraps of food they had left definitely wouldn't last if the next village had been razed.

'Guild or foe?' A woman called from the centre of the blackened rubble.

William hadn't spotted her on his approach, but could see her now, amidst the upturned spikes that had once been rafters and joists. She was sat on a stuffed backpack beside a small mound of burning detritus, warming her hands despite the heat of the afternoon sun. Goldin would have said she had skin as pale as the moon, but unlike the women in his songs, she was lean and road-worn. William couldn't decide if she was twenty nine or nineteen. Thin and pointed features were accented with grime, and her dirty blonde hair was pulled back into two messy tufts.

'Guild, I reckon,' William shouted in response, waking Goldin as he slowed the carriage to a standstill. He could just make out the definition of a knife hidden beneath the woman's ratty skirt. It wasn't too threatening, but she could have any number of weapons stowed in the large pockets of her oversized topcoat. One of her hands was in said pocket already, perhaps cradling a diminutive pistol.

'Ah, a pair of guilders. Well met.' She stood and bowed dramatically. 'I'm Gwyneth, and you?'

'William,' he replied without thinking.

'Ah, good. I'm not late then.' Her Draigish lilt would normally have put William at ease; the musical accent was often associated with farmers, priests, and affable tin miners. But Gwyneth was a long way from Draig, and was likely the reason this roadhouse lay in ruins. 'You look like you've had a rough trip.'

'Could have been worse,' Goldin replied, picking up on the tension quickly.

'You're right.' She smiled in a way that would have been reassuring had the teeth in her mouth not been black; it was as if she had been chewing on charcoal. 'Things *are* getting worse.'

Gwyneth retrieved her hand from her pocket, something glinting ominously. William snapped the scattergun up and trained it on her, but it was just a silver signet ring that had caught the sun. Even so, he kept his aim on her.

'A little jumpy, aren't we?' Gwyneth rolled her eyes and moved closer still, undeterred by the firearm. 'What are you going to do, rob me? Give me the whole "Stand and deliver, and hand me your silver!" shtick?'

She grinned. It was then that William realised that her teeth weren't black from charcoal. They weren't black at all, but the darkest mahogany replicas. She rocked her jaw from side to side and the wooden dentures shifted unnaturally.

'My cousins are hiding in the trees, and they're all armed. Maybe they'll change your mind about pointing that stolen scattergun at me.' Gwyneth planted her feet at the perimeter of the blackened earth. 'Does it make you a good thief to steal off a dead woman? Or does it just make you a killer?'

'We *are* killers, miss.' Goldin cleared his throat, shuffling a little on his seat in a way that made William nervous.

He had been with the little man long enough to know how reckless he was, and right now he could tell that Goldin was about to spring into action. He had visions of him tumbling backwards onto the roof of the carriage and slipping through the hole into the cab. Moments later, he would burst out of the doors with a hail of fire from his blunderbuss. William would be forced to join in or be killed himself. His stomach knotted at the prospect of yet more death.

Goldin surprised him then, by saying, 'We don't want any trouble, not if we can avoid it.'

'Just your privacy? That's what my cousin said, but you still killed him.' The woman reached up with two fingers and adjusted the top set of teeth with a click and a squelch. 'I'd appreciate it if you'd lower my aunt's scattergun.'

This woman knew an awful lot about what they had been doing over the last few days and William didn't like it one bit; it made his trigger finger itch. 'What do you want from us?'

'Well, you're William, I know that. Or should I call you the *False Butcher?*' She smiled and her top set of teeth fell free again, shifting a little to one side. 'Which means your companion must be Aler Goldin. Pleasure to meet you.'

'Pleasure's all mine.' Goldin couldn't even muster any sarcasm.

William felt the man's legs tense against the footrest, heard the soft creak of wood. No matter what the woman said next, Goldin was about to do something terrible.

Gwyneth's chin wiggled from side to side in an attempt to realign her teeth as she grinned. Once satisfied, she said, *'Nos da.'*

William was momentarily taken aback by the unknown comment, having expected something witty, recognisable, and well-rehearsed as was often the way with guild stand-offs. It seemed Goldin was too, as he didn't act immediately. A beat of silence passed, then there was a rush of wind from the trees. It didn't sound at all like the expected gunshot, more a branch falling through leaves. Then Goldin moved.

With a heroic cry, the little man leapt onto the back of one of the horses. William was stunned. All at once, Goldin had overcome his fear of the creatures and had performed the most bandido move William had ever seen. Then he noticed the arrow skewered through the little man's shoulder, the one that had taken him off his seat and pinned him to the back of the horse like a toothpick through a tall sandwich. The horse whinnied and bucked, spurring its partner to do the same. The carriage thrust forwards.

William might have taken this moment of confusion to blast Gwyneth's head off, but the sudden lurch of the carriage rolled him over backwards. He scrambled to stop it, but couldn't get his grip in time. He fell through the hole in the roof and landed unceremoniously on a sack of worm-infested potatoes. His back and shoulder throbbed from the impact.

The carriage rumbled out of control and veered wildly from side to side as the horses bolted. Goldin could be heard shrieking for help, and the Draig was calling orders to her companions.

Upside down on the sack of relatively soft and squishy potatoes, William couldn't help but feel that he had found himself in some tragic play. Even the scattergun had been lost to him. Too long to fit through the hole in the carriage roof, it had bounced out of his fingers and been lost on the road. It was a shame really, because nearly all the cartridges they had were those suited to it, too small for Goldin's blunderbuss and too large for his own pistol.

'Shit.' He kicked his legs and rolled onto the carriage floor. 'Shit, shit.'

Most of the old traveller's blood was dry by now, but in certain places – where it had pooled especially deeply – it was still gummy. Little surprise, given the amount of blood in a human body: fourteen pints, if the drinking challenge at the guild gala was to be believed. The idea was that you would drink enough strong ale to replace your entire blood supply. William wasn't sure that was exactly how it worked, but it was a fun challenge.

'Kill the short one!' Gwyneth shouted from a remarkably close distance, bringing William back into the fight. He surmised she must be following on horseback.

Dusting himself down, he looked about the small interior for anything of use. Goldin's blunderbuss was luckily close at hand, and his own pistol too. He tucked the latter under his belt and weighed the former in both hands. He had one shot from each without needing to search about for spare ammunition.

He moved towards the doors at the rear of the carriage, hoping to re-enact the shocking arrival of the old woman with the scattergun in his last fight. Ideally, the part where she keeled over backwards and drowned in her own blood would be omitted. Leaning closer, he peered through a crack in the splintered doors.

At just that moment, an arrow punched through the wood beside his head. If it had been inches to the left, it would have punctured straight through his skull. He cringed away, luckily avoiding another arrow that thumped through the wood. He took a step back.

A third and fourth arrow pierced the doors, the latter coming so far through that the feather flights could be seen. It likely wasn't a known attack on him, but a random peppering while the archer attempted to hit Goldin. William couldn't let it go on any longer. It was only a matter of time before an arrow found its target. He took another step back, then kicked the doors open.

As his foot met with the wood, a final arrow burst through, skewering the flesh between his first and second toes. The gleaming, blood-tainted tip protruded from his boot. He screamed from the pain, but it was too late to halt his momentum. He thrust forwards, lost balance, and shunted the doors open. One swung wide, the heavy wood moving freely on oiled hinges. As it went, the arrow pulled back through his foot until the barbs dug into boot leather and caught on torn flesh. William was dragged by the swinging door then. He fell onto his arse, slid, and was flung to the road. His weight pulled him free of the arrow and the barbs tore out in the wrong direction, rending flesh as he was cast away.

He screamed as he spiralled through the air, but it was cut short, and the wind was knocked from him as he hit the dirt. The world whipped around, a spinning blur of earth and sky, until he finally skidded to a halt in a cloud of dust. No hooves followed to cave in his ribcage or skull – a small mercy as the archer's horse passed him by.

His whole body throbbed. He couldn't see much, his eyesight was blurred with tears and grit. Even so, he could make out the definition of an oak at the side of the road; he tried to crawl for it as the only cover in the area. He didn't want an arrow in the back.

The archer's horse stomped towards him. It snorted heavily. He thought he could feel its hot breath on the back of his neck, but it could have been warm blood from an unknown gash.

'You idiot,' Gwyneth chided. 'You shot the wrong one! We could get strung up for this.'

William heard a grovelling reply, but the voice was too deep to make out against the pounding in his ears.

'Barely,' Gwyneth scoffed.

A pointed boot nudged William in the side and he groaned.

'He'll need the other one to look after him now. There's no way he'll survive on his own.'

There was another murmur from the deep voice.

'Don't be foolish. Go and get your brother, make sure he doesn't kill the little one.'

There was a stamping of hooves and the owner of the deep voice rode away. William groaned again and tried to turn his head to see the Draigish woman. It hurt, but he didn't have to look far. Gwyneth was stood with her legs astride him, leering down. She grabbed him by the shoulder and wrenched him onto his back. The entirety of his bruised body throbbed from the motion.

'It seems it's your lucky day.' She toyed with a blade. 'We'll let you keep your friend for now, but just think about your *other* friends, they need a little love too.'

As she grinned at her own cryptic message, the dentures slipped from her mouth. She reached out to catch them, but missed, swatting them away. The top set cracked William on his cheekbone, her knife hit the dirt mere inches from his ear.

'St. Brynach, I'm sorry!'

Gwyneth craned down and snatched up the teeth, dusted them off, and hurriedly stuffed them back into her mouth. The blade was stowed sheepishly under her skirt.

'Just think about your other friends,' she reiterated as she tramped away. 'They can become your worst enemies if you don't make the right decisions.'

# 1649
## CLAUDE BEECHWORTH

It was hard to mourn when there was so much jollity in the air. Secluded in the memorial garden, Claude fought to close his ears to the music, cheering, and laughter that infected the crowds. For everyone else, today was a day for celebration, but for him it marked the five year anniversary of his father's passing.

Since then, the war with Scoldland had resumed and finished. Not exactly a victory, as the majority of the northern continent was still under control of the barbarian clans. The coast, however, had been claimed and was now known only as Scold. Soon, a strict regime would be enacted to quell some of the more eccentric inhabitants; any with sense would make their way to the mainland in search of imperial fortunes.

The Empire itself had managed to survive without a wartime revolution, a product D'Elia would claim was a result of his own strong leadership. Though Claude had suspected the man to be an ill fit for emperor, when it had come to the vote, there was little choice other than him. It was the Vitulan Empire after all, and he was the senior Vitulan senator. Not to mention that the man was a renowned womaniser; nobody wanted the uncertainty of an heirless emperor again. Even if D'Elia took no wife, there would be plenty of bastards to choose from, and the Empire's future would be secure.

It followed so easily that nobody else was able to drum up enough support to garner more than a handful of votes. Claude had done the same as many of the others, seen D'Elia's impending victory, and voted accordingly. He didn't want to be out of favour with the new leader.

He had hoped to gain a certain amount of influence to force further investigation into his father's death, but once the Garlish primo had arrived, Claude lost any sway he'd accrued. Nobody cared for the opinion or favour of a lowly senator secondo. Over the years, he fell into his new role, though he didn't particularly enjoy it. Eventually, the pain of his father's death faded to a low ache, and he simply had to move on.

'Claude!' Senator Wigbert nodded as he passed for the forum. 'How's my secondo on this fine morning?'

He had golden ringlets swaying about his head, though the whole affair was slightly askew from a hurried application. Hair-pieces were the fashion with both men and women alike, for the sake of a striking visage and a variety of looks. Claude had often found it strange that a man named Wig would make his most defining feature the poorest hair-piece in the city, but the senator wore his with a swagger, as if he was the most eligible of young bachelors. In reality, however, he was rather ugly, one-eyed, and peculiar.

'Very well, Senator.' Claude nodded in response, skilfully masking his irritation at the intrusion. He had hoped for at least a few moments of peace amongst the orange trees and laurels. 'I'll be along shortly.'

Wigbert departed, humming to himself as he strolled through the memorial, seeming to think it merely a nice place to spend a morning. He was a pleasant man for the most part, a strange man certainly, but he seemed to be fairly dim. It meant that Claude had to do the majority of the work, something that irked him terribly. He didn't mind long nights ratifying papers and parchments, or he wouldn't have done if he had more autonomy over which way Garlish votes were cast. In the past years, he had been reduced to nothing more than the glorified clerk of a powerful man who bought his way into the senate. Granted, Claude hadn't earned his position either, but at least he had the skillset required.

Exhaling, he cast his eye over the marble bust of his father, the stone already touched with enterprising moss. He clenched a fist into his robes. So few still remembered, let alone wanted to pay their respects. The days marched on, and life continued. Despite his best efforts to remain true to his Garlish heritage, and to honour his father with daily arms training, Claude knew Vitulus had changed him. His dark hair was oiled and set with delicate curls, his once pale skin tanned by the long summers, and half his waking hours were spent in antiquated robes of state. Garland and its proud culture seemed so far away from the excessive feasts and virulent bribes of the capital.

Any childhood memories he had hoped to savour had fled; the interruption from his primo wouldn't leave his thoughts. He stressed and chided himself as a bad son, too preoccupied with his own affairs to even mourn. Irritated, he stood, held himself proudly as his father would have wanted, and set off for the Grand Forum.

It was only a short stroll to the senate steps, but it was a slow one. Though the memorial garden had been kept empty for the duration of the victory celebrations, the imperial square was crowded with thousands of people. There was to be two weeks of festivities, punctuated at either end with award ceremonies to celebrate the heroes of the campaign. Today, medals would be handed out to nobles and officers, and in a fortnight, the common folk would be celebrated.

With the help of a few guards, Claude made it inside the small corral at the fore of the crowd. Surrounding the great block-stage on the lower side, all the honourees were gathered waiting for their medals. Up the stairs to the rear of the stage, with the imposing columns as a backdrop, a vast bleacher had been erected for the whole senate. Claude took his place with the first nation secondos, just behind Wigbert.

Each senator would take it in turn to call someone up and present an award. Many had squabbled over who they wanted to honour, but Claude hadn't bothered. He had ended up with one of the less senior officers, who had earned a rather mundane rosette for something in the line of preserving supplies rather than heroically razing an enemy village. It suited him brilliantly.

He made little conversation with the senators as proceedings started, allowing Wigbert to do Garland's share of the inane prattle. While celebrations were in full swing in the square, with wine flowing and all manner of substances being imbibed, it was still rather muted on the senators' benches. Even the emperor's grand entrance was lost on them. D'Elia had emerged from the forum on horseback, reared it mightily and bellowed the most inspiring speech the populace had ever heard. All this was of course seen by the senators from behind, and washed out by the roar of the baying masses.

Claude took the time, while he was supposed to be listening, to wonder exactly what the emperor's motivations were for presenting his speech from atop a horse. It must have been incredibly impractical for his servants to get it all the way up the stairs and into the forum. Perhaps it was to prove how superior he was to the previous emperor, who had fallen head first from his horse. If it had been anybody else, Claude would have thought it too petty to be correct, but he could believe it in D'Elia.

The emperor's speech finished in due time and the senators began announcing their awards. A few primos went first, then the secondos – Claude would be last amongst them. After that, yet more primos would be back on the stage with the most prestigious honours. This way, the Empire's best would be awarded at the start and end of the ceremony, with those that bore forgetting taking up the midway lull.

Claude made his way out to the front of the stage, pausing halfway to bow to the emperor. D'Elia had alighted his horse, which was now back in the forum, pulling at a bale of hay and defecating on the priceless floor. The man himself was reclining on a couch. Two servant women were stood behind him, one with a jug of wine and the other holding a platter of olives. The whole thing was a caricature of how narrow minded foreigners pictured Vitulans, but the look suited D'Elia like it did no other.

As Claude made it as close to the edge of the block-stage as he dared go, he pulled an envelope from within his robe. It had been entrusted to him at the last forum and had been dusted with gold powder for the occasion. Inside was the name of his winner, along with a short speech detailing his merits. There wasn't a great deal to get wrong.

He looked over the crowd, squinting against the bright sun. The golden glint off a rooftop statue caught his eye momentarily and his heart fluttered. He swallowed a lump, and forced himself to ignore his overactive imagination.

'Ladies and Gentlemen,' he began as loudly as he could, which was only enough for the corral of honourees to hear, and opened the envelope with his thumb. 'The next award winner is a very courageous man.'

A clerk arrived alongside with the honouree's prize balanced atop a velvet cushion, but it wasn't the plain piece Claude had been expecting. A star-shaped medal in bright gold winked up at him.

'Conscripted in the latter half of the war, he was fundamental in the training of our troops at Camp Wold...'

He faltered. Camp Wold was the name given to his family estate in Garland. It had been assumed by the army and used as a training camp. The deal had been Claude's idea. He wouldn't be leaving the capital any time soon, and his grandmother had opted to reside in their Vitulan summer home, so there was little need to keep it. Freedom from the running costs alone was a blessing, and the Empire had paid a handsome sum for the privilege. It always helped when one had a chair on both sides of the negotiating table.

'And upon deployment into Scoldland, this man was pivotal in the taking of Lugrode,' he continued, ignoring the coincidence. 'He led a charge on the gates of the fort, allowing his company to circle the perimeter in secret...'

Claude couldn't help but notice that the speech he had been given didn't exactly reflect the moneywise clerk he thought he would be awarding. If the envelopes had been mixed and he was presenting a primo's award there would be bureaucratic hell to pay. For now, it was simply better to continue than disturb the flow of proceedings, and he didn't particularly care for whoever ended up presenting his rosette.

'The fort was routed from the inside out–' He was stopped by rousing applause from the audience. Looking about, he found that a uniformed man was swaggering up the steps. As many of the audience hadn't the ability to actually hear what was being said on stage, they had taken his arrival as their cue to cheer.

Claude wrote his speech off as a loss and skipped straight to the announcement.

As Prior reached the ropes that divided the honourees from the revellers, he looked back with a crooked grin and an arrogant wink. The crowd shifted, and in the blink of an eye he was gone.

Claude returned to his seat, smiling politely as he squeezed his way between two primos.

'He seemed like a strange man,' Wigbert remarked.

'He was excited.' Claude tried his best to act casual. 'And a fine soldier, I'm sure.'

He knew he should round up a group of guards to pounce on Prior the next time he showed himself. It would be so easy to lure him out at their meeting point. If the man could be captured and tortured, his secrets would flow. Claude would know his father's killer, and the law would handle the rest.

But the law was notoriously unreliable, and the senate had forgotten his father once already. Such a course of action also left little in the way of revenge, allowing none of the satisfaction in seeing the job done right, and by his own hand. He'd had a taste of it before – when he assumed the rooftop gunner dead. Metering out one's own justice eclipsed the judicial process entirely.

Claude knew he was doing the wrong thing as soon as he reached the edge of the Piazza Fortuna. Nobody in their right mind would have come; Prior Perrin was certainly a scoundrel and probably a killer too. The invitation would have been enough to send Claude crying to his grandmother five years before, but now he was desperate, and certain that the senate's bureaucracy wouldn't provide the justice he sought. Perhaps dealing outside of the law would.

The prospect of marching into the centre of one of the city's poorest districts to meet a man in need of a sharpshooter was unnerving to say the least, but Claude had taken two precautions should anything happen.

The first was a letter, addressed to his grandmother and left with his most trusted clerk. He had instructed the man to send it in two days – no sooner, and no later. If all went well, he would be back home and the letter would be on the fire. If his meeting turned sour, and he was ransomed, or perhaps killed, at least the world would know he did this for justice.

His second precaution was a palm-sized flintlock pilfered from his grandmother's purse. It wasn't entirely accurate, as the barrel was short and the mechanism quite delicate. Of course, it had the advantage of being so small that it discreetly fit into his jacket pocket, so could be carried without raising any alarm. If Prior tried anything, Claude could stand his ground and get away, and if pushed could even put a man down. The loaded bullet was the size of a pea, but still deadly if well directed. It might be possible to pierce a lung, or with a bit of luck, score a direct hit on the man's heart.

The piazza gave way to wide cobbled roads that followed the perimeter of the modest park Prior had described. It was overgrown and ill kept, peppered with rotting benches and weathered statues peering from thick, evergreen foliage. Houses crowded around it, teaming with arguments, children, and barking dogs. On the rim of a dry fountain, a stall had been opened, which was little more than an array of precious stones on a blanket, staffed by a milky-eyed old woman.

A rag-and-bone man was at the far side of the park, one tired donkey pulling his cart as it steadily lolloped over ruts in the road. He balanced carefully on the top, catching unwanted oddments tossed down from higher terraces by housewives and children.

Every building here seemed to have at least one or two others on top of it, with the roofs forming small balconies for those above. Most had little gardens with trailing plants, herbs, and clay pots, but others had been set up with chairs and tables. One such arrangement was host to a game of cards and the group there spotted Claude quickly. From the subtle muttering and apparent end to their game, they seemed to find great consternation in his being there.

He tried to pay them no mind, but found himself lingering at the old woman's stall. While he was not scared of a few wiry old men, he knew from guard reports that this district was rife with gang families, and such old men often commanded countless younger and more imposing thugs. He didn't like the thought of them singling him out and calling for their brutes to rough him up and rob him. Even something as little as eye contact could spark a confrontation, so he kept his head down and found a particular fascination with a blue-green pebble.

'Four grana,' the old woman croaked. She was trying her luck, but such an amount was nothing to Claude.

He reached for his purse then reconsidered. It was quite unwise to let the old men – who were surely still watching – see the sheer quantity of money on his person. He moved his attention to another of the worthless rocks. 'What about this one?'

Across the park, the rag-and-bone man momentarily lost his footing as one of his cart wheels dipped into a hole in the road. In an effort to save a candelabra he had been gifted, he overbalanced himself further. It was by far his most expensive trinket and, Claude suspected, part of some gang dealing. The candelabra fell safely onto a hessian sack as the man tumbled to the road. The spectacle brought a great guffaw from the old men and distracted them from Claude just long enough for him to slip by.

Once their line of sight was broken by a yellowing bush, Claude felt entirely safer. Yes, there was still every chance these men could send their thugs after him, but such men liked to parade their bravado. A confrontation would have been far more likely should he have stayed within shouting distance.

At the centre of the park, he found a bench and sat down. He was uneasy waiting for Prior to suddenly arrive, or for the old gang men to send a cutpurse his way. Nothing happened for a long time. A couple passed by, quietly talking. Another man took a shortcut through the park. Claude closed his eyes and focussed on the chirruping of a nearby bird to calm his nerves.

Deep down he knew he was being irrational about the old men, and he knew that if he should be afraid of anything, it was Prior Perrin. It was so much easier to ascribe his anxiety to something other than the man he had come to meet. If he acknowledged the knot in his gut was due to Prior, his better judgement might take heed and see him leaving the park. He didn't want to miss the chance to find his father's murderer. For now, he had to fight his inclination for flight.

Footsteps approached, but not from a distance. By the time he caught them they were almost upon him. Thick heels clicked down the path on his right, but there was also a scuffing on his left, and a low rustle through the grass at his back. At least three men had surrounded him and there was no turning back. He opened his eyes.

'Senator Claude,' Prior beamed. He was the owner of the thick, clicking heels. His smile stretched the scar on his cheek and exposed pink, delicate-looking flesh. 'I'm so pleased you could join us.'

Claude looked from Prior to his comrades. There were five in all, some lighter on their feet than others, he hadn't even heard two of them approaching. There were two big thugs with arms as wide as Claude's legs – they had been the ones dragging their feet – one was to his left and the other behind. In front of Claude was a gaunt young man with lank hair and stubble, and a pretty young woman with a crooked smile and round belly. These were the two he hadn't heard. He found it immediately disarming that a pregnant woman would be socialising with these men, but from the way she looked at Prior, Claude could tell they were together. Then he saw the pistol at her hip, and reconsidered her as a threat.

'I can't stay too long,' he said nervously.

'Of course you can.' Prior clambered onto the seat, his feet on the bench and his rump perched precariously on the backrest. 'We're all friends here. You don't have to worry.'

Claude nodded, but knew that wasn't the case. Prior was too close for comfort. The side of the man's leg brushed his shoulder and forced him to crane around to see his face. A blade could easily be slipped into his throat; he wouldn't even have time to react. Surrounded and unable to see more than two of the thugs at once, his eyes twitched in a failed effort to keep track of them all.

His mind began to run wild. The slender one in the cloak seemed like the epitome of a storybook killer and the two brutes looked as if they could twist off his head with the flick of a wrist. Even the pregnant woman had him on edge with the sizeable flintlock strapped so brazenly to her hip. If she casually strolled up and shot him in the gut, there was nothing he could do to prevent it. How was a gentleman supposed to defend himself from an expectant mother?

'You said you knew who killed my father.' He tried to sound strong and intimidating, a man not to be trifled with. The words came out shaky, with as much bite as a new-born deer. 'I'm afraid I must press you; I really need to be getting on.'

'Come on now, Claude,' Prior chuckled. 'You know we want to talk business, I told you as much. I'm not selling out your father's killer until you've paid a fair price for him. So let's talk.'

One of the big brutes shuffled on his feet. For a moment, Claude thought he would be grabbed and taken away, but it seemed the man was simply finding a more comfortable way to stand. He was that large – a great mass of fat and knotted muscle – that Claude suspected simply holding his own weight was enough to make his feet ache.

'Wouldn't your hideout be a more appropriate location?' Claude ventured, fearing the answer.

'No, I don't think so.' Prior hopped down from the backrest and landed with a creak on the bench. He slipped one arm around Claude's shoulders. 'It's a nice day out, I thought we could just talk here. We don't want to scare you, Claude. We want you to help us.'

'Your welcoming committee needs work.' Claude shied away from the man's malodourous embrace. 'Do you surround all of your friends with armed ruffians?'

Prior shrugged, then nodded to the pregnant woman. She gave an unladylike snort, rolled her eyes, and took out a lacquered pipe. With practiced hands, she began to fill it with dried herbs from a small tin, enamelled with a pastoral scene.

'And what could you possibly want *my* help with?' Claude slid further along the bench and Prior's arm rescinded.

'I told you already; do you not listen?' Prior scratched his nose with the back of his hand and sniffed. His arm was covered in old sailors' tattoos, all the colours bleeding and faded. 'We're in need of a marksman, and you're the best there is. Won a prize for it in Galmany and was Master of the Hunt before you were sixteen, I heard.'

'That may be, but to what end?' Claude had to stop himself asking who they wanted shot; he already knew what kind of men these were, and there could be little other reason for so covertly seeking a sharpshooter's services. He composed himself, and asked, *'What* do you want me to shoot?'

'Emperor D'Elia,' Prior offered nonchalantly.

Claude leapt to his feet and took a few steps away. None of the thugs surrounding him moved an inch to stop him. He could have just walked away, but something in him demanded an explanation. He turned around and attempted to wrangle his expression into a stern and superior grimace.

'What?' Prior cocked an eyebrow as he was handed the charged pipe.

'Why do you want to kill the emperor?' Claude's voice had become a loud hiss. It was a failed attempt at a whisper, ruined by his suddenly surging blood.

'Let me explain. We'– Prior pointed to his four companions with the bit of his pipe –'are, how should I put it? We possess a certain skillset that can be purchased for a price.'

'Why dress it up?' the one in the cloak growled. He hooked his thumb over his belt, the hilt of a dagger was perilously close.

Claude reassured himself with the thought of his concealed pistol. He swallowed and tried to breathe through his mouth to stop air whistling so hastily through his nose. He had to appear calm and collected, then he might subtly slip his hand into his pocket.

'Alright then… we're assassins.' Prior shrugged again. 'We kill for money, no big deal.'

'Someone hired you to kill the emperor?' This was treason. Even in standing here, Claude could face the noose.

'Not exactly,' the cloaked assassin commented. He pulled the dagger from his belt with a casual flourish and Claude inched away, his fingers fiddling with the flap over his pocket.

'One of our number was contracted to kill your old man,' Prior continued, as if he was talking of nothing more significant than buying a loaf of bread. 'It was all done through a broker – a middle man. Aside from the deposit, we never saw a single grana.'

'We tried to find out who stiffed us, but…' The cloaked assassin picked at something beneath his thumbnail with the dagger tip. 'The broker was conspicuously tight lipped until the end.'

'We've done a bit of digging since then, Claude, and we're confident it was our good old emperor who put out the contract.'

'One of you killed my father?' Claude's hand finally found its way into his pocket. He felt the handle of the small flintlock, and slipped his finger against the trigger.

'It wasn't necessarily one of us here and now. It was one of our number. There's loads of us, all over, and you can't kill us all. So don't do anything rash. You'll get your man.' Prior smiled wryly. 'I'll give up the rifleman once D'Elia is dead.'

Claude pondered on the prospect of killing both the man who pulled the trigger *and* the man behind the contract. It seemed too convenient, but damn did he want Prior to be telling the truth.

'How do you know it was on D'Elia's command?' he asked.

The line of questioning must have betrayed his interest, as Prior relaxed into the sagging planks of the bench. He reached for a flint and steel in his pocket and started to strike sparks over the dried root in his pipe.

'It seems he wanted the Scold War to continue; saw it as an opportunity to gain power, but your father wanted peace. There's not much more to it than that. Obviously, once the last emperor up and died, and D'Elia slipped into his sandals, he didn't feel the need to pay us what we were owed.'

'We can't let people get away without paying,' the pregnant woman interjected, subtly massaging her stomach. 'If we let one, then more will try. We're just trying to make an honest living.'

'And of all the marksmen in the Empire, why should I be the one to do it?' Claude pursed his lips. He knew more than ever that he was on the wrong path, but the further he ventured down it, the more things seemed to be lining up in his favour.

'You were there when our man shot your father, weren't you?' Her face softened, almost regretfully. 'Sorry about that, by the way. You know how many times he missed before he got lucky. That was before you hit him with a single shot. His sharpshooting days are over.'

'You don't have anyone else?' Claude was looking for any excuse, but even now was certain that he didn't want to find one. Everything Prior said about D'Elia made perfect sense.

'Most of our folks are a little more reckless.' Prior finally got the flame to take and sucked on his pipe. He exhaled a thick folding cloud. 'They don't have the patience for it like you do, and we thought you'd appreciate the offer.'

'I'm not sure I do appreciate you assuming me some revenge-hungry killer, but I will take you up on the offer nonetheless.' Claude smiled, almost impatient for what was to come. 'I'll kill the emperor, and your assassin too. It's what they deserve.'

# 1683
## WILLIAM OF FAIRSHORE

In the past twenty minutes, William had made considerable progress. He had shuffled to the side of the road, removed his shoe, and peeled off his blood-soaked sock and re-tied it around the gaping hole through his foot. The whole ordeal was accompanied by a lot of grunting, screaming, and crying, but now things had eased off a little. He was still bleeding, but as long as he didn't move, or sob too heavily, the pain would stay nothing more than an almighty throb.

The toothless woman, Gwyneth, and her arrow-shooting lackey had left to find Goldin. He couldn't see them now, just the carriage crashed against a tree, one of its four wheels laying on its side. He couldn't see Goldin either, but the head of a deceased horse poked out from behind the carriage. Hopefully it hadn't toppled on him, and he prayed to the gods that Gwyneth hadn't killed him. She said she wasn't going to, but guilders could be changeable at the best of times and she seemed particularly unhinged.

As he shuffled against a tree to get more comfortable, a jolt of pain shot up his leg. He ground his teeth and wondered if he would die here. There wasn't much chance of a rescuer passing by. In desperation he might stagger a short way up the road and bleed to death some two hundred yards closer to safety, or he might stay here and bleed out more comfortably.

When he thought about it, he could have died many times over the past year, and in retrospect it had been a completely foolish idea to enter the Man-Butcher Prize. Somehow, he had lucked his way to victory, but then the world had balanced out and shoved him back to his rightful place. He wasn't much of an assassin, but he'd survived guns, bombs, and that foul cult, only to be killed with outmoded technology. A damned *arrow* after what he'd been through.

He wondered whether it would have been better if he'd died in the competition. If he'd placed second he would never have been disgraced again. If he had been killed before that, he never would have seen what happened to Vesta. He lingered on her for a moment before pushing the thought away; it was too painful to think on just yet.

'Are you going to stop feeling sorry for yourself any time soon?' Goldin looked down at him, wheezing. He had managed to lumber all the way to William's side without him noticing, so deep was he in self-pity and dazed from loss of blood. 'I need you to pull this arrow out of my shoulder.'

He was hunched over and pale, and looked as if he was about to be sick. William moved his foot away with another jarring wince; he didn't want any errant bile to sour his wounds.

'She seemed nice anyway, all glossy smiles and apologies.' Goldin slumped to the floor. 'And the big one pulled me off the horse; this barb had me pinned fast.'

'A pair of saints,' William joked weakly, noting the scrap of equine viscera on the arrowhead protruding from Goldin's shoulder. 'They wanted to kill you, do you know that? They shot me by accident.'

'Why on earth would they want to kill me? *You're* the False Butcher,' Goldin exclaimed before noticing William cringe. 'No offence meant.'

'That one with the wooden teeth, Gwyneth, told me I need to think about my friends, lest they become my enemies.'

'You don't have any friends,' Goldin said without thinking. 'Again, no offence meant. You do have me though, as a friend, I mean. Unless one of us bleeds to death in the next few hours – are you going to pull this arrow out, or what?'

'I don't think they were talking about you.' William decided to think about it later. The loss of blood was making it hard to concentrate and the message had been entirely too cryptic. 'And I can't just pull that thing out, it's covered in grime. Do you have anything to plug the wound?'

'No.'

'Well, for the moment it's plugging itself.' William sucked through his teeth as he rolled onto his front. It looked quite a long way to the carriage, but they needed supplies. 'See if you can set up a campfire; we need to boil some water. And find something we can use for a bandage.'

'Yes, sir.' Goldin flicked a mocking salute, struggled up and limped into the trees to find firewood.

William headed for the carriage, crawling with purpose like an army private, but squealing like an orphaned piglet for the duration.

'Three.' William took a firm grip on the arrow shaft, blood squelching between his fingers. 'Two...'

'Wait, wait.' Goldin paused to steady his breathing. William had found a bottle of ether in the carriage, which they had considered huffing to ease the pain, but after a short debate they decided against the idea. If they took too much they might fall asleep and their wounds would go untended. Both had resorted to a nip of alcohol instead. With a grimace, Goldin took another gulp for good measure. 'Alright, do it.'

'One!' William gripped the arrow flights and yanked downwards. The shaft was sturdier than he had imagined, so his attempt to break off the end was initially unsuccessful. The wood twisted in Goldin's shoulder. There was an almighty shriek, but there was little point in stopping now. William pulled again and the feathered end snapped off.

'There, that wasn't so bad, was it?' William sighed, tossing the length of dowel onto the campfire.

Goldin mewled through gritted teeth, 'That bit wasn't even supposed to hurt.'

They had decided that removing the flights and pulling the arrow out in the direction of travel would be the best course of action. William knew from recent experience that barbs pulling out the wrong way was rather unpleasant. He didn't like to think what kind of damage could have been done to his foot: broken bones, torn ligaments. He knew he would have to see a doctor sooner rather than later, even despite Goldin's best efforts. The sock had been replaced with a more substantial bandage and the little man had cleaned the wound with white spirit. Even now, William could feel swelling, and his skin was purpling up to his ankle.

'Are you ready?' William picked a few loose splinters off the sheared wood then manoeuvred around to pull the arrow from the other end. He wrapped a rag around his hand for a better grip.

'Ready as I'll ever be. *Those bastards,* why didn't they just shoot us?' Goldin grumbled, taking another swig. 'They're dead if we see them again.'

'Three.' William started counting. 'Two…'

'Wait, wait!' Goldin protested again, but William ignored him.

He gripped the shaft as tightly as he could, pressed against the little man's chest, and heaved with all his might. The process was more of a slow drag than the yank-and-done he had intended. It was like he was pulling a leather riding boot from particularly stubborn mud. As with the boot, things got harder and then easier, before finally there was a terrible sucking noise and the shaft came free. William fell backwards, almost onto the fire. His face was splattered with blood and his leg seared with pain. Both men screamed for their mothers.

Once the pain had subsided, he tossed the half-arrow aside and began collecting what bandages they had left. He knew he had to be quick; blood was flowing freely from the wound.

Goldin was gurning and weeping, about as manly in the face of pain as William himself. As he rolled over into a position that would allow his injury to be tended, he lost consciousness – a small blessing. William packed the wound with cloth he had boiled in a pot, splashed it with clear spirit, and poured a glug of ether for good measure. He wasn't sure if that was a good thing to do or not, but it was the best he could think to do. Finally, he wrapped Goldin's torso in the longest lengths of bandage they had, and laid him on his side.

It was dark before the little man came to. In that time, William had managed to crawl about at a snail's pace, preparing their camp as best he could manage. He had also set their remaining supplies boiling in a pot. The broth was mostly beans, mouldering potatoes, and red wine.

'I'm still alive then?' Goldin grunted as he awoke.

'Barely.' William ladled a helping of what he was calling stew into a bowl and set it by the little man.

'Barely's good enough for now.' His nostrils flared at the scent of cooked food. 'Is that finest roast hog I can smell?'

'Vineyard Stew.' William deposited a wooden spoon into the bowl. 'I've heard it's a delicacy in some parts.'

'I'm sure it is.' Goldin propped himself up with a wince, finally opening his eyes. 'You look well, given the circumstances.'

'I'm alright when I'm sat down. Once I was sure you wouldn't die, I took a sniff of that ether. It took the edge off well.' The glass bottle was nestled in a nearby tussock; William picked it up. He'd wanted to take another huff, but the coloured flares in his vision told him the first dose hadn't worn off yet. 'You can have some after you've eaten.'

'Can't I have some now?' Goldin rubbed his shoulder. His eyes fixed lustfully on the bottle that somebody had so delicately decorated with a little black skull and crossbones. 'I don't know if you've noticed, but an arrow stuck through you doesn't half pinch.'

'Eat your gruel.' William set the bottle back down. 'We don't want you knocking yourself out and starving to death.'

'Fair point.' The little man tossed the spoon onto the fire and picked up the bowl with his good arm. He drank the sour contents in large gulps, broth dribbling down the sides of his mouth. 'What's the plan?'

'The plan?' William hadn't thought much about what they would do beyond tonight. His main objective had been to prevent their untimely deaths. So far, that was going reasonably well.

He looked around their sorry excuse for a campsite. There was the fire... that was probably the best bit. There were also a lot of bloodied rags, a near poisonous stew, and a fallen tree that could be used as a bench if they were feeling up to it. As it was, they were both reclined in the undergrowth in awkward and uncomfortable positions. The carriage still boasted a fine supply of spirits, so they had that going for them, but its axles were reduced to matchwood and both horses were dead. The hind quarter of one had served to bolster the stew, however, so its loss wasn't entirely in vain.

'I reckon, we eat some stew, huff some ether, get some sleep, see if we can find where our guns ended up, and *then* we can worry about how we're going to get to civilisation.' William lay back in the long grass and shut his eyes. 'Is it much of a walk to the next village?'

'I didn't mean that, although that does sound like a top plan.' Goldin dribbled broth down his chin as he spoke. 'What are we going to do about *this?*'

He gestured around them, sloshing stew.

'Plainly, someone's out to get us, or you, or me. We need to know what's going on.' He finished the broth and discarded the bowl. 'Have you thought any more about these *friends* they mentioned?'

'*No...*' William lied. While he had been crawling about the camp, he hadn't done much other than feel sorry for himself and wonder exactly who had it in for him. 'It's like you said, I don't really have any friends... other than you.'

Goldin mulled it over, nibbling on a stringy bit of horse with his pointed tooth. 'What about an old friend you had a disagreement with, perhaps? Someone you fell out with years ago?'

'Not really, everyone I know is dead. Vesta, Ojo, that half-headed slave, an old Gael called Cathal. They're all gone.' He racked his brain. There was one person he knew that was still alive. 'There's a woman, she ran a guild outpost, looked after me when Ojo died. I can't see her wishing me any harm.'

'Cathal? That wheezing gunslinger?' Goldin tongued his pointed tooth. 'Did you really know him?'

'We used to shoot targets together.' William smiled at the memory, though it was tinged with loss. 'I beat him a few times near the end, though I suspect it was more to do with his decline than my ascent.'

'I drank with him a few times.' Goldin's eyes brightened. It seemed their injuries had made the both of them sentimental sops for the time being. 'Good man, ill health... but I think we can safely rule out anyone who's dead.'

Goldin gave a little patronising raise of his eyebrows, but there was good humour in it, like with everything he did. He hadn't a spiteful bone in his body; it was a wonder he had ended up a murderer. 'Anyone before you joined the Guild?'

'I have a sneaking suspicion that my parents tried to kill me, but they surely think I'm dead, and I can't remember much before that.' He tried his best to scour through every detail of his early life that hadn't been blotted out by whiskey and orange. 'That's it.'

'Well that settles that then. We might never know, but damn do I hate being kept in the dark. I hope we find out soon. The sooner we know, the sooner we can kill them.'

'You don't think whoever it is will be waiting for us in the next village, do you?' William's fingers found the ether bottle in the grass beside him. It was about time they got properly medicated; his foot was beginning to throb horrendously. 'I just want to close this chapter and start a new one as a thief. If that means killing whoever wants to kill me, then so be it. One more for the road.'

'Fair enough.'

William propped himself up, uncorked the bottle, and splashed a fair amount onto an unused bandage. He tossed the bottle to Goldin and, lying back, draped the cloth over his mouth and nose.

The next few hours were a blur of laughing, singing, and shouted stories. They both took it in turns to fall asleep for twenty minutes at a time, only to wake for another bout of energy and excitement. The next morning, William would have sworn he stood up and danced a jig to one of Goldin's songs, but knew that was preposterous.

William groaned, all his pain amplified by the worst hangover he had ever experienced. His mouth was dry, his joints ached, and every limb sported a particularly competitive bruise, all vying for the largest, most maroon, and egregiously painful award. Words croaked out, but even he couldn't understand them. He was face down in the wet grass. It had been raining while he was unconscious, and he was sodden from head to toe. Worst of all, his foot felt like it had been punctured with a second arrow, this one the size of a broomstick. The throbbing reached all the way up to his hip, tickling his groin.

'Goldin, get me some more ether. Please.' He needed it to numb him, and was almost certain that he wasn't building some kind of dependency. Almost.

'Do you remember what I said last night?' Goldin grumbled. 'I've changed my mind. Being barely alive isn't quite good enough. I'd like a soft bed and a cup of tea.'

'Finally awake?' an unknown voice interrupted.

William tensed, sending jolts of pain through his bones. His face was still buried in the undergrowth, and his head was foggy from the night before, but he thought he could sense a hint of hostility.

'Bugger off!' Goldin shouted, straining to get up.

William gasped with relief as the great weight of his travelling companion was lifted from his bandaged foot – the throbbing had been so great he hadn't even realised the little man was atop it. He clawed his hands into the dirt in an attempt to get away from the surging pins and needles and flopped with a shudder onto his back. His world turned from dark and hazy grass to a bright and hazy sky.

It looked like it hadn't been long since the rain had stopped and that it might start again at any moment. Everything was grey and covered in cloud, but the sun was at its back, illuminating the mist to an intensity that ached his eyes. He reached for his pistol, which he had still not managed to locate, and grabbed a handful of damp grass.

'Are you looking for this?' The stranger's voice drew William's gaze away from the clouds. The man who he found was tall and slim, dressed in a black suit and top hat, and was indeed holding a silver flintlock. It was even engraved down the barrel with wild flowers. 'One of my horses nearly trod on it.'

'You're not here to kill us, are you?' Goldin was stretching all his joints as if he was about to start a brawl with the man, even though he was only a third of the height and with half as many functioning arms.

'Not if I can help it.' The stranger smiled. 'This is your flintlock then?'

'Depends if you're going to give it back or not,' William croaked through dry lips, wondering if that was a product of the ether abuse, or if he had polished off the whiskey too. 'Do I know you?'

'No, no.' The stranger scuffed the sole of his shoe casually in the damp earth. 'I'm just a friend.'

William groaned. That word prickled at him, and he suspected the man's use of it was quite intentional. He wasn't ready for mysterious conversations. Propping himself upright, he cast about for the ether to quell the still thrumming pain. The nearest tree, and the next three or four, had been reduced to nothing more than blackened stumps. Clearly he and Goldin had a little accident involving the ether and the campfire last night. He thanked the gods for rain.

'I should say, we have a mutual acquaintance. A nice young lady, but a little eccentric. She sent me to find someone with a silver flintlock. You, I suppose.' The stranger pursed his lips, turning the corners downwards.

Goldin raised his fist, ready to fight. The other stayed limp at his side.

'I'm just a coachman.' Palms up in defence, the pistol rocked limply on one of the stranger's fingers. Only, it didn't look quite right, and no matter how William blinked, his vision wouldn't clear. The man had an extra digit on each hand. He flipped the pistol around in a way that looked precise and familiar, and then held it out, handle first. 'I was told you might need help getting to D'Arnao.'

William and Goldin shared a glance. They were both eager to get this journey over and done with, but it was hard to entrust themselves to the coachman. It was hardly a wise decision to board the transport sent by the person that had almost killed them the day before. If they didn't, they would surely die where they lay, sprawled on the roadside.

'Fine.' William took the flintlock and opened the chamber with a grimace; the loaded cartridge had been taken. He and Goldin were as good as prisoners, but at least they weren't dead. 'Take us to D'Arnao. It can't be much worse than here.'

# 1649
## CLAUDE BEECHWORTH

After the initial meeting in the park, Claude sent away his clerks, maids, and butlers. The house needed to be free of prying eyes and ears if he was to plot the emperor's death. A fortnight of paid leave for the victory celebrations was reason enough for his staff, and before the end of the first day, the vast townhouse was empty. Prior Perrin and his retinue of killers moved in the morning after.

Assassination proved an easy sport for a senator, and it was exciting to be working on something so clandestine. Claude acquired new weapons – five pistols and an artisan rifle – for a fictitious hunt planned two months hence. Under the guise of imperial renovation grants, he was gifted architectural drawings for the buildings around the square. He had even backed a timely bill, proposed by the New Gods' Order, to keep armed guards from sullying the sanctity of their cathedral. It made choosing a vantage to shoot from all the easier.

Over the course of a week they schemed and spied. The dining room had become their base of operations, and the polished walnut table was strewn with plans, maps, and gathered intelligence. It was impressive how rapidly their plot was coming together.

The assassins had claimed a bedroom each, but took care to mind their manners and appreciate the luxury around them. Claude learned that the brutes were brothers and not entirely as brutish as he had first suspected. In fact, one of them was a fine chef who prepared the majority of the meals in the absence of any staff. The shady killer-type didn't look nearly as threatening outside of his cloak, and had been a woodworker's apprentice before a string of misfortunes had seen him take up a dagger in self-defence. The woman, Nadalia, was Prior's wife and a former customs officer from

Thego. She was intelligent and kind, and took an instant liking to Claude. Although she mocked his uptight demeanour, it was in an amiable way that he quite enjoyed to play along with. She was a delight, but even so, had killed many men.

Claude had always thought of killers as monsters, but to these people it was just business. Yes, there could be a thrill in dancing with death and taking another man's life, but there wasn't any bitter emotion in it. He came to see the assassins as just people; they weren't scary, or vile, or threatening. When the final day of victory celebrations arrived, and it was time for the emperor to die, Claude felt no trepidation in becoming an assassin like them.

'You're sure you're ready?' Nadalia asked as she straightened his jacket. She was only a few years older than Claude, but saw him as less worldly and had taken to mothering him.

'Yes. I need to do this. It's for my father.' As Claude voiced the reasons, he couldn't help but feel immature, and not just because Nadalia had taken to smoothing a curl in his hair with spit and a rough palm. These assassins killed as a job, and they didn't condone emotional murders. They said you had to remove all feeling from a killing or it could eat at you, and here he was letting it steer him. He shook his head and sent the thought away. He didn't want to be a professional; this was revenge, plain and simple. Once he was done, he would return to the senate, to his paperwork and the comforting drawl of bureaucratic deliberation.

'How do I look?' Prior came into the entrance hall, wearing one of Claude's father's old suits. He had a rifle slung on a strap over his shoulder.

Nadalia hummed appreciatively and embraced her husband.

'Good then?' He smiled, and once released, passed the rifle to Claude. 'You'll be needing this.'

He didn't take it.

'I've been thinking,' Claude ventured, 'it might be better if I use my old rifle.'

'Will it cover the distance?'

'Most assuredly… It's not for any sentimental reason, you understand?' Claude felt a need to defend himself, to align with their warped standard of ethics. 'I'm more comfortable with it; I can make the shot. Definitely. That one, it's good, but I'm not proficient with it. It's still new to me, and–'

The doorbell chimed, cutting him off. He swallowed spittle. A carriage had arrived to take him to the Grand Forum. As it was the last day of celebrations, there was to be another tedious ceremony. Claude was to present an award to a soldier who had lost an arm and a leg in service to the Empire. The man was surely courageous, but proceedings would be cut short long before it was his turn to hobble onto the stage.

'Very well.' Prior shrugged. 'We'll leave this one behind, we're less likely to get caught with just the one. You remember the plan?'

'Of course I do,' Claude sniped, his nerves getting to him for the first time. 'It's not particularly complicated, is it?'

'I suppose not.' Prior slipped his pipe and a small pouch of dried root inside his jacket pocket. 'We should go.'

'Good luck,' Nadalia called after them. 'Tell Lukasz, when he's buying wine for a job well done, save mine a few months.'

Claude took his rifle – which was enclosed in a hard case – and led the way, escorting his guest as a senator would. Strangely, he found it hard to slip back into the character of himself. He couldn't quite remember how he should behave and was too nervous to act casually. Even some of the etiquettes, that were normally second nature, slipped him by. He opened the carriage door before the driver had the chance, and allowed himself inside before his guest.

'Fine day, isn't it, my lord?' The driver was an affable man with an honest face, and keen to provide a good service. He held the door for Prior, who squeezed inside and settled on the opposite seat.

Claude nodded tersely and pulled the rifle case onto his lap. The weather was hardly a concern on such an auspicious day. Bright blue skies, a faint breeze, and a pleasing kind of heat. Just as it should be at this time of year.

'Would you prefer that on the luggage rack, my lord?'

'No. We're quite comfortable, thank you.' Claude felt the need to expand on his cover story. 'It's only a clarinet.'

Prior shot him a look, then added, 'I'm here to play at the ball after the ceremony.'

The driver wished them luck before softly closing the door.

'Keep your mouth shut. The more you say the more suspicious you sound,' Prior hissed. 'Just stay calm and this'll all go as smooth as you like. Trust me, with your connections, this is child's play. It took nearly six months to get our man on top of the senate last time.'

Claude shuffled uncomfortably. After an enjoyable time with the assassins, he had almost forgotten it was their organisation that had seen his father killed. He set the rifle case on the seat opposite and tried to take his mind off what was to come next.

'How many of you are there?' he asked.

'How many what?' Prior was staring out the window, one hand stroking his newly-shaven chin.

'Assassins.' Claude smoothed down his suit, not wanting a thing to be out of place. 'You said you had assassins across the Empire.'

'Oh, right. There's about a hundred of us, and there are more joining every day. It's a growing profession.' Prior spoke casually, more concerned with keeping track of their progress through the city. 'It got to the point where assassins were killing each other for poaching contracts. We wanted a greater stability, so we formed a sort of gang.'

'I've never known a gang so large, sounds more like—'

'We're here, hold on.' Prior braced himself against the doorframe and propped his feet against the opposite wall.

Claude followed suit and a breath later there was a deafening crack of wood splintering. The carriage juddered sharply, throwing him from the seat despite his attempts to stop it. He tumbled into the footwell, cracking his shoulder blade painfully against the seat. A wheel collapsed and the carriage listed dangerously to one side, its iron axle screaming over cobbles. Claude was rolled over, jerked about like a rag doll. The metal buckled and dropped the wooden cab to the road, the rough material curtailing their momentum.

When the carriage came to rest, and the grating and splintering, along with the screaming of all involved, had subsided, an eerie silence was punctuated by a horse galloping away. Its bridle had snapped and it was bolting for its life.

'That went well,' Prior commented, pulling a small knife from his belt. He wasted no time in slitting his palm and promptly daubing fresh blood over Claude's face.

'Get off. That's enough.' Claude struggled away and righted himself.

'You ready?' Prior wiped the knife on his shirt and sheathed it. 'Moan a bit; you look like the weeping sort.'

Claude grimaced, about to defend his honour, when Prior jabbed a meaty finger into his left eye. He swore and began shielding his face, blinking rapidly as tears streamed down his bloodied cheeks.

'Perfect.' Prior beamed.

Half blind, Claude shunted the door and fell out onto the road; he had expected the thing to be jammed closed, but the crash had weakened the latch. He landed in a heap, yelping as he struck his shoulder again. When he looked up through bleary eyes, his face twisted in discomfort, he was surrounded by concerned onlookers. Thankfully, his co-conspirators were nowhere to be seen. The plan was going well.

It had been the job of Prior's two thugs to heft a great plank into the carriage wheels as it passed. A task they had attended to expertly and then disappeared without a trace. Now, Claude would be seen publicly injured and well away from the city square with no means of transport. It had been a risky but most ingenious plan, cooked up by Nadalia.

'Let me through!' a man proclaimed in an out-of-place Lothagian accent. It was Lukasz, Prior's usually shadow-skulking, cloak-swaddled companion. 'Let me through; he needs a doctor.'

The small crowd bustled as Lukasz pushed his way closer. One old woman was thrust aside and only kept her footing as she fell against the press and was caught by helpful hands. Lukasz emerged at the front, ill-fitting white coat about his shoulders and brown leather medical bag in hand. The outfit was a bit much, but it played well for the gawping crowd.

'Oh, my gods!' Lukasz wasn't the best actor – his skills more suited to remaining unseen than drawing attention – but the crash was dramatic enough to justify his over-the-top demeanour. 'Senator Claude Beechworth, is that you? My gods! I must get you to my surgery immediately.'

Lukasz slipped an arm under Claude's and hefted him to his feet. At the far side of the coach, Prior had alighted, rifle case in hand,

and quickly hurried to join them. The pair dragged Claude unceremoniously across the road while he wailed sorrowfully and fussed at his weeping eye. Anyone watching would see his bloodied face and easily assume his dismay was a natural reaction to the accident.

Claude's stomach turned at the sight of the second horse – the one that had not been released from its bridle. It had been partially dragged under the sliding carriage. Its head was folded under unnaturally, bone jutting out. Further down the road was the driver. The crash had ejected him and his body had collided with an iron lamp post. He was in a similar state to the horse.

Claude looked away. That man was dead because of his actions, but somehow he couldn't bring himself to care, his mind was entirely occupied by the task at hand. As the body went out of his sight, it went out of his mind.

He was dragged onto the flagstone walkway and into a building with a freshly painted sign that simply read "Surgery." He had bought the place when it was determined they would need a safe house to change their clothes. When the door to the street was shut behind them, he found his feet, pulled himself out of the assassins' grip, and took out a handkerchief to clear the blood from his face. His eye was still sore, but he was confident there would be no lasting damage.

Inside was bare. The place had been a family home less than a week earlier, but when Claude had offered the occupant four times the market value to vacate within two days, they had stripped the place with abandon. The only thing that remained was a cracked mirror that had been damaged when it was removed from the wall. It was a shame; the wood frame was thick, oiled, and carved with grapes, rolling hills and detailed vineyards. It was plainly an expensive piece, but easily forgotten compared to the windfall the family had received.

In his reflection, Claude noted the stitching on his sleeve had pulled away. It didn't matter; he was done with it anyway. He pulled off the jacket and tossed it onto the burning hearth, then tugged a rough brown robe over his head to cover his shirt, suspenders, and trousers. Once he was done, he appraised himself. As far as he could tell, even under a wide-brimmed hat, he was still unmistakably Senator Claude Beechworth.

'Are you certain this is going to work?' he asked Prior, who was already straightening a similar robe in black, fringed with red and gold embroidery.

'Nobody will pay us any mind once the ceremony starts.' Prior opened the rifle case, slid the weapon under the fabric, and secured the strap over his shoulder, hidden by the robe. 'You'll have the incense anyway; keep your head down and if anyone looks your way, wave it about and get some smoke going. How does this look?'

'Your shoulders are a bit lopsided.' Claude could easily tell the rifle was there, just as he could easily tell it was his face under the low hat brim, but he knew what he was looking for. He had to hope the preachers in the New Gods' Cathedral had taken the celebrations to heart, and had supped more sweet wine than was ordained.

Prior took a discarded curtain from the rail and tossed it about his shoulders. 'What about now?'

'Better.' Claude was surprised, but the rich velvet actually looked like just the sort of blandly extravagant thing a priest might wear.

'Let's go,' Lukasz called from the back room. He had divested himself of his surgeons garb and was now dressed as plain as any working man. Fitting, as he was to be the driver for the modest carriage they had stowed at the rear of the building.

Claude snatched up the incense burner and hurried out through the back door to the small cobbled courtyard. They wasted no time in departing for the city square.

Though the roads were busy, it wasn't long before their carriage reached a private road, reserved for the guard and those that still had to conduct business in the square – gods' men included. There had only been two weeks to plan the assassination, but Prior's team was skilled in scheming, and Claude's connections had proven invaluable. For a man as trusted as he, with wealth he had accrued as senator, it was all too easy.

As the carriage passed through unguarded gates into a quiet courtyard behind the cathedral, the thrum of the crowd in the square became a roar, signalling D'Elia's arrival on the stage. Claude had seen a draft of his speech, and even had a part in writing some of it. He had ensured it was long and dawdling so he had plenty of time to position and shoot.

When he alighted and approached the rear of the cathedral, he began to feel restless. He forced himself to breathe steadily and keep his mind on the job at hand. At least Prior would be accompanying him to the roof.

The worldly assassin led him confidently through a small rendered office building appended to the rear of the marble edifice. They weaved through a vast room of uneven desks and stacked papers, each one reporting of some relic to be documented, investigated, or procured by any means necessary. From the height of the papers, it seemed the clerical duties of the clergy could be never-ending.

Entering the southern transept, Claude swung his incense burner nervously. It drummed up plenty of sweet-smelling smoke, but all of it seemed to trail in his wake rather than plume up and obfuscate his features. He had half a mind to slow down and let it envelop him, but the other half was determined to hurry across the nave. He mastered his apprehension, lowered his head, and kept pace with Prior.

The cathedral was one of the most ornately designed and beautiful structures the Empire had ever built. The roof in particular was a marvel, with frescoes coiling up into the eaves of every spire on the roof, of which there were nearly fifty, each one built in dedication to one saint or another. Claude didn't see any of it however, his eyes fixed on the swinging incense burner and away from any of the clergy who may recognise him. The devout were often interested in the business of the Empire. Their gods' fates were intertwined with its success, so many attended public forums.

Noise built and faded as they passed by a rehearsing choir and soon they were through a door and into a spiralling stairwell. While Prior barred the door with the golden stem of a tall candelabra, Claude extinguished the burner and shook off his robes. It was no good to have them weighing at him while he took his aim. Everything was tucked neatly underneath the steps for later retrieval and the pair hurried upwards, pausing only to bar a second door that led onto a balcony.

'This is going well,' Claude commented as they made the roof. It was as much an affirmation to himself as anything. He needed his nerves steady if he was to shoot straight.

'Don't voice it, for crying out loud. Think it, but don't voice it,' Prior chided him. 'The gods have a bitter sense of humour about these things, you can't go tempting Fate.'

'I won't.' Claude rolled his eyes at the superstitions and took his rifle.

He had to resist the urge to break it open. He had loaded it that morning with the most meticulously wrapped paper cartridge he had ever made. It had slid snugly into the breech, and he had even taken the time to trim the back of the cartridge, rather than letting the gun mechanism shear it off. He had one shot and he had to make it count. There would be no time for a second, not if he was to flee quickly enough as to keep his anonymity.

They followed a narrow walkway that weaved between the spires until they reached a small parapet at the front of the building. It was there to enable access for maintenance and cleaning. The gods wouldn't be happy if their pristine white house was allowed to go green with moss. The parapet was also the perfect perch for an assassin.

'I wish we'd known about this place last time.' Prior toed the stone wall. 'Solid, good vantage. Would have made our lives a hell of a lot...'

He trailed off at the sight of Claude's glower, clearly remembering that last time it was Senator Beechworth who had been killed.

Claude moved to position, knelt, and mounted his rifle on the wall. He peered through the scope. It was an old thing, fashioned by his father from a sailor's telescope. Long range optics had become all the more common now, but back then the use was fairly niche. Claude had never changed it for a newer purpose-engineered optic. He had grown used to this one and feared that should he try to shoot through anything else, his aim would be off and might never recover.

As a precaution, he checked the surroundings. There didn't appear to be any sharp-eyed guards that had seen him, and the sun was at such a high angle that it wouldn't reflect off his spyglass and betray his position. He found the senators and his empty seat just behind Wigbert, who was conversing with the Conejan primo. Claude wondered if news had yet arrived of his carriage crash. He hoped that it had, but his alibi was secure enough either way.

The emperor was orating from horseback again. He seemed determined to secure himself in the minds of his subjects as a great warrior-leader, despite never having lifted a blade or fired a shot in his life. The man was too used to relying on others. He couldn't even pluck a grape himself; he was doted on by servants, and had to hire assassins to murder his enemies.

Claude tensed on the trigger. He was in the perfect position. The shot was lined up, but his finger refused to budge. He had seen a man die so he could be here and hadn't felt any remorse then. It had all been in the cause of justice, but now he was here he couldn't be so certain. Hiding on a roof, preparing to take a man's life for revenge didn't feel like the justice he had expected. It made him feel cheap.

'I can't do it.' He lowered the rifle with a sigh.

In that moment, it was as though a great weight had been lifted. For the first time in years he felt as though he was the master of his own destiny. He had been helpless in saving his dying father, he had been forced into the senate and held very little sway there. Now, he had the power over a man's life, and not just any man, the emperor himself. This was a gamble in which he held all the cards, and he was folding of his own volition before Prior could make him lose any more. It was pointless to live in such a bitter way.

'What?' Prior scowled.

'I can't do it.' Claude shifted away from the wall and reaffirmed his decision. 'I *won't* do it. It's time to be the bigger man and move on.'

'If you'd wanted to move on, you wouldn't have come to see me in the park.' Prior sneered. There was a fiery glint in his eyes that made Claude nervous, as if the outgoing commoner he had come to know was just a front. 'It's too late to change your mind now.'

'History cannot be rewritten.' Claude became a little bolder, remembering that amongst him and the irate assassin, he was the only one with a firearm. 'It's done; my father is dead. It doesn't matter.'

'This is to settle the score a bit! If someone wrongs you, you have to wrong them back. You can't let people walk all over you or you'll end up at the bottom of the pile.'

'If that was true for everyone… how many people have you wronged?' Claude's features were as stone, his tone acidic. 'You must have a hundred wishing you dead, would you have them settle the score too?'

'I'm an assassin, Claude. I'd love to see them try. Now, if you don't have the bollocks for it, give me the damned gun and I'll kill him myself.'

Claude wanted to refuse, but he could see Prior's hands clenching into trembling fists. There was no chance he would win if it came to blows, and he didn't want to shoot him. He still liked the man. Somehow, in his rising panic, he strung together a new convoluted logic. If the emperor died by Prior's hand, that wouldn't be a bad thing. Perhaps it was what Claude truly wanted; justice would be done and his hands would be clean. He could still be the better, more forgiving man. Not the man who thrilled at the thought of killing – the man he feared he was.

'Take it.' He tossed the gun to Prior, and the assassin shunted him out of the way.

His form wasn't as good as Claude's. It was awkward, but he seemed practised enough with a firearm in his hands. Prior rubbed the light scar at his temple, clearing beads of sweat from his sight. The rifle clicked and scratched on the stonework as he adjusted his aim. His breathing was measured and whistled softly through his nose.

Claude's breath was rapid and shallow, as manic as the distant crowd in the square below. He chewed on his thumbnail, nervous for the outcome as he waited.

As Prior fired, Claude felt a pang in his chest, like shears had snipped a taut string inside him. At the same time, the assassin recoiled with a guttural yell. The rifle clattered to the floor, and Prior staggered backwards holding his shoulder. Instantly, Claude was searching for a wound. He could only assume an imperial sharpshooter had spotted them on the roof and fired just as Prior took his shot, but he found no blood.

'That thing kicks like a bloody mule!' Prior brought himself up, his face pained but not deathly. He was rubbing his shoulder and rolling the joint. 'How much powder did you put in it?'

'I…' Claude quickly realised that the old gun's recoil had jolted Prior's unready shoulder. 'I did put a little extra in… I wanted to ensure the bullet flew true over the distance.'

'You could have bloody told me.' Prior was loosening himself up now, but it was plain from his grimace that his shoulder still ached. He might have even broken his collarbone from the reaction it caused. 'Check the stage, did I get him?'

Claude hurried to the edge. There was a lot of frantic activity, but he couldn't quite make out the details. He snatched up the rifle and peered through the scope. D'Elia was being led away by his guard, limping, but there was no blood. It seemed his horse had reared up in panic and thrown him from its back. A few guards were attempting to wrangle it to poor effect.

'Well?'

'You missed him.' Claude swept the scope over the scrambling senators and found Wigbert tending to the Conejan primo. The pair of them were covered in blood. Half of her neck had been blown out and she was long dead. Wigbert was just too shocked to see it.

A flurry of movement below drew Claude's attention to a guard, pointing for the cathedral roof. It wouldn't take long for men to assemble with rifles; others would be approaching on foot through the crowd. Claude ducked behind the wall just as a bullet took a chunk out of a nearby statue. It wouldn't have hit him if he hadn't moved but the near-miss was enough to encourage him to run nonetheless.

# 1683
## WILLIAM OF FAIRSHORE

William chewed on the last heel of stale bread, turning it from a tasteless husk into tasteless mush. He swilled it down with a dribble of his equally stale water. He was curled up like a beaten dog in the corner of the coach. It was richly upholstered, but his body ached enough that even the plumpest pillows were uncomfortable.

The roof was made of thick canvas, supported by black-iron rods, and had been folded away to enable the passengers some fresh air. The driver had insisted the sun would do him good, but William suspected it was so that he and Goldin could be watched. Their severe injuries made them reliant on the man and William knew better than to trust him. Though the coachman had made the gesture of returning their weapons, all powder and shot had been lost.

Goldin munched sullenly, finishing his rations. He belched and winced at the pain from his shoulder.

When the coachman had set out to find them, he had brought a selection of cured meats and olives, along with two loaves of bread and three urns of clean water. It was all in aid of getting them back to civilisation alive, and he had given it willingly. For himself, he had procured two bottles of fine wine and yet more preserved meat. All of it was gone.

'Vitulan wine.' Goldin swilled down the last of the crisp white. 'Dish water compared to the stuff in Lex, but it fills a hole nonetheless.'

William rolled over with a groan. He had opted to forgo the wine in favour of water and had allowed Goldin to polish off both bottles himself. The little man wasn't particularly drunk; he was aware of the danger and had paced himself over the four days travel. William hadn't even wanted a sip. Although he couldn't fight and was in no condition to run with his foot in tatters, he wanted to be alert when the coach reached its destination.

When the labouring horses finally drew the coach over the brow of a low mountain slope and D'Arnao came into view, his stomach bunched. The place didn't look particularly threatening, in fact it looked idyllic. A cluster of red, orange, and yellow buildings all clinging to the far mountainside, a green-blue lake spread out below. It didn't change the fact that he and Goldin were as good as helpless, and therein waited those responsible for of his current predicament.

The horses made light work of the remaining leg of the journey. With it all being downhill, and the weight of the cart now working with them, their pace seemed to almost double. William wasn't grateful for the change and once or twice considered jumping from the cart. The road itself switched back and forth down the mountainside, bordered by steep banks of shale. He imagined that if he threw himself right, he could slide down the shale to the point the road next passed, and get far ahead of the trundling coach. The only problem then was that he couldn't walk, and would have to rely on luck. He would need to find a well-proportioned branch for a crutch.

In the end, he spent so long deliberating on his escape that the coach was at the foot of the slope and circumnavigating the lake. It was too late. He sat back, watched the boats bobbing about the pristine waters, and awaited his fate.

'I'd love a swim,' Goldin mused wistfully. 'Can't remember the last time I went swimming.'

'I'm not sure you're in good health for swimming.' William noted the slung arm and shook his head with a smile, but the notion did give him pause. There was a possibility that *he* could swim. It might hurt, but it didn't require him putting any weight on his foot.

'Perhaps not,' Goldin agreed.

William nodded, but was at least open to the possibility, not as a leisure activity, but an option should they need to leave in a hurry. Fleeing on a stolen carriage would be easier, though the initial theft might prove impossible.

The dry dirt roads gave way to bumpy rounded cobbles. The coach lurched on the uneven surface, jolting improperly tended wounds despite the best efforts of its sprung steel suspension. William winced and turned back the other way, trying to get a modicum of comfort out of the padded leather.

'Not far now,' the coachman announced as they turned onto a winding market street. 'Would you do me a favour, and keep low? The guard here can be a bit keen and I don't want to be caught with a pair of guilders in tow.'

William sank low in his seat, but kept his eyes high enough to peer over the side. Goldin grunted as he tried to keep pressure off his shoulder in the new position.

The way was narrow, crowded with townsfolk in bright linens, and huddled with stores that spilled into the roadway. Wooden hangers boasted fine dresses, and tables were arranged with homemade jewellery. One carpenter's shop was stacked high with dining sets, each made out of different hardwood and stained a bold shade. With the horses gusting hot breath and struggling with the incline, the coachman had to take particular care to steer them through it. As such, progress slowed and became as painful as William's foot.

The coach almost came to a standstill when navigating a particularly unwieldy display outside a small fishers' guild. A placard-bearing scarecrow, hemmed in by small canoes, took up half the roadway.

William found his gaze drawn to a young woman tending a stall of worthless trinkets. Coloured stones, string-and-feather hangings, and wind chimes were the main stock, but he wasn't particularly interested in those. Her flowing dress and wavy chestnut hair were far more interesting, not to mention the smooth olive skin revealed by a wide neckline.

He almost called out to her until she turned and he realised that it was not Vesta at all. He swallowed a bitter lump. Vesta's body had been left in Blackbile along with so many other sponsors and assassins. Perhaps, if he had been faster, smarter, a better killer, maybe she would have joined him on the road.

A glance from the woman was enough to bring him back to the reality of his situation. He looked away, self-conscious for the first time in weeks. His hair was long, lank, and choked with grease. It had started to look mousy rather than its usual blonde. His body was sticky with old grime and sweat, and his clothes were torn and crusted with blood. In the sudden bout of self-pity he wondered if he would ever walk properly again, or if the barbed arrow had done irreparable damage. He looked like a roadside beggar, so easily ignored.

'Oi,' Goldin whispered and elbowed him in the ribs. William thought it was a reprimand for base lechery, but Goldin was pointing to the fishers' guild scarecrow.

The figure held a placard with a very simple design. At the centre was a crude drawing of a man. Below, it said "William of Fairshore, the False Butcher. Three hundred gold pieces." Above – in large bold letters – were four words: "Wanted. Dead or Alive." William came to realise that the scarecrow was in fact tied to a stake, with logs arranged around the empty holes at the bottom of its trousers; an effigy of a fiery death. He sank even lower into his seat.

'Who in the hells would want to kill you?' Goldin grunted. 'What kind of fishermen put out a bounty?'

'Could be a front?' William posited. He tried to ignore the anxious knot in his gut. It seemed his fears were finally being realised; the Guild had issued a contract on him.

Goldin sneered at the coachman's back. 'Do you know anything about this?'

'Know about it? Of course I do,' the coachman replied, snapping the reins. 'My employer was quite perturbed about it. Hence, sending me. He didn't want anyone getting to the pair of you before he did. You're already beaten up enough as it is.'

William weighed his options: he didn't have any. It was either stay with the coachman and be at the mercy of his employer, or leave the coachman, and be at the mercy of any number who sought his bounty. It felt wrong to do nothing, to just sit here and accept his fate, but there was nothing else.

'How are you feeling?' he asked Goldin.

'Better than you, I'd wager.' His voice was low so the coachman couldn't hear. 'I can walk at least, and if I get a pistol, or something, I can fire one handed. I *think* I'll be able to handle myself.'

'Take this then.' He passed the silver flintlock to Goldin, who slipped it inside his jacket. It wouldn't be of much use now, but Fate might see fit to supply a few cartridges, and Goldin might be able to shoot them out of a tight spot.

The coach arrived in a flat square surrounded by narrow hotels. Vines and flowers of all colours bloomed in window boxes and trailed from high balconies. Tables and chairs were arranged in the sunshine outside open-fronted eateries. If William and Goldin had arrived here uninjured, they might have cut short their travels entirely. It seemed D'Arnao was suited perfectly to the holidaymakers William had hoped they would be. Even after their respite, they might have stayed here; rich imperials on holidays of their own would always be good targets for budding thieves.

'We're here.' The coachman slowed his horses to bring them to a rest beside a vibrantly painted statue cradling a cornucopia of purple grapes.

William looked about nervously, from the imposing hotels with any number of onlookers, to the packed eateries, crowded with diners. The man who had sent for them could be anywhere. The driver got down from his bench and rounded the coach on the far side.

'I trust you can handle yourself,' he said to Goldin, opening the semicircular door as he passed.

William wondered if his wording was a coincidence or if he had heard them whispering about his pistol, but there was no time to linger on it. The coachman rounded to his side and opened the door.

'If you get yourself down, I'll help you across the square.' The coachman sniffed and flicked at his nose with his sixth finger. 'It's not far.'

William grimaced and lowered himself. If he thought the padded leather was uncomfortable, the lip of the coach was downright painful. When he had come tumbling off the carriage during the attack, it wasn't just his foot that had been injured. His whole body had been battered and bruised. He felt like an overripe fruit, the flesh beneath his skin soft and delicate. It didn't take much to make his eyes screw shut and his teeth grind. As the lip dug into the back of his ribs, he pushed off with his hands to alleviate the pressure and dropped down. He landed on one foot and trusted most of his weight to the coachman. It was an effort to keep upright and instinct brought down his injured foot for balance. An eye-watering spasm was sent up his spine. He gagged.

'That wasn't so bad, was it?' the coachman said patronisingly, tucking himself under William's arm and supporting him with his shoulder.

'For you, maybe.' William shuffled forwards.

The coachman practically carried him across the square, William's one good foot hopping in tow. Goldin followed slowly. He was in far better shape, but by no means fighting fit.

They moved to a vast dining area outside one of the eateries. Warped wooden chairs were arranged around mismatched tables, all protected from the sun by large parasols. There were at least thirty diners: local workers and foreign tourists. William eyed each group sceptically. Anyone could be the coachman's master, and any number of others could recognise him and be interested in his bounty. One man glared at him over a half-finished dish of mussels, but soon resumed his noisy slurping. William thought he spied an assassin's mark on the man's wrist. It tightened the knot in his stomach, but he hoped it was only a birthmark and his paranoia playing tricks.

Inside, the eatery was gloomy, lit only by sparse wall lanterns that were stained black from ill use. It was empty for the most part, save for one waiter tending a small bar and a group of diners who – contrary to everyone else – had opted to stay out of the sun. William spotted them early, a collection of oddly shaped silhouettes in the dark. He could tell just from the feeling in his gut that they were the ones who had sent for him. One stood up. Tall and slim, he had to stoop under the low ceiling. With a hand outstretched to shake, he met William on the threshold.

'William, I'm so pleased you could make it in one piece.' The spindly man smiled, stretching wrinkles. His shoulders were lopsided and his suit was tailored to fit his crooked frame. He looked positively demonic, with his unnaturally white teeth and his eyes glinting in the low light.

William recognised him easily. After the public humiliation in Blackbile, mere moments after he had been stripped of his victory and disqualified from the Man-Butcher Prize, this man had thought it a good idea to offer him employment. Naturally he'd refused. Anyone else in his position would have done the same. He clamped his mouth shut and kept his hand at his side. This man was certainly no *friend*.

After an awkward pause, the spindly man returned to his table. 'Come, sit. We have much to discuss.'

William shared a glance with Goldin, then hobbled to an empty chair. The coachman deposited him then sloped off with a sarcastic, 'You're welcome.'

William felt a pang of guilt. He hadn't meant to be so ungrateful for the man's help; he was just in so much pain it was hard to maintain common courtesy. He called after the man, 'Thank you, uh—'

'It's Dunstan.' The coachman sighed, then retired to the rear of the restaurant to nurse a glass of liquor.

William observed the array of oddities at the table before him. Alone, each one might not have looked so strange, but together they made an unusual and unnerving group. There was the spindly man and his lazy-eyed little companion, a white haired squat fellow with port stained skin across half his face, and another, rotund with a bullfrog neck. William feared for the man's oesophagus and chair in equal measure, both appeared to be under tremendous strain.

'First things first.' The spindly man tucked a napkin into his collar, perhaps to hide the immense jewel on his shoestring necktie. 'Allow us to introduce ourselves. I'm Alwyn Finchley, this is Deegan Finchley.'

The white haired man nodded.

'And this is—'

'I'm sorry,' Goldin interrupted, 'but what are we doing here?'

'If you would allow me to finish.' Alwyn twitched.

'Why should we?' William scowled, emboldened by Goldin's interruption. 'Your men have been trying to kill us since we left

Blackbile, that's patently obvious. Is this revenge because I wouldn't take your contract?'

Alwyn considered for a moment, then snapped his fingers. The bartender swooped in to fill everyone's glasses with rich, red wine. Others came through doors at the back, carrying platters of freshly prepared fish, both scale and shell.

'That was a simple misunderstanding on our part.' Alwyn shrugged. 'Let's talk, eat, and we can put this sorry business behind us. We should move forward.'

'Move forward?' William scoffed. 'I can't even walk.'

'Just hear me out, and we'll attend to such ailments. I know some of the best doctors, and have one in my employ, right here in town.'

William folded his arms. The smell of garlic and butter-slathered fish made him salivate, but he didn't want to give his hosts an inch.

'Will you let me explain?' The spindly man cocked an eyebrow and, as William didn't reply, he took the answer to be yes. 'I came to you with an offer in Blackbile…'

He reached out with a pair of metal tongs, selected a langoustine from a platter and transferred it to his plate. Then, taking up a delicately slender knife and fork, proceeded to part its shell and carve out miniscule portions of flesh. His portly companion, on the other hand, had taken to eagerly slurping and crunching to get the most meat from each carapace. The young boy had a similar messy aplomb towards a cut of fish. Tentatively, Goldin joined in. Only William and Deegan, the white haired Gael, abstained.

'You said no. I didn't like that. I'm not bitter about it, but I didn't like it. I came to my cousin and proposed we put a little pressure on you.' He gestured to Deegan with his fork. 'The idea was to burn down every tavern and roadhouse between here and Grod. Hence you might arrive desperate, starving, and all the more eager to accept my offer. Obviously that went a little skew whiff when the pair of you killed his wife and children.'

William's eyes met Deegan's; they were filled with a cold fury. He looked away.

'There was a little bit of retaliation on his part. I wouldn't allow him to kill you, but he could have your diminutive friend killed. No hard feelings, Mr Goldin.' Alwyn sent a sickly smile the little man's way. It wasn't returned or acknowledged. 'Our niece and nephews set out with revenge on the cards. You know how that went.'

Alwyn was orating as if the events were some tremendously exciting anecdote.

'And?' William glowered. 'Where exactly are you going with this?'

'I'd like you to take my job, my contract.' He turned his smile on William.

'You want me to kill a man for you? I'm nigh on a cripple.' William wasn't impressed with this strange family, and he didn't like the thought of working for them one bit. 'I doubt I could even shoot straight given my condition.'

'Fiddlesticks, we'll have you right as rain in no time.' He carved another small portion from his langoustine. 'And as far as I'm concerned, you more than proved yourself in killing Deegan's loved ones; they were ever so tough.'

Both William and the Gael flinched.

'As for your loss against our niece and nephew, you were hardly on form. You did come out with Mr Goldin still living, so you must have done something right.'

'What if I say no?' William toyed with the edge of the tablecloth nervously. 'Will you send your killers again?'

'You can go.' Alwyn shrugged as if it all mattered nothing to him. 'I've precious little time to waste any more on you. We'll find someone else. I'm not sure who. You've killed all the good ones, but we'll find someone. Your wounds, however, will be your own. I'll be taking my surgeon and his medicines with me when I leave town.'

'If I say yes?' William pressed. He could feel Goldin's eyes drilling into the side of him for even asking, but they weren't really in a position to confer.

Alwyn deposited the morsel of shellfish into his mouth and chewed it thoughtfully, before announcing, 'Five hundred grana.'

William felt a shiver go down his spine. He had hoped that he had killed his last, but five hundred grana was an awful lot of money. He could start again with that much, maybe even become something more than a thief.

'For expenses,' Alwyn continued. 'Weapons, food, accommodation. Then, when the job is done, there will be a payment to the tune of, let's say, five thousand.'

Goldin choked a little on his salt fish and took a healthy swig of wine to clear his throat. William swallowed phlegm.

'Each,' Alwyn added smugly.

William risked a glance at Goldin, but the little man was back to eating and ignoring the Finchleys. His poker face was impressive, so much so that William couldn't be sure if the man wasn't all that interested in the offer; he surely had to be. Five thousand grana was, for a simple assassination, a frankly ridiculous amount of money. Not to mention it was five thousand *each*.

'William of Fairshore?' someone called over the hubbub of the diners.

William tensed and slowly turned in his seat. Stood amongst the tables was the man he had seen glowering over a dish of mussels. He cocked a large black-iron flintlock. 'There's a price on your head. Come peaceably, or I'll be forced to shoot. I don't want to spoil luncheon for these fine folks.'

Alwyn sighed deeply, pulled the napkin from his neck and folded it onto the table. He worked a scrap of his meal from between his teeth with a squeeze of sallow cheeks, and fixed the intruder with a black-eyed gaze.

'Everyone, stay calm,' the gunslinger barked. 'You've a liar and a cheat dining with you. Come now, William. Don't keep me waiting.'

'Silence this fool,' the portly one beside Alwyn commanded.

Half of the people at the eatery stood and drew a weapon of one form or another. There were easily twenty in all. Pistols came from inside jackets, short scatterguns from under tables, and a selection of blades from beneath napkins.

'Thank you for your concern, but we're all tremendously calm.' Alwyn picked up his wine glass and swirled the liquid with a casual roll of his wrist. 'Perhaps you'll just toddle off and leave us to our business.'

'Five seconds,' the portly Finchley growled.

The gunslinger recoiled, but made his decision quickly enough. He lowered the hammer on his pistol, slipped it into a holster at his hip, and backed away. As he reached the periphery of the tables, he mustered up enough courage to add, 'You won't always be so protected, *False Butcher*. There's hundreds of us baying for your blood. You won't disgrace our guild or our prize again.'

He turned and fled. Moments later, everyone sat and stowed their weapons as if nothing had happened. William suspected the gunslinger would be followed and killed. The Finchleys didn't seem the sort to let an infringement like that drop so idly.

The low hum of luncheon chatter resumed. William turned back to his hosts, his eyes slow to adjust in the gloom.

'What do you say?' Alwyn sipped his wine. 'Kill a man for me?'

'If I'm to make a decision, I need to know the details. Let's start with: which man?' William tried to look calm and collected. Five thousand grana was a lordly sum, enough to keep him comfortable for a very long time.

'I thought we were going to be thieves?' Goldin interrupted; he looked concerned. 'I thought you didn't want to be an assassin?'

William thought about his life before he joined the Guild. What he could remember had been a constant torture, whether it had been slaves trying to gut him, or that pawnbroker making a slave *of* him. More recently, since he had given up being an assassin, he had been accosted twice on the road and almost killed. It seemed in the Empire, if William wasn't the one doling out the death and despair, he was the one it was being heaped on top of.

Right now, he felt weak. As helpless as that little boy he used to be, forced to wear a ball and chain and work every hour the gods gave. He didn't want to return to that. Ever. And if that meant he had to compromise his morals this one last time, it was a sacrifice he was willing to make.

'It's five thousand, Goldin,' William hissed, surprised the little man wasn't tearing off Alwyn's arm for it. 'Each.'

'I thought you were done with killing.'

'Yes, but...' William lingered on his time as apprentice under Ojo and the life he had led before entering the Man-Butcher Prize. Yes, the kills filled him with regret, but was guilt really as bad as what he had been through before he became an assassin?

'It's… it's what we're good at,' William reasoned. 'I was trained by the great Ojo Azul, and I'm as good as a man-butcher. There's no point giving up on that. And if we kill this one man, we'll be set, we won't have to kill anyone else ever again.'

Once the contract was done, William would have enough money to get away from the Vitulan Empire and to keep himself safe. He could go somewhere there wasn't a price on his head, a place where nobody knew who he was. He would never again have to worry where his next meal would come from, and could live a better life.

Turning back to Alwyn, he asked, 'Who's the target?'

'A senator. Senator Sepo Falade, Numinian primo.' Alwyn's voice was calm and level as if this was all perfectly normal. William knew that it wasn't. For guild members, senators were strictly off limits. 'It'll be a tough contract to fulfil, I'm sure, but the fee is well worth the risks. Beyond his death, I have only one requirement: you take my best schemer with you. What do you say?'

'I'm not sure.' Goldin spoke first. 'This is too big for us, and… Will, these people tried to kill us, how can we rely on them?'

'I'll put the money in a trust. Make payment conditional on the target's death.' Alwyn twitched again. There was a look of scorn across his face, and William suspected the man would have much rather succeeded in Goldin's killing. 'We have connection enough to make it all official with the bank. Then it's out of our hands.'

'I still think it's a bad idea.' Goldin harrumphed. 'But if you want to take the contract, I'll help.'

William swallowed another clot of phlegm. He knew this was too good to be true, but if it wasn't, he would never have to kill again. One man's death might prevent him killing hundreds more. He had made up his mind quickly and impulsively, he just hadn't dared voice it so hastily. There was only one right decision, and this had to be it. 'We'll take the contract.'

'Excellent.' Alwyn clapped his hands and wrung them together. 'I'll send word to my surgeon that you'll be ready for treatment presently. Once you're fit enough, you can head for the capital.'

He raised his glass. 'To a job done right. *Saluti.'*

# 1649
## CLAUDE BEECHWORTH

'Reload it,' Prior hissed. He had thrown himself to the floor after the guard had blasted a statue's head into dust, and was still trying to recover from the excitement of it. Claude had planned to run, but it seemed Prior had anticipated this, and was now clutching at his ankle and preventing his escape.

'Reload it?' Claude balked. 'If I try for the emperor, I'll lose my head.'

'No, that ship has sailed.' Prior pushed up to his hands and knees. 'We might need to shoot our way out, so reload it before you go dashing off.'

Claude swallowed; he had vastly underestimated his likelihood of dying. Quickly, he fished into his pocket, retrieved one of the well-made paper cartridges and slipped it into his rifle. He clipped it shut with care and readied the hammer.

When he looked up, Prior was almost out of sight, crawling away as low and quick as he could. Claude followed suit. He shuffled along the walkway and only stood to run once he was certain to be hidden by the spires. Any number of imperial marksmen would have their sights trained on the cathedral roof by now.

'You lead the way.' Prior panted at the doorway to the stairwell, still struggling to fully regain his breath. 'With any luck… the guard should… the crowd.'

'The panicked crowd should stop the guard getting to us. Yes, I know.' Claude hurried past and down the spiral stairway. 'I did pay attention to the plan.'

Their feet rumbled down the wooden steps. Heavy breathing seemed to amplify in the tight, round tower. He could hear distant shouts, but nothing in particular was discernible. This mad dash for freedom had always been part of their plan, there was little else to do once one had shot a rifle over a crowd, but it was far less straightforward than in theory. It was hard to account for the sheer panic one felt, especially when the wrong person had been killed, and it felt as though everything was rapidly unravelling around them.

Claude made it to the next floor and unbarred the door. He waited to open it until Prior was ready; the man was still clumsily trailing down the stairs. He took position across the small room and aimed the rifle at the door in case any guards came through.

'You paid attention to the plan?' Prior wheezed as he arrived alongside. 'I thought you must have missed the part where you were supposed to shoot the emperor.'

'Admonishing me is hardly conducive to escape.' Claude spat on the floor. Fear, or the sudden rush of adrenaline, was collecting phlegm in his throat and he had to cough to dislodge it. He spat again. In his frenzy, all thought of etiquette had gone out the window.

'It was only a joke, Claude. No need to get your britches bunched up. We can try again. Call this a trial run.'

The door to the stairwell burst open, the gilt candelabra Prior had used to bar it proving useless against a charging monk. He staggered in and stopped, startled at the sight of the two men.

'Senator Beechworth?' the monk scowled. He was plainly confused by what he had found, but he didn't have to wait long before Claude made it obvious.

There was a clap of smoke and the monk staggered backwards. His hands clutched about his stomach, but despite his efforts, his thick robe was quickly blackened with heavily flowing blood. By the time he crumpled to the floor, Claude and Prior were halfway across the transept.

To the left, the nave was crowded with frightened people. They had come inside to shelter from the gunman, unaware that this very building had been his vantage. Thankfully, the monks had made a barrier of pews to stop the crowd spilling too far inside and damaging the relics. There were only a few in Claude's path for the exit, and all of them were incapable of stopping him. They would, however, be able to identify him to the guard. There was nothing he could do about that now; there were too many witnesses forcing their way inside.

Prior barged a monk out of his path and shouldered the door to the small cleric's office at the rear of the building. It was only seconds before the pair of them were through it and into the coach. Lukasz snapped the reins and the carriage lurched into motion. Claude loaded another cartridge into his rifle and aimed it out of the window, ready for any pursuing guardsmen.

'You'll kill a damned priest, will you?' Prior shook his head, bitter disappointment creasing his brow. 'But the emperor's off limits, is he?'

'I don't know.' Claude kept his eyes on the swiftly passing streets. 'I didn't have chance to think about the monk.'

'Perhaps you thought too much about the emperor. You were certainly aiming at him long enough.'

'Perhaps I did.' Claude rounded in anger. He didn't mean it, but as he turned, he brought the rifle with him and trained it on the surly assassin. 'And perhaps if I had the time again, I'd do it. *And perhaps, assassinating the emperor is too much for a first-time killer?*'

Prior's lip twitched, his eyes drifted slowly to the rifle. Calmly, he asked, 'Are you thinking of shooting me with that thing?'

'Perhaps.' Claude let the tension draw out and watched the assassin's eyes quiver like gelatine for a moment longer. 'If you keep on carping, I might have to.'

He lowered the rifle and pinched at his closed eyes.

'My head's beginning to ache, so just keep your whining to a minimum.' Claude took a breath. 'It's not all bad though, is it? We've scared D'Elia well enough, he may just pay you what he owes.'

Prior sighed, tried to start a few sentences, but they all faltered after one or two syllables. Claude hoped these were the failed apologies of a too-proud man. Finally, Prior spat out something cognisant. 'It's just so frustrating. We were so close; one trigger pull.'

'I know.' Claude nodded. 'I'm sorry too.'

He checked out of the window; the carriage was still hurtling along. It seemed – as Claude had ensured in the senate – the lion's share of the guard had been focused in the square. There were few out in the city to set up barricades or to prevent their escape.

'We're nearing the surgery,' he confirmed as a local landmark sped by.

'And?' Prior lay back in his seat.

'We can get changed out of these grubby clothes, finish the plan.' Claude shrugged, feeling the weight of his shirt. It was made heavy with a saturation of nervous sweat. 'We can celebrate a – not a job well done – a job survived. I have a case of Chateau *Something* at my townhouse.'

'You've been compromised, Claude,' Prior said softly. 'You can't just go home. We've got to get away from here.'

Claude choked on a bit of saliva. There had been a sense of doom and regret twisting in the pit of his stomach ever since they had left the cathedral. He had known it was there, but had refused to acknowledge the cause. Now, Prior had voiced it: he had been seen, and not just by one person that could have been mistaken, by a whole score of people. His gun had still been smoking.

'Yes,' he mumbled distantly.

Not only had he failed to enact revenge for his father, he had forfeited his position in the senate. Probably his holdings, too. He would be a wanted man for the rest of his days and it would all end in blood, or dancing at the end of a rope.

'It's not all that bad, Claude.' Prior clapped him on the back. 'You might be a wanted man, but that's not the worst thing you can be. It's certainly more exciting than senate parchments.'

He jabbed a jovial elbow into his ribs, but Claude was having none of it. He turned away. 'What in the hells am I supposed to do now?'

'There's a village to the north east; in Grod.' Prior seemed to have lost his irritation over the failed assassination, and was almost merry in his fresh plotting. 'I've got some unsavoury friends up there, the boys and I were planning to meet them. Best place we could think of for a hide out. Not too far, but outside the Empire, and the folk there have more allegiance to Stark than the Vitulans.'

He dipped his head to try and catch Claude's eye.

'It's no different now. We'll be hunted, yes, but it's not a bad life.' He sat back and propped his legs on the opposite bench. 'Anyway, now you're over the first hurdle – killing that old monk –

you might make a decent rifleman-assassin. There's good money in it.'

Claude moved through the old wooden house, ducking beneath lintels and dodging tightly crammed furniture. It wasn't much, and was on the verge of falling down, but it was well positioned. The village of Czarny was high on the slopes of a volcano, not too far from the Landslide River, and from the house there were views for miles. Transports could be seen coming and going, and should a small army come in search of the would-be killers of the emperor, there would be plenty of time to escape.

There were only two bedrooms, but it was enough to make do. Prior, as the leader of the group, stayed in the larger room with his wife and new born child. Claude had been given the other, because, in Prior's words, he was used to the finer things in life and it wouldn't do to have him sleeping in the attic or draped over a moth-eaten couch. It was slightly embarrassing to be given his own space, but he appreciated it nonetheless. The other gang members slept where they could, squashed together like forgotten luggage bags. As such, Claude felt it right that he do his part and earn his private room the only way an assassin could.

He had killed two that day and accrued funds enough to keep himself in the finest wine and food Grod had to offer. It was still foul, bitter-tasting tripe, but it was slightly *less* foul, bitter-tasting tripe. He would also contribute his share to the group's coffers.

He had grown accustomed to killing, and was surprised at his lack of remorse. Prior had been right. It was simple business, and that was all there was to it. The only regret he had was that he had faltered at the crucial moment. If he had kept control of his emotions, the emperor would be dead, and he would have the name of the man who shot his father. Killing was better without emotion, but now his initial trepidations had passed, he craved the indulgence of a little revenge.

He set down his rifle case and went to find Prior. He nodded to Lukasz and a few others, then proceeded out of the back door to the yard that came with the property. Prior and his wife were sat at a small table scattered with bullets, powder, and coins. She was nursing their infant son, and Prior was nursing a hangover. He was hunched over, drinking some apothecary's green concoction from a wooden cup, and counting their gold pieces to make himself feel better.

'Gods, it's ripe today.' Claude pulled a handkerchief out of his jacket pocket and shrouded his mouth and nose. 'Is there anywhere in this damned country that isn't on the banks of that fetid river?'

'Of course there is.' Prior grinned. He seemed to take great enjoyment in the former senator's discomfort.

'I find it hard to believe.' Claude sat at the table with them. 'I've been to a dozen different villages and I can't get away from that pervading stench.'

'I would have thought we'd be used to it, practically living on top of it as we do,' Nadalia remarked.

'I don't think there's much getting used to Czarny.' Claude looked out over the winding little village. He didn't like it here, and not many of the others did either. He had heard one of the assassins refer to the place as the arse of the world, and he didn't disagree. Considering the smell, the locals, and the ash, there were no redeeming factors. He changed the subject, lest he lament his change of circumstances any further. 'How goes the watch?'

'Grand.' Prior made a little stack of coins then knocked them over. His hair was greasy from the night before and he was letting it hang in his face to shield darkly circled eyes from the sun. He wasn't even sat in a position where he could look over the village. 'A cart went out first thing from the blacksmith's. There's not been much since.'

'No?' Claude observed a carriage trundling up the dusty track. It was certainly not one of the locals – the paintwork was clean for a start. 'No new transports have come into the town, let's say, over the plains to the south? You would need to have not looked for over an hour to miss something like that.'

Prior scowled up at him, then twisted to look for the carriage. After a moment of searching, he found it and leapt up, knocking the table half a foot. The coins jostled. Another stack fell over and one rolled onto the floor.

'Is it imperial?' he asked, scrabbling for his gun. 'I knew they'd find us eventually, not this soon, though. Nadalia, get Walter out of here, we'll fight them off.'

'Calm down, would you?' Claude reached across for the wooden cup and sipped the green juice. He shuddered at the taste of it, but it was quite refreshing. 'I don't think we'll be fighting today.'

'You want to run?' Prior was whey-faced from his over indulgence, and skittish. At a word he'd bolt.

Claude smiled, enjoying the fact that it was he of the three who was cool and collected. Since he had taken to killing, he had found a power and confidence in himself that he had previously thought impossible. The others hadn't noticed it yet, but they would soon enough.

'Not at all, dear fellow. Look closer. That's a Daschinger coach, designed to hold four, maybe five at most.' Claude took another sip of the green juice. 'As we outnumber them fivefold, I wager they have a message for us. There'll be no fighting today.'

'What kind of message?'

'Something from the emperor, I suppose.' Claude shrugged.

'What makes you so sure?' Prior snatched up a handful of freshly folded cartridges and stuffed them into his pocket.

'A hunch.' Claude had seen the carriage on the road that morning, and while he had been initially unnerved, had followed it and watched. He knew there were only four men: one coachman, two guards, and an envoy. Once he had established that the envoy was intended for none other than Claude Beechworth, he hurried back to the presumably compromised safe house to await the message.

'A hunch?' Prior shook his head.

'Sit down Prior, you're making the place look untidy.' Claude settled back into his seat.

For a moment Prior frowned, then churlishly did as he was told. 'Nadalia, you should take Walt to the market; I want you safe should anything go wrong.'

She seemed to consider arguing that she was the best gunslinger he had, but decided against it. She bid them both farewell, belted a pistol to her hip, and sauntered off with little Walter in her arms.

Prior appraised Claude with a sceptical eye, then reached for his wooden cup. He groaned as he leant for it, then tipped it back, downing what remained in one gulp.

'You're sure there won't be any fighting?' He smeared the dregs from the corners of his mouth.

'I'm sure.' Claude smiled. 'Not unless we start anything. I suggest we hear them out, let them leave, then leave ourselves. An imperial spy must have picked up our trail, they clearly know where we're staying.'

'You don't think there's a rat amongst us, do you?'

'They're your men, you tell me.' Claude shrugged. 'Let's not worry about it today.'

'You're right. We'd better prepare for this carriage.' Prior tossed the cup and thrust himself to his feet. He still looked incredibly tired, but he held himself purposefully.

The pair headed inside and quickly gathered their posse. Some were out in the market, or completing what few contracts had come their way, but most were there, enough to put two armed men in each window and five more on the veranda. Claude walked out into the street to observe them from the envoy's perspective.

'Positively fearsome,' he confirmed, then headed back inside for his rifle.

After a short wait, the carriage came back into view. It progressed slowly at first, with the driver peering at each building in turn. He was trying to find an address, but when he saw the five armed men waiting for him, it all but confirmed it. He took the horses to a trot to reach his destination and stopped outside.

Two guardsmen alighted first, big brutes with old-fashioned leather jerkins and antique matchlocks at their hips. The envoy came after, dressed in a traditional Vitulan robe. The sweeping white wool looked ridiculous against the filthy grey backdrop of the Grod village. If any locals saw him – retrograde as they were – he might have been beaten for dressing as a woman. Of course, none of Prior's killers would mind if he had been wearing a dress; there were a several amongst them with a penchant for the finest in women's jewellery and soft fabrics.

The envoy straightened; he appeared to think himself thoroughly high blooded. He had a scroll of parchment clutched to his chest, sealed with purple wax. It mattered little that he was stood in a slew of mud and the discarded excreta of twenty substance-abusing outlaws.

'Is the former senator, Lord Beechworth, at this residence?' The envoy's nose wrinkled as a spear of local odour punctured through the oppressive volcanic sulphur. He looked across the five armed men, dismissing each one with a sneer.

'I'm here.' Claude stepped onto the porch. He held his rifle lazily. To anyone who didn't know him, it would look as though he weren't ready to shoot, but that wasn't the case.

'I have a missive for you.' The envoy affected a sour smile, intensified by his disgust for the surroundings. 'I am Demetri Georgio Nomikos, imperial envoy–'

'Hand it over, then.' Prior was at Claude's back, pistol aimed at the envoy. 'We haven't got all day.'

'I'm supposed to read it.' The envoy swallowed and shuffled nervously, deflated that his long-rehearsed introduction was dismissed.

'Go on then, read it,' Claude instructed. 'I'm on tenterhooks.'

The envoy cracked the wax seal and unfurled the parchment with as much ceremony as he could muster with trembling hands. He cleared his throat and began. ' *"For Claude Beechworth, former senator secondo of Garland."* '

The envoy stopped, his fingers fidgeting about the parchment.

'Yes?' Claude raised an eyebrow.

'It says, *"Pause for dramatic effect,"* ' the envoy explained, tapping the text in question with a manicured nail.

One of the men in the windows cocked his flintlock. It made a brilliantly menacing sound, though it just meant that the man had simply forgotten to do it sooner. Even so, the effect on the envoy was palpable.

'I– I have to read it as intended, it's my duty.' His air of superiority slipped away with his cowardice. 'I apologise.'

He looked about for a reply but none was forthcoming.

' *"You missed – Pause for dramatic effect."* ' He read the instruction aloud as if to explain himself, then shuffled the paper in his hands. Once the required pause had passed, he continued. ' *"You bloody well missed, didn't you?"* '

Claude and Prior exchanged a look. Prior muttered something about not missing a second time, but it wasn't loud enough to deter the envoy.

' *"I trust this letter, and my envoy, find you in rude health. My informants advise that you are going from strength to strength in your new career. I am alive and well, though the same cannot be said for our Conejan colleague."* '

An image of the primo's gushing neck flashed through Claude's mind. He sneered at it, which made the envoy quail behind his parchment.

' *"Enemies of the Empire are everywhere."* ' The envoy coughed to clear his throat again. ' *"Expansion is inevitable and essential, and the senate cannot allow for internal dissidents such as yourselves. Enemies of the emperor will be expunged with swift and fiery prejudice."* '

Prior looked across, weighing his pistol in hand. Claude gave a slight shake of his head.

'Would you get to the point?' Prior sneered.

'I have to read it as written.' The envoy scanned the scroll, unfurling it even further. 'But it does go off on a bit of a tangent. I'll skip ahead.'

He shimmied the parchment in his fingers, skipping a good third of the text, then continued, ' *"As you have demonstrated, I am in need of protection and require a means of despatching my enemies. And, as I recently found great success in co-opting the Merchants' Guild to remove a fierce pirate from the waters about Wisteria, I got to thinking – pause for dramatic effect."* '

Claude sighed and toyed with his rifle.

' *"As I use the merchants as a whip to lash unruly businessmen and rivals, there is a great need for a guild of assassins with which to whip whomever else I choose. I need killers I can utilise in secret, people who can remove certain political inconveniences. You see where I'm going, I'm sure."* ' The envoy pulled a conspiratorial expression that was certainly both instructed on and well-rehearsed. ' *"Should you choose to accept this offer, every so often, my envoys will come to you with targets. You will kill them for me. In return, I will ensure that no more imperials come searching inside the borders of Grod."* '

'Protection and free licence to kill whomever we want'– Prior's words were intended to sound sceptical, but it was obvious he was interested –'what's the catch?'

'I'm getting to it.' The envoy bristled at the interruption. ' *"By all means continue your business. I encourage you to grow your guild to something greater. The more killers you host, the better you might serve my needs. However, you will ensure the safety of the senate, and protect the lives of key individuals as and when you are instructed."* '

'It sounds too good to be true.' Claude was still doubtful.

'Let me reiterate.' The envoy cleared his throat for a third time; it was a wonder the man's gullet wasn't red raw. 'The alliance is to be kept secret. As such, you will remain outlaws. While any efforts to rout a guild of killers in Grod will be strangled with red tape, assassins may still be hanged for their crimes if caught within the Empire. This is the extent of the offer.'

'I don't like it,' Prior hissed subtly to Claude. 'I became a killer to avoid service to my betters.'

'What other choice do we have?' Claude shrugged. 'D'Elia is offering an olive branch. I suggest we take it.'

# 1657
## CLAUDE BEECHWORTH

Claude refilled his glass, but his return to the card table was forestalled by the view through the window. Things were going well for the Assassins' Guild: membership numbers were up, and their town had become more than just a collective of killers. With a vast market, profitable factories, and even a theatre for those too distinguished to find their entertainment in the brothels, the place was a hotbed of budding commerce.

Granted, Claude wasn't so enamoured with the name. He had wanted to call the town Aldermoor after his childhood home, but others had taken to calling it Blackbile for the indiscriminate volcanic sludge that flowed down the Landslide River.

A dockside crane hefted crates from a steel-bottomed barge, built to withstand the heat and the abrasive rubble that was carried on the current. Claude sipped his sherry and marvelled at the wonders that could be achieved when progress wasn't hampered by regulation and morality. Only the other day, a promising young doctor had arrived in the newly finished town hall. He had proclaimed that, in exchange for test subjects, he could provide the Guild with the most wondrous tinctures and restoratives. The man's efficacy remained to be seen, but Claude was hopeful.

Just then, with the distant sound of splintering wood, the crane collapsed. A great steel pulley flung out under the tension, carving a path through a waiting horse and cart. A length of rope followed it, entangling workers and dragging them into the steaming torrent. Claude sighed, but at least now the guild artisans knew the minimum width for the reinforcements required on such cranes. In the Vitulan Empire, the limits were never tested so thoroughly.

'We haven't got all day, Claude,' Prior called from behind him. 'It's your turn.'

Claude turned to see the self-proclaimed mayor looking up at him expectantly. He was sat at a table piled with polished gems, grana, and exquisite jewellery. The streaked remnants of powdered intoxicants could still be detected amidst a clutter of playing cards. Claude noted the backs of his cards were now dog-eared and adorned with red crests; he was quite certain they had been plain blue before.

He stepped closer, set down his sherry, and picked up his cards. He had an ace and a queen, and with the trio of aces on the table, that made four of a kind. Given the other cards on offer, he couldn't be beaten. It was a strange move on the part of whoever had cheated him, as his hand had been woeful and he'd expected to fold. He eyed his three companions. It was obvious who the cheater was.

The man on his right, one of Prior's brutes, was now sheepishly clutching two blue-backed cards. He glared as if it was Claude who had wronged him by returning before he had the chance realise his mistake. It was his own fault for being too addled to realise he'd held the winning hand to begin with. The man tossed down the cards with a grunt and stormed out of the room, slamming the door behind him.

'And then there were three!' The player to Claude's left chortled. It was the fresh-faced, young doctor. He reclined in his chair and folded one leg over the other. 'What's your play?'

'All in.' Claude pushed his pot into the middle of the table. He had won the majority of hands so far and his plunder far outstripped that of the young doctor. He smirked. 'Barnaber, what's *your* play?'

'Ah, too rich for my blood. My father always said: don't gamble that which you aren't willing to lose.' Barnaber slapped his knees and stood. 'What say we have a tipple of my aniseed liqueur? I see Claude is sated with his sherry, but you *Mr Mayor?*'

Prior inclined his head, more interested in studying his cards at that moment.

Barnaber approached the bookshelf. Prior had it built because it seemed like the mayorly thing to do, but it hadn't taken long after its construction for him to remember that he didn't own any books.

The shelves had promptly been repurposed into a display for fine foreign liquors. Barnaber snatched up the bottle he had brought from his homeland and picked at the wax seal with a hand that only sported three fingers.

'Cut it off with this.' Prior pulled a gold plated flick knife from his boot and tossed it to the doctor.

Barnaber fumbled the catch, accidentally pressing the button and extending the blade. He almost dropped the bottle too, but managed to save that at the expense of the knife. It landed point first in the carpet, a fraction of an inch from his foot. Awkwardly, the young doctor bent and retrieved it, rubbing over the rug with the heel of his polished shoe to obscure the hole he had made.

'If only my serums knitted carpet the way they knit flesh.' He chuckled, embarrassed, but neither Claude nor Prior reacted. They were both too drawn into the game by then.

Prior took a last look at his cards, then said, 'Well, *my* father always said fortune favoured the bold. All in. Let's see what you have then.'

Claude tapped his cards on the table, eyeing the ace, but didn't reveal it to Prior. 'I think we'd better steer clear of fathers, don't you? And, look at your pot, it hardly equals mine. Do you even have enough to call?'

'We're trying to have a friendly game here, Claude. Can a man not passively mention his father? There's no need to be so sour about it.' Prior leant back in his chair and the wood creaked in protest. 'What if I add my knife to the pot? The gold in the hilt is worth plenty. You can have that if you win. When Barnaber's got his bottle open, obviously.'

'I still don't think it's enough.' Claude sniffed. 'Offer me something worthwhile.'

Prior chewed on the inside of his cheek. Then, with a grunt, said, 'Speaking of fathers, what say I tell you who killed yours? If you win, that is. If you lose, I don't want you to mention it again. It's unbecoming of an assassin.'

Claude mulled on it. He hadn't sought the information out in all the years he had been part of the Guild, but now it was laid before him, his need to learn the truth was overwhelming.

'Deal.' Claude dropped his cards, finally revealing his queen and ace.

'Four aces and a high queen; a fine hand.' Prior laid his own cards with a flourish. He had an ace and a king. 'But it's not good enough.'

'You cheating swine.' Claude shook his head. Should he have expected anything else? Probably not.

'Always got an ace up my sleeve. You know that.' Prior shrugged. 'That's what you get for gambling with killers. We don't often play by the rules.'

'You forget, I'm a killer too,' Claude said quietly. He set a finger on his ace and slid it aside, revealing a second ace concealed between his two cards. 'A queen and *five* aces; that *is* a fine hand.'

'You crafty bastard.' Prior accepted his knife and a glass of spirit from Barnaber. He slurped a measure and waited for the doctor to return to his seat before continuing. 'I suppose you should know. Come collect your prize.'

Prior beckoned him. Claude arched a brow, wondering exactly what the assassin was planning.

'Come here, and I'll give you what you've won.' Prior fiddled with the golden knife so that it reflected the light from the open window.

'Very well.' Claude rounded the table to loom over Prior, who still reclined in his chair. 'Who killed my father?'

'I'm letting you have this as a sign of faith.' Prior pursed his lips, offering the flick knife hilt first. 'I'm sure you know anyway; you're clever enough. It was me who killed your old man.'

Claude smiled. While Prior had gambled and lost with his wealth, he hoped to gamble and win with his life. It was an exercise in extreme trust, something to be admired. Claude took the flick knife, studying its gilding and the subtle ivory inlay. A tiger was depicted clawing an elephant in a miniature engraving. 'I had my suspicions. When you shot D'Elia and missed, your reaction was a little… extreme. You said my rifle "kicked like a mule," I remember that like it was yesterday. It was almost as if you had a wounded shoulder. I clipped my father's killer in just that spot.'

Barnaber shuffled uncomfortably.

'Let bygones be bygones, eh?' Prior beamed, but he didn't seem so relaxed anymore. 'We're in this together now, me and you. This is our town. There's no secrets between us.'

Claude flipped the knife to inspect the inlay on the reverse. This side depicted the elephant hefting the tiger overhead with its trunk. The cat's back was broken.

'Claude?' Prior sounded downright nervous. It didn't suit him. 'You didn't kill D'Elia, and your father's death was on *his* say-so. You understand, don't you? We'll move past this and the Guild will be stronger for it. You can't hold your father over me. We're both killers. We're both assassins. Senator Beechworth was just another contract. There's no ill will in a killing.'

'Sometimes there is.' Claude plunged the blade into Prior's chest, feeling the sharp edge scrape between ribs. Once it was buried to the hilt, he stepped back to admire his handiwork.

Prior writhed and gasped. His eyes bulged with shock. He tried to speak, but in the immediate his breathing was too rapid to allow the formation of words.

Claude pulled a handkerchief from his pocket and cleared flecks of blood from his knuckles. He wasn't pleased with himself, but he didn't regret his actions either. The sensation was of mundane accomplishment, as if he had just signed the last of a stack of parchments. A job had been done. A chapter had been finished. He could move on to bigger and better things.

Turning to the doctor, he asked, 'Can your elixirs save him?'

Barnaber was pressed so hard into the back of his chair he might snap the wood. His hands were fidgeting, his feet shuffling. When he couldn't force a reply out of his stuttering jaw, Claude snapped, 'Spit it out then! Can you save this man or not?'

'I– I– If I could get to my medical bag, yes.' Barnaber wrung his hands. 'I'd remove the blade and pack his wound with a serum that encourages the flesh to knit. It really is quite something. He would be well again in mere days.'

'Did you hear that?' Claude leered at Prior. The man hissed hot breath through clenched teeth, his hands gripping white-knuckled on the arms of his chair. 'This man can save you.'

'Shall I get my bag?' Barnaber scraped his chair back.

'No.' Claude drew the blade from Prior's chest and pivoted on his heel. He directed the tip for the young doctor; blood dripped onto the card table. 'Sit down.'

Barnaber slumped onto his seat. He had the defeated look of a man who had only just realised the depravity of the organization he had aligned himself with. He wouldn't cause any trouble.

Claude regarded Prior coolly. He gulped for air like a landed fish and one hand clutched his chest as if he might hold the wound shut. His fingers were slick with blood.

'I just wanted you to know before you bleed out, this wasn't an impulsive thing. I don't regret it. You can be saved by the doctor's miracles, even now. That won't be happening.'

Just then, small feet drummed on the floorboards outside. Before anyone had the chance to act, the handle was yanked down and the door barged open. A boy in a linen one-piece burst in, holding a threadbare teddy in one hand and a toy rifle in the other. He tossed down the bear, threw himself behind an ornamental globe, and peered out from his cover with the rifle held sloppily to his shoulder.

'Bang, bang!' He giggled. 'Daddy, Uncle Claude, can we play Assassins and Imperials?'

Claude and Prior shared a look. The boy couldn't see the extent of his father's wounds as Prior's chair faced away from the door. Prior gritted his teeth and forced himself to level his breathing.

Claude spoke to cover what remained audible of the dying man's struggle. 'Walter, that was a tremendous entrance, I must say! If we were imperials, I'd wager we'd be struggling for life right now.'

'Can we play?' the boy pressed, moving out from behind the globe.

'I'm afraid your father is very busy. Why don't you run along? Myself and this fine young gentleman'– he gestured to the squirming doctor –'will be out shortly. We can have a game then.'

'Dad?'

Prior swallowed and screwed his face tight. With an effort, he spoke as evenly as he could manage. 'Do as Uncle Claude says now, Walt. You be a good boy for him. Run along to the square. I'll be watching over you.'

Claude tensed as the boy stepped closer, but he simply picked up his teddy, and dashed out of the door. He waited until the boy's footsteps faded before locking eyes with Prior. He owed him that much. 'Don't worry, old friend. I'll look after young Walter. I know all too well what it's like to lose one's father.'

# PART 6

## 1673
### GWYNETH FINCHLEY

It was late by the time the coach entered the grounds of the Manor, and Gwyneth was far beyond tired. Sleep evaded her because travelling made her ill if she looked anywhere but out of the window. There was something about feeling the motion, but not seeing it, that turned her stomach. It meant that closing her eyes for a quick nap was well out of the question. Now they had arrived, there was little she wanted other than a private room and generous quilts. That too was out of the question.

Finchleys from across the Empire and beyond had gathered for a family reunion. A celebration, her father had said, though he seemed more fraught than jubilant. In contrast, Gwyneth's mother was brimming with excitement, her eyes sparkling with the prospect of the night ahead.

As Gwyneth pondered on what could elicit such conflicting manners from her parents, the tree-lined road gave way to a vast expanse of gravel.

It seemed they were some of the last to arrive. At least twenty carriages were arranged on the gravel and even more had been taken to the rear of the property. As they reached an awaiting footman, valets in red velvet hurried to make room for them between a gaudy yellow vehicle and a highly sprung gig.

Gwyneth leant out of the open window and looked up, more interested in the grand house than the toiling staff. In the dark, it looked like the lair of a blood-sucking beast from one of her storybooks. The sight of high spires and slouching, half-rotten gargoyles sparked her bitter imagination. Even from a young age she had drawn delight from the macabre.

The footman opened the carriage door and Gwyneth slipped out, her attention drawn from the daunting architecture by the ceremony of it. Standing to the side, she waited for her parents. As regally as any distant queen, and giving no indication of the club foot that pained her, her mother disembarked. Gravel crunched pleasantly as she stepped. Her bosom was powdered white, and her angular face was softened with subtle paints. Green brocade skirts fell in a broad bell around her, cut to display the custom, emerald-studded shoes beneath.

Dressed to match, Gwyneth fell in pace with her mother and attempted to emulate her grace. Even her father, who despised such formality, wrangled with a cravat and refastened his waistcoat buttons. He thanked the footman quietly, then puffed as he jogged the short distance to catch up.

Lifting her chin proudly, Gwyneth was determined to make a good impression on her extended family. If she behaved well, she was sure they'd let her play the grown-up games her parents had only hinted at. She just hoped the carnival atmosphere would be enough to keep the fatigue at bay.

Lofty mahogany doors were flung wide, spilling light and music into the evening. A dozen footman lined their route, bowing in turn as Gwyneth's family entered. Beyond, was a grand hall filled with guests holding tall flutes of sparkling wine, all talking and laughing with the familiarity that came with shared blood. Each man was dressed in a fine black suit with long tails, and the women wore a variety of garish evening wear that made Gwyneth's frock look drab by comparison.

Once inside, her mother was tugged by the elbow into a circle of gossiping aunts, while her father reacquainted himself with distant relatives. Gwyneth waited patiently, albeit shyly, unsure of what to do. She recognised almost everyone in the gathering, but had been so young when they had last met she couldn't put names to faces. She shared a smile with a woman who had a purpling, swollen neck, and waved at a one-legged man who was propped on an ornate, bone crutch.

'Gwyn.' Her mother knelt down with considerable effort. Gwyneth had always been small for her age, and at only ten years old, was dwarfed by many at the gathering. 'Your cousin, Fortuna, is in the study. You might go ahead and find her there? Your father and I need to talk with your Uncle Alwyn. Is that alright?'

Gwyneth nodded as her mother stood and shuffled away. Her father squeezed her shoulder as he passed and was gone. Without their coat tails to hang onto, Gwyneth felt strangely liberated. She wouldn't have to endure the tedium of aged relatives, and was free to seek out Fortuna and the other girls. She pushed through the murmuring crowd with abandon.

Finchleys of every shape and size were represented, all huddled together in celebration. She hadn't a clue where the study was, and given the size of the Manor, didn't think she would find it in a hurry. Everybody here was family, and while most could point her to the study in seconds, asking for directions spoiled the adventure. She thrust between legs and stomachs and arms, marching with determination to find her cousin.

Drops of wine were sloshed down her back by a great aunt with bony forearms and quivering fingers. Another rather rotund uncle took some circumnavigating, with an additional detour around a herniated lump. She managed to weave about her relatives quite well, with most shifting to allow her access, and others simply requiring a friendly greeting in each of their native tongues.

Through a complex history of war and conquest, the language of the Empire had finally settled on Garlish, but the Finchleys could be a traditional bunch. Each branch of the family liked to at least be fluent in their country's mother tongue. As the family was so old and wide spread, with clusters of relatives in almost every nation, Gwyneth had picked up a reasonable amount of every known language. It would have proven a valuable skill had the bureaucrats in Vitale not mandated that all imperial subjects be fluent in Garlish. There was little reason other than ceremony to speak any other way.

As she moved through the crowd, she caught snippets of their conversations. One man claimed to be intolerant of sunlight, another had accidentally turned their child orange with a diet based exclusively on carrots. Others were debating the upcoming festivities. Two, who Gwyneth heard mention a game of fates, became conspicuously quiet as she passed. She slowed to see if they would resume their conversation, but she was not yet of age, and they were diligent with the family's secrets.

After greeting an old woman in Scoldlandic and receiving a reply in Draigish, Gwyneth slipped by to continue her search. Her path was blocked then by a tall, round-bellied gentleman in a tweed suit. His face was striking, with a bulbous, port-swollen nose and a frayed leather eyepatch. The hair atop his head was thinning and white, and when he knelt to speak with her, his breath was laced with both fortified wine and pungent cheese.

'Well, if it isn't young Gwyneth.' He smiled. His mouth was foul, cluttered with uneven brown teeth; the gaps were the only saving grace. 'You're lucky, you know?'

'Am I?' She tried to remain polite despite the waves of odour as the man spoke. Her mother always said that politeness was next to cleanliness, and everyone knew what cleanliness was next to.

'Not many get to come here so young. I wasn't invited until I was fifteen – my first game night.' He looked into the distance, quietly reminiscing.

'The Patriarch said it would do us good to see how things are done. That's what my dad said.' She peered around his bulk in search of the study door, forgetting her manners momentarily. 'Fortuna is here too.'

'Yes, but she's of age. You're not.' He took a sip of sherry from a small glass, and continued, 'You will learn a great deal, however. The Patriarch is right. This night, it's a good thing. And though my brother might not know it, it's an honour and a privilege to expunge the bad blood.'

Gwyneth shuffled a little, unsure of exactly what he was talking about.

'After all, we must keep the family strong.' He stood up and puffed out his barrel chest, making a sort of impromptu speech for the few around him that turned to look. 'I'm glad I had the honour, and my brother will be glad too… one day. It takes strength to progress as we do, to keep things pure and right.'

He inhaled sharply, swallowed, and then downed the last of his sherry. His eye was a little glassy by that point; Gwyneth assumed it was a symptom of his familial pride.

'Do you know where Fortuna is?' she enquired, sensing an abrupt end to his little speech.

'In the study with my young Mina, I believe. It's through there.' He pointed to the far side of the room, traced his finger about the lip of his empty glass, and shuffled away.

Gwyneth watched him go, and craned to look to where he had pointed. She couldn't see over the huddle of towering relatives. Spotting a small table, on which resided a single vase, she hurried over and clambered up. She did take the time to remove the vase and place it on the floor before she did so, cautious as to not smash the thing in front of her whole family. It was a wise decision too, as the legs were uneven and she nearly upended the table pulling herself on top.

She scouted over bald pates, luxuriant wigs, and greased coiffures, until finally she spotted a boar's head mounted to the wall. Below it was a wide door with double panels that looked suitable for a study.

Before she had chance to climb down and hasten across the room, a spoon chimed against glass, signalling an announcement or start to proceedings. Everyone curtailed their conversations and turned in the direction of the sweeping staircase. There was a woman stood halfway up with a charged wine flute in one hand. A manservant was quickly retreating with a silver spoon, having done the duty of striking the glass for her.

The woman was familiar to Gwyneth. It was Fortuna's mother, known to most as the Matriarch. She was second only to her husband, and was certainly the most important woman of the esteemed Finchley family. She stood tall, taller than nearly every man in the family, even despite the distinctive slalom of her crooked spine. Gwyneth had often thought that the Matriarch might become the tallest woman in the Empire if she opted to have her spine straightened on a rack. Even so, she looked regal and imposing in her fitted black silks, and ever so handsome with her grey mane fashioned into a tall beehive.

'Unfortunately,' the Matriarch began, 'our Patriarch is indisposed this evening. Hence, I shall be directing formalities.'

The study door opened and Gwyneth watched as a group of girls made their way into the hall. There were a few that she recognised, but couldn't remember the names of. Then Fortuna emerged in an exquisite mauve dress, trimmed with lace. Her glossy hair bobbed around her in golden curls. As she turned to close the door, Gwyneth noticed a burn scar down the side of her face. The flesh was warped, red and mottled, and there was a stripe of hair missing from her scalp. Gwyneth nearly dropped off the rickety table at the sight of it, but curiosity kept her upright and fixated.

'We've all heard the terrible news by now, I'm sure.' The Matriarch took a sip of wine to moisten her cracked lips. 'News of infidelity travels quickly, especially when one is unfaithful to both one's spouse *and* one's family.'

'She should burn in the lowest hell,' slurred the uncle with fetid breath.

'Now, now, Freddy.' The Matriarch pursed her lips and wrinkled her nose as if she had smelled dog's muck. 'We all know how passionate you are, and passion is what we shall need… but not just yet.'

The man muttered something, then elbowed his way petulantly through the crowd in search of a fresh beverage.

'We need to discuss the evidence first. Then, as a family, we may pass judgement.' The Matriarch handed off her glass to a footman, who swooped in with impeccable timing, then clapped her hands twice. 'Bring in the condemned!'

Gwyneth knew what condemned men were. They were criminals, prisoners, those sentenced to death by hanging. She had seen one once. Not the hanging of course, her father was too much of a spoilsport to let her see anything as tantalising as that, but she had caught sight of a man being led to the square. His dogged look would stay with her forever, though she was certain he had earned his fate.

A door opened near the top of the stairs and a group of Finchleys bustled onto the landing. Three of them were brothers, distant cousins from the Scoldish branch of the family. Each of them was as broad as a bull. One had short black hair and a flat-topped head. The others had ginger manes, twins from the look of them, but one was cross-eyed and the other had quite the opposite problem. His pupils were directed outwards and were so widely spaced that Gwyneth imagined he could observe the whole hall without turning his head. The trio grunted and muttered as they hefted two prisoners into view.

Gwyneth was shocked; the prisoners were not masked bandidos with eyes as narrow as their moustaches. One was a slender woman and the other a boy not much older than herself. They were bound at the wrists and ankles and their mouths had been gagged. Gwyneth knew them. She had played with the boy years before. He was her cousin, and she was fairly certain the woman was his mother. She was wearing an exquisite white dress, and though at first Gwyneth thought it was her outfit worn to the gathering, it didn't quite fit. The dress looked more suited as wedding attire.

The pair were wrestled down the stairs until they were level with the Matriarch. The woman was snarling through her gag and fighting all the way, but the boy was too frightened and confused. He walked as he was directed and stood there, obedient under the gaze of the extended family.

'Uncover the boy's face, let us see him,' the Matriarch ordered.

The flat-headed brother quickly untied the gag and pulled it away from the boy, who took a ragged breath, but didn't scream.

'Let's get a good look.' The Matriarch lunged like a panther and wrapped her long bony hands around the boy's head. Her fingers squashed his cheeks and pushed his lips into what would have been an amusing expression had the atmosphere not become so dower.

'See here.' The Matriarch steered the boy's head so that everybody in the room could get a good angle. Her long painted nails dug into his nose and chin. 'His first hairs, thin mind, but there they are. A thin covering across his top lip.'

She released him and stepped away. His head had gone a purplish red in all areas not marked white by strongly pressing fingers.

'Does anybody see anything else remarkable about this boy? Anything unusual?' She thrust her finger at the man with the eyepatch, returning with a fresh sherry. 'What about you, Freddy? What do you see when you look at this boy?'

'I see...' He took a sip as he contemplated. 'I see a healthy boy. No, a healthy young man. Blonde hair, brown eyes, short. Nothing in particular out of the ordinary. Nothing special.'

'Exactly.' The Matriarch snapped her fingers, looking almost eager, then reined herself in. She stood as tall as her crooked spine would allow and addressed the crowd as a whole. 'I think you have all seen enough to form your own conclusions.'

The bound woman kicked out and screamed through her gag. One of the ginger brothers clamped his hand over her mouth and the other gripped her arms. Even between their shared might she fought well enough to cause a significant stir.

'We shall put it to a vote. There is little reason to hear the excuses of an unfaithful witch.' The Matriarch sneered. 'All who believe this child to be impure and the mother unfaithful, say aye.'

There was a resounding "Aye!" from all those gathered there. Only Gwyneth kept silent, still not fully certain of what was happening. Clearly, it would be bad for the mother and child. While she had been eager to see the punishment of a stranger caught poaching in the grounds, these two were family and that changed everything. Family were supposed to protect one another.

'All those who believe the condemned to be innocent...' The Matriarch eyed the crowd. 'Say aye.'

There were no "Ayes," though some in the crowd jeered. Gwyneth held her breath.

The Matriarch snapped her fingers and a curved blade was instantly deposited into her grip by the efficient servant. For a heart-stopping moment, Gwyneth thought the Matriarch was about to turn it on the bound family members, but she descended the stairs instead. Gwyneth took a breath, shaken. The thought of a blade being used to punish her kin filled her with dread.

As the Matriarch's foot tapped onto the parquet floor, a man was wrestled into the hall by two more hulking Finchleys. He had a hessian bag over his head and his arms were fastened behind his back. He was struggling almost as much as the bound mother, but it seemed there was less desperation in his movements than hers. He was positioned in front of the Matriarch.

Gwyneth craned to see better and almost slipped as the table wobbled on uneven legs. A distant relative with a swollen scalp noticed her plight and reached out to steady the table. He offered a brief smile before turning back to the tense display. Given the circumstances, his nonchalance unnerved her even more.

'The vote was unanimous. You know what to do.' The Matriarch pulled the hessian bag off the prisoner's head and slit his bindings with the knife.

The prisoner was another of Gwyneth's uncles, the father of the bound boy. His struggling stopped; without the bindings to stop him there was nothing to struggle against. He looked down, helpless, as the Matriarch pressed the handle of the knife into his cupped palm.

'Please,' he muttered. 'Please don't make me do this, not in front of the whole family. Can't you at least afford us our dignity?'

'We gave you the chance to solve this matter on your own terms. You failed.' The Matriarch stepped aside. 'Now, we do things our way.'

'I believe in you, brother,' the sherry drinker slurred his encouragement. 'It's time to cut out the rot. Cast it out!'

The condemned father nodded pensively, then mounted the first step. He weighed the knife in his hands with the same dogged look of a man led to the gallows, only Gwyneth didn't draw any morbid glee from this. With each footfall and creaking step, the boy and mother struggled more to escape.

'Do the boy first,' the Matriarch instructed. 'The mother should face the consequences of her actions.'

The father approached his son slowly, and as he stopped before him, the room fell quiet. The boy stilled, save for a quivering terror and the rapid whistling of breath through his nostrils. There were no words exchanged between them, but their eyes were locked for a long time, one set wide as a startled hare's, the other resigned like those of an old mule. Gwyneth wanted to look away, but she was transfixed on the gleaming blade as it raised into the air.

The brute holding the boy yanked his head back to expose his neck. The skin was pale, unblemished.

The mother kicked out and her muffled screaming escaped from beneath a cupped palm before she was wrestled into submission. Her head was wrangled and eyelids forced open to watch. Then the dagger punched into the boy. For seconds, it appeared as though no damage had been done. The hilt sat perfectly against young flesh; not even a bead of blood trickled down. Solemnly, the father tugged the blade and it bit through the boy's windpipe.

Gwyneth dropped her gaze, but it was too late. The gushing torrent of blood was burned onto her vision. She recoiled, upsetting the table, and was forced to jump to prevent from falling with it. The vase smashed as the table tipped onto it. She didn't stop to assess the damage. Sickened, confused, and scared, there was no time to think, just run.

She weaved between the family members that, only moments before, she would have trusted to the ends of the world and back. Now, she cringed away from each and every one of them in her attempt to get out. Perhaps she would be next. After all, she seemed to be the only one who hadn't expected the terrible event.

As she darted around the rotund uncle, she spotted the open doors to the gardens. It was a straight sprint to freedom. She doubled her efforts, but something caught her by the scruff of the neck and nearly took her off her feet. Her collar half-strangled her, then she was gripped under the arms and hoisted into the air.

'You're not going anywhere, yet.' The stomach-churning sherry breath of her Uncle Freddy washed over her. 'Like the Patriarch says, "you have a lot to learn this evening." '

# 1683
## WILLIAM OF FAIRSHORE

'I'm sorry I couldn't do more for you.' The surgeon sighed as William hobbled to the doorway with his crutch. 'Restoratives don't keep well on the road and aren't readily available in a quaint little place like this.'

He smiled as much as his drawn features would allow, which wasn't very much. He had sunken cheeks and forward-pouting lips that made it look as though he was trying to suck mud through a reed.

'I have a cousin in Vitale. He will have restoratives to hand, if you still need them.'

'I should be alright.' William tested his weight on his bad foot. Even the slightest pressure on it sent jolts of pain through him, but if he grit his teeth the leg would support him. It was definitely a step in the right direction. 'It's a long way to Vitale and I'll be able rest up in the coach. I might be fit enough to walk by the time I get there.'

'We can only hope.' The surgeon stroked his chin, his pouted lips shrinking thoughtfully. 'Good luck.'

With a thump and a click, the door was closed and the latch set. William exhaled heavily and looked upwards as he took a lungful of clean air. Although the sky was gloomy and the clouds were threatening rain, he couldn't help but grin as he limped into the square.

He had split his time almost equally between bedrest and sleep and hadn't had a gasp of fresh air for days. Back in Blackbile, Dr Barber's elixirs and serums would have seen him up and on his injured leg within minutes, but it seemed things weren't so simple without his well-guarded knowledge. The Finchleys' physician had opened and resealed his wound with neat stitching and applied stinging salves, but it wasn't nearly as effective. The old surgeon had even dosed him with mind-dizzying drops, applied directly to the tongue, and the pain still wouldn't fully subside. Yet only a week had passed, and with a carved branch for a crutch, he could just about walk.

As the first specks of mist-fine rain started to fall, William set the tip of his crutch in the crux of four cobbles to make sure it didn't slip. Even rain was preferable to his stuffy little room, and it would certainly wash away the medicinal stench from his clothes.

He did a few steady laps around the statue at the centre of the square, eager to test himself and encourage blood flow to his bandaged extremity. It had been decided that he, Goldin, and Dunstan – the Finchleys' coachman – would set off to the capital post haste. All the contracts had been signed; Goldin had even been taken to the nearest city to witness the creation of the banking covenants required for their payment. Now the little man had returned, it was time to begin the job.

William made his fifth lumbering lap, pondering on exactly what he might do with five thousand grana. He could buy a fine house with that amount and still live comfortably. He wouldn't have to kill ever again, and if he spent it wisely, might never have to work either. If everything turned out in his favour, he could be like one of those rich imperials with servants, maids, butlers, and chefs. It was all he could ever want. Most importantly, he would never need to worry about where his next meal was coming from, or what he might have to do to afford it.

'Will!' Goldin yelled from somewhere behind.

William turned around a little too fast. As he put his weight on his bad foot, a needle of pain shot up his leg from bone to bone. He took a moment to steady himself, teeth clenched and his whole body rigid. Slowly, his muscles relaxed and he settled his weight back onto the crutch.

'Will!' Goldin shouted more urgently.

William traced up one of the slender hotels to find the source of Goldin's shouting. The little man leant precariously over one of the upper balconies. He had a wide grin, tousled hair, and was wearing only a bedsheet over one shoulder. It didn't hide much, but a mercifully placed vine climbing across the balustrade saved William from a sight he would rather avoid. It made the little man look almost imperial from his high perch, in a garb reminiscent of a robe.

'I'm glad to see you up and about.' Goldin looked over his shoulder as distant giggles carried down on the breeze. 'Sounds like we're setting off soon. I'll be down in... let's say, forty five minutes? We can have some luncheon before we go.'

Goldin tipped back into his balcony and disappeared with the merest flash of hairy buttock between the vines. He called back, 'It's all on the Finchleys' silver, mind!'

William rolled his eyes. It seemed that while he had been convalescing, the little man had been living it up at the cost of their new employer. The arrow wound through Goldin's shoulder had been patched up and left to heal quickly and with seemingly little discomfort. William supposed he might be in a similar position if he hadn't the need to stand on his wound, but it hardly seemed fair. Goldin hadn't even wanted to take the job and now he was the one reaping all the rewards.

William hobbled across the square to the eatery. There were a few familiar faces sat at tables there, those who had confronted the gunman. They were presumably in the employ of the Finchleys and would no doubt protect him should anyone else seek his bounty.

He still wasn't certain who had put the price on his head, or what his value was. If it was a lot of money, there could be hundreds of assassins out there scouring every town, village, and ditch for any trace of him. He tried to push the thought away but it refused to go, lingering long enough to occupy him until Goldin arrived – which was a good hour and a half later.

'You're frowning well,' the little man commented as he hopped onto a wobbly wicker chair beside him.

'What?' William didn't turn to look. He was barely even listening, still fretting on the unknown details of his bounty.

'Means you must be thinking about something,' he clarified. 'Are you planning the assassination?'

'No, uh...' William shrugged, snapping out of his thousand yard stare and finally taking a sip of the whiskey and orange he had been coddling – during his fixation on the bounty he had managed to order a drink and meal when prompted by the waiter. It was warm from being sat in the sun, but was refreshing nonetheless. 'I was just *thinking.*'

'Well, I've been thinking too. With that money we're getting for supplies…' Goldin flagged down the waitress as he mused. 'Maybe we could buy a scoped rifle? It might be easier killing a senator from a distance. You know, like Lord Beechworth did years ago.'

'I thought he was aiming for the emperor?' William scowled, toying with his glass.

'Not in the version I've heard. You don't think he'd miss, do you? He was the best sniper the Guild ever had – and if it worked for him, why not us?'

'You might be right, but I'm no good with a rifle.' William downed his whiskey and orange, feeling a little better with his friend at his side. 'What about you? Can you shoot over distance?'

'I'm not sure I'd know where to start, but I've seen you with a rifle. You're better than you think.'

'You have to get a feel for the range, know the gun, and see how it's affected by the wind. It seems a bit technical.' William picked up a roll of bread and tore into it. 'I'd probably miss.'

As the waitress returned with a drink and plate of food for Goldin, another pair of boots approached from behind. They were so close by the time William heard them, that a knife could have been slipped between his ribs. It startled him and sent another jolt of pain up his leg.

'Don't drink too much,' the person behind him commented. 'I don't want to be sharing a coach with drunkards, let alone drunkards with sore heads. They make poor companions.'

William could hear the subtle clicking of wet wood and he recognised the distinctive Draigish lilt. It was the woman who'd had them shot. He turned measuredly.

'What do you want?' He scowled at the Draig.

'Me?' Gwyneth smiled. The ill-fitting wooden dentures clicked in her mouth as she spoke. 'I don't want anything, but Alwyn decided that I'll be escorting the pair of you to Vitale.'

'You and your damned brother nigh on killed us!' Goldin sat up, furrowing his brow.

'I'm sorry about that, but can we move past it?' She took a vacant chair beside Goldin, her blonde bunches swaying as she sashayed around the table. 'You're almost better now.'

'Almost better?' Goldin scoffed. 'Look at him, he can hardly walk.'

'Well, the surgeon said you'll be better by the time we reach Vitale, so there's that.' She flagged over the waitress and leant back, setting her heavy boots on a chair. They were covered in mud. As she crossed her feet over roughly, dried clods shook loose, dirtying the delicate wicker. 'I'll have a small red, I suppose, if these boys are drinking.'

She sent the waitress away with a wave of her hand, and turned to William with a brown smile as she tidied the rucks in her dark linen dress.

'So,' she began, 'I was thinking–'

'I'll stop you there.' Goldin shuffled his chair out. 'We're not going anywhere with an attempted murderess. Where's your uncle, where's Alwyn? I'm going to speak with him. We don't need anyone to chaperone us, especially you.'

'Goldin.' William held out a steadying hand. While he wasn't particularly happy about having Gwyneth join them on the road, it was a stipulation of the contract. If the pair of them were to complete the job and enjoy their riches, for now, they would have to endure her. 'She did say sorry.'

'Well, it's not good enough.' Goldin hopped off the chair. 'I'm going to see Alwyn. This is ridiculous.'

'You can't. He's gone, left town already and left me in charge. This whole assassination is now *my* operation, and we're going to Vitale as a trio or not at all.' She smiled in an annoyingly smug fashion. 'If I don't accompany you, there will be no payment.'

She cocked an eyebrow, not even turning away as she received the small glass of wine from the waitress. 'I'd like this to be quick and painless. Is it possible we can all get along? Or at least act like it?'

William looked at Goldin pointedly. He realised the little man was only looking out for him, but it wasn't necessary. For the sake of five thousand grana and the freedoms it bought, William was willing to put up with just about anyone.

'Fine.' Goldin sat back down with a grunt.

There were plenty of rest breaks on the way to Vitale, and scheduled stops where the surgeon had mandated William disembark to exercise his leg. The journey was also timed so that each night they would reach an extravagant roadhouse at dusk. There was good food and even better wine in the vineyard-strewn hills, but little enjoyment to be had. Gwyneth had forbidden the assassins from drinking more than two glasses each, and while Goldin had initially insisted that he drank his wine in pints, he eventually relented.

On the fourth day, Goldin spotted a signpost to a place called Sabbia and it sparked a distant recollection.

'That's the place,' he announced with a click of his fingers.

'What is?' William looked over lazily; he was incredibly bored and his foot was dully throbbing with the bounce of the coach suspension.

Gwyneth had offered him a numbing serum from a medical bag under her seat, but he'd refused, opting to keep his wits sharp. Whether right or wrong, he supposed that pain meant healing.

'The place I was on about.' Goldin wagged his finger. 'I was on a fair few substances at the time. It makes it harder to recall, but it's coming back to me.'

William inclined his head.

'I thought it was on the coast, but it's not. There's a big lake at Sabbia, massive it is, and the shores are white sand.' He stared into the middle distance, briefly lost in nostalgia. 'Best whores you've ever seen, William.'

'Unfortunately, it's not on our route.' Gwyneth cocked an eyebrow at William. 'You'll have to sate your urges elsewhere. Chiesa is the next town on this road, they might—'

'I don't... I'm not...' he tried to protest.

'Ladies of the night aren't really Will's cup of tea, but it means there's more for me, doesn't it?' Goldin giggled. 'Shame though, to think we were so close to our destination. A four day ride. Still, we should come back here once the job's done. We'll have a bit of spending money then.'

The little man stared into the distance again, perhaps imagining what kind of good time could be afforded with five thousand grana.

'I met a woman there, in Sabbia. Can't remember her name; I'll just call her Winnie. Strongest thighs I've ever known, and a show off about it too.' There was a twinkle in his eyes as he recounted old memories. William shifted to better follow the story. The little man tended to gesticulate when he got going, and it always brought a smile.

'How can you *show off* strong thighs?' Gwyneth snorted, showing those brown teeth again. 'Run up a hill?'

'Put it this way: you wouldn't let her tend your pumpkin patch.' He made a made a squelching noise from the corner of his mouth.

Gwyneth laughed, teeth clacking.

Goldin adjusted himself to include her in the telling of his story, and William was surprised to notice the initial animosity between them had all but vanished.

'Anyway, one day we wanted to go out on the lake, make a romantic day of it. I'd planned to steal a rowboat from one of the marinas. Then I could call for her on a nearby beach. The only problem was, I had to sneak in with my supplies.'

The more he spoke, the more Gwyneth seemed to soften. She leant forward, eager for the break from travel boredom. She smiled and giggled in all the right places, and William soon found himself warming to her. You couldn't hold a grudge against a killer when you were one and the same.

'I had this picnic basket. I'd stocked it with wine and cheese, and a few substances that we might enjoy together. A bit of spark powder or something.' Goldin giggled at his own story. 'I'd bought this thing, a fruit from the southern continent, and it cost me a good few silvers, mind. They called it a watermelon. I'd got it in my head that Winnie could do what she did best, but I couldn't scale the fence with the basket *and* the melon…'

'What did you do?' Gwyneth prompted.

William gritted his teeth through a jolt of the coach and twisted to get a more comfortable seating position.

'Well, first I tossed a rope over a branch and tried to hoist my supplies over,' Goldin continued. 'It was quite easy with the basket, what with its handle to fix the rope to. The watermelon was another matter.'

William was enjoying the story, but having rocked onto his side found it hard to look back at Goldin and follow along. Instead, he closed his eyes and tried to relax. It wasn't long before he drifted to sleep. Whatever else he heard of the little man's tall tale was forgotten, but he did have a tremendous dream of dockyard infiltration.

By the time they arrived at that evening's tavern, a thatched inn that slumped quaintly to one side, William was keen for his supper. It was incredibly painful to move after so long in the coach, but he was determined to disembark unassisted. Goldin lingered nearby, and when William appeared to struggle, took his elbow.

'What are you doing?' William hissed through his teeth as he tentatively set weight on his bad foot.

'Helping?' The little man faltered.

'No. I need to do it.' William waved him off; he was worried that now he was on the road and out of the surgeon's supervision, his foot was getting worse rather than better.

Goldin scowled and looked as though he was about to say something, but William realised the way it had sounded and clarified.

'It's not a pride thing.' He leant on his crutch and lifted up the bad foot, swinging it back and forth with a wince every time the muscles pulled taught. 'I just need to get used to doing these things myself. I thought a bit of sleep might help, but it's gone tight.'

He stretched out the leg, opting to change the subject. 'You're getting on well with Gwyneth.'

'We're working with her, aren't we?' Goldin shrugged. 'What are we supposed to do, sit in silence?'

'I thought you were angry because she tried to kill you.' William tested weight on the foot again and whimpered.

'People try to kill me all the time. I try not to let it bother me.' He grinned, his cleft lip pulling tight across the protruding tooth. 'She's good fun anyway, now we're on her side.'

'I'm glad you like her.' William shunted himself forwards, wincing through the first few strides. It really wasn't so bad once he got going; the pain from each step turned to a lesser but more constant hum. 'Just be wary of her. She's allied to us for now, but it's only on the strength of ink and parchment.'

The coachman, Dunstan, called to Goldin for assistance, and as the little man left to haul luggage, William limped into the tavern.

'I don't think you understand what you're doing.' Gwyneth was at the bar, posturing like a peacock; chest puffed out, narrow shoulder's squared up, finger brandished like the keenest blade. Anyone else would have needed to duck under pitchers that hung from hooks on a beam, but at her height she could stand straight.

'I know exactly what I'm doing, darling.' The portly woman behind the bar gestured with a particularly girthy arm, encompassing the tavern's run-down interior.

The copper pitchers above were dented and a few hooks hung empty. A display of pint glasses behind the bar was half gone, and the few that remained were chipped. William noticed then, that despite the relatively large floor space, the tavern only had two tables and three chairs between them. One of them only had three legs and the patron atop was balanced precariously to partake in his card game.

'You can't turn us away, there's not another road house for miles.' Gwyneth was angry, but the tone of her voice betrayed desperation. She sounded like a pleading child.

'You can sleep in a ditch for all I care, now sling your hook and piss off.' The barmaid jutted her thumb with such force it wobbled her second chin.

'You'll regret this.' Gwyneth sneered and turned to go, spying William who had only managed to shuffle three paces inside.

'Don't think I'll regret turning you away as much as I regret allowing the others to stay.' The barmaid turned and shouted through a curtain of beads to the back room. 'Arthur, get down here, and bring your pistol.'

'Sorry about this,' Gwyneth addressed William. She had lowered her voice, but was still seething. One hand was clenched and the other was caressing her leg; the folds in her skirts revealed a small dagger hidden there.

'What's happening?' William's brow furrowed, he didn't fancy his chances should a fight break out. He wasn't particularly athletic at the moment and had forgotten his flintlock in the coach.

'I told her my name and she – well, look.' She tossed her head to the barmaid, shouting for retribution. 'A few relatives of mine came through here last night and trashed the place.'

'Alwyn?' William couldn't imagine the man touching a glass in the place without gloves on, let alone tossing it across the room in some kind of brawl.

'No, he had business elsewhere.' She bit her lip, almost nervously. 'I think it's the Badger Sett.'

'Badger what?' William scoffed. 'You think a group of badgers came through here and trashed the place?'

'Don't be facetious.' She rolled her eyes, still fidgeting with the folds in her dress.

'I'm not being–'

William was interrupted by an old man stomping down a stairway behind the bead curtain. He emerged, grey brows bristling and pale eyes narrowed to slits. He was as slight and gaunt as his wife was plump and red, and looked positively sick – not much of a threat had he not been waving a sizable flintlock.

'Where are they?' the old gunner asked the barmaid, tipping his head to peer through small round glasses perched on the tip of his nose. 'We don't want your sort in here. Leave now, or I'll be forced to shoot.'

Gwyneth whipped around, her hand flashing with steel from under the hem of her skirt. A small knife flew across the room and punctured the man's throat. The strike had the deadly accuracy of a sharpshooter who could take an apple off a man's head at fifty yards, only it was the apple in the old gunner's gullet. Blood sprayed and the flintlock tipped from his fingers. He crumpled to the floor, his last breaths quietly hissing though the tear in his windpipe.

The barmaid staggered back, her mouth agog. Likewise, the card players were stunned to inaction and silence. The one on the three-legged chair tipped over, hitting the floor with a thump. None of them had expected, nor were used to, such a display of death and violence in their rural tavern. The only sound other than fearful gasping was the scrape and clunk as Goldin found his way inside.

'It's not half as nice as it looks from the outside,' he announced his entrance loudly. 'It's a bit shabby, isn't it? I thought we were supposed to be living the high life. Has your uncle's coin purse run dry?'

He rounded William and spied the barmaid.

'Still,' he continued, 'they do have some impressive whores.'

The barmaid burst into tears over her murdered husband, prompting confusion in Goldin.

'We're leaving,' Gwyneth announced, then addressed the stunned crowd. 'You would all do well to forget my name. This is a time for grieving, not revenge. Bury your man and breathe no word of this again. Misfortune has a way of finding folk who cross my family.'

She about turned and stomped out of the tavern.

'You're joking, aren't you? I don't mind the place really,' Goldin called after her. 'I'm sure Alwyn has a few spare coins. My tastes in whores are awfully economical!'

William pivoted on his crutch and shuffled after Gwyneth. He was lingering on exactly what "the Badger Sett" might be, but couldn't fathom it. With luck, he might be able to tease it out of her on the road.

# 1674
## GWYNETH FINCHLEY

'I… uh–' Gwyneth's father had tried to start a conversation three times now, but each attempt ended similarly and quickly. 'No matter.'

He squirmed and looked away.

Gwyneth rolled her eyes and turned her attention out of the window. They were soon to arrive at Adelaide Bennet's Finishing School and, unlike Bennet's Independent, it meant she needed to board. It was a prospect Gwyneth was quite pleased about. Things had become tense between her parents over the past few months, and she was glad to escape the shouting.

Browning needles, dropped from tall pointed trees, muffled the cartwheels as they progressed. The trees themselves were green despite the season, though a darker shade than the woods in Draig. An ominous, heavy fragrance carried on the breeze. Gwyneth was used to rolling hills and uninterrupted fields for grazing or crops; it seemed they had travelled through this spear-like forest for miles. Even the ground was different: lumpy and rutted, punctuated with jagged grey rocks and spans of moss. It made her feel even more distant from home, which was a relief.

Nothing had been right in their little cottage since they had visited the Manor. Not because she was jealous of the luxury of it, but because she wasn't sure how to feel about her family. Her parents had both watched placidly while a mother and son were killed. The death hadn't even been the worst of it. The slow sawing with the knife until each of the heads were free of their bodies made her retch, even now.

'Nerves,' she muttered quietly, coughing and swallowing back what little had made it to her oesophagus.

'I…' Her father tried again. 'I wanted your mother to speak to you about something; something important, but you know how she is. Especially now. I can't talk to the woman without her spitting fire.'

Gwyneth kept her gaze out of the window. She didn't want her parents' disagreements weighing on her more than they already were. If she just pretended not to listen, she hoped her father wouldn't load his worries on top of hers.

'I need to ask you something.' He fidgeted in his chair and played with a cloth cap in his hands. 'It's about your bloods.'

Gwyneth cringed further away and set her sights on a little pool as they passed, hoping against hope that he would just give up and they could forget the whole thing. Her bloods were still intensely embarrassing for her. When they had first come, almost two months prior, she hadn't known what they were. Nobody had ever told her, and she had assumed there had been something wrong, even to the point of worrying the cause was demonic – which was a ludicrous notion. In the end, she had covered it all up through a combination of frantic wiles and disinterested, arguing parents.

Unbeknownst to her father, Gwyneth's mother had, days too late, hobbled into her room to teach her of menses. At that time, sat on the edge of her bed, with the offending bloodied clothes hidden under a loose floorboard nearby, Gwyneth pretended her bloods hadn't yet come. Now, she had to sit through another parental monologue.

'I wanted to make sure that you know what they are.' He fussed with his handkerchief.

'I know what they are,' she scoffed as if she had known all along, but kept her attention away from her father. She followed the little pool until it drew out of sight. How she wished that she could just tumble out of the coach window and slither into the placid waters.

'You know? Have you had your first?'

Now was her chance to own up, to admit that she was – as her mother described it – a new young woman. She didn't think she was ready for that. The feeling of shame was still fresh in her, even though she knew now that it was perfectly normal. And new school nerves made her feel particularly green and childish. She chose to lie. 'Mother spoke to me the other week. She told me what to expect: the bloods and all that.'

'Good. I didn't know she had.' He paused a moment, then continued. 'Did she tell you about the change?'

'From a girl to a young woman? She mentioned it.'

'No. The *big* change.' Her father seemed a little more comfortable with this subject than when he was focusing directly on the bloods. 'You know how the Patriarch taught you about the evolution of man?'

'Yes.' She turned to see her father, unsure of exactly what that had to do with her menses.

'Well, the Finchleys are special. We evolve faster than the common folk. That's why we have gifts.' He flexed his hand to show webs of skin that linked each finger together. 'While others are little more than apes, we are already taking the next step. That's why I can swim faster than anyone you've ever known. That's why your uncle's a genius. That's why your mother has fits that come with visions.'

Gwyneth thought about it for the first time. Her family had always been a little eccentric and each relative always had their own niche or talent, but she had never realised that was anything out of the ordinary. When one uncle had sprouted boils that contained just the type of yellow bile he needed for surgical experiments, she had always considered it a coincidence, but there were many such coincidences in her family. Everyone had something special. Except her.

'I know what you're thinking, but don't worry.' He patted her on the shoulder. 'Some are born with it, like that young Mina, did you see her head? Looked like a bad potato, but I'm sure she'll grow up a smart one. Others, it comes later. For girls it's no later than first blood, and it usually comes with it. Your cousin, Fortuna, it happened to her – that mark on her face came overnight.'

Gwyneth wasn't listening. She had drifted back out of the window again. Her father had said that the gift would come with her first blood. She scowled, deep in thought as the grand schoolhouse came into view through the trees. She wasn't even focused on that, and it was to be her home for the next six years. Instead, she was racking her brain for any other Finchley as regular as herself. There were none, or perhaps there was *one*.

'I just wanted you to be prepared. Especially as you're not going to be at home anymore. It's a big change you've got coming, and I want you to write to me when it happens.'

'That boy,' Gwyneth broached tentatively.

'What boy?'

'The boy at the Manor. The Matriarch said he was ordinary.' Just like herself, Gwyneth thought.

'That he was.' Her father swallowed sombrely. 'Sometimes bad blood gets into the family and we need to expunge it before it affects us all. That's why that mother and son needed to go, but I wouldn't worry about that. You're safe, I'm certain.'

Gwyneth nodded, despite knowing that the opposite was true. It was only a matter of time before her father found out, and would be forced to put a blade to both her and her mother. Her breath whistled through her nose.

'Please, don't...' Her father gripped her shoulder. 'I can see you're worrying and there's no need. Your mam's been true to me, I assure you of that; a reliable wife and sister both. I've known her since all I can remember, she wouldn't sully our bloodline.'

Very few words were exchanged after that, even as the carriage stopped and Gwyneth's luggage was offloaded from the rack. Her father simply bid her farewell, gave her a brief hug, and then bundled himself back inside. He perhaps sensed her mixed feelings, and being a man lacking in any understanding of such complexity, had opted to remove himself from it. Once inside, he stared straight ahead in the empty cab, not daring to look out of the window and catch her eye.

'I hope you enjoy it, young miss.' The carriage driver set her luggage on the floor beside her. 'I'd help you in, but your father intends to be on his way. Good luck – my sister schooled here too; she said it was... an *experience*.'

Gwyneth thanked him and watched as he returned to the carriage. With a snap of the reins, it began to trundle away. Only then did her father dare look, offering a weak smile and cursory wave. She nodded – all she could sum up for him in that moment.

Then she turned, putting her back against family worries, and facing the fresh anxiety of an unknown school.

It was strange that nobody came out to meet her; no tutor or footman to assist with her luggage. Gwyneth tried to shift her trunk alone, but the two miniature wheels weren't tall enough and the brass corners quickly dug into the compacted dirt of the roadway. She decided to leave it. There would be someone inside who could help.

The main building stuck out like a sore thumb at the centre of the forest clearing. It was made of a bold, red brick and all its windows and doors were framed with light sandstone. The main entrance was an archway between two towers, above which was a large gold and black clock. It occurred to Gwyneth that the archway was broad enough to have accommodated her carriage, and nobody had come out to meet her because the dolt of a coachman had dropped her off too soon. She rolled her eyes and paced through the arch.

Her polished black shoes – ornamented with a silver buckle each – clicked with a satisfying retort, and she skipped the latter half of the journey to lift her spirits. After all, a new school should be exciting. There were new friends to make, new crafts to learn. Still, it didn't improve her mood. Once inside the passageway, she felt an overbearing sense that something was not quite right. It was dark and quiet; too quiet for a school filled with children her age. A rusted drainpipe dripped noisily into a blocked gutter, unnerving her further. She pressed on for the light beyond.

The courtyard was cobbled in a dark grey with lighter stones marking paths that linked each doorway in straight lines. It was still quiet, devoid of any children or tutors, but there was a caretaker nearby, diligently painting the uprights of a noticeboard. She headed his way.

'Good morning.' She smiled, rocking onto her tiptoes. She was wearing the uniform of one of the best schools in the Empire, and that lent a certain confidence when addressing the menial staff members. Where he was in oil-marred, paint-smeared overalls, she was in a smart black skirt and jacket, silver buttons gleaming. 'Sorry to trouble–'

'You'll be causing me no bother miss, but I dare say you'd better clear off.' He snorted and spat, then turned back to his painting.

'I'm sorry.' She scowled. 'I just wanted to know where to find the headmistress.'

'Look...' He dropped the brush into his paint bucket with a grunt. It sank, leaving only the tip of the handle exposed. He sighed as he turned to face her, but his expression changed as he spotted something behind her in the distance. 'She's right there.'

'There you are!' The headmistress' tone seemed needlessly harsh. 'I've been waiting for you in my office for half an hour. Your father and I agreed eight o'clock precisely.'

'I'm sorry, miss.' Gwyneth turned sharply, kept her back straight and made herself look as presentable as possible. 'I only just–'

'And here I find you dallying as if my time is worth nothing to you.' The headmistress approached, her stride long and quick. She was heavily set, with a man's square frame under scholarly robes. There was a belt through loops on her jacket, positioned high on her waist and pulled tight to accentuate her bosom. It was an attempt to give her a more hourglass-like figure, but it didn't give the impression that she would have hoped for.

'I can tan her thighs, if you'd like?' the caretaker offered.

Gwyneth glared at the man, taken aback by the merest suggestion of him striking her. Of course, corporal punishment had been present at her last school, but it had been reserved for extreme cases. Once, a boy had sourced gunpowder from a teacher's cabinet and had used it to blow up an expensive porcelain toilet. Even then, he had only been caned five times, and the teacher had taken no pleasure in it. This caretaker's eyes twinkled at the prospect.

'Thank you, Mr Tunn,' the headmistress agreed and the caretaker began to hurriedly search through a small wooden toolbox.

'It's here somewhere.' He pulled out a few tools which clattered on the floor: a hammer, a rusted pair of pliers, and a few bent nails.

The noise sent irritated twitches through the headmistress, who exhaled steadily, then snapped, 'It's quite alright, Mr Tunn. We don't have time to be waiting for you to find your slipper. I'll deal with the girl myself – make sure you have it on hand in future.'

'I will, headmistress.' Mr Tunn wrung his cap in his hands, his eyes darting to Gwyneth. 'My apologies.'

'Come, girl.' The headmistress pointed to her feet, the way one might beckon a dog, and said, 'You're late for morning assembly.'

'Yes, miss.' Gwyneth hurried forwards, head down. She had seen this type at her previous school, and was keen not to upset her further.

'What's your name, girl?' The headmistress about turned and strode off before Gwyneth drew alongside, forcing her to break into a jog to catch up.

'Gwyneth.' It was hard to keep pace and maintain the ladylike manner that was expected in such finishing schools. 'Gwyneth Finchley, miss.'

'Finchley, eh? Well, don't think that you'll be getting any special treatment here.' A strand fell free of the headmistress' tight bun and she wrestled it behind her ear.

'No, miss,' Gwyneth agreed, hoping to spare herself any further ire. 'I'm sorry I was late, my dad dropped me outside the gates and I wasn't certain—'

'No excuses, please. They spoil your apologies. Through here.'

The headmistress shunted through a pair of double doors with mottled glass and pale green woodwork. They swung wildly on their hinges, struck spring stoppers and came flying back closed again. Gwyneth had to dart aside to avoid being struck by one and almost fell. The highly polished floor inside was slippery under her smooth soles. Thankfully, the headmistress was far enough ahead as to not notice the display. Gwyneth trotted after her.

They hastened down a corridor lined with classrooms. Each door had a rectangular window etched with the classes taught within. Etiquette, Needlepoint, and Home Economics were just the start. While the subjects didn't exactly set Gwyneth's heart aflutter, they were safe in a way that distanced her from the horrors she had seen. She just hoped that, during her time here, she might scrub the vision of her cousin's death from the tableau in her mind. Maybe if she did that, the possibility of her own father being forced to do the same to her might seem a little less realistic. She peered into the classrooms in an attempt to ignite a girlish glee in the blandly domestic.

Most rooms were blocked with closed blinds, but she spied into those that she could. Most were empty, but a few still had teachers at desks, reading or scratching notes with quills. All the students were at the aforementioned assembly, and as such there was little of interest to be seen.

'In here.' The headmistress stopped at a pair of double doors and ushered Gwyneth through.

Stepping into the hall, Gwyneth stopped dead. She hadn't been led into the hall at the rear, as she had expected, but at the front. The headmistress blocked her retreat.

'Savages really, the lot of them.' An old man was at a lectern, speaking to an assembly of disinterested girls and young women. 'I remember another campaign–'

'Sorry for the interruption, Mr Davies.' The headmistress allowed herself into the hall and closed the door with a subdued click.

The man at the lectern craned around, half-moon glasses slipping down a sweaty nose. He grumbled, but gathered up his papers all the same.

'No matter.' He stepped away from the lectern, his back returning to a natural stoop as he deferred to the headmistress. 'I was just recounting my time in the First Scold War while we waited. The girls responded well, but I can finish another time. Perhaps I'll make a lesson of it.'

Gwyneth cast her eye over the crowd of watching girls. At least two were asleep, though a few seemed interested in her sudden arrival. Fortuna drew her attention with a subtle wave; Gwyneth offered a sheepish smile in return.

'Maybe another time, yes.' The headmistress strode forwards, but stopped short of the lectern to address the students. 'I apologise for the late start. Our new student was dawdling in the courtyard when I found her.'

Gwyneth pursed her lips. The embarrassment was mounting, and it took all she had to shuffle alongside the headmistress where she presumed she was supposed to be. Though the girls had been muttering before, an oppressive silence fell over them like a heavy blanket.

'While we usually encourage a brief introduction, I'm afraid we don't have the time today. You will each have to get to know Gwyneth on your own time.' The headmistress clicked her fingers impatiently at a teacher lounging on a chair beside the front row. He leapt up, wild, mousy hair bobbing. 'There is, however, a simple lesson I would like to impart.'

The mousy-haired teacher picked up his chair and carried it onto the stage.

'It is a lesson integral to all learnings undertaken at this finishing school.' The headmistress paused as the chair was set down before Gwyneth. In the quiet of the hall, the clunk on the stage boards echoed all the more. 'It is of respect and punctuality. Lean on the chair, please.'

Gwyneth's heart sank. She knew what was coming, even before the headmistress started to unbuckle her belt. She looked to her cousin for help; Fortuna was a prefect and well respected, and perhaps she could do something to stop this. Gwyneth hadn't done anything wrong, after all. It was her damned father who had caved to his own embarrassment and left her on the road without assistance or instruction.

Fortuna looked away. Perhaps her intention was to let Gwyneth preserve a little dignity, but as all the other girls were now brimming with fresh excitement, it felt more like cold indifference. Perhaps Fortuna was as complicit in their family's dark rituals as Gwyneth's parents were.

Gwyneth leant forward, her hands braced on the seat of the chair, and stared out at the whispering, giggling mass of hostile girls. She grimaced, determined not to show any weakness, and then turned her face downwards. In the lantern light she could see the reflective sheen of sweat left by the teacher's rump. It drew a perfect curve between each buttock, and now that she could see it, Gwyneth was almost certain that she could smell a hint of something foul. It was disgusting, but she didn't have long to focus on it.

The belt came cracking down on her rear with ferocious speed. Leather snapped against her skin, leaving a white-hot band of pain.

The impact jolted her, made the chair screech forwards against the stage. A childish squeal was pushed from her, and it was all she could do to prevent it from naturally progressing into floods of tears. She bit her lip, swallowed her anguish. Tears flowed freely down her cheeks nonetheless, but she managed to prevent herself from bawling like a new-born.

Two more strikes came in quick succession and with each she managed to contain herself less. Thankfully, there wasn't a fourth. If there had been, she might not have been able to keep herself upright against the pain.

'Up, girl. Back straight. Take your punishment with decorum.' There was a whistle of leather on fabric as the headmistress pulled the belt back through the loops on her jacket. 'I take little pleasure in disciplining you, only the satisfaction that this might steer you right. Listen, pay your elder's respect, and we'll get along just fine.'

Gwyneth forced herself upright. Her legs were trembling, her eyes spilling tears, and her breath carrying unstoppable whimpers.

'Are we agreed?'

'Yes, headmistress.' Her voice wavered, but she kept her face as placid as her trembling lip would allow and tried not to twitch at the subtle jibes shared between girls in the crowd.

'Are you sorry for your disrespect and dallying?'

'Yes, headmistress.' Gwyneth found her cousin again in the crowd. Fortuna was looking now, exchanging words with a few other girls. She wasn't laughing or whispering as the others were, but there was no forthcoming support.

'Are you thankful for my lesson? Will you act correctly from now on?'

'Yes, headmistress.'

'Well?' the headmistress' tone sharpened.

'Thank you, headmistress.'

Gwyneth was spared from attending classes for the remainder of the day. The headmistress had deemed the flogging lesson enough.

It was a small mercy, but Gwyneth was glad of it. She didn't think she could have coped with the hard chairs.

The boring, old teacher with half-moon glasses had led her to a dorm. Once he left, she promptly dashed to the nearest bed and sobbed into the sheets. She cursed the callous headmistress, and her stupid father for making her late. It all felt so impossibly unfair and the thought of six more years here made her feel ill.

A knock at the door interrupted her tears; three heavy-fisted thumps that set her on edge, more likely a teacher than another student. She held her breath and kept quiet, hoped that whoever it was would just leave. There was another knock, this one gentler. She stayed still, worried that the slightest rustle in her bedsheets might confirm her presence. It wouldn't be too long until lunchtime, and she feared a teacher might have come to collect her. She couldn't face the other students yet, not with her face fresh from tears and the flogging so keen in everyone's minds.

Floorboards creaked as the visitor left. She realised then that her sobbing had been so loud prior to the first knock that it had drowned out the visitor's arrival. Whoever it was certainly knew she was in here.

Minutes later, she sat up on the bed, the intrusion having broken her downward spiral of self-pity. Her backside ached even against the generous padding of the quilts. She looked about the room; there were four beds in all, and now that she took them in – specifically the one with the empty nightstand and unfitted sheets – she realised she had been crying on another girl's bed.

Gwyneth stood up, wincing at the spike of pain in her rump. She didn't know what to do; all her belongings were in her trunk, and that might still be sat at the side of the road. She couldn't keep soddening another girl's sheets with her tears, and the prospect of making her own bed just to cry in it seemed wrong. Just as she considered venturing outside, she heard footsteps in the corridor.

All of a sudden, the thought of leaving the room seemed preposterous. She couldn't face those sneering glances of the other girls, and she damn well hoped whoever approached wasn't coming in here. She danced about, looking for somewhere to go. Not to hide necessarily, but make herself more presentable. She didn't want anyone to know she'd been crying.

The door burst open.

'Are you going to move that thing, or what?'

Fortuna came through, two other girls in her wake. She hastened over to the bed Gwyneth had been crying on and threw herself atop it. One of the other girls followed, slumping onto a bed of her own and crossing her legs. The last knelt down and started searching through the top drawer of her bedside table.

'Well?' Fortuna pressed. 'Are you leaving it out there or not? You know, if you get in trouble in the dorm, we all do.'

Gwyneth blinked; she hadn't a clue what her cousin was talking about.

'Bring your bloody trunk in!' snapped the cross-legged girl – a Gael with long pigtails and a thick layer of face-powder.

Gwyneth moved to the door and found that her trunk had been set outside. It must have been brought by her earlier visitor. She cursed herself for not having been brave enough to answer. Now, she had to drag the damned thing inside herself.

She grabbed one of the handles and heaved. It had little wheels set into the underside that enabled it to roll, but to do that she had to lift one end, and it was terribly heavy. The effort made her backside ache all the more. After two failed attempts, she looked back into the dorm for help. The three girls were deep in conversation, something about boys from the nearby village and the potential for sneaking out one night. Only the Gael paid her any mind and she just tutted.

Gwyneth returned to the trunk and heaved again, this time making about two feet of progress. She had managed to get the trunk halfway through the door.

'Found it.' The girl who had been rifling through the bedside table produced a fine hairbrush triumphantly.

'Oh, that looks wonderful. We'll take it to her now.' Fortuna jumped up as quickly as she had thrown herself onto the bed, and hastened to the door. 'Come now, cousin, you're in the way.'

'Sorry.' Gwyneth grimaced, lifted the end of the trunk and tried to drag it a pace further into the room.

The Gael jumped from her bed onto the top of the case, thumping it to the floor and dragging the handle from Gwyneth's fingers.

'Watch yourself with that, it's heavy,' she snickered as she hopped from the far end and disappeared down the corridor.

'Margot!' Fortuna called after. 'There's no need to be so harsh. She's our dorm mate, and my own cousin, after all.'

The blonde tossed the brush to Gwyneth, who caught it awkwardly. Then she came forward and heaved the trunk out of the doorway. While Gwyneth had made it look particularly difficult, this girl dragged it in like there was little inside but a few undergarments. She winked at Gwyneth.

'Don't tell anyone I helped you.' She snatched the brush out of Gwyneth's grip, then turned and hurried away.

'What?' Gwyneth muttered. The girl didn't hear.

'You're not exactly flavour of the month.' Fortuna shrugged. 'There's a few girls here… cruel girls. And with that little display at the assembly… I'd appreciate it if you wouldn't talk to me outside the dorm. Despite my scars, I've cultivated a superb reputation around here. I wouldn't want you sullying it with, you know… yours.

'Anyway.' She grinned, showing a set of pristine wooden teeth that Gwyneth hadn't noticed before. 'I must be off. We've a surprise for one of the girls; she just got her first blood and she's missing home. We're throwing her a little party at luncheon.'

Fortuna sashayed around the trunk and into the corridor, but paused a moment.

'We'll have to have a little shindig for you.' She offered a weak smile. 'You know, when you get yours. In the room of course, can't have anyone seeing us talk.'

She swallowed.

'Mine was hellish.' She indicated the side of her face that looked half-melted by fire. 'It's always worse for Finchley girls. But you've got a good friend in me, I'll help you through it… privately.'

The door clicked shut.

# 1683
## WILLIAM OF FAIRSHORE

Chiesa wasn't as idyllic as D'Arnao. It was certainly nicer than many towns William had frequented, but there was a subtle hint of squalor and industry to the place. While the main cobbled streets were sided with terracotta-roofed buildings, rendered in handsome shades of beige, white, and brown, one had only to look down the ivy-hemmed alleyways to see oily gutters and shunned beggars. There was a smell too: a combination of improper drainage and waste left out in the heat.

'My uncle recommends a gunsmith here.' Gwyneth was propped up in her seat, head darting about like a small bird, excitedly taking in all the comings and goings on the main street. 'Well, it's more of an emporium for *hunting supplies.*'

She slid the last two words out of the corner of her mouth in a way that made spittle hiss between her teeth.

'I've not used them before myself, but I'm sure they must be decent.' Gwyneth ducked her head to peer inside a barber's shop as they passed. The barber was currently wrapping a bloodstained bandage around a pole to dry. He had presumably used it to stem the flow of an accidently sliced neck or ear. 'They're certainly expensive enough.'

'I didn't see Alwyn as the hunting type,' William commented. His nose twitched at a fresh sting of burnt hair and chemicals that emanated from a tannery hidden somewhere down a winding side street.

'Not him,' she replied. 'Not one for blood, Alwyn. Another uncle.'

'They're not in short supply are they, uncles of yours?' William noted.

'They're not all uncles, it's just easier to know everyone as aunt, uncle, or cousin. The Finchleys predate the Vitulan Empire, and we never lose touch with our own. My grandmother says a Finchley was present when they invented the calendar.'

'When the gods made the world?' Goldin scowled.

'I didn't take you for a religious man.' Gwyneth looked a little amused. 'And no; I mean when people dragged themselves out of the muck and invented days, weeks, deadlines and responsibilities – for good or ill.'

William shared a shrug with Goldin. They had never spoken about such things before, but both had a good idea of where the other one stood. It was the same for everyone on the continent: gods and devils were just another fact of life, whether you worshiped them or not.

'I'm not *religious*,' Goldin said. 'The gods are bastards to a man, woman, and whatever else in-between. Do you think I'd be a killer if I cared where I was going?'

'I just didn't think you'd believe that prattle.' She blew dismissively like a braying horse.

'If the old gods weren't real then who did the new gods kill?' Goldin rolled his eyes, his grin barely holding back a laugh. 'Who made the world, even? Your great-great-great-grandad? I bet he makes fallen bread land butter-side-up too, doesn't he?'

William let out a laugh.

'Oh, piss off the both of you,' Gwyneth harrumphed.

William smiled at her. Not because he and Goldin had gotten one over on her, though they most certainly had. It was because, in spouting something so outlandish, he recognised the same mad spark in her that made the assassins so special. All different in their own way, and never entirely accountable for their actions.

'Maybe you're right.' He humoured her. 'Maybe the gods aren't hiding and they just don't exist at all.'

'What's worst about you patronising me, is that I know that I'm right.'

'Of course you are.' Goldin winked. 'It's us, we've got it wrong. Us and the emperor and the high cardinals and my very own mother.'

'Stop it now.' She pushed him sullenly, but there was a hint of play in it so she wasn't entirely at odds with being dead wrong. 'We're here, anyway – Shoulster's.'

William looked over as the coach slowed. What he saw, in a row of upmarket stores on the main road, was a small shop with a black sign and two narrow window displays. The sign indeed read "Shoulster's" in whorls of golden script. The same writing was on the windows, touting weapons, ammunition, warm outdoor clothing and other such hunting supplies. Behind, in the little displays, were collections of fine rifles, some brilliantly gleaming in silver, others with a buffed, black sheen. More still boasted lacquered wooden grips and stocks. Though the frontage was only small, the fine display spoke of the weapons' quality.

William took his flintlock out of a trunk and tucked it under his belt. He was of a mind to get himself a new holster and needed the pistol to make sure it fit. And it didn't hurt to ensure it was loaded in the event of emergencies. There was only a slim chance he would need it for protection, but he did have a price on his head.

Getting out of the coach was a challenge, requiring the assistance of both Goldin and Dunstan. Gwyneth headed inside while the three struggled, the shop bell tinkling lightly after her. William was glad of the small mercy; he couldn't handle her watching him gurn and wince with the wound she was responsible for. Despite this, he also hoped her departure was motivated by similar awkward feelings, rather than a callous disinterest. He was still trying to remain sceptical, but it was easy to grow fond of road companions.

'Can you stand?' Dunstan tentatively released his grip from William and paused a moment, ready to catch him if he fell. 'Good. I'll get fresh horses and fodder, unless you need assistance inside?'

'That's not necessary,' William replied hurriedly, shifting the crutch under his arm, then added, 'Thank you. I'll ask if I need it.'

Goldin strode ahead, opened the shop door and held it for William. The pair shared a smile as he shuffled slowly by and the little man patted his back.

Shoulster's was larger inside than it had appeared. The floor space was wide, with four rows of glass cabinets, each stocked with different instruments of death. The walls too were cluttered with weapon racks and shelving. Everything on display was exceedingly expensive, from antique suits of armour, to golden ornaments and foreign trinkets arranged on high shelves. There were also taxidermies of at least ten southern beasts William had not dared believe were real. One of the creatures looked like a tree; its skin was rough as bark, and it had a long mouth rimmed with a hundred jagged teeth. Even the most modest of the beasts was astounding. It looked similar to a cat but the head was almost as big as Goldin, and its fangs were as long as some of the more generous knives on display.

Gwyneth was at the counter speaking with the old proprietor. The man was suitably loud and well spoken, Garlish despite the proximity to the Vitulan capital. He was prattling on about the esteemed legacy of the establishment and how his forebear, Timothy Pendleton-Shoulster, had helped establish the ivory trade that made it all possible. Gwyneth kept trying to butt in with enquiries about more specialised weaponry, but the man was dead set on recounting the challenges his ancestor faced in procuring hardy slaves at a fair price.

William made his way down the nearest aisle, which was stocked with an assortment of artisanal rifles. Goldin detoured for a wall rack of scatterguns and blunderbusses. The pair browsed for a time, testing mechanisms, checking the ergonomics of grips, and posing for each other with their favourite guns. Once William had decided on a nice but eye-wateringly expensive rifle, with a clean telescopic sight that looked easy to use, he moved to look through some accessories.

Gwyneth finally managed to interrupt the proprietor's monologue and intimate that she was into more nefarious dealings. The man caught on quickly and gave his acknowledgement with an obvious wink. With aplomb, he ushered her from the counter to a door beside a small mirror where William was trying on a new holster for his flintlock.

'Ah, a shoulder holster, we call them *shoulsters* here.' The old proprietor barked a laugh, spraying spittle and projecting foul breath that was rich with whiskey and vinegar. 'They're a bit of a speciality of ours; the finest stitching and leather you can get. Nominative determinism, I think they call it. You end up doing what your name says of you.'

William smiled and nodded, hoping the old man would take his breath of pickled onions and herring elsewhere. He pulled his flintlock from his belt and slipped it into the "shoulster", fastening it with a stud that was designed to pop open when drawn. He noted the quality of the thing and was impressed that it seemed to be about the right size for his pistol.

'What's yours?' the man pressed.

'My what?'

'Your name, boy.' The man's yellowed teeth showed; there was a little flake of something stuck to his canine. 'What's your name?'

William panicked a moment, realising that he probably shouldn't be sharing his name with anyone he didn't know. He reached for the first thing that came to mind.

'Bill.' He shrugged. 'Bill of… Brightsands?'

'Brightsands? Perhaps you'll end up on a beach someday, I don't know.' The old proprietor patted his shoulder and shuffled off into the back room with Gwyneth in tow. 'Through here, young miss. We've got ether, garrottes, a selection of poisons…'

His voice faded as the pair headed down a narrow corridor.

'That's a good omen, I suppose.' Goldin weighed a blunderbuss in his hands. 'A beach is exactly where we want to be, once this is all done.'

'Sabbia, was it?' William twisted, despite the pain, to get a better angle of himself in the mirror. With his flintlock tucked subtly under his arm, rather than so brazenly on his hip, he might be able to conceal it under a jacket.

'Sabbia.' Goldin cocked and fired a different blunderbuss with a satisfying click. 'It's coming back to me now. There's a grand house, just back from the sands. Some rich bastard used to live there, not so sure now. Still, there's plenty of wealthy folk there, and there'll be fine food and pretty baubles for sale. That money's burning a hole in my pocket, and I haven't even earned it yet!'

There was a chuckle from the little man.

The shop bell tinkled and William looked over. He had assumed it would be the coachman, and wanted to thank him again for his assistance, but it was somebody else. William noted the man's eyepatch, but tried not to focus on it for fear of offending. He nodded a polite greeting and turned away, more concerned with finding a handsome jacket.

He set down his crutch, balanced on his good leg and tested himself on the bandaged foot; he couldn't try on any clothes with the length of wood wedged under his arm. Finding a nice light jacket on a rack, he tried it on and did his best to admire the sorry-looking individual he found in the small, round mirror. All in all, the jacket fit well. It was a dark red that was almost black – smart with subtle embroidery. It would be easy to hide in, and a good shade for concealing blood, but the price tag made his gut lurch. He wasn't sure he could afford it.

'I think he's just popped in the back.' Goldin was talking to the one-eyed man, who was patiently waiting at the counter for service. 'Not sure how long he'll be.'

'Oh, thank you very much.' The one-eyed man's voice was gravelly, but weak and a little breathy. William could imagine it carrying a similar stench to that of the Shoulster's proprietor. 'Hang on a minute. Are you Aler Goldin?'

'That I am!' Goldin puffed out his chest and leant the blunderbuss on his shoulder casually.

'It's a pleasure to meet you.'

William watched the man subtly in the mirror. Not for any fear of him, but because he was rather strange and he didn't seem at home in the high-end shop. He was dressed in worn-out linens and dirty leathers – a long brown coat, far too warm for the climate, and a shirt with stains on it. William wondered if he was one of the homeless people he had spotted in the back alleys, and entertained the thought that perhaps the man was here to rob the place.

'I cross paths with your folk sometimes in my line of work. Well, I say *work*. Play's more like it.' The one-eyed man shook Goldin's hand with gusto. 'I've even been to watch a Prize or two in my years. Didn't get there last year, but I heard you did well.'

'Not as well as our William, here.'

William closed his eyes and cursed the little man under his breath. He could thump Goldin sometimes, and right now he felt like kicking him somewhere sensitive. Had it completely slipped his mind that William was a wanted man? When he opened his eyes, he found the stranger peering at him through the reflection in the mirror.

'You're that False Butcher I've heard about. William… what was it? Fairmount?' The man's one eye surveyed him, from crooked stance, to bandaged foot, and finally the crutch leant against the racking. 'Looks like you took a beating in the Prize.'

'It's William of Fairshore, actually.' William saw no problem in correcting the one-eyed man now; his cover was already blown. He plastered on a false smile, and hoped the conversation would be done with quickly.

'William of *Fairshore?*' The one-eyed man scowled, apparently distracted by something in one of the glass displays. 'Right.'

William wasn't surprised the man wasn't overawed with a twice-disgraced, blacklisted assassin. On a more positive note, he seemed unaware of the bounty.

'Nice to meet you, anyway,' the one-eyed man added seconds later as a distinct afterthought. He was already weighing a rifle in his hands and eyeballing the minute script on a list of prices.

'The pleasure's all mine,' William muttered under his breath, and turned back to his mirror.

Upon second appraisal, he decided that he would buy the jacket after all. It was rather smart, and with a new shirt and trousers he might blend nicely into the Vitale crowds. As he tried to stand up more squarely, he caught a glimpse of movement behind him in the mirror. The one-eyed man took the rifle by the barrel and swung it like a club. The stock cracked over the back of Goldin's head and knocked him to the floor.

'Have some of that!' the one-eyed man bellowed, a mad smile in his voice.

William spun around, staggering from the pain of it. His hand reached instinctively for his hip, but his flintlock wasn't there. It took precious moments to remember he had affixed the thing to his chest with the new holster, and by then One-eye was upon him.

'And you.' The man swung with the rifle. 'I'll put you where you belong.'

Thankfully – perhaps because of the man's missing eye – when he came to strike William, he missed. The stock passed mere inches from William's nose and caused him to stagger backwards. The rifle twisted the one-eyed man around, its momentum unimpeded. It tore out of the man's grip and spun across the room. The front of a glass display case smashed into glittering beads.

As William finally found his flintlock, his foot touched the floor. Agony jerked him over. He mewled through clenched teeth and collapsed into a heap, his arm tangled beneath him. He hoped it wasn't broken; he didn't think it was – his fingers could still flex. In the moment, it simply bolstered a hundred other pains, aches, and agonies.

More glass shattered; no doubt the one-eyed man was rearming himself. William cringed in anticipation of a blow. He started to crawl, hissed through the pain of it. Then he rolled himself over with a grunt that swelled to a guttural yell as pain lanced up his leg. He pulled the flintlock from the holster and aimed it, blinking frantically to stop budding tears from obscuring his vision.

As the room softly faded into focus, he found that the one-eyed man was sprawled on the floor some four paces away. He wondered for a moment if the momentum of the rifle had twisted him right around and sheared his spine, but that was ridiculous. He spotted Gwyneth then, toting a bottle of ether, and the smashed glass and liquid that drenched the one-eyed man.

'My head's killing me,' Goldin groaned from the far side of the room, staggering up. Blood wept from the back of his head, but otherwise he seemed to have his faculties. He took up the blunderbuss he had been eyeing.

'Where's the shopkeeper? I'll have this, two boxes of paper cartridges, two boxes of shot, a pouch of powder, and a pack of rolling papers.' Goldin wiped trailing snot from his nose. 'Better get yourself a mop as well, this eyepatch-wearing son-of-a-cock is about to make a sizeable mess.'

'Wait.' Gwyneth stepped into Goldin's path.

'He could have staved my head in if I wasn't blessed with such a thick skull!' Goldin touched the back of his head and brought his fingers away, bloody. 'I'm going to turn his head to jam.'

'He's my uncle.' She held on to Goldin's gun. 'I can't let you kill him.'

There was something of a stand-off as the two wrestled for the blunderbuss in the close confines of the shop. William wobbled upright, his stomach clenching awfully as his foot throbbed. The proprietor, meanwhile, was busy ringing in the sale, unperturbed by the altercation.

'He must have figured out who you were working for. We've done things like this before, he probably put two and two together.' Gwyneth yanked the gun free with a growl. 'Or he saw Dunstan leaving, I don't know.'

William propped himself against the wall. 'Is he a *badger?*'

'Yes.'

'I'm guessing that's bad news for us,' William commented with a sour chuckle. He closed his eyes and swallowed a sudden jolt from his foot. 'As much as it pains me to agree, Goldin's probably in the right. If this badger is going to be a problem for us, maybe we'll have to kill him.'

'We're not killing him. There are rules.' She sneered at the unconscious body and appeared to consider it a second, before continuing, 'Alwyn wouldn't like it, and you'd end up in a ditch somewhere.'

'Then, let's go. I'm sick of this shit-hole town.' Goldin snatched his Shoulster's-branded canvas bags from the counter and peered inside to check his purchases.

'We can't let him tell the others. Then we really will have a problem.' Gwyneth pursed her lips. 'We'll have to take him with us. If he goes missing, the Badger Sett will know something of our operation, but they won't know everything.'

'Sounds like a brilliant plan.' William retrieved his crutch. 'I love travelling with people who tried to kill me.'

'I almost killed you once, to be fair,' Goldin remarked.

'No, you didn't.'

'I thought about it.' The little man shrugged. 'When you held up my cart on the way to Blackbile, it could have gone either way.'

'Brilliant.' William blew air through pursed lips. 'Me and my three would-be killers; I wouldn't miss it for the world.'

# 1674
## GWYNETH FINCHLEY

'Here she is!' One of the girls snickered. 'How's your rear, dear?'

Gwyneth looked away, tried to ignore the pointed comments. As chance had it, her eyes found her cousin's.

Fortuna was sat at the back of the room with the other rich and beautiful young women. Although half her face was besmirched by scars, the preened and powdered half was perhaps the most beautiful "good side" in the room. The usually shallow young ladies saw it reason enough to see past her imperfections. She teetered precariously atop their social pyramid, and even talking to Gwyneth outside the dorm might bring her crashing down. She turned away, and let the other seniors continue their derision.

'It's a good job the headmistress used her belt. Look how bony she is,' another commented.

While these girls had been at the school a good few years longer than Gwyneth, curricula weren't divided by year but by House. As such, classes contained a wide age group from old veterans to new starters. The idea was that the older girls could help teach the young, but the imbalance of knowledge only served to foster ill will.

'If Mr Crane had used his paddle,' the girl continued, 'he'd have snapped it on her.'

'Or snapped *her,*' a third added.

It had been over a month since Gwyneth had been marched in front of the whole school and flogged, but some girls wouldn't let it drop. Days could pass without mention of it, but now and then someone would awake in a particularly vindictive mood and dredge it all up again. It seemed today would be one of those days.

Gwyneth was thoroughly bored of the same uninspired and endlessly repeated comments, but they still cut her deeply. In addition, she was convinced she'd never find a friendly face in all her time at school. Being associated with her seemed akin to contracting leprosy. The injustice of it made her all the more irate.

Taking her usual table – in the rear corner with only one stool – she tried to ignore any further muttering and jibes that came her way. She slumped forwards, elbows on the bench and hands propping up her cheeks, as unladylike in her posture as she could get. It was hard to keep faith in the whole finishing process when even her most accomplished classmates had the same vicious taste as badger baiters.

'Good morning, girls.' Mr Kohli swept in, embroidered and sequined silk smock trailing airily in his wake. 'I've such an exciting challenge for you today.'

He rifled through a drawer in his desk, pulled out handfuls of scissors, bobbins of silk thread, and a small, stuffed doll he used as a pincushion.

'I'm sure you are aware that the Winter Gala is coming up.' He practically danced to the edge of the room and began to unspool a wide sheet of fabric from one of the rolls on a wall mounted rack. 'I have spoken with the headmistress and have secured the privilege of creating the banners for our class.'

There was a genuine hum of excitement from every girl except Gwyneth, who sulked. She could hardly be eager for a mandatory party with the students that despised her and the loving family that might also kill her.

'To that end'– Kohli slipped a sharp pair of scissors through the fabric, cutting off a length in one smooth motion –'I would like you all to get into pairs.'

Gwyneth's heart sank into her stomach and was caught in its sickening roll. Needlepoint was usually one of her least hated classes. While there were often jibes at her expense, she didn't normally have to interact with any of the spiteful young women.

The tutor clapped his hands twice in quick succession. 'Come on girls, we haven't got all day.'

There was a flurry of whispering and movement as the other girls bartered to join up with their most treasured friends. Gwyneth stayed still at her table in the back and hoped that she would be forgotten. Even the humiliation of pairing with Kohli was preferable to joining with one of the girls.

Minutes later, with most of the bargaining complete, it became apparent that aside from Gwyneth, there was one other sans-partner. Gwyneth cursed even numbers and tried to shrink even further into the corner, hoping against hope that a cloud would pass by the window and bathe her in shadow.

'Can Tabitha, Hattie, and I make a threesome, sir?' the spare girl posited. Another humiliation, but a humiliation that suited Gwyneth just fine.

'I said pairs not trios, girl,' Kohli retorted with a flamboyant wave of his arm that upset his glittering smock beautifully. 'Look, Gwyneth there, she is in need of a partner. Sit with her.'

Gwyneth's heart sank even further, so low that if there was any more upset it was in danger of falling out of her backside. The only reprieve was that this spare girl hadn't been particularly cruel to her before. Perhaps that lack of cruelty was exactly why Gwyneth hadn't come to learn her name. It was a sorry state of affairs when her worst enemies were her only associates.

The girl sighed and traipsed to Gwyneth's bench. She acted as if it took all the strength she had to prevent herself from keeling over dead. At the realisation that there was no stool waiting for her, she huffed and returned to fetch her own. It was dragged over, legs squealing against the floorboards. The moment seemed to last forever and poured on humiliation like so much scalding water. Gwyneth could bathe in it if she was that way inclined.

The girl sat and kept her gaze dead ahead, glaring at Mr Kohli.

'Good.' Kohli thumped the tip of his closed scissors onto his desk to draw the class's attention. 'I want one three by eight banner – feet, that is – from each of you, and there will be a prize for the best, so try your damnedest. I'm heading out for more supplies. Get planning! There are papers, inkpots, and dip pens in the bureau at the back if you want to draft anything.'

With that and a snap of his fingers, he flourished out of the room.

The class burst into activity, with girls gathering supplies and gushing over the Winter Gala. The small table in the corner, however, was devoid of such jubilance. The girl next to Gwyneth shuffled uncomfortably.

'So.' Gwyneth smiled, hoping to make something good of this sour predicament. 'I'm Gwyneth.'

'I know,' the girl said, not even bothering to look at her. There was an Eastern lilt to her voice that the finishing school hadn't managed to beat from her yet.

'Look, you don't want to work with me, and I'm not exactly... At least tell me your name.'

'Sidonia.' She drummed her fingers on the wooden bench: a rhythmic tapping. Gwyneth couldn't help but notice that her nails were false. They were thick, with a pleasant rainbow sheen across the pearlescent white.

'I like your nails,' she commented, hoping that flattery and a feigned interest might help relations.

'You do?' Sidonia cast a derogatory eye over Gwyneth. 'I did not think you were interested in pretty things.'

'I like pretty things,' she lied. It wasn't her fault she hadn't been born with prominent cheekbones or a neatly pointed chin. 'I just haven't had a chance to get settled here yet. It's hard to–'

'Well, these are Kamandi.' Sidonia splayed her fingers and wiggled them so that colours danced across her nails. 'Shells: hand-picked on the black sands and worn down just-so in their work camps. Beautiful, aren't they?'

Gwyneth nodded, but before she could say anything, the girl was talking again.

'These.' She indicated diamond studs in her ears. 'Are from Gan Salawi. I'm told the mines are openly contested and change hands daily. A complete bloodbath, apparently.'

Gwyneth smiled. It seemed that while this girl was immensely self-centred, that she actually had something in common with Gwyneth – or at least the morbidly curious girl Gwyneth used to be before she saw her cousin's head parted from his body. Sidonia was more enamoured with the ugly histories of her trinkets than the beautiful facades.

'This was from a swordmaster's hilt.' She indicated a large square brooch. 'My father bought it off a big Gael we met in a roadhouse

– we found ourselves there after a storm. He was a traveller, said he took it from a dead man in the Amaris Isles. They actually slice open their own bellies if they don't get their way, can you believe that? Talk about big sulks!'

They both chuckled.

'I've heard that. They have special swords for it.' Gwyneth mimicked plunging a blade into her guts, complete with lolling tongue and crossed eyes. 'They stick it in and pull up, slicing through all the important bits.'

'I can't imagine being such an incredible sourpuss. "I can't protect my village" dead. "My porridge is too cold" dead. "I forgot to buy flour" dead.' Each time Sidonia said dead, she mimicked the same impaled gurn that Gwyneth had. 'It's true, you know? The Gael said he stole a sack of flour from a swordmaster and he just up and killed himself.'

Gwyneth's mouth spread from an optimistic smile to an out and out grin. She dared not hope it, but she might actually make a friend of Sidonia. They certainly shared the same interests – interests that Gwyneth thought she might have lost the stomach for.

'I don't have all that many things, but I do have a nice necklace...' Gwyneth trailed off, noticing that Sidonia's attention had drifted away. The pair of them were being watched. Sidonia stilled for a moment, like a hare in the light of a coach lantern. She had been caught being nice to Gwyneth.

'Oh, my gods.' Sidonia suddenly recoiled, her face changing in an instant. Any trace of mirth was gone, replaced entirely with a scowling distaste. 'Your mouth; it's disgusting. You have foul, rotting enamels like a stinking pauper.'

It appeared Sidonia wanted to distance herself, lest she be thought a sympathiser. While subtle indifference had worked for Fortuna, she had been careful to never be seen talking with Gwyneth outside the dorm. Sidonia, on the other hand, had shared a laugh and a friendly smile. It seemed there was only one way to counterbalance the kindness: a fresh torrent of spite.

'My gods, they're actually browning at the edges. I might just be sick.' Sidonia turned away dramatically and feigned a gag. 'Your breath...'

Originally, wooden replacement teeth were intended to prevent dental problems, but the procedure was incredibly expensive. As such, implanted incisors, carved canines, and modelled molars had become somewhat of a status symbol.

Gwyneth was dumbfounded. She hadn't a clue how to react. There was no reason in replacing teeth that still had a few decades in them, but as wealthy heiresses, almost all her classmates had been through the procedure. They took it as a badge of honour – proof that they were among the most rich and influential. Now Sidonia had mentioned it, the other girls were certain to be loading bullets of scorn. They would cut her down for sport, the way their fathers hunted pheasants.

Gwyneth cringed into the corner as the others started to join in. "Rot mouth" was amongst the slurs hurled by the refined young women, along with various jibes on poverty and the lower classes. While Gwyneth had found the old insults tawdry and uninventive, this fresh volley was too sudden and too much to bear. She thrust to her feet, sending her stool screeching across the boards, and dashed out of the room.

Tears were pricking at her eyes as she fled down the corridor and out through double doors to the courtyard. She didn't stop there, determined not to show her hurt to the callous girls. Tramping through puddles and mincing fallen leaves, she hastened down a short passage, crossed the racket courts, and ran into the parkland beyond. Maybe she could lose herself in the forest that hemmed it, or perhaps drown in the lake at the far side.

She kept running and gasping and crying until she could stand it no more. Finally, she collapsed into a pile of dried leaves and huddled herself tight. She sobbed openly, hands clutched to her streaming face. It was a cathartic jettison of emotion that had weighed on her like an ever-growing millstone. It felt as though she might cry for eternity, wallowing in her own self-pity until her tear ducts bled dry and she became as brittle and arid as a leaf in the heap. But as powerful as the torrent was, it was stopped in an instant by the sound of a breaking stick and the sudden notion that she was not alone.

She sat up, startled and snivelling. Leaf litter clung to the fabric of her jacket and was embedded in her hair. She looked out to the nearby lakeside: nothing, not even a ripple on the placid waters. Closer, there was a small, red-painted shed with doors hanging open. One creaked subtly in the gentle breeze, displaying various gardening tools inside. A long handled pair of shears were leant against the wall.

'Sorry to be bothering you, young miss.' A voice startled her from behind.

She whipped about, kicking up dry leaves and causing half the pile to slump. The caretaker was stood ten paces away, chewing something brown, possibly root or tobacco. It looked as though he had been maintaining a boundary fence. When she came running in fits of tears she had stumbled right by him on the opposite side.

'You're not supposed to be out here. If a tutor finds you, and in a state such as that, they're liable to have you flogged. At least I have my slipper handy this time.' He brandished a tired slipper from his back pocket.

Gwyneth pushed onto her knees, ready to run should he come for her. 'Do you mean to beat me with it?'

'Only if I'm forced to.' He flexed a finger under the sole and folded it back so that only soft leather remained at the tip. 'Doesn't hurt half as much as the faculty thinks it does.'

He chuckled and shoved it back into his pocket. 'I carry it with me everywhere since last time we met. My reckoning is: it's a win-win-win. Your arse is saved the pain, the headmistress is saved the effort, and I get to maintain my ruthless edge.'

He spat root slime to the dirt.

'What's the matter, young miss?'

'The girls here are vile.' She sniffled and struggled to contain rapid breaths. Saying it out loud was harder than simply feeling it. 'And, I'm not sure I'll ever make any friends.'

'Sounds like this finishing school has up and finished with you.' He started to move away. 'Come over here, I've got to be getting on with my work, but I'd like to talk. Talking's good when you feel bad.'

He walked to the fence, took up some tools, and set back to his work. Gwyneth dusted herself down and cautiously followed. When she got there, he was getting a new plank into position and worrying a trio of nails in his lips.

'What does that mean?' She frowned at his hammer as it purposely thumped a nail home in one strike. 'The school has finished with me?'

'I mean,' he mumbled from the corner of his mouth. 'There's a good portion of folks my age with no friends. It just happens as you get older, once you leave school, I imagine – although I never attended school in any capacity other than taking care of the grounds.'

He drove another nail powerfully into the fence. 'You're just starting a little early, I suppose.'

'That's hardly comforting.' Her scowl continued. 'The girls here torment me daily.'

'No,' he agreed, then plucked the final nail from his mouth and hammered it into the fence. 'I'm not much of a philosopher, if I was I wouldn't be mending a rotten fence now, would I? Though I do find a little manual labour helps to alleviate the drudgery of life. A good project is all the companion you need sometimes; something to occupy your hands, which occupies your thoughts in turn.'

He cast an eye at her. 'Perhaps if you threw yourself into your studies you wouldn't find yourself so upset.'

'I have little interest in deportment or elocution.' She sneered.

'Then find something you do like.' He pulled a rusty pair of pliers from a tool belt and offered them. 'Try these. This next plank's rotten and I need to get the nails out. I find mending things highly comforting, maybe you will too. Not all girls are born to be prim and proper, my sisters certainly aren't.'

Gwyneth blew air through pursed lips and scowled. The man was right, he was no philosopher, though she was under no illusions that she was meant to be a young lady of taste. Perhaps she *was* more suited to men's work. There was no harm in trying.

Even in two hands the pliers were heavy, the hinge stiff. She gripped a protruding nail on the board and tugged. It didn't budge.

'Hold them sideways and lever against the wood.'

She adjusted her grip and pulled. The nail slipped outwards with a satisfying squeak. She tried another, and as it came away the board fell from the fence. She tipped it onto the pile of those the caretaker had already removed.

'Good?' He pulled a leather pouch from his pocket, took out a pinch of dried root and pushed it into his mouth. 'There's not much in life more satisfying than pulling nails.'

'It is satisfying. Diverting, even.' She nodded, and sniffed to clear her nose. She hadn't thought about the bullying at all while preoccupied with the fence. It gave her clarity. 'I'd rather be pulling Sidonia's nails, I reckon.'

She giggled at her little joke, then took a moment to seriously picture the girl screaming as the beautiful shells were plucked from her fingers. There was something awful about her being so amiable before the bullying started – it was more personal. Perhaps the fakes would be secured to the natural nails with some kind of adhesive and they would be plucked away too, leaving only pink and gummy welts. She smirked; Sidonia could be the ugly history to Gwyneth's own pretty trinkets.

'I'm not sure that's a good idea.' The caretaker mirrored her mirth and patted her on the back. 'Though, I suppose if the thought gives you a little solace, who am I to argue?'

He chewed a moment. 'Why not try fitting that board?'

He picked up a fresh piece of wood and positioned it against the supports. 'Take that nail, hold it to the – just there; that's right. Now, strike it. You can go lightly at first to get it started, then, give it some hammer.'

Gwyneth did as she was told, and found the whole thing quite enjoyable. It was far more gratifying repairing a fence than it was sewing a stoat or sheaf of barley onto a napkin. This was more worthwhile.

She drove two nails into the board at the top, but found it difficult to get into a comfortable position to secure the bottom. Still, she followed the caretaker's instructions and got one more nail home. Positioning the final nail, she decided to drive it into the wood with a single strike as he had, only to rap herself on the thumb. With a yelp, she dropped the hammer and stuffed her throbbing digit into her mouth.

'Damn it. I'm sorry.' The caretaker winced. 'I didn't mean for you to get hurt. Let's have a look.'

Reluctantly, she let him see.

'You gave yourself a good crack, I'll give you that.' He smirked, pulling a little glass jar filled with cream from his toolbox. 'You broke the skin a little, and your nail might go black, but there's no lasting damage. Here…'

He unscrewed the jar and daubed her thumb in the cream.

'This stuff is gold dust when it comes to numbing wounds. I use it all the time. It would set me back a hefty coin purse, but I won the recipe in a bet. I grow the herbs down by the lake and make it myself.' He sealed the jar and tossed it to her. 'Keep it, I've got loads of the stuff, and I reckon you might be better suited to pulling nails than driving them. Best keep away from hammers in future.'

'It doesn't hurt too badly.' She gave him back the hammer and offered the pliers. 'That salve's working already, I think.'

'Keep them; they might give you what you need, help you cope with the bullying. I don't know. My sister had an awl she liked to hold in times of strife, perhaps my pliers will do the same trick for you. You've definitely perked up somewhat. I'll tell the headmistress I dropped them in the lake; I'm surely due a new pair on Adelaide Bennet's pocket change by now.'

Gwyneth grinned, flexing the pliers open and closed on the rough hinge. It was a nice stress reliever and it put her in mind of metal spheres her mother rotated in her palm when agitated.

'It's good to have something real, something to keep yourself sane when life's beating at you. Just make sure to keep them hidden. We don't want you getting thrashed.' He pushed a few nails between his lips and set about securing another board. 'And you'd better be getting back to class.'

'Thank you.' Gwyneth stood and dusted off her knees. She wasn't sure if the caretaker was wise or just one of those low born types that rambled with unearned confidence. Either way, she liked him.

She strolled back to the school, enjoying the resistant flex of the pliers.

# 1683
## WILLIAM OF FAIRSHORE

William eyed Gwyneth as she danced about with a knife. It was curved and she held it with the blade down, springing back and forth on the balls of her feet like a ring fighter. She slashed upwards, flourished the blade, and caught it in her other hand. Her enthusiasm was catching, but William found himself a little stunned. It was still a fact she had tried to kill his only friend in the whole continent. It was right that he should hate her for it, but with Goldin's rough edges ever softening for her, William found it hard to remain cautious. He genuinely liked having a second companion.

'What do you think of this one?' She swiped upwards again, then returned to a neutral pose. With her tatty woollen sleeve hanging low and hand turned just right, you couldn't even see the blade was there. 'It's a little pricey because of the jewel in the handle, but it fits right in my palm.'

Perhaps Gwyneth saving him from the one-eyed man could cancel out her attempted murder prior. It seemed a scale that was easy to balance and made the prospect of trusting her all the more reasonable.

William toyed with a flintlock that was far too expensive for even his generous budget. While he hadn't been in the market for a replacement, or even an accompaniment, to his silver pistol, this one was undeniably fine. It had a revolving chamber that could hold and fire three brass cartridges – the same ammunition he would need for the rifle.

'I have to admit, I was a little sceptical in letting you join us on this job – I've had bad experiences with clients in the past.' William thought it best to explain himself, if only a little. 'But you saved me and Goldin both. I'm glad you're here, and not just because I'm in no state to fight yet. It's good to have you around.'

William pushed a little lever with his thumb and tilted the gun so that the revolving part tipped out to the side. It really was a smooth action; a testament to superior build quality. He set the chamber spinning with the flick of a finger.

'Thank you.' Gwyneth nodded, a smile turning up the corners of her mouth. 'Dunstan's not really one for frivolity, so it's nice to have a bit of fun on the road.'

'Thanks, lass,' Goldin added. He was shopping one handed, taking multiple trips between the shelving and counter for items he had forgotten to purchase previously in his ire. He was also pressing a blood-blackened towel to the top of his head, having shrugged off the wound as little more than a scratch. 'You enjoy a good tale or sing-song as much as I do. When this contract is done, and Will and I are rich beyond our wildest dreams, you're welcome to call by my villa any time.'

Goldin's head wound had bled profusely, as many blows to the cranium tend to do, but his skull was intact, and the contents didn't seem too badly affected. William supposed that, in very much the same way palms callous and become tough from hard labour, brains go through a similar toughening when subjected to the life of drink and drugs led by Aler Goldin.

The little man snapped his fingers as if something had only just occurred to him.

'Do you sell bandage?' he asked the proprietor, who promptly whisked him away into the back room.

'Get rope, too!' Gwyneth called after. 'We don't want my uncle wriggling too much. With William's leg sticking out, there's barely enough room in the coach as it is.'

'Sorry about that.' William flicked his wrist and the bullet chamber snapped back into the firing position; it was so satisfying to watch.

'No, it's my fault you got injured, and I'm sorry.' She gathered up the knives, garrottes, and bottles she had collected together and hauled them over to the counter beside the till.

'We should be in Vitale in a few days, we'll find Uncle Alwyn's contact, and then I think we'd better find you some restorative medicine. We might be able to get a message to the surgeon general. He's an uncle too, and he might send us a supply.'

'I hope so.' William cast his mind back to the salves employed by Dr Barber. It was more than possible to work medical miracles if certain ingredients were combined. He might even be healed overnight with the right concoctions. 'I've had enough of limping.'

He picked up the rifle from his own collection of goods for purchase and shuffled across to the wall display. He had so painstakingly selected it, taking time to get accustomed to the scope and complicated reloading mechanism. Now, he wasn't so certain it was right. He set it back on the rack and selected another model that was substantially cheaper. It was surely just as accurate; these rifle makers had to build to a certain standard, no matter the price. It would be frivolous to spend any more. It was also a turn of luck that the money saved would enable him to indulge in the three shooter.

William had often detested Vitulan architecture, damning the white-block monoliths that eroded any charm Garlish cities might have once had, but they looked damned impressive in Vitale. Rather than the odd fake and gaudy façade of white stone nestled between red brick in Valiance, every building here was of the same style and crafted with impeccable quality. It changed the impression made by the bold white buildings from that of indecently hoarded and boastful wealth, to a higher class of living for all. Even meticulously hidden work houses looked finer than the imitations occupied by Garlish lords.

'I didn't think anything like this was possible,' William found himself saying. 'Valiance is big, and it's horrible there.'

'It never ceases to amaze.' Gwyneth smiled that crooked wooden smile of hers. 'I've been here a couple of times; the scale of it doesn't really sink in until you try to get from one place to another. Going across a district can take a good hour or two by coach.'

'I'm going to crick my bloody neck at this rate.' Goldin was craning upwards, focused on a golden statue at the pinnacle of a banking house's roof. 'I bet there's some money to be made here, eh, Will? If you fancy trying out thievery again. That golden goddess has awfully thin ankles, wouldn't take too much work with a hand saw.'

William smirked at the idea of the pair of them up there, toppling the thing onto a waiting flat-bed carriage far below.

'There is plenty of money to be made here.' Gwyneth's teeth clicked. 'Unfortunately for you two, that involves the death of a senator.'

Their one-eyed prisoner wriggled and grunted at that. He had been trussed like a hog and gagged for the benefit of them all. In addition, those bindings had been fastened to the coach side so that he couldn't flail or strike a blow to William's aching leg.

'Damn it all. I've said too much, now.' She rolled her eyes, then addressed their prisoner directly. 'I guess that means we can't be letting you go until this is all over.'

He mumbled something spiteful through the gag, his one eye staring viciously at the assassins. William sneered; Gwyneth's uncle seemed to have taken a particular disliking to him, perhaps judging him – correctly – as the leader of this whole operation. He would often catch the man staring at him in what ways were afforded to a bound and gagged man: lazily, ferociously, with the one eye bulging, and worst of all, piteously.

'We'll add him to the list of things to do.' Gwyneth nudged him with her boot. 'After Dunstan finds our contact and we get a message to the surgeon general, I'll get that gag off him and find out what the Badgers are up to.'

'We could ask him now, there's little else doing.' Goldin shrugged. 'These plain white blocks aren't holding my attention as I hoped they might.'

The elegant terraces were arranged like frills of lace over steep hillsides, making even the poorest homes seem grand. Their route took them through avenues of towering columns and meticulously shaped topiary that gave way to plazas awash with grand fountains and statues. At intervals, modest parks added a splash of greenery and glimpses of brightly dressed citizens, and though many horses traversed the wide roads, the way was remarkably clear of faeces.

'He might lie. I'd rather get him somewhere we can ensure he tells the truth.' Gwyneth leant forward. 'I'm not really allowed to harm him, but I've always hated this drunken old twat.'

'I can thump him, if you'd like?' Goldin patted a fist. 'Maybe crack him over the head like he did to me.'

'It might be better if we don't do that in the open.' William noted the guardsmen on street corners. 'I'd rather keep a low profile.'

Each guard had a traditional weapon of one form or another – mostly rapiers, but a few of the bigger ones had maces or hammers. He imagined the traditional arms did well to dissuade the citizens from violence and crime, and they could be employed to deadly effect. It was the subtler black-iron flintlocks that gave William pause. They were more worrying than a spiked ball, even if the image they conjured was only that of a blood-darkened shirt, as opposed to a caved-in face or cranium.

'We'll tie him to a chair once we get to the safe house and I'll interrogate him personally.' Gwyneth sounded almost giddy at the prospect. 'Is that alright with you, Uncle?'

Dunstan grumbled at being acknowledged, and sullenly replied, 'I'm not interested in these silly games you play.'

'Excellent.' Gwyneth clapped her other uncle – the one bound with rope – on the knee. 'You and I are going to have a *painfully* good time.'

The bound man's eye bulged again, this time with indignation and fear. The amount he could convey with a solitary eye and the tone of his laboured grunting was impressive. It was a wonder that those without ropes and gags found it so difficult to express themselves. William was glad in the least that he had put his initial trepidations with Gwyneth aside. Sure, she was unhinged, but she shared that same morbid glee that he so admired in Goldin.

# 1674
## GWYNETH FINCHLEY

'Damn it all,' Gwyneth cursed as she woke, feeling a familiar dull pain in her abdomen.

It was that time again. She was in for a day of pain and discomfort, and to make it worse, she had to carry on like nothing was wrong. It was taught in the finishing school that it wasn't ladylike to give in to the menstrual forces. One had to remain dignified and strong as to not upset the delicate sensibilities of the husbands that were to keep them. Gwyneth thought it a tremendous amount of tripe, though she was in a similar position to would-be ladies of taste: if her maturity was discovered by her family, she would be deemed bad blood. Her father would be forced to kill her.

'Are you alright?' Fortuna asked. She was sat at the end of her bed brushing some expensive scented oil through her golden locks. They always seemed to sit just right, even when she had only just rolled out of bed.

'It's nothing.' Gwyneth stretched with a groan. 'I just remembered I'm supposed to be running today.'

'I thought you enjoyed it.'

While heavy exercise and sweat certainly wasn't considered tasteful by the headmistress, a good figure was desirable in a young lady, and it had to be achieved one way or another. Gwyneth was already scrawny enough, so the rationing imposed on some was not viable for her. She had to exercise in the hope that repeated exhaustions would somehow hammer her into a perfect hourglass.

'I just feel a little... off today.' She risked a peek under the covers. Another girl in the dorm had woken up one morning with bloodstained sheets, her menses coming as an early surprise. Since then, Gwyneth had taken to sleeping with a folded cloth in her underwear at all times. Today, it had thankfully held. 'I might have a cold.'

'Well, don't share it around.' Fortuna shuffled to the far end of her bed. 'A running nose and a powdered face do not a good match make.'

Gwyneth asked Fortuna to inform her tutors that she was indisposed that morning and stayed in her bed until the dorm was empty. Only then did she risk the trip to the lavatory. She had gotten rather expert at disguising her bloods over the past months, having had only one near miss when someone had stumbled across her in the laundry room. Slashing her leg to account for the blood may have been rash, but it was certainly preferable to a sliced neck. A light daubing of the caretaker's salve had seen to the pain with miraculous effect. Her leg went numb within minutes, and she had been unable to detect the jab of a fork into her calf for two weeks. She had started to worry that permanent damage had been done, but the feeling came back as the last of her scabs peeled away.

Arriving in the lavatory, Gwyneth was relieved to find that her flow hadn't started quite yet, though the ache in her stomach remained a grim portent. Hiding herself monthly from the other girls was far from a solid long term plan; she was getting old now for a girl who hadn't received first bloods. Surely, her family would start to suspect her soon. Perhaps they already did. She just had to hope her gifts were late coming and wouldn't be too much longer. Either that, or accept her mother had bred outside the bloodline, making her bad stock and bad blood. Gwyneth didn't feel like bad stock.

'There you are.' Sidonia was waiting for her when she returned to the dorm. 'Miss Hounshire wants no excuses today. She said that if you weren't knocking on death's door, you were to come to class, and here I find you up and out of bed.'

Sidonia had been recently elevated to prefect and she wore the badge with a pompous pride. She stood there, flawless in prefect greys, regarding her with disdain. It made Gwyneth realise exactly how rough she must look: hair dishevelled from her pillow, nightshirt sweaty, she could almost feel the dark circles under her eyes.

'I've just been to the toilet. I've been sick.'

'Somehow, I don't believe that. Let me smell your breath. Show me those pearly whites.' Sidonia smirked, displaying her own teeth: expertly carved.

Gwyneth opened her mouth and exhaled.

'Ugh.' Sidonia recoiled. 'I can smell the tooth-rot setting in, but there's no smell of vomit. Get your skinny arse down to the field.'

Gwyneth had initially hoped that Sidonia might remain on good terms with her away from the judgemental girls. It had been a foolish notion. Sidonia needed to prove her superiority to herself as much as the others, and had taken it upon herself to be Gwyneth's most cruel and scathing tormenter. Whether they were observed or not, she was abhorrent.

'Fine,' Gwyneth relented. 'Give me a minute to change.'

Sidonia regarded her for a moment with a cocked eyebrow, then about turned and swanned out of the room. 'I'll be waiting downstairs. Wrap up.'

Gwyneth frowned. Usually, the uniform for physical activities was a short skirt and light shirt. She peered out of the window for the first time. The forest and field were coated in a thick layer of snow and a good portion of the lake's surface was frozen. The girls were gathered on its bank and the tutors were striding out to test the integrity of the ice.

As a result of the boiler in the finishing school's cellars – that sent steam up through pipes disguised in the walls and floors – the dorms had been fairly warm. Gwyneth hadn't even realised how cold it had gotten since her run the previous week, and she certainly hadn't noticed the beginnings of the snow the previous night. Just looking through the window to the frigid scene made her shiver. Her guts cramped at the prospect of ice skating at such a time, but there was little else she could do. Sidonia was a prefect and would make damned sure Gwyneth didn't get out of class so easily.

She dressed in the heaviest clothing the school's uniform charter would allow. A long skirt, shirt, and smart jacket, covered with a woollen robe. It was all quite warm from the top down, but a gust of wind could easily curl under her skirts and lash her legs. To that effect, she had worn two pairs of bloomers. It was all the armour she could equip to combat the cold and it still didn't feel enough.

She met with Sidonia and they walked across the field in silence. As the bitter winds began to set in, doing battle with gloveless hands and legs poorly fortified under ridiculous winter skirts, Gwyneth began to feel that she might actually be sick. The cold certainly intensified the needling in her abdomen.

As they reached the lakeside, the physical education tutor, Miss Hounshire, was out on the lake with the caretaker. She was directing him where to hammer iron spikes into the ice. Topped with little red flags, they presumably indicated the perimeter for where it was safe to skate. Girls were stood waiting, wrapped up in coats and cloaks, each trimmed with the fur of a different exotic animal. Four times as many girls as normal had joined for the day's activities, drawn in by the novelty of the frozen lake.

Sidonia found a pair of skates from a box beside the caretaker's shed and tossed them into a thick pile of snow.

'Put those on,' she instructed, then left to speak with the popular girls.

While others seemed to have new boots, with pristine bleached-white leather and fur trim, Gwyneth's were old, brown, and worn though on the toes. The first was easy enough to put on, but when it came to the second it was too hard to balance on a single blade. She winced as she sat in the snow, feeling another spike of discomfort that set her stomach rolling. Once the laces were tightly knotted, she stumbled up against a tree for balance.

'Ah, Gwyneth.' Miss Hounshire had arrived on the bank and was clapping imaginary dust from her hands as though she had any part in the caretaker's manual labour. 'I'm glad you were well enough to join us. It should be good out there today.'

Gwyneth nodded and forced a smile that caused a crack in her rapidly drying lips.

'Come on girls, gather around.' Miss Hounshire was a large woman, built similarly to the headmistress. She had the same square shape to her, only her body was harder and formed of dense muscle. She had a tight leather jacket on, and leather trousers that were usually for riding. Small ear muffs were her only concession to the cold, made from fox fur and vibrantly orange. 'As you all know, the Winter Gala will be upon us shortly, and by then the whole lake should be solid as a dock man's thigh.'

A few girls tittered at Miss Hounshire's bawdy humour.

'The headmistress expects there will be skating abound.' Her puckered mouth tweaked up at the edges. 'This is your chance to get a little practice in, and have fun while you're doing it.'

She clapped her hands, rubbed them, cupped them, and blew in a cloud of steamy breath. 'Well, what are you waiting for? Have at it!'

Slowly but surely, the girls moved onto the ice. Some were well versed in skating, those unfortunate enough to be born in the colder reaches of Garland or Lothagia. There was a Scoldish girl who made it all look so easy, gliding out with one skate in the air. She hopped and weaved about, spun on the spot with one foot.

Some others weren't so competent, Gwyneth included, though she was far from the worst. While a couple struggled to even stay upright, she managed to maintain a steady pace, arms stretched wide for balance. It might have been the fact that she knew that falling over would be detrimental; the pain in her gut was keen enough already.

She skated by the shore for a few minutes, testing her balance before venturing further out. She built confidence quickly and while she was no competition for the Scold – doing twirls and skating literal rings around her – she did get on par with others that seemed to have prior experience.

'Watch out, rot mouth!' One of the prefects arced around her.

Gwyneth grit her teeth, praying the others would leave her be. So many days had passed without them even acknowledging her, why did it have to be today that they reiterated their stale jokes? She sneered and changed course for a less populated stretch of ice.

She couldn't help but notice that wherever she moved to, a gaggle of girls followed at a not-so-subtle distance. After a few minutes, one girl skated right at her, only to swerve away at the last second. Little flakes of ice kicked up from her skidding blades. Gwyneth recoiled and nearly toppled over in an effort to avoid the clash. Only by sheer luck did she manage to stay upright. She held her arms out for balance and dared not even move, lest she slip onto her rump.

Suddenly, another girl hurtled by. Then another. They missed her by inches. The game was obvious: cause Gwyneth to fall over despite never touching her, then relentlessly mock her while she was down. She wouldn't let that happen, and the best thing she could do to stop them from winning, was to stay still and refuse to flinch or falter. It was easier said than done.

Two more girls swept past, their blades gliding over fresh ice. Then another girl came by. There were three more after that, coordinated to come simultaneously. Gwyneth nearly flinched that time. Sidonia joined in then, and while her skates were amongst the best, she wasn't as proficient as some of the others. Her skate caught in a groove in the ice and she collided with another girl careening in the opposite direction.

They clashed in a mess of limbs, spiralling with their own momentum. Sidonia managed to stay upright, but the other girl fell halfway down. There was a tear of fabric as she gripped Sidonia's coat to haul herself up. Slowly their rotation stopped, and, as their abashed faces found Gwyneth, their embarrassment quickly turned to ire.

'What in the hells are you doing?' Sidonia shoved the other girl away and looked down at the torn pocket on her woollen coat. She fiddled with the flap and worriedly looked about. Her prefect badge had been ripped from her and had skittered ten feet beyond a perimeter flag. She rounded on Gwyneth then, her hubris making her all the more ferocious. 'That was your fault, Rot!'

'No, it wasn't.' Gwyneth balked.

'Yes, it was.' Sidonia's cheeks blushed red and her eyes bulged. She was huddled-in, balancing like she hadn't thought that falling over had been an option before. 'Go and get it back, now!'

'Piss off.' Gwyneth stood up straighter, perhaps now was the time she should deal with her tormenters once and for all. A skate to the shin would soon quiet Sidonia and make any others think twice about bullying her again.

'What's going on here?' Miss Hounshire skated close.

'Gwyneth won't do as she's told, Miss,' Sidonia carped.

'Come now, Gwyneth.' Miss Hounshire took on a stern tone, gliding between the pair of them. 'Do as Sidonia says. She's a prefect now, you know that.'

'Yes, but she wants me to–'

'I don't care what she wants. This is about authority and your lack of respect.' She enunciated every word as if each was more important than the last. 'Now, you will do as Sidonia asks, or I will be having words with our headmistress. Is that clear?'

'Yes, Miss Hounshire.'

'You're on thin ice dear: I heard that vulgar language of yours. Make sure I don't have any trouble from you again.' Miss Hounshire spun on her blades and skated off, hands clasped behind her back.

Gwyneth looked down, her anger washed away by the futility of it all.

'Well?' Sidonia spat. 'Are you getting my badge then? Or do you wish for another lashing? I heard Miss Hounshire has quite the arm.'

Gwyneth sighed and skated to the perimeter flag. A small red triangle of linen was tied to the end of a rusted iron spike that reached her shoulder. She held it for a second to steady herself and looked out to the badge beyond the perimeter.

'Miss Hounshire!' Sidonia called for the tutor, but not loud enough to actually get the woman's attention. It was more of a warning, but it was all the warning Gwyneth needed.

'I'm going.' She pushed out past the flag.

Progress was slow, not because the ice outside the perimeter was harder to skate on, but because she was terrified of how thin it might be. She shuffled as delicately as she could. The few feet stretched out and seemed much further as she neared the lost badge. A subtle cracking noise, muffled as if the underside of the ice was beginning to split, set her on edge. She could feel the weight of nearly ten girls watching her, silently wishing for her to fall through. Nervous phlegm collected in the back of her throat; she swallowed.

Cautiously, she reached down. When her fingers found the badge, they snatched it and she lurched upright. The simple act of bending at the hip flared a pain in her abdomen and she had to steady herself. Her fist clenched the prefect badge tight. Her lips pursed. After the moment of tension subsided, she pivoted and shuffled back to the perimeter flag.

There was a collective sigh as she returned to the safe ice. Hers was of relief, but those of the onlookers were of disappointment. Gwyneth couldn't help but smirk as she made her way to the still huddled Sidonia.

'Here's your stupid badge.'

As Gwyneth's skate passed over the channels the girls had made dashing around her, there was a terrible crack and the ice from beneath her fell away. Her stomach rolled, her fists clenched, and she tried to leap to safety. Plunging into the clawing, frigid waters, her body flopped forward onto still-sturdy ice. All at once, she was stunned and winded, left gasping like a fish. She clutched for the ice, fists bunched and unable to release in the shock. Her legs kicked, splashing uselessly in freezing water. She reached out for help from whoever was nearest – Sidonia.

Some girls were laughing, but the prefect retreated. Her face was a picture of horror; she had barely missed falling through the ice herself.

Gwyneth wriggled and scrambled until she managed to heave herself onto the ice. Free of the water, she was promptly sick. Shivering, unthinking, with her head down, she crawled towards the shore. Only when she touched the shale bank did she feel safe enough to collapse onto her back. Her guts and head were throbbing. She gasped for minutes, eyes skyward, trying to block out the whispers and titters and torment.

A girl, one of Sidonia's friends, and a particularly cruel one at that, skated to Gwyneth. She loomed over her a moment, her features indistinguishable with the bleak sun at her back. Gwyneth feared the girl might spit on her.

'Are you alright?' she asked, kneeling. 'Can you get up?'

'I'm fine,' Gwyneth wheezed.

'Good, good.' The girl offered a guilty smile. 'Let's get you back to the dorms and get you cleaned up.'

'Was I sick on myself?' Gwyneth asked, pushing herself to a seated position with the girl's assistance. 'The headmistress–'

'It's not the vomit.'

Gwyneth looked down. Her skirts had ridden up around her waist and her bloomers were on display for all to see. The water had caused the wad of cloth inside to leech. They were pink with blood, darkening as they drew up between her legs. She threw herself away from the girl helping her and was sick again onto the ice, this time for the very real prospect of her own filicide.

Gwyneth thrust upright, driven by a wild, panicked energy. She kicked off her skates and ran painfully across the shale. Reaching the field, she lost a woollen sock to a frigid puddle, and kept running despite Miss Hounshire's calls.

The whole run was a mad blur. When she reached her dorm, she slammed the door and managed to drag her heavy case across the floor to bar it. Somehow, the prefect badge had managed to stay in her bunched fist for the duration. She tossed it onto her pillow and promptly ripped off her wet and bloodied clothes. Once naked, she tore the sheet from her bed, sending the badge flying again, and wrapped herself tightly for warmth.

She juddered with the cold, teeth chattering, both frozen and terrified. It was a blessing that Fortuna hadn't been skating; if she had, it would have been too late. There was only a short amount of time to spare. Soon, Fortuna would find out, and then her parents, and then the Matriarch. With no evolutionary gifts self-evident, Gwyneth would be proven bad blood. Killed.

She racked her brain for any kind of gift she could easily fake. Her mother's fits: not convincing enough, and her mother had the club foot too. Fortuna's scarred face: difficult to replicate. Countless crippled cousins. That duct on her uncle's chest that spilled precious bile for his experiments. An uncle that inflated like a pig bladder on contact with certain foods. Dozens of extra nipples. Handfuls of webbed fingers. Footfuls of webbed toes. Granted, some gifts weren't as obviously positive as others, but they were still evolutionary advancements. Surely, they were. Regardless of the usefulness of their gifts, they all had one, and she would need to counterfeit one if she hoped to stay alive.

Flinging open the lid of her trunk, Gwyneth started to search. The numbing salve gifted to her by the caretaker was wrapped in a scarf, and would surely help her do whatever she needed to do. She set it aside, considering that perhaps she could hold her face against a steam pipe and copy Fortuna's scars after all. It was a little derivative, and not so believable.

Then she found the pliers. Those could do some damage. Perhaps she could tear out her fingernails the way she had dreamed of doing with Sidonia. It was a good idea, and she actually started dipping her fingers by turn into the salve, but was it really enough? Her late bloods and the sudden arrival of her self-inflicted gift would surely arouse suspicion, and what would happen when they started to grow back?

She looked down at her salve-smeared fingers. Perhaps she could break them and make herself double jointed, or use her sewing kit to join the skin and make them webbed like her father's. Fingers didn't just go webbed overnight; that was the kind of gift you were born with.

She realised then what she had to do: something so extreme that no one in their right mind would ever do it to themselves. She took the salve and started smearing it about her gums. It wouldn't be particularly obvious what the benefit of her gift would be, but her family could be endlessly creative when it came to determining their unique traits as evolutionary advantages.

The salve tasted strange. There was a slight tingle to it for a minute, then nothing. She couldn't feel the touch of her fingers against her cheek or the scrape of the pliers as they passed between her lips. Her breath heightened as she gripped the first tooth, but there was no doubt in her mind: it was this or death.

She would claim they just dropped out.

# 1683
## WILLIAM OF FAIRSHORE

William limped around the room in circles. He had been without his crutch since they had arrived in Vitale, and was just managing to walk without wincing. It helped that he was on a lush carpet.

Gwyneth had tried to get him an appointment with the surgeon general, an uncle of hers, but the man had been too busy. He had instead sent William a few vials of a sickly concoction. Having taken his first draught only an hour before, William wasn't feeling the effects just yet. It was clear the tincture was in no way as potent as those administered by Dr Barber, but William imagined such things would be as closely guarded by the Empire as they were by the Guild. The best restoratives wouldn't be given out so freely. William was hopeful, however, that after a night in a comfortable bed he would feel a lot better.

Looking around, he didn't know how to fully absorb the luxury in which he found himself. From the vast couches to the expansive hearth, everything was sheened with gold, or padded and coated in red brocade. The carpet itself looked too fine to walk on, the seats too plump and perfect to sit on. Even the fire roaring in the hearth seemed out of place amid the grand gilded surround. Absolutely everything in the room was far too expensive to even consider using. Even being here and exhaling used air probably depreciated the place by a handful of gold each minute.

The safe house he had imagined Gwyneth taking him to was a kind of dusky, dusty, cobweb-adorned warehouse. The kind of place with disused machinery: a mill or smithy. Somewhere that had been shut down for taking more fingers off its child labourers than you could count on both hands. William had been prepared to make his own bed from news-sheets and old rags, to stack crates for a table, and would never in ten lifetimes have guessed they might have taken refuge in one of Vitale's finest hotels.

'I like it.' Goldin launched himself onto a chaise longue, muddy boots and all. 'It's homely, just the sort of place I'm accustomed to.'

William winced as the little man proceeded – now that he had already dirtied the expensive leather – to kick off his boots in opposing directions. One landed on the marble fireside and the other clunked against a cabinet holding crystal glassware. The delicate flutes jingled dangerously.

'Can we set him over there?' Gwyneth directed two porters, who were hauling their bound and gagged captive. 'No, actually, leave him in the bathroom. I don't want him sullying these carpets if he pisses himself.'

She followed the two lumbering porters from the lounge.

William suspected that it was blood rather than urine that Gwyneth wanted to protect the carpets from. She had been grinning for hours at the prospect of interrogating the prisoner. As for his easy transportation into the well-renowned hotel, he had been brought through a back door and carried up service stairs with the luggage. William hadn't bothered to ask, but assumed, as with a startling amount of enterprises, this was a Finchley hotel.

At first, he had found it hard to believe that one family could have spread like a weed through the Empire, though it was a known truth that money comes to money and power to power. If the Finchley family really was as old and unified as Gwyneth claimed, it made sense that they had amassed so much. In fact, thinking of it in such terms made the prospect seem inevitable for those lucky few dynasties. He wondered how many other families there were with the wealth and power to steer the Empire.

'This is nice, isn't it?' Goldin flexed his toes in the direction of the hearth. One of his woollen socks had a hole in it and his big toe was protruding, the nail black from an old injury.

'I suppose.' William felt uneasy with the whole arrangement.

'Here.' Goldin tossed over a hard jelly wrapped in gold foil. A box of Prospor delight had been set on a small table as a welcoming gift and Goldin had already eaten two. He champed and smacked his lips with gusto as he devoured the third.

William unwrapped his own jelly and popped it into his mouth. It was quite toothy, more so than he had expected and he had to chew rather than let it dissolve. It had an overwhelming taste of roses, and was far too rich compared to the bland fare he could usually afford.

'Thank you for that.' Gwyneth remerged from the bathroom with the porters. One of them was still pocketing a gold coin. 'These two are a little worse for wear, and I couldn't carry him up here myself, not even with my coachman to assist.'

'It's no trouble really, *Madonna,*' one replied in a florid Vitulan accent.

'Your secret is safe with us, ma'am.' The other winked, his own Garlish accent the antithesis of anything ostentatious. He tapped the side of his nose.

'Yes, yes.' She ushered them out. 'There's no need to lay it on thick, he'll be well looked after. We just need to keep him out of our way until this is done.'

'I understand, perfectly.' The Vitulan porter bowed then swept the door closed, leaving only the trio in the extravagant penthouse.

'Right.' Gwyneth took up a small leather bag that she had stowed by the door and stalked back into the bathroom. 'Time to see what my uncle knows.'

William rounded the room again, unsure whether it was a good idea to sit down or not. He was still taking in all the little details on the carved columns and frescoed ceiling. The room was so cluttered with expensive trinkets and incredibly detailed patterns it was too much for his eyes. All this decadence just felt wrong; living like a king while others struggled to survive. Though he supposed, coming from an assassin that had killed more than a score of men, that sentiment was as rich as the rose jelly.

'We should probably go in.' Goldin stood from the chaise and stretched.

William nodded. He hadn't wanted to watch their prisoner tortured for his information, but if he did have anything of value to give it was better to hear it first-hand. The pair headed into the bathroom, with Goldin making only a brief detour for the drinks cabinet. He selected a fine Smelters' brand bottle of whiskey and didn't bother to collect any glasses.

The bathroom was equally as impressive as the lounge. The space was tiled in pristine white, as large as some entire homes. There was a freestanding bath in the centre, with wide clam shell sweeps of porcelain and golden lion's feet.

Their prisoner was in the bath, huddled up and trembling. Though he hadn't been fed or watered for a good day and a half, he still had enough spare moisture to sweat profusely. It beaded on his forehead, made his hair lank, and darkened the fringes of his eyepatch. His one eye betrayed fear and hatred.

'So…' Gwyneth pulled a few cloth pouches from her leather bag. 'I've been spending my hard-earned coin this afternoon, all for your benefit.'

She set one pouch on a slatted table between a dried-up sea sponge and loofah, and started opening the other.

'Granted, I do enjoy a nice spree now and then.' She pulled a waxy purple cube from the pouch and presented it. 'I got this from Pesci's, made from whale oil. None of that pig tallow rubbish.'

She thrust the cube of soap at the prisoner.

'Smells of lilac,' she commented. 'I thought, afterwards – in theory – the blood should come right off and I can treat myself to a nice bath. I imagine my beating arm may require some rest and relaxation by then.'

She set the cube on the table and withdrew a pair of stockings from the other pouch.

'High denier.' She winked. 'Don't want it ripping after a few swings now, do we?'

Goldin passed the bottle of whiskey to William and he took a swig. Silently, the pair watched as Gwyneth deposited the cube of soap into one of the stockings and fidgeted to get it right down to the toes. William almost choked on his second mouthful as Gwyneth started swinging the thing for practice; it was like a damned flail.

Gwyneth caught the soap in her hand and crouched down to meet the prisoner's eye. 'I am reliably informed that this shouldn't leave any bruising.'

William wasn't so sure about that. He passed the bottle back to Goldin, then limped across the room. He wanted to stand where the prisoner couldn't see him. The man's one eye kept glaring at him and he didn't like it.

'Let's play nice, alright?' Gwyneth reached forward and tugged the gag out of the prisoner's mouth.

'Gwyneth!' he spat, drool spluttering over his chin. 'I need to tell you something.'

'Oh, don't spoil it,' she harrumphed. 'You've got to resist a little or it's no fun. I've been looking forward to this.'

'Gwyneth,' he snarled. 'This is important. I need to speak with you, only you. I can't talk with them here.'

'That's more like it.' She took a few more practice swings with her impromptu flail. 'Though it is terribly rude to exclude my friends here, wouldn't you say? We'd all like to hear what you and the Badger Sett have been up to.'

'Some things are better kept between us.' The words hissed between clenched teeth. 'A family matter.'

Gwyneth scowled a moment, but kept idly swinging the soap as she considered him.

'We'll step out.' William decided for her.

He didn't want to see any bloodshed if it wasn't required, and this man seemed perfectly happy to talk if his conditions were met. Gwyneth could relay the information afterwards and perhaps provide a little explanation. As far as William was aware, this Badger Sett was determined to stop the assassination, but there was little explanation as to why either side of the Finchley family cared so much for the fate of a senator.

He limped out of the room. Perhaps he was better off knowing none of it. Some contracts came with explanations, usually when patrons needed to justify their actions, but most came without. An assassination should be a simple killing, no emotion spent or context required. He had been willing to accept a few wrinkles in the contract for the sheer price of the thing, but it wasn't exactly wise to involve himself in the Finchleys' politics.

'That was a bit of an anti-climax.' Goldin clunked the bathroom door shut behind him and pressed his ear to it. 'Not sure I've ever seen an interrogation before. It would have been nice to tick it off my list.'

'We're better off out here.' William gestured for Goldin to join him on the couches and finally sat in one of them himself. For all its beauty, the couch he had selected was terribly uncomfortable. 'Ojo used to say there should be no emotion in a killing, we're better off not knowing the details.'

'Sod Ojo.' Goldin waved the thought away with the whiskey bottle in hand, sloshing a few drops onto the expensive rug. 'I want to hear.'

'If it's anything important Gwyneth will let us know. Just come and relax.' William shuffled to get more comfortable.

'Can't bloody hear anything anyway, this door's thicker than…' Goldin walked over to the couches and shrugged. 'A barn door?'

He slumped onto the chaise as the door from the hallway opened. The coachman strolled in, locked the door behind him, and quickly divested himself of his coat and hat. True to his usual self, he didn't say hello.

'Evening, Dunstan.' Goldin raised his bottle in greeting.

'Did you find – who was it you were looking for?' William asked. 'Alwyn's man?'

'I did,' he replied in a clipped tone, brandishing a small briefcase. 'These are for Gwyneth – spare teeth. Where is she?'

There was a commotion in the bathroom: a loud shriek of pain and a dull thump. Then there was another. The blows came hard and fast, as if Gwyneth was swinging wildly with the soap-flail and leaving no space for questions or replies. While each man in the room had expected the prisoner to receive a beating, no one had anticipated anything as punishing and relentless as what could be heard through the door.

Dunstan lurched towards the bathroom at the same time that William jumped up. They rushed for the door together, with Goldin lagging someway behind.

Gwyneth didn't even look up or acknowledge their arrival. She was panting and grunting with each swing, beating the one-eyed man about his face and body. His nose was broken and bleeding profusely, and more blood was leaking from a split above his eye.

Dunstan grabbed Gwyneth from behind and dragged her away from the bathtub. She took two more futile swings as she came out of reach of the prisoner, then tossed the soap away. She was panting and snarling, but didn't resist.

'What do you think you're doing?' Dunstan turned her around and gripped her by the shoulders. 'You know this isn't allowed.'

'He deserved it.' She shrugged.

'What in the hells are we going to do with him now? If the Matriarch finds out—'

William didn't know what to say. He didn't understand these people one bit, but it was clear that the coachman's anger was fuelled by fear.

'I don't know.' Gwyneth shrugged Dunstan off and rounded on the prisoner. 'I suppose if we let him go, he'll tell the Matriarch what happened. If that's the case, we'll have to kill him. I saw a nice bridge as we came into the city, we could toss him into the river and claim ignorance.'

'I don't think we'll be doing that.' The coachman sighed.

'I won't talk,' the one-eyed man added with a whimper.

'Let's just calm down.' William racked his brain for a solution. 'We don't need to worry about it now. We took him prisoner so that he couldn't inform the Badger Sett of our plans. We'll just keep him until this is done. Then, once you've had time to think about it, we can deal with him accordingly.'

William swallowed, hoping to avoid more death than was necessary.

'I want him out of my sight.' Gwyneth spat at the bound man and Dunstan had to wrestle her back.

'I'll take him,' he offered. 'I'll keep him in another room. Next door. William's right, we need to cool down, and we can deal with him later.'

'Fine.' Gwyneth relaxed, and as Dunstan let go of her again, she sloped out of the bathroom.

William followed first this time. With a guiding arm around her, he led her back to the couches. He wasn't sure what the Badger Sett could be up to, but it had riled Gwyneth. Whatever it was, it couldn't be good for the contract's success.

As he sat down, William realised that for the past few minutes his foot hadn't hurt at all. Even when he had dashed into the bathroom to stop Gwyneth there hadn't been so much as a twinge. He subtly wiggled his toes, and made an effort to hide his glee given the dower circumstances.

Goldin offered the bottle of whiskey to Gwyneth and she took a large gulp.

'I'm sorry,' she muttered, her breath wavering as if she might cry. 'I shouldn't have hit him. I didn't mean to complicate things. They're already too complicated as it is.'

'I managed to get those aliases, if it makes any difference.' Dunstan produced an envelope from his pocket. 'All backdated in guild records.'

It was Gwyneth's idea to procure aliases. The Guild could have vital information that would help them in their upcoming assassination. With Gwyneth not a member, and William with a price on his head, they wouldn't have been allowed entry to a guild outpost without them. Even if Goldin had gone alone, he was a known accomplice of William, so his presence would have attracted attention.

'At least we have some good news.' Gwyneth took the envelope and slid her thumb under the flap. 'I hear the Guild keeps architectural drawings and such; it should make our lives easier.'

'What's my new name then? I've always fancied myself as a Horatio.' Goldin smirked. He always had a way of lightening the mood. 'I'm not sure I could do the silver-spoon drawl it deserves though.'

Gwyneth's mouth twisted up at the sides, but as she read the details on the documents her smile quickly turned to a grimace.

'What about you, Will?' Goldin continued. 'You're quite good at that Conejan accent. You could be a Santiago.'

William smirked, but the last time he had played a Conejan it hadn't gone so well. He didn't feel like pretending to be Francisco Asino, or any other Conejan ever again. It just brought back too many bad memories, both of Ojo and his monumental downfall, of which he was only just recovering from.

'I'm better at Gaelish.' He tried to change the subject.

'Go on then.' Goldin straightened up in his chair and rubbed his hands with glee. 'I've not heard you do Gaelish.'

'These won't do.' Gwyneth folded the papers and thrust them towards the coachman. 'You'll have to take them back. Get something different.'

'I'm not your errand boy, and I don't like your tone.' Dunstan pouted. 'Take them back yourself if it's that important.'

'I…' Gwyneth sighed. 'Please, just take them back. I know it's not your fault, but these aren't right.'

'What's wrong?' William tried to look across at the papers.

'The–' Gwyneth rifled through them too quickly for William to see any details. 'The dates are all wrong, and the descriptions; it says here that Goldin's six foot three. If outpost security is tight and they check their records… We shouldn't use these.'

She folded the papers over. 'Please, just get some new ones.'

'Do you have any idea how long it takes to get names put into guild back records?' Dunstan walked away and started helping himself to a drink from the expansive liquor cabinet. 'They have to contact our man in Blackbile for starters. That takes long enough, let alone wait for the ledger updates to be sent to the outposts.'

'If it takes so long we should get right on it.'

'Be my guest.' The coachman took a draught of something brown. 'I've helped you enough already, I'm not even supposed to be involved.'

'Please, Dunstan?' Gwyneth implored him and shoved the papers into her pocket.

'Fine, but there's no point rushing. I'll get Freddy set up next door first and I'll find our man tomorrow.' He paused, thinking for a moment. 'And if the new aliases come back before the senator is dead in a ditch somewhere, you owe me a drink.'

'Done.' Gwyneth nodded.

'Can we pick our names then?' Goldin's eyes were already darting as he mulled over potential candidates.

'Write something down.' Dunstan reclined against the wall. He didn't look happy, but then again he never did.

Gwyneth pouted. 'We'll have to plan this killing without guild help, at least until the new aliases arrive.'

William didn't like the way that this job was going. There was far too much information flying around that he just couldn't understand. He'd rather be killing the senator alone, with nothing more than a name and a deadline. It felt like the Finchleys were intentionally keeping him in the dark for their motives, and that made him all the more nervous. Not since he had been contracted in Fairshore had he felt a job would turn so sour. His gut had been right then, and he had ended up blacklisted for not listening to it.

Deciding it would be better to get some fresh air, William said, 'We should leave while the prisoner's moved next door. We can get a lay of the land before it gets dark.'

'Can't we start tomorrow?' Goldin shuffled deeper into the cushions. 'I'm comfy now.'

'This place is...' William was at a loss for words. He was stood on a small plinth in the memorial garden at the centre of the city square. From here, he could see beyond the diligently groomed poplars to the buildings bordering the white slab expanse.

'Big?' Goldin offered.

'And then some.' William pivoted slowly, taking in the vast square in very much the same way he had taken in the grandiosity of the hotel room: dumbfounded and awestruck.

On one side was the Imperial Palace, set behind an ornate garden and threatening black-iron fence. The whole facade was pocked with alcoves, each inhabited by unique statues of great imperials, long dead. The gardens were of course populated with countless guards, patrolling or standing sentry. The extreme amount of security on display didn't matter much, however, as William had no intention of killing the emperor.

'It certainly looks a very pricey neighbourhood.' Gwyneth was studying the senate building itself. She had cheered up since they had left their hotel room and prisoner behind. William longed to find out exactly what had drawn such a reaction from her, but decided he would rather stay in her good graces.

With his mind on potential assassination strategies, William about turned to look at the New Gods' Cathedral. 'That's where Lord Beechworth took a shot at D'Elia.'

'If you believe that sort of thing.' Goldin shrugged, causing the whiskey in his bottle to glug pleasantly.

'Why wouldn't I?'

Everyone in the Guild knew one version of the story or another, and while there was no consensus on the details, everyone got the gist. Lord Beechworth tried to assassinate the emperor, failed, and somehow the Guild was born as a result.

'I've never been convinced.' Goldin closed one eye to size up the cathedral roof. Even now there was a scaffold erected around one of the many spires. 'From that vantage, I doubt he would have missed. He was the best rifleman the world ever knew. I think it's just made up: a cautionary tale to stop aspiring assassins gunning for those with the power to squash the Guild.'

'You don't think there will be any repercussions after we kill the senator?' William felt a pang of guilt.

'Who am I to say?' Goldin took a swig of liquor.

'There won't be any repercussions,' Gwyneth declared. She was still sizing up the senate.

'And what makes you so sure?' Goldin pursed his lips, wet and glossy with too much dribbled whiskey.

'This little killing will be easily forgotten. Sepo Falade has few friends and many enemies.' She rounded, perhaps sensing the scepticism from the two assassins. 'He's a war monger, wants the Empire to expand further into Nok. The continent is fairly barren, so most tend to disagree. I imagine half the senate will be glad to see the back of him. Anyway, it won't be left up to chance. My uncle will see us right.'

William radiated yet more scepticism. He'd had clients renege on payment before and his suspicions about this family were growing. He was confident they would pay him, they had set up a covenant with the bank after all, but the Finchleys seemed duplicitous. Perhaps they would sell him out to the Empire to raise their status further. He couldn't see Gwyneth having part in something like that, but Alwyn was another matter. Still, if he had the gold on hand it wouldn't be too difficult to get somewhere distant and safe.

'You've gotten a feel for my family now. If there's a pie without a Finchley finger in it, I certainly haven't smelled it.' Gwyneth shrugged. 'Just know that the right palms will be greased and life will go on as normal.'

William didn't know what to say to that. The Finchleys inhabited a world all too complicated for a simple killer to comprehend. A world of endless bureaucratic greys, as opposed to the easy black and white he found in a life of kill or be killed.

'Let's review our options.' Gwyneth twisted on the ball of her foot, her attention firmly on the senate. 'I'm not sure repeating the great Lord Beechworth's missed-shot is an option. What about infiltrating the senate? Falade will surely spend most of his time there.'

While in years long past the senate had been open, a wrought-iron fence had been erected around the whole building. Guards patrolled it as they patrolled the emperor's grounds, walking the perimeter at the bottom of the steps up to the high building, and standing sentry on the great plinth stage where the emperor made his famous speeches.

'I don't think sneaking in will be easy,' he concluded.

'What about getting a job there? A wine pourer, or something?' Goldin offered. 'We could slip him some poison or knife him if the opportunity presents.'

'It's possible.' Gwyneth chewed her lip.

She had changed her dentures for a fine row of carved pearl teeth that had arrived in the briefcase with the coachman. From what William had seen, she had upwards of ten sets, all different colours and materials. These made her look far more presentable and somewhat pretty in a way he had never noticed before. Though he could now appreciate the threatening nature her usual pair gave her and realised exactly why she chose to wear them on the perilous road. Without them, she looked like any other unassuming young woman.

'There sure are a lot of guards, though,' she mused.

'Getting out would be nigh on impossible if the alarm was raised.' William grimaced. 'We might be better getting to him on his way to the senate, or out in public somewhere. Maybe at his home.'

'His home might be difficult.' Gwyneth hopped down from the plinth. 'That will be guarded too. We should still seek it out and see, but I think a cloak and dagger in the street is a better option.'

'They love a stroll in a park, these rich types.' Goldin took another swig of whiskey. 'If we know where he's going to be, we can get set up with that rifle.'

'One forms a strong love of nature when they aren't forced to sleep in it regularly.' Gwyneth smirked.

'You're right there.' Goldin jumped down. 'There's not much point sticking around here then, is there? If we're not killing him here, let's go out for a drink, enjoy ourselves. We can find this Senator Falade tomorrow.'

'I'm not sure Gwyneth wants us getting drunk on our first night in the city,' William remarked, still studying the buildings around the square.

Gwyneth scoffed, 'That's very presumptuous of you.'

'You said you didn't want us drinking.'

'No. I said drunkards with sore heads make poor travelling companions,' Gwyneth corrected him. 'You can throw up and groan all you like if you keep to your room in the hotel. We're about to start a big job; we can let our hair down just this once.'

William wasn't happy that the pair were so keen to retire on their first night actually hunting for the senator. He looked down to chide their laziness, but as he found them, Gwyneth glanced away. He wasn't certain, but the knot in his gut told him that she had been lingering on him. It was the same persistent stare followed by nervous reluctance to maintain eye contact that he had made at a few girls himself. Suddenly, the prospect of frequenting one of the capital's many taverns didn't seem like such a bad idea after all.

# 1680
## GWYNETH FINCHLEY

Once Gwyneth turned seventeen, she was no longer required to attend classes as a student. She did, however, need to act as an assistant in various lessons. It was a scheme on the school's part to keep her occupied until the coach arrived from Draig to take her home. As a girl could leave the finishing school at any point once betrothed, most of Gwyneth's peers had already departed, taking their demeaning attitudes with them. Only unmarried girls remained.

Fortuna had returned to the Manor some years ago. Though Gwyneth was sad at the time to have lost the poor friendship they had, she had made at least two equally poor friends since. They would make idle conversation occasionally, but neither spent any time with her outside their roles as assistants. There was one, however, who was as spiteful as ever.

'You're with me today, slack-tooth.' Sidonia walked into the little assistants' room, a box in her hands overflowing with old brown laces. 'We're taking class G out on the lake. The headmistress thinks boating will be nicely diverting for the girls.'

Gwyneth sneered and as she did so her teeth slipped sideways in her mouth. She hadn't been granted the implants she had expected – the ones that Fortuna, Sidonia, and all the other girls had. Her father couldn't afford the procedure, so had instead sent a pair of ill-fitting dentures and a pot of tree-sap adhesive that was as useless as the flavour was foul.

'Now?' Gwyneth looked up from her book.

'Yes, now.' Sidonia tossed her hair then stomped out of the door.

Gwyneth considered not bothering. A few days prior, she had received a letter from her father stating that a coachman would be with her soon. She expected his arrival that afternoon or perhaps even the next morning. If that was the case, she could easily shirk her duties and get away with it. Should he be delayed, there was a very real chance of a caning. Keen to avoid such humiliation in her final days, she traipsed out into the cold and across the field.

There were ten rowboats lined up on the banks of the lake and a huddle of girls waiting nearby.

'Late, as usual,' Sidonia commented. She was already handing out life jackets to the girls from a large box.

The jackets were old and cumbersome, made from thick bars of cork tied together with the brown laces. Each fitted like a corset and was about as uncomfortable as one. They had become compulsory on the lake after Gwyneth had almost fallen in, though the school hadn't seen fit to buy new, instead acquiring the old cast-offs from a decommissioned imperial frigate.

'You seem to be doing fine by yourself.' Gwyneth saw no need to put on a friendly face for the younger girls' benefit. 'Are you sure you need me here?'

'You know the rules. Two tutors are required at the lake.' Sidonia tossed a life jacket to the last girl and helped another tie the laces behind her back. 'As Miss Hounshire is not feeling well, that leaves me with you.'

'I hope she's not knocking on death's door,' Gwyneth replied sarcastically. 'There's only one acceptable excuse for not attending physical activity, as far as I recall.'

'Quit your whining and get some oars from the shed!'

Gwyneth stormed off and collected as many oars as she could carry – three. Ideally, once the boats were set up, Sidonia would be happy enough to let her wait on the bank while she and the girls had tremendous fun on the water. Gwyneth wasn't particularly in the mood for tremendous fun. She was more inclined towards a long and tedious journey, one that would take her all the way back to Draig where she could forget this place. There was no threat there anymore, it seemed her family had bought her ruse and accepted her sudden lack of teeth as a gift. Things could be like they were before she came to this horrible school, and more importantly, before she saw her cousin killed.

'I have been out on the lake plenty of times before, and I'm quite the sportswoman.' Sidonia was chatting with the girls and checking their life jackets as Gwyneth trudged past with the oars. 'We can have a race when we're out there.'

'What about you, miss?' one of the younger girls asked.

Gwyneth set two of the oars in a rowboat and moved to the next before she realised the question was intended for her. She found the girl, and replied, 'I'm not much of a rower, if I'm honest. I usually keep away from the lake.'

'I can show you, if you'd like?' The girl offered a wide smile that pushed her cheeks into chubby, freckled bunches.

Gwyneth smiled back, although the glimpse of kindness at this late stage of her school life only increased her melancholy.

'You've been on the lake.' Sidonia grinned. 'Maybe not as a rower, but you've skated here.'

'Have you, miss?' another of the girls asked. 'I love to skate. I hope it's cold this winter.'

'I've skated here.' Gwyneth smiled; it was actually quite nice to have the girls genuinely interested in speaking with her. 'It was before the Winter Gala, a few years ago.'

'Gwyneth dropped my prefect badge through a hole in the ice.' Sidonia knotted a girl's lifejacket so tight it made her gasp. Her usual sly smile had slipped from her face and her cheeks were beginning to blush with anger. 'The headmistress made me search for it. She refused to give a new one. I spent hours wading in the freezing water under her supervision. Every week we would come out; every Wellensday for two months. When I couldn't find it, I was no longer a prefect.'

The atmosphere soured rapidly. The girls had stopped giggling and whispering and chatting. All was quiet, save for the wind whistling through the pointed tree tops.

'You know that, don't you?' Sidonia took a step forward, fixing Gwyneth with a steely glare. 'I saw you watching me every week. It wasn't hard to mistake you, your head all bandaged up.'

Gwyneth bared her wood-carved dentures. There was little that could soothe her pain better than that of her enemies. While she had been recovering from the loss of her teeth, seeing Sidonia wading in the frigid waters was better than any tincture or salve. Perhaps now was the time to let Sidonia in on her little secret. She reached up and gripped the lapel on her blazer, slowly turned it over to expose the prefect badge hidden beneath.

Sidonia swore, and then lunged forwards. Her hands were outstretched like she might grip Gwyneth by the hair or gouge out her eyes with those beautiful nails. It wasn't to be.

Gwyneth took the last oar in both hands and hefted it from right to left, lifting it as she did so. The paddle struck Sidonia across the face as she barrelled into it. There was a crunch and spray of blood. Delicate wooden teeth sprayed out. Her body crumpled and she fell into the nearest boat, her legs over her head.

A few girls screamed and ran, others stared in horrified amazement.

'I think boating is off for the day, girls,' Gwyneth concluded, spying a man approaching across the fields. It wasn't her father's coachman as she had expected, but Uncle Alwyn's. When she realised who it was, she threw the oar down, stepped out of the grounded boat and strode off. 'Someone get Sidonia some salve for her mouth, losing teeth can smart… and say goodbye for me. My coachman's just arrived.'

Gwyneth was taken straight to the Manor from the finishing school. Not because she had knocked the sense out of Sidonia – the coachman had greased a few palms and that had been covered up easily enough – but because there was an important meeting there. She had been worried at first that another child was to be killed, or worse still that she was being taken to her own execution. From a few subtly probing questions, she found that wasn't the case, and by the time she got there, it was clear that some kind of celebration was planned.

She arrived before most of the extended family and stayed in a guest room across the hall from her cousin. She and Fortuna passed the time as young ladies do: in intense boredom – at least that was how Gwyneth felt. She hadn't picked up the love of needlepoint that her cousin had, so their days spent decorating cushions weren't quite as thrilling as she'd have hoped. Fortuna did apologise for not being there for her at the school, which was nice of her. Gwyneth accepted, but didn't think she could ever truly forgive being abandoned to her tormenters.

As more guests came, Gwyneth used it as an excuse to distance herself from Fortuna, and when her parents arrived she spent almost all her time with them. Her father inspected her new teeth, looked over her bare gums, and was pleased that her gift had finally presented itself. Her mother was keen to learn of her experiences in the finishing school, but quickly dismissed the tales of bullying as the wild imaginings of a teenager. Gwyneth realised then that she drew as little enjoyment from her parents company as she did from Fortuna's.

'Ah, young Gwyneth.' Uncle Alwyn found her in the study late one afternoon. 'You're with us tonight.'

'What do you mean?' She scowled up at him. She had been trying fruitlessly to fix a daffodil needlepoint intended as a gift for her mother. It wasn't particularly fun, but once she had set out to make something she wanted to see it finished right.

'You're seventeen, aren't you?' He smirked. 'It's time for your first outing. You'll be in my party.'

Gwyneth blinked and scowled deeper, frustrated by her failing handicrafts and the unusual announcement from her uncle. It sounded very suspect. She hoped Alwyn wasn't trying to marry her off to someone, especially as she had no intention of settling into this pointless domesticity. She tossed the cushion cover aside, and inquired, 'What party?'

Alwyn brought a hand to his temple. 'Heavens, Rhys, have you taught this girl nothing?'

Gwyneth's father had been dozing in a chair, a glass of spirit slowly tilting in his grip. At Alwyn's outburst, he sat bolt upright and straightened his glass so fiercely he tossed more than half the contents into his crotch.

'She didn't have her bloods until she left for Adelaide Bennet's,' he blustered. 'I didn't want to tell her… in case, you know.'

Gwyneth swallowed. She knew exactly what he meant: he didn't want to inform her of the family's inner workings on the off chance she had bad blood. The joke was on him, because she did have bad blood and was going to find out anyway.

Alwyn sighed. 'Come through to the dining room. You're sat with Fortuna; I'll have her explain the details to you.'

'Are you coming, Dad?' Gwyneth asked as she arose. The two men shared a quiet glance that was loaded with hidden meaning; Alwyn left with another sigh.

'Your mother and I aren't allowed to join in.' Her father shuffled uncomfortably. 'The only reason we were invited tonight is for your support. We want to see you do well.'

'What do you mean?' Her stomach began to churn ominously.

'Some Finchley's dedicate their lives to it, but not everyone gets to play. Just know that if you don't impress, you'll be back home with your mother and I.' He patted her slender hand in his best approximation of fatherly support. 'Relax, use that cunning of yours, and knock Uncle Alwyn's socks off.'

The dining room was a grand hall sporting three huge tables; two that ran the length of the room in parallel and one curved at the head of the room. The three together made a kind of horseshoe shape. Alwyn sat at the head of one of the long tables, blue banners adorned with hares hanging above him. The other long table was decorated with red banners and snarling badgers, beneath which was Fortuna's Aunt Fortitude, the sister of the Matriarch.

Gwyneth was relieved to see the man who had sliced open the throats of his wife and son was on that table, far away from where she was to sit. His one-eyed brother was there too, the one who had encouraged him to expunge the bad blood. She knew that, if they knew her loss of teeth was self-inflicted, they wouldn't hesitate to kill her too.

A place card marked her seat in fine calligraphy, sitting her next to Fortuna. They said a quiet hello and Gwyneth went straight back to inspecting the room.

It seemed that the top table, marked with neither a badger nor a hare, was reserved for only the purest family members. Five of the most powerful Finchleys were there, including the twisted

Matriarch, along with her husband and father, Wigbert Finchley. Known to all as the Patriarch, he looked almost as old as time itself. He raised a glass of wine in quivering fingers and toasted it right at Gwyneth, his eyes sparkling bright beneath bushy white brows and hooded skin.

'What's happening?' Gwyneth nudged her cousin.

'It's the start of this year's game,' Fortuna hissed excitedly.

'What game?' Gwyneth craned down the table trying to see who else was in her group.

'The Game of Fates.' Fortuna let out a squeak. 'The most exciting, intriguing, political, strategic, and high-stakes game of all. The fates of men are on the line.'

She was making fists of her dainty hands. Gone was the girl who so loved to do needlepoint of sweet little bunnies, although Gwyneth was sure it was Fortuna's handiwork on the banners.

'Why would anyone stake their life on a game?' The bi-annual Man-Butcher Prize and its hundreds of competitors was brought to mind. People staked their lives on gambles and games all the time.

'Alwyn was right!' Fortuna giggled from the excitement of being able to teach someone the ways of the game. 'You really know nothing, do you?'

'I suppose not.' Gwyneth leant aside as a butler filled her glass with wine.

'Well, once papa positioned that fool D'Elia as our emperor and got the Assassins' Guild protected in a tangle of red tape, he could basically do whatever he wanted.' She took a hasty sip of her wine, then continued, 'Bureaucratically speaking, the Guild was his sword and the emperor his shield.'

An uncle on the far side of the table, who had a fat lip and purplish growth under one eye, interjected, 'For a man who thrived on backstabbing political rivals, once he got to the top and secured himself many means of onslaught and protection, things became a little dull.'

'Hence, the games were born.' Fortuna was positively brimming with excitement. 'One team tries to elevate a man in society: get him a promotion or a medal or some such. The other team seeks to disgrace him.'

'We play with men's lives like prawns in chess,' her uncle added, misnaming the game pieces. 'Little knobbly buggers, they are! And we have the whole Finchley treasury and leverage at our disposal. It's Finchley versus Finchley. There's no better opponents out there. The Badger Sett against the Burrowing Bunnies!'

'I came up with the new name,' Fortuna added gleefully.

Gwyneth swallowed. Her family's excitement was catching. The Game of Fates sounded like the most exhilarating thing she could ever imagine. It definitely beat needlepoint or going back home to tend to the flock with her mother and father. All she had to do was impress and her whole life could be a game, bought and paid for by the Patriarch. She sucked thoughtfully on her wooden teeth and swallowed her nerves.

# 1683
## WILLIAM OF FAIRSHORE

'My first was a money lender.' Goldin sipped the foam off his ale. 'Ignorant sod, he was. He'd come into The Mop and Bucket every night and sling threats at any man that owed him. It was a nice little tavern; rural place with rickety tables and a blunderbuss over the bar – nothing like this place.'

He gestured around at the fine tap room the three had found themselves in, complete with lacquered mahogany bar, copper pipes, and brass pumps. There were four different ales to choose from, and so many bottles lined up on the shelves at the back, the owners needn't have papered the wall. Such an extensive range perhaps detracted from the experience as the murderous party had all opted for simple ale: two light and one treacle black for Goldin.

'There was none of this fancy stuff there. Just five jugs of the same swill lined up going stale.' Goldin slurped and hummed in appreciation. 'It was the third seediest ale house in Penton at the time, which suited me down to the ground. Simple pleasures, modest folk, and only one problem: any time this money lender came in he'd spoil the mood by bullying folk.'

William lifted his mug and scowled at the leather mat that had stuck to the bottom. He shook it free. There wouldn't have been such inconveniences in the establishment Goldin described, though it likely would have offered a large helping of fleas and vomit-scented straw on the floors instead.

'I didn't even owe him any money and he would still come over and vex me.'

'Why's that?' Gwyneth prompted, ever the diligent audience.

Her interruption caused William to glance over. She looked away as he did so, suddenly immensely interested in the brass banding on the edge of a large barrel. As far as he could fathom, they were all the actions of a shy girl who was starting to become more than a little interested in him. He let his gaze linger on her a while longer, emboldened by the ale in his belly. After a time, she dared to peek at him again, but as their eyes met she quickly turned back to Goldin. That all but confirmed his suspicions.

'He was always pestering me to see if I wanted to borrow any money. I always said no.' Goldin flicked his nose with the back of a finger. 'Well, always, except once.'

He took a swig of ale to draw out the tension that was building around them. 'One night, just after he had roughed up an old fellow and tossed him to the gutter, I thought, why not borrow some? I'll head on down to Fairshore, to one of their rich men's gambling houses, and blow the lot. I'll either make my fortune, or I can move on. Mr Moneylender's not going to find me, not if I don't want to be found.'

'As you'd expect,' he chuckled. 'I lost the lot.'

'So he came looking?' William huddled closer to distract himself from Gwyneth with Goldin's tale. Whether the stories were true or not, it mattered little. He loved the way Goldin told them.

'No.' The little man grinned. 'I went back home and took my last coppers to The Mop and Bucket. I suppose I'd just been looking for an excuse all along. I don't think I wanted to kill him, just have a scrap and get back at him for all the folk he'd hurt.'

William grinned. Somehow, when Goldin talked about killing a man, it was as guilt-free and righteous as anything that happened in a legend or myth. Not at all as muddy and fraught as William found when he killed men himself.

'He came in as usual, and when he spotted me he came right over to collect his repayment.' Goldin shrugged. 'He antagonised me, I antagonised back. He threw a fist, I threw a few back. He grabbed the blunderbuss from above the bar, but I didn't let him shoot it. I pounced on him, wrestled it from his fingers, and when I kicked him away I just pulled the trigger.'

He made the sound of a gunshot with his mouth.

'I don't think I expected it to be loaded, but I'm glad it was.' He set down his mug, now empty. 'Blasted him right off his feet and he was dead before he hit the ground. There was a kind of stunted silence after that. I thought I might have to run, then one of the old drunks started cheering.'

'You weren't run out of town?' Gwyneth grinned, her pearl teeth straight and white, more so even than natural teeth.

William swallowed a lump that had collected at the back of his throat. He wasn't sure if it was her sudden interest in him, or simply a combination of youth and alcohol, but he was beginning to get a little flustered. He fidgeted on his chair and tried to focus on his mug.

'Quite the opposite. The folk in Penton loved me for it. I never had to pay for another ale at The Mop and Bucket again.' He raised an eyebrow and shot William a gleeful smile before attempting to take another gulp from his empty mug. 'Speaking of ales, does anyone else want one?'

He stood up unsteadily.

'I will.' Gwyneth smiled, a subtle rainbow dancing across her pearly whites.

'And me.' William was only halfway down his own drink, but he could easily catch up while Goldin was at the bar. Between them they had finished over ten ales and William was starting to feel the effects. He paused to stifle a burp. 'Same again.'

The little man nodded and wobbled off to get three more drinks. William watched him clumsily navigate a table of Kamandi traders in fine silks, then realised that without him the conversation had dried up.

He tried to think of something to say, but the part of his brain that stored any and all interesting conversation starters had become a locked cell. He turned his attention back to Gwyneth, smiled, and hoped – in that brief moment of mild spontaneity – words would come to him. They didn't. He took a hasty gulp of ale and sighed, trying to appear content with the quiet. Maybe if he pretended the silence was a comfortable one, rather than an awkward one, it might just become so.

'So…' Gwyneth broached. Her eyes were on him and he suddenly felt incredibly self-conscious. 'Do you have any heroic stories?'

For a second, William thought the tension might have been about to ease, but he was right back on the spot again. He opted to tell the truth rather than make up some exciting fiction. 'Not really; at least nothing you don't know. I almost won the Prize, that's about my only crowning achievement...'

He stopped himself before he told her exactly how horrible it was. It was better to keep the mood light.

'Here we are.' Goldin returned, sloshing ale onto the table as he set out three glass mugs. He stopped before sitting down, picking up on the stilted atmosphere. 'Everything alright?'

'I was just asking William if he had any epic tales.'

'Ah.' Goldin cleared his throat. 'Probably better to avoid that subject. When it comes to killing folk, Will can be a bit of a stick-in-the-mud.'

'A stick-in-the-mud?' William balked.

'Exactly.' Goldin grinned, then did his best imitation of William. 'What have I done? Precious, sacrosanct life! Who am I to take it away? I must be miserable for at least a week.'

He blew foam off the top of his ale with spluttered laughter. Gwyneth laughed too, though not quite as raucously as Goldin. William only scowled. He wasn't upset by the little man's comment, but it did needle at him – life *was* sacrosanct... for the most part. Though he supposed that letting his emotions torment him was pointless if he was just going to accept contracts anyway.

'What about you then?' Goldin turned the question back on Gwyneth. 'You must have some good stories. You knocked the snot out of us two.'

'It was a few lucky shots, and that was my cousin mostly. He's won prizes for his archery.' She shrugged. 'I manage contracts when men need killing. Though, when the need has arisen, I have taken a few lives personally – bureaucrats mostly. They're not as easy to get as you might think; a few had a fairly robust guard detail.

'There was one gentleman, a preacher. I managed to get a chandelier dropped on him.' She smiled, light glinting off her teeth in a dazzling sheen. 'My cousin and I were up in the rafters, a wrench on the fastening, just waiting for him to pass underneath. Halfway through his sermon, he stepped forwards and pleaded to the old gods for a sign.'

She slapped the table. 'Crash!'

There was another round of laughter, and the stories continued through two more ales. William even managed to recall a story worthy of sharing, about a time when he found himself trapped in a broom cupboard with the corpse of a man he had just despatched. At the time, and ever since, he had always considered it a horrific experience. In recounting it, he began to see a lighter side to the ill-fate that had led him there.

'Shall we move on?' Goldin slurred.

'Back to the hotel?' Gwyneth was starting to blend her words too.

'No.' Goldin pushed the empty mugs to the centre of the table. 'Somewhere else. This place is nice, but it's a little *too nice* if you catch my drift. We're starting to get disapproving glances and I'd rather not rock the boat by flooring someone. It might be a bad idea considering what business we have in the city.'

'Where then?' William expected that Goldin might suggest a brothel and didn't really want to leave the fine tavern.

'I thought we might try the guild outpost,' he suggested.

While William hadn't liked the idea of moving to another tavern, a guild outpost might suit them. The booths were usually small and private for the purposes of negotiating deals, and Goldin could easily be distracted talking to any other killer at the bar. William imagined huddling with Gwyneth in a corner booth, not too far from the fire, and decided that going to an outpost was a tremendously good idea.

'We can't,' Gwyneth protested, 'the aliases aren't ready yet.'

'We can get in without. Me and Will have the requisite branding.' He rolled up his sleeve to display the scarred mark of the Assassins' Guild. 'Most of the time they don't even check the ledgers. We'll make up some fake names and get straight in. If not, we'll just come back here.'

'William has a price on his head, if you don't remember.' Gwyneth leant forwards and lowered her voice. 'If we get found out, there won't be any coming back here.'

'A little peril never hurt.' William was all for the venture now, the dash of danger even added to the frisson. 'And the aliases can't be that bad, maybe we could make them work?'

'No. Let's just stay here.' Gwyneth shuffled in her chair.

'Well, I think we should use them.' Goldin nodded his head, groggily. He was so drunk that he only had one eye open, and was tilted so far to the left that he might fall off his stool. 'I've been blessed with a silver tongue, give me the names and I'll get us inside. Even if they do check the ledger they never look at the fine print.'

'This is Vitale,' Gwyneth asserted. 'They do things differently here; they'll do it right. And when they find out we're not who we say we are, I'm sure it won't take them long to figure out who William is.'

'Let me see them.' William held out his hand expectantly and nearly knocked over the empty mugs. 'You two can get in without aliases, it's only me who needs disguising. I'm sure we can figure something out.'

'No!' Gwyneth snapped, standing with her fists bunched on the table.

The sudden outburst stopped half the conversations in the tavern. The atmosphere had suddenly soured and William wasn't quite sure why. They were just having a bit of banter, there was no point getting angry over a minor disagreement.

'I'm sorry.' Gwyneth sat back down.

William thought for a moment, collecting his wits through his ale-fugue. Her being so defensive made him suspicious; there was something wrong about these aliases, more than a simple clerical error. She didn't want him or Goldin to know exactly what.

'We're supposed to be in this together.' William held back a small hiccough. 'How can we work as a team if you're going to keep something from us?'

'I'm not keeping anything from you. Can't we just forget it? It's not important.' She raised an arm to signal for the barmaid, but was ignored. 'Let's just get another drink here and head back.'

'Show me the aliases,' William repeated sternly. Perhaps as a result of the ale, the words came out with even more spite than intended. Fear flashed across Gwyneth's eyes as a result. It was enough to sober him and he was about to apologise when Goldin stepped in.

'Look.' The little man drew Gwyneth's attention. 'I'm sure it'll be no big problem. Just show us the aliases and we can all move on. We'll put this little episode down to drink and we can laugh about it later.'

'I can't show you,' Gwyneth protested.

'If you don't show us, we'll just believe the worst.' He pursed his lips. 'Like Will says, we've got to trust each other, and I don't want a piece of parchment coming between the three of us.'

Goldin was right. Only minutes ago, William had been thinking about something more with Gwyneth. Now, because of too much rich ale, he had allowed something so small to rile him up. It didn't matter what was on the aliases really, but trust went both ways.

With a huff, Gwyneth reached for her pocket. She slapped three envelopes onto the table and paced off to the bar.

Once the aliases were out in the open, William had to see what was inside. Hesitantly, He slipped his thumb under the first fold and levered it open. It felt wrong to be doing it, as if he was betraying Gwyneth despite the fact it was her keeping secrets from him. Steeling himself, he started to read.

Gwyneth's alias was Gwen Evans. It wasn't a particularly exciting name, but there didn't seem to be any issues with it or any of the associated descriptions. Goldin's alias, in the second envelope, was similar. His name, Reiner Schulte, was a little bit of a strange choice as it was Galman, but it wouldn't cause too many issues. The details all seemed correct too, even his height – which Gwyneth had previously claimed to have been incorrectly noted at over six feet.

He peeled open the final envelope, his own. It was empty. He scowled over at Gwyneth, just in time to see her depositing a crumpled document into the fire.

# 1681
## GWYNETH FINCHLEY

'I'm looking forward to this year's game,' the uncle across from Gwyneth announced. He had been helping Fortuna to explain the games for the past few minutes. 'Last year, we were on the side helping the subject – that is *the subject* of our endeavours.'

He enunciated every word precisely and punctuated it with a wave of his hand as if each one was the most important. He was so overt with his gesturing that at one point he unsettled a glass holding crisp napkins and knocked his silverware into disarray.

'Yes, last year's subject was a man called Enzo Ricci,' Fortuna continued for the red-nosed uncle while he took a moment to decide which of his seven disturbed forks should be the outermost. 'He was a private in the Empire's army, stationed on the short border wall between Eldeen and Jernbakken. We managed to get him promoted twice in as many months.'

'It was going so smoothly.' The red-nosed uncle sneered at a little spoon. 'Then the Badger Sett got him caught *in flagrante delicto*. Dishonourable discharge. Had to find his way to the mainland off his own back. Of course, our agents were there to lend a helping hand – that is *the agents* of our team's desires. They enact on our behalf to further the goals of the team.'

While Gwyneth was new to the Game of Fates, the idea was straightforward. It was appreciated that her uncle was explaining it all to her, but he seemed to be going into detail in the most unnecessary areas. She nodded in the hope that he would understand that *she* understood, and would stop talking.

'So, Enzo Ricci,' Fortuna cut in to continue the story proper. 'We got him free passage on a ship, and when he got to Conejo we'd arranged for the Merchants' Guild to offer him a job.'

Fortuna was bubbling with excitement. 'I was a part of that bit. Aunt Felonia offered a guild officer a bribe and I fluttered my eyelashes at him from the carriage. Obviously he only saw my good side.'

She traced her jawline with a finger.

'Obviously,' the uncle agreed, 'there's no eyelashes on the other side.'

He cleared his throat, then said, 'It was a valiant effort from the Burrowing Bunnies, but our man Ricci ended up stabbed in a tavern brawl. We lost: dead is technically a lower status than alive. This year, however, will be different!'

'How so?' Gwyneth slid her ill-fitting teeth around her jaws to try and make her smile less crooked.

'We're the ones trying to disgrace this year's subject.' He took a sip of sherry, the sleeve of his jacket caught on a knife handle and dragged yet more cutlery out of position. 'Which is the side the Bunnies have always been best at.'

'So, who's this year's subject?'

'Ah, that's the thing—' The red-nosed uncle stopped as he noticed the Matriarch standing to address the room.

'Good evening, ladies and gentlemen.' The Matriarch was like a different person than the one Gwyneth had seen the night her cousin had been killed. She was smiling, full of festivity and cheer. It was almost hard to believe it had ever happened. How could a family that killed one of their own all sit together to drink and eat and celebrate? 'You all know why we're here, so I won't draw things out with a long speech. All I have to say is well done to the Badgers, and good luck to the lot of you for this year. Bring out the wheel!'

A large upright wheel was carried from behind a curtain at the back of the room by two burly footmen. It was supported in the middle by a metal bolt that attached it to a stand. Even as it was being carried the thing was turning subtly about its axis. Blue and red alternating segments were labelled with names. Gwyneth squinted to read them, but didn't recognise any in particular.

'Eighteen candidates,' the red-nosed uncle whispered excitedly, 'all from different stations in the Empire, from a prince to a pauper, from a farmer to a pharmacist. There's a general on there, a simple handmaid, and even a circus sharpshooter.'

'I'm hoping for the Lobotian Postmaster.' Fortuna grinned. 'I've never been that far east. You'll come with me, won't you?'

'I think I have to prove myself first.' Gwyneth shrugged.

'Oh, don't worry about that, just put a few ideas forward and you'll be a shoe in.' She tossed her hair. 'I got in easy enough.'

Gwyneth didn't see the point in positing that members of the core family got in on principal, and pretended that Fortuna's encouragement was reassurance enough. 'Thank you.'

'Quiet now,' the Matriarch commanded. 'It's time to spin the wheel. This year *my grandson* has the honours.'

The Matriarch gestured to an ill-looking boy sat near Uncle Alwyn. Uncle Richtus, one of the family's leading medical minds, came from the top table to take the boy's hand and lead him to the wheel. Gwyneth wondered if the doctor was allowed outside fifty feet of the boy, he looked so malformed. His eyes were wide set, bulging in opposite directions, and snot drooled from his snout-like nose. How anyone could see his misshapen form and deem it an evolutionary boon was beyond her.

The boy reached up with grasping hands and tugged at the edge of the wood to spin it, giggling as he did so. It was a weak pull and the thing only turned a quarter of the way, but that was enough. As the wheel came to rest, a name was indicated by a red pointer, which the Matriarch promptly announced. 'This year, it's Osmond Snee!'

'Who?' Gwyneth found herself saying, but it was drowned out in a grumble of conferring players.

'Cogitate your first moves while you masticate. Now is the time for supper.' The Matriarch bent her crooked spine and kissed her grandson on the forehead, then strode back to her position at the top table. 'After the cheese course, the Badger Sett will have the drawing room and the Burrowing Bunnies will take the study. Only then can you lay your plans in detail.'

What followed was an array of the most delicious and exotic fare Gwyneth had ever tasted. It was hard to eat with her ill-fitting dentures, with weak sap holding them in, but she didn't let it stop her. She was privileged to be here and knew, as with her parents, it could all be so easily taken away.

She tried to ask a few more details about the subject, but the red-nosed uncle shushed her to silence. It seemed that now was a time for personal reflection and conferring wasn't allowed. Fortuna tried to tell her after the soup course, but she was shushed by their uncle too. She quietly mentioned that she had a pamphlet with details on all the potential subjects and that she would fetch it for Gwyneth when they adjourned.

The rest of the meal passed quickly enough. Eleven miniature dishes came and went with precision. There was one course with a single prawn slathered in garlic butter, sat atop some green foam. Gwyneth could have eaten a whole bucket full, but that would have spoiled her appetite for the succulent marbled beef, and it was definitely worth saving herself for the two mouthfuls of creamed peanut and banana cake.

When the one-eyed uncle on the opposite team offered out his own cake as a trade for somebody's cheese and biscuits, Gwyneth was tempted to take a second helping, though decided against it. She didn't want to deal with a man who encouraged his own brother to commit filicide.

After the cheese, biscuits, and coffee were consumed, the teams adjourned to plot. Fortuna quickly left for her rooms to retrieve the pamphlet and Gwyneth took the time to visit the lavatory. She knew it would be bad form to arrive last in the study, but it wouldn't do to have a bulging bladder distracting her at such a time. If she impressed, her family's wealth would be made available and her life would be all the easier. Every scrap of acceptance distanced her from being labelled bad blood.

She emerged from the lavatory and was relieved to see some of her older and more infirm relatives still being assisted down the long hallway for the study. She hurried after, and in her eagerness, barrelled into a man as he emerged from the dining room.

'Damn it, girl.' The one-eyed uncle recoiled and sneered down at her. He had been smoking a pipe and ash had spilled onto his lapel. He tried to dust it off, but only succeeded in making it worse. The dots of ash became long streaks.

'Sorry, Uncle.' Gwyneth did an awkward curtsy and made a move for the study.

'Wait,' he barked. 'Let's get a look at those teeth.'

Gwyneth stopped and pivoted on her heel. There was a hostility in her uncle's voice and she didn't want him to cause a scene. He was well respected in the family – had proven himself expunging bad blood. Even if she found him sickening, his approval would help her into the inner sanctums. She bit back her distaste and fixed him with her best toothy grin.

'Not quite as fashionable as Fortuna's,' he leant closer. She could smell liquor mixed with the root-smoke on his breath. 'But terribly convenient.'

'What do you mean?' Gwyneth took a step backwards.

'I don't mean anything.' He shrugged. 'You got your bloods late. We were starting to think you were one of the bad ones. Your father was terrified that your mother had bred outside the family. I don't think he wanted to end up like me or my brother; he thinks us broken men. It matters not, anyway; at the eleventh hour, your gift came and all was well.'

He followed Gwyneth as she slowly backed away, leering ever closer. The shadow of burgeoning stubble combined with those under his eyes made him look skeletal.

'When I learned my son was not my own, I didn't want to believe it. I tried to think of ways to conceal his bad blood, perhaps counterfeit him a gift. He could be burned, or lose the use of an arm. I could even pull his teeth; that's an easy ruse.' He pulled up his eyepatch, revealing the white eye beneath. 'You can't fake this, can you? One eye whitened by pus: that is my gift, and what I lack in perception of depth, I gain in perception of people.'

He reached out and snatched Gwyneth by the arm of her dress. She might have screamed if she hadn't been so petrified. This uncle wasn't fooled; he knew her secret, and all he had to do was tell the others. She was bad blood, and if she wasn't expunged, a terrible fate would befall the family. At least that was what *he* believed. One word from this foul creature and she would be killed, likely by her own father's hand.

'I see right through you, bad blood.' Flecks of spittle sprayed across Gwyneth's face. 'I will find proof of it. My all-seeing-eye has you now.'

There was a light thumping of feet down a nearby staircase and Gwyneth was released by her uncle.

'Gwyneth, Uncle Freddy.' Fortuna greeted them warily and slowly padded down the remaining stairs.

'Fortuna.' The one-eyed uncle retreated, smiling and nodding like nothing had happened. 'Good luck in this year's game, I must retire to the drawing room.'

He adjusted his eyepatch into position and sloped off down the corridor.

'What was that?' Fortuna hurried over and pressed the pamphlet into Gwyneth's hands.

'Nothing.' Gwyneth measured her breathing. 'It was just… pre-game banter. He was trying to get in my head.'

'I shouldn't say this.' Fortuna glanced over her shoulder. 'But I find him a vile human being. Cruel. I do hope he gets what's coming to him one day. Let's get to the study, this is your chance to prove yourself.'

Gwyneth allowed Fortuna to take her by the hand and lead her down the corridor, still reeling from her uncle's accusations. She had thought pulling her teeth would be enough to convince them all, but perhaps there was more to it than that. Perhaps she had to play the model Finchley, a Finchley beyond reproach, someone who couldn't have aspersions cast on their lineage. Not only did she have to impress in this game, for the sake of her life, she had to become Alwyn's star player.

# 1683
## WILLIAM OF FAIRSHORE

'What are you doing?' William yelled as the edges of his crumpled alias caught the flames and started to turn black.

'I'm sorry.' Gwyneth shrugged pathetically. 'It was written wrong – contained things I can't tell you. Not yet.'

William thrust to his feet, his face made hot by anger and the alcohol he had imbibed. Perhaps if he was sober, his temper wouldn't have been so quick to bloom, but it was too late now. He felt betrayed, untrusted, and was disappointed in Gwyneth all at once. He dashed his mug against the wall churlishly, staining the fine paper and sending shards of glass flying.

'William, please.' Gwyneth tried to hurry back from the fireside, but the small tavern was too cluttered.

William wasn't interested in hearing her explanations any longer. He thought they were friends, or at least allies, but apparently it wasn't so. She was hiding things from him. Storming away, he kicked over his chair and upset tables in an effort to get out. He needed fresh air and space, time to think the evening over in detail, without his alcohol empowered low-mind barking over rational thought.

Outside, his face, ears, and forehead felt even hotter against the cool night air. He didn't know where to go or what to do. If he stayed, he would only cause more trouble, but he couldn't go back to the hotel room. For now he had to stamp about, brood, and curse.

A thin rain started. In bleak humour, William stalked off to find temporary shelter. He would make plans to set out on his own. This venture was clearly a fool's errand and was better off abandoned.

He might feel different in the morning, but right now his mind was made.

He walked far away from the pristine palaces and cathedrals of the city centre. The streets were no longer a perfect promenade of white slabs, but were heavily cambered and cobbled, reminiscent of the dumps in Garland. The buildings were still fairly grand but simpler, and the street was dimly lit by too few lamps. It made the glow of a seedy tavern entrance all the more inviting. Inside would be warmth and drink, perhaps a bed for the night. He headed through the door.

The ceiling inside was low and festooned with ropes, netting, and trinkets. Despite the fact that Vitale was one of the furthest places from a coastline, the tavern had been nautically themed. Walls were cluttered with paintings of frigates, schooners, and little fishing boats. A wooden life ring, painted in white and red, was hanging on the wall and a vast anchor was put in pride of place behind the bar. William noted that the clientele were not unlike those one would see privateering or being marched from an imperial ship in chains. Most men here had more facial scars than limbs.

'What'll it be?' A gruff man behind the bar was trying fruitlessly to clean a mug with a cloth draped over a rusty hook he used for a hand.

'Something strong.' William sat on a stool at the bar, next to a man who looked a little too up-market for the place. 'And a room if you've got one.'

'Rum,' the man concluded, turning to an array of misty bottles. 'Dark or white?'

'Dark.' William shrugged.

'And me, *monsieur,*' the man next to William added.

He held up his empty glass to be filled. Dressed in a fine shirt and blue tailored waistcoat, complete with golden watch chain, he looked nothing at all like the other patrons in the dingy little tavern. His beard and hair were neatly cropped too, styled with expensive rose scented oils. It might have been because William was angry already, but he took an instant disliking to the man.

'What about the room?' William pressed the barman.

'Sadly not.' The man hooked a small glass from a peg and deftly flipped it so it sat upright before William. 'All our rooms are taken. There's some shindig happening nearby, we're booked up.'

William wondered exactly what kind of event could attract men such as these, but didn't linger on it. It wasn't his business, and what *was* his business needed some thought.

He sipped his foul tasting rum while he considered his options. He could leave town, forsaking the contract and the riches it promised. He could try again to change his career, resume thievery again, or he could find something else, maybe even something legal. Toiling away for a pittance was hardly an attractive option, and it would also mean leaving Goldin behind. He didn't want to abandon his only friend.

Or, he could suck it up and finish the contract. It would only be a few weeks and the job would be done with. Some bad memories he could ignore while enjoying his piles of gold.

'This is dishwater, isn't it?' The man beside William leant forwards to insert himself in his eyeline. He held up his glass and wiggled it, sloshing rum dregs in the bottom. 'I've had better spirits in the worst dive in Blackbile. Wouldn't you agree?'

'Me?' William prodded himself in the chest.

'I assume you're here for the meeting tomorrow.' The man eyed something on William's chest and winked. 'With a fine pistol like that, you must be a guilder.'

William realised that in his drunken state he had allowed his jacket to fall open and expose the holster and three shooter within. He had left his more conspicuous hip holster and silver flintlock back at the hotel room – yet another reason why he couldn't simply flee the city.

'Yes.' He nodded, trying to remember Goldin's alias. 'I'm a guilder; Reiner Schulte. Pleased to meet you.'

'Galman?' The guilder cocked an eyebrow. 'I'm Yves Kaplan, from Aurinne. I've not spent much time in Galmany, or outside Lex, to be honest. I find most of my business in the Golden City, but–'

'My mother was Garlish, I was raised there.' William cleared his throat and turned his attention back to his rum in the hope that Yves might leave him alone.

'Are you looking forward to the meeting?' the man continued. 'I'm the one who called the Hunt as a matter of fact. It's a damned disgrace I have to stay in this rat hole, but others snapped up the outpost rooms quickly.'

'Hunt?'

'I suppose the term is a little barbaric, but these are barbaric times.' Yves pouted. 'We have assassins killing one another once every two years, man-butchers, and now the False Butcher. I understand the appeal of it, truly. The best foe can only be another assassin. I'm just not foolish enough to stake my life on the slim odds of winning something like that.'

'Some people don't have the same luxury as you.' William swallowed the last of his rum. 'For some, it's their only option.'

'True, but why cheat?'

William turned to face the assassin, expecting Yves to be directly accusing him. The news-sheets had claimed that he intentionally killed Genevieve before her sponsor, and that was how he had been disqualified. There was no mention of Genevieve's son miraculously crawling from beneath a blown-up building.

'That's why I called together the Hunt.' Yves flagged the barman down for another rum as he returned from one of the booths with a tray of empty glasses.

Strangely, amongst the glasses for spirits and the mugs for ale, there was a delicate wine flute. Something that William hadn't even expected to be an option in this maritime dive.

'It enables assassins like us – too smart to enter the Prize – to get a little taste of the action,' Yves continued. 'Now we get to know exactly what it's like to hunt for a trained killer. And, as we're working together, I don't think it likely we'll get bested by this lone butcher.'

'You're hunting William of Fairshore?' William's rum threatened to come back up and he had to swallow it again. As he wasn't yet dead, and hadn't been threatened, he was confident that he had not been recognised. He risked a look over his shoulder at the surly looking patrons and suppressed a shudder.

'It wasn't too difficult to arrange – ah, excellent!' Yves paused as a plate of grey meat and potatoes was deposited in front of him. 'He was blacklisted anyway, so it wasn't too hard to put a bounty on his head. There was a little bit of push back from a few members on the guild committee, but rules are rules and bureaucracy prevailed. Once I put the price on him, arranging the Hunt was easy. We should have a good time, and I hear he's been spotted near the city. Are you staying for something to eat?'

'He's nearby?' The revelation that people were still looking for him, and that someone had spotted him, made William feel ill. 'And, no. I haven't the appetite tonight.'

'I know. It's exciting, isn't it?' Yves grinned and stabbed a steaming potato with a two-pronged fork. The tines screeched against the tin plate and made William wince. 'I hear he's an ugly bastard; all scarred and deformed; six foot tall and broad to boot. Fine prey for a team of assassins.'

'I heard he slaughtered an entire chapter of Sacrificial Lambs.' William tried to stay calm as he embellished Yves' false information. He had to get out of this place and quickly, though once he'd left there would be nowhere for him to go.

'Amateurs. But if I find him first, I'm going to do something brutal.' Yves toyed with a straggly bit of meat, winding the sinew about the fork before depositing it into his mouth. He continued around his chewing, 'Maybe cut out his guts and string him up with them. Nobody cheats in our prize, or makes a mockery of our guild, and gets away with it.'

The anger that had been boiling in William ever since his falling out with Gwyneth finally bubbled over. He swung his fist for the Lexman, caught him completely off guard, and knocked him off balance. Another fist came behind the first, which knocked Yves to the floor. William followed him down, straddling him and thumping him in the face and head. He was shouting something about how the Guild were meant to protect their own, but it came out as an unintelligible roar.

Yves' hands fell limp and William stopped hitting him. He was panting, drunk, and tired, but he leapt up, ready for any other guilder who might have come to the man's aid. Nobody had moved from their chairs, but all eyes were upon him.

'Are there any other guilders here?' He wiped blood from his knuckles onto his shirt. 'Any that want to fight?'

'Yes, but no thank you.' An old guilder flashed him a gold-toothed grin. 'We're quite alright drinking, if it's all the same to you.'

One of the younger assassins looked keen, but the calming hand of a wiser man kept him in his seat.

'Good.' William clenched his teeth. It seemed that a group of guilders who had gotten together for the sole purpose of hunting and killing one of their own weren't exactly thick as thieves. Perhaps another reason to try out the thieving life and the comradery that came with it. 'Enjoy your drinks.'

William rounded on the man behind the bar, expecting to be facing down a pistol or blunderbuss, but the old sailor-type was just stood there, awkwardly cleaning glasses with his hook.

'Do you want me to leave?' William panted.

'Leave?' The barman frowned. 'You won. We don't kick out winners here. As a matter of fact, if you drag that chap on the floor outside, we'll have a fresh vacancy. If you're still interested?'

William rolled up his sleeves, swallowed yet more phlegm, and set about dragging Yves Kaplan from the tavern. It was fairly hard going as the tables were cramped close together and the men sat at them were the type to sprawl out and not bother to make way for a man dragging a body. Not to mention the fact that William wasn't too steady on his feet, even without Yves weighing him down.

'Help him, will you, Silvio?' someone called from the back of a shaded booth.

William looked across as a rather large Vitulan, presumably Silvio, unfolded himself from the booth. He was a mature man, with oiled, silver hair on his head, top lip, and chest. William knew this because Silvio had his leather jerkin open and wore an exceptionally airy shirt. At his hip, there was a rapier as thin as his moustache, and beside it, a three shooter as slender as his pianist's fingers – a pianist's pistol perhaps. He had to twist awkwardly to get his knees from under the table, but once upright he towered over the half-crouched William with all the bravado of a famous ring-fighter.

'Would you like me to take his feet?' he asked calmly.

William didn't respond. He was looking beyond Silvio to the other towering brutes, all crammed into the booth. If these men were here to hunt him, he would have little chance of escape. They looked to be the three most enormous people within the Empire or without. One had a big round breastplate over a bulging gut. Another had scale-tattooed forearms as thick and muscled as stout salmons – which was entirely appropriate in the nautically themed tavern. The third had a mop of orange hair and shoulders broader than an ox. Each one of them was crimping themselves in, making themselves as small as possible, all for the benefit of a young woman in the deepest recess of the booth.

'Answer the man then,' the young woman commanded. She was spread out across the bench at the back, one foot up on the padding and the other outstretched. While she had the largest friends in the Empire, her hair was larger still, a great ball of shimmering curls that bobbed around her shoulders as she moved. 'Are you ill?'

'No, ah– just drunk, sorry,' William stammered. 'Yes, take his feet, please.'

With that, Silvio doubled over and hefted up the man's feet. Once he was back upright, he braced one arm under the back of Yves' thighs and took nearly all of his weight. William was just there for show at that point, but he performed his part brilliantly, guiding the assassin's torso through the door and out into the street.

'One.' Silvio started to rock the body. 'Two.'

William hadn't the intention of actually tossing the man into the gutter, he didn't possess the strength to lift him alone, but it seemed Silvio had other plans.

'Three.'

They released the man and he flew through the air, far beyond any distance William had thought possible. He landed in the road with a jarring crunch then rolled back towards them, stopping in the wet shallow of the gutter.

William winced, stretched his back, and stood upright for the first time since taking on Yves' weight. Silvio still towered over him.

'Would you like a drink?' The old fighter set his hands on his hips and offered a broad smile.

William wasn't convinced it was a question despite the man's intonation, but thought it was best to reply: 'Yes.'

The pair stooped through the door, one far easier than the other. Inside, the barman was already bringing a tray of ales to the shaded booth. William could tell from the quantity that one of the glasses was for him. His stomach gurgled. He didn't think he could handle another heavy ale, especially squeezed between these giant men in such close confines.

'Move out, Yerik.' The young woman at the back kicked the portly man's chest plate playfully. 'Go and prop up the bar with Donal, I think I'll be alright here with… What was it, again? '

William considered another outing for Reiner Schulte, but it invited too many questions about his origins. He decided to use the alias that had worked well enough in Chiesa, at least before Goldin had given the game away to Gwyneth's deranged uncle.

'Bill.' It came out husky. He coughed to clear his throat, and had been about to add "of Brightsands" when he realised it sounded entirely too similar to Fairshore. Instead, he added, 'Bright… man. Bill Brightman.'

'I'll be fine with Bill, here.' She grinned and cocked her head so that the vast ball of her hair all shifted onto one side.

'As you wish,' Yerik grunted, shuffling out of the booth.

The one with the orange thatch followed him out, each scooping up a mug from the arriving tray as they left. William took the portly one's place and shuffled across the bench as Silvio sat beside him. He was hemmed in now, pushed towards the woman in the dark recess; any attempt at a swift exit would be blocked. Worse, the man with the scales tattooed on his arms – sat across from Silvio – hadn't taken his eyes off William since he'd sat down.

'You made for quite the show,' the woman commented. 'I've seen some brawls in here before, but nothing quite so decisive.'

'You come here often?' William found that hard to believe. This party looked more like a band of roving heroes that had stumbled into the wrong dive than typical regulars.

'I like to people watch.' Though her accent was mostly Vitulan, now he was close, William could see she had the complexion of a

Numinian. 'I find the colourful characters in places like these make the best tableau.'

She sat back, her arms folded. She was draped in a fine cloak of white silk, trimmed with blue and gold ribbon. It was reminiscent of a Vitulan robe, but far more stylish and no doubt expensive. Both her accent and clothing were an indication that she came from extreme wealth, but her comfort in the perilous dive – and the company of four brutes – suggested there was a more cutthroat side to her. It all spoke danger to William, but like the spectators in Blackbile, he was transfixed. Her eyes were like golden-brown pools, sinkholes that were drawing him in.

'There's not many more colourful than the type that find themselves here,' Silvio added. 'We were excited to see assassins in here tonight, but it seems they get their action elsewhere. They're content enough to drink and laugh. Yours was the only enjoyment to be had.'

'When we watched you come in...' The woman picked her slender wine glass from the tray, exposing fine golden bangles as they extended from the folds of her silk. 'You were all red and angry, but not too far from tears. You put us in mind of a wounded field mouse – soft as the day your mother birthed you.'

'We shared a bet.' The tattooed man's eyes bulged with menace. 'We wondered how long you'd last here.'

William noted then that the man's eyes were different colours. One was blue and the other was green. One nostril had a gory split in it too, he presumed from where a ring had been pulled out.

'I lost; I've never been good at betting.' The woman shrugged. 'It turns out you're harder than I thought. We like men like that, don't we Silvio? Soft men who can be *hard* when needed.'

'That we do.' Silvio chuckled.

William took a sip from his drink. After so much alcohol it tasted simply awful. He didn't know what to say, he was too drunk and words were escaping him. These people were friendly enough, but they gave off an aura entirely too confrontational. William couldn't say what it was exactly, perhaps his own fragile state, but he just wanted a bed, and sleep, and an end to this conversation.

'We're playing with you,' the woman giggled and patted him sympathetically. The touch of her fingers on the back of his hand was impeccably soft. 'We like to rile up some of these stuffy old fighter-types sometimes. You seem… different. You're as drunk as one of them certainly, but you're not spouting nonsense and drooling. Are you with these visiting assassins?'

'No. I'm a sharpshooter.' William thought it prudent to lie; he felt as though a wrong answer would see Silvio's blade emerge. He also had a good idea that the more menacing man would have spotted his pistol. 'I work in a circus. I shoot at targets and bottles. Fruit sometimes.'

'That sounds exciting. Is there a circus in the city then?' The young woman's face lit up and her tone changed. 'Or for the parade?'

'No, I came alone.' William struggled to concoct more lies. 'I'm between jobs; taking time out to travel.'

'Oh.' The woman looked disappointed, but quickly rallied. 'That must be wonderful, to see the world. I'm stuck here in this damned city. It's terribly dull, even the excitement of this little dive is starting to wane. Where have you been?'

'Garland – that's where I'm from – and Lex, Conejo, Galmany, Grod, Vitulus obviously. I went to Wisteria, once.'

'I wish I could go travelling.' She crossed her legs and leant one arm across her knee, letting her hand hang loosely at the wrist. A candle on the table made two jewelled rings glitter. 'I was born in Numin, but brought up here.'

'I spent some time in Numin.' William tried to keep his answers short and as close to the truth as possible. It was easier to remember that way.

'What was it like?' She cocked her head at him, her hair shifting pleasantly, oils shimmering even more beautifully than her rings. Perhaps she appreciated him for not being the dullard she had expected; maybe that was wishful thinking.

'I was young.' He thought back to that terrible pawnbroker. 'I didn't see too much outside the Silken Coast. I don't remember it well.'

'Fair enough...' She took a sip of her wine, glancing at him. 'So...
how did you get to be a sharpshooter? I'd love to be able to do
something like that. All my hobbies are entirely too pedestrian.'

'Well, I...' William had been about to create an off-the-cuff
fictional account of how he had joined a circus, when he spotted an
opportunity and pivoted the conversation towards it. 'I could teach
you. I'm in the city for a while, and I like to practice as often as
possible. You can join me, if you'd like?'

'Really?' Kupela's eyes sparkled at the suggestion. 'I'd love to.'

'Are you sure that's—' Silvio started sternly, but the young woman
cut him off before he could finish.

'Calm yourself, it's just a bit of fun.' She rolled her eyes. 'Gods
know it's the only fun I'll be having over the next few weeks. My
leash will no doubt be tightened during the festivities.'

'Festivities?' William couldn't quite figure out the dynamic; the
men seemed all at once servants and keepers. He thought it best to
keep the conversation light until his drink was done and he could
slip away without causing any offence. Finishing his drink, however,
was proving a larger challenge than expected. The longer it sat there
the staler it got, the froth gathering like scum on the waters of a
poorly cleaned bathhouse.

'Do you live under a rock when you're not in that big tent of
yours? It's the twenty five year anniversary of the victory in Numin.
There's to be a parade, speeches from the emperor and senators. *All
superbly exciting.*' She added the last part with heavy sarcasm, then
swilled down the last of her wine.

William feared for a moment that she might order another, but
a stern glance from the tattooed brute made her choose otherwise.

'I have to be getting home shortly. As far as my father is aware,
we've been for a stroll in the park and a late night reading binge at
the library.' She giggled, all of the animosity gone. Maybe it had gone
some minutes ago and William was only drunkenly beginning to
realise now. 'You should come find me, show me some of your
moves. A damned sharpshooter in Vitale, that *is* exciting.'

'Alright.' William nodded. He might have been separated from
his only friends, but that didn't mean he couldn't make himself some
new ones. 'Where can I find you?'

'Come to the Via Principale Forum around noon, I'll be there any day this week. Ask for Kupela Falade.'

'Falade?' William almost choked on the word. 'As in Senator Falade?'

'So you don't always dwell under a rock!' She shook her head, laughing as the two large men shuffled out from the ends of the booth. 'He's my father and an absolute dolt, but that's another story.'

She slid her way delicately around the table and stood, joining her hulking entourage.

'I'll look forward to meeting you again. Properly, next time.' She gathered her silks about her in preparation to tackle the cold night air. 'Don't forget your pistol, I really would love to see what you can do with it.'

Flushing under her scrutiny, William tried to look anywhere else but her. Instead he consigned the names and places to his memory and bit his tongue, determined not to say anything that would make her rescind her invitation.

'Goodnight, Bill *the sharpshooter.*' She winked. 'It was a pleasure making your acquaintance.'

William burst into the hotel room, panting. Goldin was sat on the chaise again and Dunstan was leant against the drinks cabinet. It looked like Gwyneth had been pacing, but she'd stopped now. For a moment, a dumb silence fell over them.

'William, I'm so glad you came back.' She rushed towards him.

'Stay over there!' He pulled the three shooter from the holster in his jacket. He intended to level it at her as a threat to keep her back and make a show that he wasn't ready to forgive her just yet. Instead, the thing slipped from his fingers and skittered across the floor. It hit the edge of the rug and bunched it up. In retrospect, it was a foolish idea to pull it out in the first place, but he really was very drunk. Still, it had the desired effect; Gwyneth had stopped in her tracks.

William noticed then that Dunstan had pulled out a small flintlock, and was casually aiming it at him.

'Don't point that thing at me.' William sneered and marched in from the doorway. 'Since I took your contract, I've never been anything but nice and honest with you damned Finchleys. I don't like your secrets and games.'

'William, I'm sorry.' Gwyneth reached out for him as he strode past, but he shook her off and kept moving. 'I can explain.'

'Save it.'

He reached a chair, then realised he was too angry to simply sit down and relax, no matter how much he wanted to. His legs were tired, his eyelids heavy, and he felt more than a little sick. All he wanted to do was curl up and fall asleep, but this had to be dealt with first. He stared into the flames dancing on logs in back of the vast fireplace.

'I know we…' Gwyneth swallowed.

'Save it,' William repeated. 'You're my employer and I'm your employee. We are not friends. You can keep secrets from me, it's perfectly reasonable. I was just drunk… I still am, so let's just leave it. I don't want to lose my temper again.'

'But, Will–'

'I'm here to finish the job,' William interrupted. He put a hand to his forehead, tried to force himself to sober up. 'Something's happened… something's fallen into my lap. I want to finish this job quickly, get my money, and then I never want to see another Finchley again. That is, if I can trust you to pay.'

Gwyneth looked like she was about to protest again, but with a sigh, she said, 'The money's in a conditional trust at the bank. You'll get it.'

'There are no Finchleys in the banking house, are there?' He stopped, one hand on the wing of an armchair to steady himself. 'They won't change the deal at the last minute?'

'Well.' Gwyneth took a pace towards him. 'There *are* Finchleys that work at the banking house, that's how we can get clauses that hinge on the death of a senator, but you can trust us. You can trust me. I like you – barring your behaviour tonight. I'll see you right, I promise.'

'Good.' William kept his response clipped. His chest was suddenly filled with a rising sensation of sadness. Perhaps it was floating on the contents of his stomach that was threatening to spew forth. His lip trembled and his eyes welled up. He had to bite down hard on his feelings and swallow them. Damned liquor. He cleared his throat to cover any involuntary sniffling.

'Did you see the news-sheets?' Goldin scooped a paper off a small glass-topped table. 'Is that why you came back?'

'There's a parade and speeches at the senate.' Gwyneth took another step forward. 'We were thinking, and I know it might sound insane, but what if we tried that sniper from the roof tactic? Like Lord Beechworth did.'

'No.' William tried to step back and nearly fell over the armchair. His flailing arms made the coachman raise his pistol. 'I was thinking of something else – please stop pointing that thing at me.'

'Well don't leave us in suspense.' Goldin tossed the news-sheet back down and slouched onto the chaise. He crossed his bare feet over. The soles were nearly black.

'I met someone: a girl,' William paused. Gwyneth had been glancing at him all night and might not like the thought of him meeting someone else. Still, he had said it now, and it didn't matter how she felt. He had to tell himself again that they were just colleagues.

'Go on,' Gwyneth prompted.

'It was Kupela Falade,' he continued, 'the target's daughter. We spoke, we got on – I think. I told her I was a circus sharpshooter. She wants me to meet her, *with* my pistol, tomorrow.'

'Kupela...' Gwyneth muttered to herself, nodding.

'I thought I could uh… make friends with her?' He didn't want to lay it out any more plainly than that. 'Then, if I get near her father, I can slip him a blade, or poison his tea. Anything.'

'I don't like it.' Goldin folded his arms. 'We should stick to Gwyneth's plan.'

William rounded on Goldin, but the way the little man cocked an eyebrow calmly was incredibly disarming. William pursed his lips and steeled himself. 'If I'm here, we're doing this my way.'

'You're not thinking right, Will. You're too drunk.' Goldin guided William to the end of the chaise and sat him down. He offered a small glass with some white spirit in it.

'And you're not?' William took the glass and drank. He cringed. 'Water?'

'It's good for you. And yes, I am drunk, but I know you better than you know yourself right now.' Goldin sat in the wing-backed armchair opposite. 'Doing something like that: befriending a girl and killing her father. It's not you. It takes a cold man, a man like Ojo Azul. I've seen the way you obsess over the simple kills. You're not tough enough for it.'

'I am.' William turned to Gwyneth for backup. 'I can do this; Ojo was my mentor.'

'Stop kidding yourself, William.' Goldin leant forwards, his elbows on his knees. 'Who taught you to shoot? It damned well wasn't no Ojo Azul was it? Cathal Doorley was a friend of mine a long time ago, he had a kind heart and was a devil with a flintlock. When I look at you, I know whose shadow I see. You're just trying to step out from the wrong one.'

William took a sip of the water and swallowed it slowly. It took an effort to keep his breathing measured and half a dozen subtle blinks to keep his eyes from spilling tears. He might have just broken down and cried right there if Gwyneth hadn't interrupted.

'We should do it.' She sat on the chaise next to him. 'It's a good plan. We couldn't have expected anything like this, but when something so perfect drops in your lap… we've got to go for it. He'll have a sad daughter either way.'

'Gwyneth, are you sure about this?' Dunstan butted in. Some time ago he had exchanged his pistol for a glass of dark spirit and was nursing it scornfully. 'Alwyn assigned you to Senator Falade, not his daughter.'

'Why don't we have a vote?' Goldin perked up. 'If we can't come to an agreement, we'll just have to think of something else.'

'I'm in favour of using Kupela,' Gwyneth said decisively.

'I think we should use the rifle.' Goldin ignored William and fixed the coachman with a pointed stare.

'I shouldn't be involved. In fact, I should be getting back to my room. Your prisoner could do with some supper.' Dunstan abandoned his drink and retrieved a coat from an ornate hanger. 'And I'll have to tell Alwyn about it.'

'About what?' Gwyneth was visibly distressed.

'I was going to say your change of plans, but everything, I suppose.' Dunstan shrugged on his heavy coat. 'Family prisoners, the senator's daughter; Alwyn will not be happy.'

'Hang on.' Goldin stood and rolled up his sleeves. 'You can't be "not involved" one minute and involved the next.'

'I tell you what.' Gwyneth snapped her fingers. 'We try to get to the senator through Kupela, but if the parade comes around first, we go to the backup plan. We'll leave her alone after that.'

'And what about the prisoner?' Dunstan glowered.

'You can release him. Just wait until after the parade. We should be done by then, whatever plan we end up going through with.'

'Fine. You have until the parade. If you can't get to Sepo Falade before then, leave the girl out of it.' He sighed. 'I'm entirely too lenient with you.'

'That's because you know I'm Alwyn's star player.' Gwyneth flashed a grin; she had switched back to a more modest set of pale wooden teeth. The pearl ones had been stowed in her carry case. 'And you know we're going to get our man.'

'I hope that you do, or all this anguish will have been for nothing. For what it's worth, I agree with Goldin. A sniper shot from a rooftop is a lot cleaner.' Dunstan let himself out and closed the door with a click, adding a muffled, 'But don't pay me any mind, I'm not allowed to play.'

Stirred into action, Goldin belched loudly, bid Gwyneth goodnight and took a fresh bottle of sherry to his room. William knew the little man wasn't entirely happy with the new plan, but it would work. He couldn't remember the last time things had lined themselves up so perfectly. He wasn't about to let such an opportunity pass him by.

Now it was settled, a wave of fatigue swept over him. William swayed slightly, met Gwyneth's gaze, and then looked away. There was an expectant atmosphere now it was just the two of them. He stumbled down the hallway and fiddled with the lock to his room. Gwyneth followed him, her room adjacent.

'I can trust you, can't I?' he voiced his concern.

'Yes.' She gave a close-lipped smile, hesitating at the threshold. 'I'm on your side, more so now than ever.'

'No more secrets?' He finally managed to disengage the lock and the door to his room swung inwards.

'I swear I'll do my best.' She fiddled with the handle on her own door. 'You just have to remember I'm working under Alwyn. I can only tell you what I'm permitted.'

Perhaps if he hadn't been drunk, William wouldn't have gotten so upset about the aliases. He still wondered what had made her so secretive, but she had been drunk too, and just as rash. He nodded to himself and slipped into his room. Things weren't perfect right now, but they had been a lot worse, and he was thankful for the four poster bed that awaited him.

# 1683
## GWYNETH FINCHLEY

'So…' Gwyneth pulled a few cloth pouches from her leather bag. 'I've been spending my hard-earned coin this afternoon, all for your benefit.'

She shot a grin at her uncle. She had worn her oldest, most crooked set of teeth for the occasion and presumed she looked quite mad. Her uncle certainly seemed to think so, as he shrunk into the far recess of the bathtub, fear in his eye. She set one pouch on a slatted table between a dry sea sponge and a trio of linen cloths, then started opening the other.

'Granted, I do enjoy a nice spree now and then.' She supposed that she was mad in a sense, though it was anger rather than derangement that she felt. With a flourish, she presented a cube of soap, impressed with tiny pink petals. 'I got this from Pesci's, made from whale oil; none of that pig tallow rubbish.'

Thrusting it in her uncle's face, she added, 'Smells of lilac.'

This menacing charade continued until she had compiled her items into an impromptu flail. She glanced at William and Goldin who watched from some distance while sharing a bottle of whiskey. For experienced killers, neither one seemed all that thrilled to be party to an interrogation, though they didn't know the extent of their prisoner's depravity. If it wasn't for him and his persistence in proving her bad blood, she wouldn't have needed to throw herself so wholeheartedly into the games. She might have preserved a little more of the innocent girl she used to be.

'Let's play nice, alright?' She tugged the gag from her uncle's mouth.

'Gwyneth!' Saliva dribbled down his chin. 'I need to tell you something.'

'Oh, don't spoil it,' she harrumphed. 'You've got to resist a little or it's no fun. I've been looking forward to this.'

'Gwyneth,' he snarled. 'This is important. I need to speak with you, only you. I can't talk with them here.'

'That's more like it.' She took a few practice swings with the soap stocking. It felt heavier than expected. 'Though it is terribly rude to exclude my friends here, wouldn't you say? We'd all like to hear what you and the Badger Sett have been up to.'

'Some things are better kept between us.' The words hissed between clenched teeth. 'A family matter.'

Gwyneth scowled. Then, as she thought about what her uncle might know, and what he could tell her assassins, she realised it had been incredibly foolish to allow them into the bathroom in the first place. All it would take was one or two words and it would all come crashing down.

'We'll step out,' William offered, already ushering Goldin to the door.

'That was a bit of an anti-climax,' she heard the little man grumble as the door shut.

'Right.' She sighed and swung the soap flail. 'Out with it.'

Her uncle actually shuffled closer to her and lowered his voice. He was still filled to the brim with fear, but she could tell it wasn't her who the source of his terror.

'It's about–' He swallowed. Sweat beaded on his brow.

Gwyneth wondered whether this man's wife and child had wept and fidgeted this much before he killed them. His brother's had certainly remained more stoic in the face of a beheading. It was only justice that this one-eyed murderer would see the same fate. She would, however, need to satisfy herself with merely beating him. He was of good stock, his lineage proven by a gift. Killing him would only bring death upon herself.

The eye not covered by a patch flitted about nervously, then the man hissed, 'It's about your assassin.'

Gwyneth suspected as much. She shrugged. It seemed the man was just hoping for more information to take back to the Badger Sett should he escape. 'Is that all?'

'I recognise him!'

'And?' She started to swing the flail again.

'He has his mother's face, his mother's eyes. I know it's him. There's no mistaking it.' He swallowed. 'He's my son – or he would have been, if my wife hadn't bred outside the family.'

Gwyneth let the flail fall limp.

Her uncle's fear seemed unlike anything Gwyneth had seen in a man. His hair was lank. His eye was bulging. Snot was dribbling from both nostrils. It all betrayed the insanity within.

'He's bad blood, back from the hells I sent him to.' He spat as he spoke, his voice fighting with the mania to keep low. 'You know the rules as well as I do. Finchleys must breed with Finchleys to keep the bloodline pure. Those cursed with bad blood must be expunged. It's for the good of the family.'

'Don't be so dramatic.' Gwyneth sneered. 'Hells and heavens are just an imperial tool.'

'Gwyneth!' he snapped. 'You're not listening to me. I killed the boy – drowned him. I didn't wait as my brother did, until forced by the Matriarch. As soon as I knew William was bad blood, I threw him off the bridge at Fairshore. His mother too. It was the right thing to do. Now he's back from the dead, and no doubt he's working against us. That's what bad blood does.

'Cut my bonds. We'll slit his throat together. There's no telling how powerful he might be.'

The cube of soap cracked against his cheekbone. He cried in pain, but before the sound could finish, it was cut off by another blow. His head twisted from the impact. Blood sprayed out of his mouth. Gwyneth swung again, this time striking his body. What she had been told about it leaving no bruising had been a lie, but she didn't care. This man was evil and deserved to be punished.

Swinging the flail again, she poured out all her hatred. From the day she had seen that boy's throat sliced in two, with this man cheering encouragement. From all the years spent worrying that it might also happen to her. This man had tried to kill his own son, had encouraged his brother to do the same, and wanted to do it again. He deserved death, maybe more than any man in the whole empire.

She beat him until his face was crumpled, until his body was shrivelled in defence. She didn't even stop when Dunstan barrelled in, nor when William and Goldin followed. She kept lashing out, even when she was grabbed from behind and dragged away from the bathtub.

Two swings made no contact. She snarled and panted, then threw the stocking flail away.

'What do you think you're doing?' Dunstan turned her around and gripped her by the shoulders. She slumped in exhaustion, letting him hold her up. 'You know this isn't allowed.'

'He deserved it.' She shrugged, face hot with tears, trying not to let her gaze linger on William. Though the man in the bathtub wasn't William's true father, his mother was a Finchley, and that meant he was her cousin. Bad blood, just like she was.

# PART 7

## 1679
### KUPELA FALADE

A silken hiss of lacing and the creak of corset boning was punctuated by the expulsion of Kupela's breath from her lungs. She gripped the bed post as her maid cinched her tighter still.

'Gods.' Kupela gulped as the maid yanked each cross of thread.

Inch by inch, her ample curves were squashed into the odious torture device. As a child, she'd longed to join in the parties and balls reserved for the ladies of the senate. She'd dreamed of dancing the night away, and ached to wear the illustrious gowns and swags of jewels. If only that child had known the truth of it.

'We'll have no complaints, miss, you want to look pretty don't you?' The handmaid smiled tersely, and reduced Kupela's waist by another finger width. 'There's nothing finer on a young woman than a form-fitting dress. I learned that at Adelaide Bennet's – finest finishing school in the Empire, don't you know?'

'I don't.' Kupela grimaced, sipping air until she grew accustomed to the restrictive garment. 'You know my father has no inclination of sending me away. I'm stuck here.'

'Give it a rest with the stranded princess routine. This isn't a dragon tower or hell-fire keep.' The handmaid turned her about and added liberal amounts of powder to her face and chest. 'Your father will be busy at the ball, so you can spread your wings a little there. I hear a few young men of your age will be attending.'

'I can barely spread my arms.' Kupela grunted and twisted herself inside the bodice in a vain attempt to get a little more room. She was beginning to regret the plate of macaroons she'd enjoyed mid-afternoon. They sat heavily in her stomach and it felt like one stiff breeze would crack a rib, which was troubling as Kupela's bedchamber was one of the airiest rooms in the house.

Fine gossamer curtains danced on a breeze allowed in through four lofty doorways. All were open, leading out onto an ivy-hemmed balcony that looked over the grassy courtyard at the heart of the city-centre estate. Inside was decorated in white and gold, all pristine curves and decadent plasterwork. There were more paws carved into the furniture legs in this one room than she had seen on any lions back in Numin. The room was grand, but it was the little trinkets and keepsakes cluttered on the dresser and side tables that made it her home.

'If there's one thing dragon-tower princesses and senator's daughters *do* have in common,' the handmaid continued, 'it's the need of a good man.'

'I don't want one just yet, thank you. I'm fine as I am.'

Kupela endured her handmaid's ministrations for a short while, but soon swatted her away. No matter how much the woman practiced, styling curls was beyond her. Kupela wasn't sure why; she had seen many ladies with hair almost as buoyant, and hers might as well be considered straight when compared to her father's. She started to un-pick a tangle of the handmaid's design.

'If you don't find yourself one, no doubt your father will line one up.' The handmaid sashayed away to retrieve a velvet-lined jewellery case. 'It's like this book I've been reading: The Milliner's Boon. It's about a young woman who falls in love with a dashing hat maker.'

'Sounds thrilling.' Kupela offered her best approximation of high-born enthusiasm, then diligently lifted her curls so the handmaid could more easily access her neck.

'It is, truly.'

A string of sapphire cabochons set in gold were secured about Kupela's throat.

'There's one part where the milliner has this top hat hiding his —
it's immaterial.'

'His material?' Kupela frowned, letting her hair fall back down.
'Fabrics for the hats?'

'It doesn't matter, dear.' The handmaid paraded her to a full
length mirror, fussing over the drape of her skirts. 'The point is,
there's a *fine* hat maker and an old baron with a foul disposition. You
can guess which one the young woman wants to marry and which
is politically convenient, can't you?'

'I can,' Kupela said flatly as she examined herself in the mirror.
Her hair was sat just right, despite the handmaid's best efforts, a
little tiara nestled high in the curls. She twisted at the hip, played
with the ruched fabric of her skirts. The corset did make a fine shape
of her, though she was certain it wasn't worth the pain, and she
might land herself a husband looking like this whether she wanted
to or not. 'The company of a fine milliner might suit me, but I've
no interest in marrying.'

'I think that's for your father to decide, dear.' The handmaid let
go of the mirror and it tilted downwards under its own weight. 'Until
you have a husband you're his responsibility and I've heard whispers
he wants you to marry sooner rather than later.'

Kupela sneered as the handmaid turned away; the woman was
far too enamoured with tradition. When it came to women, tradition
took a lot and gave little.

While the ball was one of the more exciting events of the year,
Kupela couldn't help but feel she wasn't enjoying herself enough.
Everyone she knew was there, including all her father's fellow
senators and their families, but the atmosphere was more restrained
than at many parties she had attended before. A few senators had
recently been caught up in various scandals and it seemed everyone
wanted to be on their best behaviour. As such, the evening was filled
with pleasant, yet uninspired conversation.

Kupela tried to alleviate the tedium by dancing with various acquaintances: an old woman who worked as a clerk in the senate, the Oster secondo, and another senator's daughter. In previous years, the primo for Gael and Draig had brought a fiddle player. Kupela had found that entirely more entertaining and had danced until she dropped, sharing laughter and joy with anyone who would accompany her. Today, the music was as safe and slow as the conversation.

When the son of the surgeon general asked her for a dance, Kupela made her excuses and left the slowly drifting press of the dance floor. Though she knew the young man from around the senate and didn't mean to be rude, she didn't want to be caught dancing with any potential suitors. Especially now her handmaid had put her in mind of marriage. She didn't want to be reduced to a mere wife.

Overlooking the torch-lit gardens was an area filled with couches and cushions. Even so, everyone was standing amongst them. Gone were the days of senators drinking their fill and drunkenly collapsing over one another. Each was sensibly sipping and having the most refined conversation. Her father had deemed her too young to drink casually at these gatherings, though the night would pass quicker with a glass or two to warm her belly. She had taken wine in previous years of course, when he and his fellows had drunk so much that they could barely slur let alone talk.

She found him in the crowd easily. It wasn't only that he stood a head above everyone else in the room, but that he wore the most vivid fabrics. Where others wore white or plain pastels, Sepo displayed his heritage with honour. He was the only senator to be born outside the Empire and was determined to not only have Numin thrive under the imperials, but to expand his influence south, assimilating his homeland of Djurundi.

His robes this evening were cut in the style worn only by Vitulan senators and Leneecian philosophers, but were tailored from the finest Djurundi silk, patterned with red stripes, orange dots and black chevrons. There was a thick sash of leopard fur hung over one broad shoulder, with a paw for a clasp, fashioned in pearlescent opal. He looked over as Kupela found him and nodded a greeting before turning back to his conversation.

She waved at him then drifted on through the party, making idle chatter with one dignitary or another, doing her best approximation of a lady of taste despite lacking any training. After a particularly wearisome conversation with an agricultural clerk on the importance of crop rotations, she was approached again by the son of the surgeon general.

'Kupela.' He always looked well when he smiled, and it came so easily to him. 'A few friends and I are invited to the observatory, if you'd care to join us? I hear the remains of Wrath can be seen tonight.'

He indicated behind him with his thumb to a few important progenies grouped near the entrance. There were a few senator's sons and daughters and a couple of young clerks' assistants.

'I...' She paused and glanced at her father. He was deep in conversation with the Conejan primo, planning the next southern conquest no doubt. Certainly distracted enough for her to slip out for a few hours. 'I'm terribly sorry, but I don't know your name.'

'It's Richter.' He flashed a grin again and then looked down in a way that seemed bashful. His sweep of black hair tumbled forwards and he had to push it back again. There was something about the way it bunched between his fingers that was entirely more captivating than talking diplomacy at a senators' ball. 'About the observatory?'

'I'd love to.'

The telescope was a conical structure of wood and banded metal that stretched from the floor to the high, domed ceiling. The whole thing, roof included, sat on iron rails set into the floor so the apparatus could be rotated in a full circle. Kupela had gasped as the attendant cranked a wheel to adjust the telescope eastwards, then turned another to adjust the upward angle. She couldn't imagine the hours of work needed to design and build something so incredible.

The attendant rotated a few iron bands and levers, apparently adjusting the lenses, then invited each guest to take a look in turn. Kupela was third to peer into a tube that jutted from the side of the telescope. There was a small disc of glass set into the end and inside it looked as though there was nothing but black. Once she pushed her eye up close, the heavenly body emerged. Her breath stopped.

Wrath was a beauty. Only small, hanging just so, like a droplet suspended on a spider's web. It was red, swept with orange and brown. She could just make out smaller flecks of red and the trail of dust behind it. According to the scriptures, Wrath was cracked when the new gods eradicated the old; it was amazing to not only have it on faith, but to see the proof for herself.

She moved away to let others take their turns peering into the glass. A group had formed around a second attendant who was fielding questions; Kupela joined them.

'How does it work?' One senator's son craned his head upwards.

'Have you ever used a magnifying glass?' The attendant started searching through a shelf cluttered with wooden stands, vials of coloured liquids, one brown potted plant, and numerous books. 'Ah, here we are.'

The attendant pulled out an object that looked almost like an unfinished picture frame. It was square, flat, and made of aged wood. When rotated, Kupela could see that it housed a bulging pane of glass.

'My grandfather has one for reading the news-sheets.' The senator's son moved in closer. 'Just like this one, only smaller.'

'Exactly.' The attendant held up the wooden carrier to display the lens to those watching. 'Using this telescope is just like holding a magnifier to the skies, only far more complex. These lenses are made by the finest glaziers the Empire has to offer. I would let you hold it, but replacements are prohibitively expensive.'

Someone tapped on Kupela's shoulder: Richter. 'Want to have a look around?'

Kupela had been enjoying the marvels of the observatory and had been interested to discover more about the telescope's uses and operation. Though Richter wanted to take her away from what was possibly her only opportunity to learn, her answer was an obvious, 'Yes.'

Richter led the way up a staircase of iron plates and onto a gantry that skirted the edge of the room. There were rows of bookshelves, all custom built to follow the curve of the walls. Kupela suspected it made alphabetising a pain.

'Are you enjoying the observatory?' Richter asked. Dark blue suited him very well, and made him stand out from his peers. He wore a suit of the Garlish style, with a long-tailed jacket and shimmering silken lapels.

'I am.' She looped her arm through his as they strolled. 'I've never seen the heavens in such detail.'

'I like it here; I come often. The attendants asked me if I'd invite a few of my contemporaries.' Richter smirked at the group below. 'I think they're hoping for a grant from the senate. If we become sufficiently enamoured with the heavens we might convince our fathers to open their purses.'

'My father is too concerned with conquest.'

'And mine medicine.' Richter shrugged, leading them through a doorway into a small cobbled courtyard. At the far end was an ornate building of white painted iron and multitudes of glass panes. 'Though it does have its benefits, such as this place.'

'What is it?' Kupela peered through the glass. It was hard to see inside as the panes were speckled with droplets and clouded with steam. She could tell greenery was crowded within, but it looked like no simple greenhouse, and one leaf that was pressed up to the glass was nearly as wide as her arm span.

'It's a solarium. The attendants here used to do more than simply watch the skies. This place was used to observe the effects of solar exposure. Needless to say, nothing pleasant. Now, my father uses the place for exotic flora and fauna – for medicinal ingredients and such. Do you want to go in?'

'I'm not sure.' She thought she noticed one of the leaves move against the glass, stirred by something unseen.

'I assure you, it's perfectly safe.' His wicked grin implied otherwise. 'I'll keep you safe.'

'I suppose…'

'Before you change your mind then?'

She sighed. 'Lead the way.'

Richter took her by the hand and set off for the door.

Kupela staggered in his wake, laughing and clutching her skirts in her one hand to prevent from tripping. They barrelled inside, ducking under low branches. There was a small path that wound between trees and little pools; it forked and narrowed. Richter darted right; Kupela was dragged after. Butterflies cast upwards as they disturbed a thin branch. Other insects chirped. She thought she saw something shift in the trees overhead.

They emerged into a small clearing made by a mosaic disc in the floor. A trolley was pushed to one side, stocked with gloves, secateurs, and sample vials. To the other side was a bench, angled towards a pool containing colourful fish. Richter collapsed onto it, and took Kupela with him, his hand still clasped firmly on hers. She tried to fall beside him, but their momentum carried her halfway onto his lap. She gasped and quickly shuffled back. Richter, just as mortified by the accidental overstepping of bounds, released her hand, stammering an apology.

Abashed, Kupela stared into the trees, unable to match his gaze. Then, she spied a grey-haired beast peering right at them. It had thick, curved claws and black, beady eyes. The shock of it made her yelp. 'Richter, look!'

'It's harmless.' He chuckled. 'And a lot slower than you.'

She moved to playfully push him, but he caught her hand again in his. For a moment, they fell quiet. Richter teetered like a tightrope walker, his dusky eyes flickering to her mouth. Then he broke away to retrieve a tin from the floor beside the bench.

He opened it with a pleasant pop and a collection of brown pellets were revealed. He scattered a handful into the pool, drawing fish to the surface, then offered the tin to her. Kupela threw a few helpings to the most colourful specimens.

'This is fun.' She smiled, marvelling at the gossamer-like fins.

'My father has places like this all over the city.' Richter tossed another handful. 'I'd love to show you them. There are much more exciting creatures to be seen than that slothful beast over there.'

The grey mammal beyond Richter watched with placid eyes as it slowly minced a leaf.

'I'm not sure I'll be allowed.'

'Why not?'

'It's something my handmaid said.' Her brow furrowed. 'I'm not sure I'll be free to do as I please much longer; I think my father wants to find me a husband.'

'Anyone nice?'

'Shut up.' She jabbed him in the ribs with her elbow. 'You know as well as I do it won't be anyone nice.'

'I'm sure you can find a way to get out of it.' He pressed the lid of the tin closed.

'Maybe if I marry someone first.' Kupela shrugged, watching a fat shimmerfin emerge from beneath the overhanging bank. It raised to the surface, dispersing the smaller fish, and swallowed the remaining pellets ten at a time.

Richter shifted in his seat to face her. His thoughts were plain across his face before he even opened his mouth. 'What if *I* marry you?'

'Don't jest.' She slapped the back of his hand softly.

'Well, why not? I'm an eligible bachelor, aren't I? I'm apprentice to the emperor's chief physician.' He smirked. 'You're only a senator's daughter, but I'm prepared to marry down.'

She punched his arm, slightly harder than she meant to.

'What?' He grinned, his eyes holding hers.

'You're sweet, but you're still a fool.'

She felt her whole chest tighten as an impulse took her. Pushing her anxieties down into the tight press of her corset where they might suffocate and die, she leant forward and planted her lips on his. Richter was surprised at first, but after a moment he kissed her back. His lips locked about hers perfectly and it went on entirely longer than Kupela had intended. When she pulled back, she gasped, exhaled a breathy giggle, and thrust to her feet.

'We should be getting back.' The words came out far quicker than Kupela intended. 'The others will be wondering where we've got to.'

Her face was hot. 'But you can come find me tomorrow, if you'd like? We can go for a stroll together, maybe come back here. I like these, um, creatures.'

She caught a glimpse of the spying mammal again and looked away.

'We can come back here.' He reached out and took her hand. 'But the attendants have a tendency to drawl; there's no reason to head back just yet.'

Kupela swallowed, smiled, and delicately lowered herself back to the bench.

# 1683
## WILLIAM OF FAIRSHORE

'How are you feeling?' Goldin leered over William, his breath strong with sour ale. The little man's eyes were bloodshot, but he seemed to be coping with his hangover fairly easily.

'I'm fine,' William lied, massaging the side of his head with the palm of his hand.

The coach bounced over an uneven cobble, making things ache that had no reason to. Sure, his foot was well within its rights to throb, but what had he done to his teeth to make them so embittered against him? Gnawed a plum stone perhaps? Even his extended slumber and late breakfast of fruit and grains hadn't helped his constitution. By the time he had managed to scrub the scent of stale sweat and liquor from his pits, noon had come and gone. Kupela would have probably expected him in the morning; mid-afternoon would have to suffice.

'No, I mean: what are your opinions on the upcoming job?' Goldin grinned; his teeth were tinted green from some herbal remedy he had consumed with his breakfast. William had tested it and refused to drink one himself; he was regretting it now. 'You look like death.'

'I feel optimistic about the contract,' William lied again. It wasn't guilt or any of the things Goldin had alleged he would feel the previous night. It was because he couldn't possibly impress the senator's daughter when he felt so wholly awful. 'It's just a bit of target shooting. I can probably do it with my eyes closed.'

He shut his eyes, which was a pleasant relief from the glaring brightness of the late morning sun. Perhaps the target shooting *would* be easier this way.

'Do you have everything you need?' Gwyneth prompted.

'You know I do.' William replied carefully, considering going back to sleep. 'There's a knife under my belt, digging into my hip, another equally as uncomfortable in my boot. I think there's a garrotte in my jacket somewhere.'

'It's in your inside pocket.' She smiled. She had switched back to the crooked brown teeth, which meant she was up to no good. 'I just want you to be ready.'

'What about the pair of you?' William knew she and Goldin had been planning something that morning, but had been paying more attention to four cups of orange juice than any of the conversation.

Gwyneth leant back and propped her foot on the bench opposite. She groaned and rubbed her face as if she was only now beginning to wake up. 'We're going to the guild outpost; see if we can find any records or blueprints for the backup plan. Ideally, we'll be ready to go if you don't get a chance to kill Sepo Falade before the parade.'

'And it keeps us out of the hotel room.' Goldin put on a mocking tone and rolled his eyes. 'Which is a *good thing*, apparently.'

'You don't want to be sat on your backside all day just waiting for news from William, do you?'

Goldin cocked an eyebrow and smirked as if the answer was too obvious to voice.

'I thought you had to wait for the new aliases?' William leant his elbows on his knees. He frowned at Gwyneth, trying to keep the sun from his eyes.

'Only yours, but you aren't going to need it just yet.' Gwyneth gave him a reassuring pat on the knee, then diverted her attention to a gaudy fortune teller's wagon trundling by. Clearly, she was avoiding the subject.

'Did it say we were married or something?' William grinned, but the stretch of his facial muscles made his head throb.

She swore at him, aiming a fist at his arm and told him to mind his own business. It was all in good fun, though she was doing her best to watch the passing buildings. William was fairly certain she was blushing.

He had been foolish to consider abandoning them so readily, he realised. Spending time in their company was enjoyable and he definitely didn't like how the ale had affected him the night prior. It would have been so easy to end up with nothing again. Still, once Sepo Falade was dead and he had a lifetime's worth of gold, there would be plenty of time for soul searching.

After some time, the coach rocked to a halt. William opened his eyes, realising only then that they had been closed for some time. He looked up to see the coachman staring back at him, witheringly. Goldin had fallen back to sleep too and was subtly snoring. Gwyneth was turned away, but the way her cheek was resting heavily on her hand suggested she was no longer conscious. Some first day on the contract this was shaping up to be.

William alighted the coach and tried to close the door as quietly as he could. He didn't want to disturb his companions – he would much rather be asleep himself. The subtle click woke Goldin with a gasping snore that sounded like the grunting of an irate pig. Gwyneth was woken in turn.

'Good luck, the pair of you.' William waved as they both squinted at him groggily. 'Though I hope we don't need your backup plan.'

'With any luck, Kupela will take you straight to Sepo.' Gwyneth yawned and stretched. 'See you tonight.'

'Don't wait up.' William smirked as the coach pulled away, leaving him alone.

The Via Principale Forum was only a single storey, but was wide and expansive. It looked ostensibly like a small senate, although it was made of more regular bricks and had been whitewashed to maintain the effect. The building was still a meeting place for the high-minded and wealthy, but it hadn't been financed by the bottomless vault of the Empire. It seemed purse strings drew tight when it came to funding more community facing endeavours.

William was eyed suspiciously by a street corner guardsman as he entered. The foyer was open, surrounded on three sides by columns. A white wall spanned the far end where a woman was pinning notices to wooden boards. As William came close, he spotted that the little parchments boasted of thinkers' conferences and Mythday evening thespians' clubs.

'Excuse me.' He cleared his throat as he came alongside the woman. 'I was told to ask for Kupela Falade, but I'm not sure exactly who to ask.'

The woman rounded with a big smile, her fashionable hair piece listing dangerously. 'Ah, she said she was expecting a young gentleman. She's in the courtyard, follow that passage through to the left.'

William thanked her and made his way through the building. Most rooms were empty, but a few housed groups of one discipline or another. There were bald and bearded men in one room, studying symbols they had drawn on a board with chalk. In another room, children were being taught how to use a potter's wheel by a woman with wild hair and hands too coated in clay to do anything about it. As William passed another room, that was seemingly just a place for men to drink liquor and talk about hunting foxes, he spied a way through to the courtyard.

When William had heard the word "courtyard" it had conjured up the image of a small cobbled square, not a decently sized park. There was grass and small, rolling hills, delicately pruned trees, and bushes. There was even a small pond attended by a family of ducks. Somehow, a jet of water emitted from a pipe in the centre, going straight up. Droplets fell back down to the water making a pleasant rain-like splashing. What had been saved on the modest exterior, had clearly been spent here.

The low building stretched all the way around. William supposed it did technically make this a courtyard, although it might be in excess of two acres.

'She's taking a stroll amid the poplars,' Silvio muttered in his ear.

'Bloody hells!' William jumped back. 'You're light on your feet.'

'I can be, when the mood strikes.' The tall fighter flashed that superior grin of his and strode away towards a shaded pergola. His three burly companions were sat at a round table inside, holding cards and looking over impatiently. It was Silvio's turn. 'Have fun. We won't be far.'

William considered that some kind of threat, but it was a particularly friendly threat and not one that worried him all that much. He didn't mean to do any harm to Kupela anyway, he only wanted to kill her father.

He made his way for the pointed poplars.

'Mr Brightman!' Kupela spotted him before he saw her. She was sat on a gently rocking bench, suspended from a wooden frame, but she leapt up as he approached. 'I wasn't sure if you'd come. I'm glad you did.'

Skirts swayed about her as she came closer. She wore a fine Vitulan dress, complete with frills and studded pearls. William wasn't particularly interested in the fashion of it, but the casually perfect form she struck was enchanting.

'I am too, and you can call me Wi– Bill.' He rested his hand on the holster where he kept his silver flintlock. 'This place is certainly different.'

'It's a veritable cornucopia of activities; I practice archery here sometimes. I'm sure you'll suit the place nicely, Bill. Or was it Will?'

'Well…' William paused a moment, wondering whether he had been identified.

'You don't look much like a Bill to me. Bill is an older man's name.'

William took a breath, reasoning that Bill was so close to his real name already that it didn't really matter if she knew. He cursed last night's drink-degraded imagination, and said, 'It is Will, actually. William.'

'I knew it.' She smirked. 'If I didn't know any better, I'd assume you were trying to impress me last night.'

She slipped a hand through his projected elbow, linking his arm. Suddenly then, William's mouth became incredibly dry. He looked at her, but her head was momentarily turned away, watching the flight of a passing bluebird. He studied the curve of her nose, the coil of hair that fell free and trailed by her ear, the dimple in her cheek. He prayed that he didn't lose his nerve before the time came.

'So, tell me, *William.*' She started walking, pulling him with her. 'How does one get into circus sharpshooting?'

'I didn't have many options when I was younger. I had a pretty rough start, really.' He opted to keep things as close to the truth as possible. 'I ended up collecting glasses in a tavern for coppers. There was a regular there, used to practice shooting in an old tunnel underneath. I think he was a retired assassin. I followed him down once and he ended up teaching me.'

'Weren't you scared of him?'

'There's not much to be scared of when you have little to lose.' William realised that sounded a little dramatic. 'And I was young, wasn't smart enough to be scared.'

'So, you were taught by an assassin and joined a circus?' She led him through a gap in a hedge to a small enclosure with woven straw targets at one end. They were certainly much more upmarket than the ruinous barrels and trash he'd used during his training with Cathal all those years before.

'There's not much honest work you can find when shooting is your only skill.' He shrugged. If only he'd thought of joining a damned circus sooner, he might have made a career of it. He peered to the side of the straw targets and noticed that hessian sacks of sand had been heaped at the back for the purposes of stopping their bullets.

'I suppose not.' Kupela appraised him in a way that made his ears feel hot. 'Though I imagine it's good for self-defence, and – I'm hoping – tremendous fun. Will you teach me?'

'It's why I'm here, isn't it?'

Kupela tossed him a look that implied she had other plans for him.

William's stomach rolled and he had to pause to collect himself. He pulled the silver flintlock from his holster. 'You can use this one.'

She took it delicately in two hands, twisted it in the sun to study the etched wild flowers. 'It's pretty.'

'It is,' he agreed, although next to her flawless skin it looked tarnished. 'It's *pretty dangerous,* so be careful with it.'

'Pretty dangerous.' She snorted, amused. 'You are a joker.'

That was the first time William saw through her haughty demeanour; it was oddly endearing. He pulled out the three shooter from inside his jacket. 'I mean: it's *very* dangerous. So don't point it at anything you don't want a hole through.'

He took aim at the bales and pulled back the hammer on the pistol, rotating the cylinder to the next chamber. It was a nice action.

He squeezed the trigger, dropping the hammer and igniting the powder in a brass casing. With a familiar clap the bullet shot forth in a spear of flame. It struck the target inside the second painted ring – not quite as impressive as he'd hoped.

'Good shot.' Kupela jumped with glee. 'Is it my turn?'

'Be careful with that thing,' William chided her softly. 'Right, just do as I say and take it slow. First, plant your feet like this.'

He displayed a typical firing stance, not that it was often assumed in the midst of a fire fight. She copied him well.

'Take aim. A little higher.' He walked around her. 'Keep both eyes open. Little higher.'

He reached out and adjusted the pistol with a nudge. It drifted low seconds later. He adjusted her aim again, but this time it strayed a fraction to the left as he let go.

'I can't seem to keep the thing steady, it's terribly heavy.' Kupela pursed her lips, frowning. 'Could you help?'

Her eyes darted to the ground behind her. He followed her direction, and peered over her shoulder; her aim was further off than he'd thought. Reaching around, he cupped his hands around hers, steadying the gun. 'Better?'

'Yes.'

William thought he could detect a slight pressing of her dress into his pelvis; he swallowed saliva and tried to keep his attention on the gun. Her breath tickled the hairs on the back of his arm, her perfume sliced through the fugue of his hangover. Steeling his resolve, he put his finger on the back of hers and squeezed. Somehow, despite every distraction, this shot was entirely more accurate than his first.

Kupela jumped forwards and pumped her fist. She rounded on him, grinning. 'That was a good shot, wasn't it?'

'It was a great shot for a beginner.'

'*For a beginner?* It's closer to the bullseye than yours,' she teased. 'Maybe I should join the circus.'

'Maybe you should.' He took the silver flintlock and offered her the three shooter. 'But can you do it again?'

'Of course I can.' She quickly assumed the firing stance and raised the pistol for the target. 'But... you'll have to help me again, this one's even heavier.'

He knew that wasn't the case. While the three shooter was slightly bulkier because of the rotating cylinder, certain advances in the metals meant it was actually lighter than his silver flintlock. Still, he didn't mind wrapping his arms around her again.

'Up a little,' he guided Kupela, feeling that pressure of her skirt and the subtle warmth of her body. 'About there. You pull the trigger this time – when you're ready.'

As Kupela settled in to fire, adjusting her sight about the pistol William had in a fixed grip, he had a sudden sinking feeling in his chest. Could it be untimely indigestion? Kupela was making him tremendously nervous with her advances. Or was it a pang of Goldin's foretold guilt?

Kupela pulled the trigger. This bullet struck a target right on the outer edge.

'You threw me off on purpose.' She wheeled away again, this time in mock outrage. Letting go of the pistol, she left it in William's hands. 'You just can't stand losing to me, can you?'

'I wouldn't put it like that.' He fired the last shot for the target. It hit wide, marginally closer to the edge than the last shot. 'Looks like you win.'

He grinned, though the three shots all but confirmed his fears. This new pistol, while capable of firing three shots in quick succession, was wildly inaccurate.

'Well, you're going easy on me then.'

'You can't have it both ways. I didn't even realise we were in competition.' William started reloading the silver flintlock with a supply of cartridges from his pocket. 'Want to try again? For real?'

'I never back down from a challenge.'

They took it in turns, each using the silver flintlock. William sent a few shots into the bullseye to display his prowess. Then purposefully sent a few shots wide to make the competition a little closer. It was clear Kupela knew what he was doing, but neither one of them mentioned it until William came to take his final shot.

'This is the decider.' Kupela came behind William as he took his aim. She rested her chin on his shoulder and peered down the sight of the pistol. 'I wonder if you'll score a bullseye and win, dashing this young woman's hopes of a life in the circus. Or you might shoot wide, which would be incredibly patronising.'

William's mouth worked. He hadn't a clue what to do. He didn't want to upset her and spoil his chances; he was really starting to like her. And of course he didn't want to jeopardise the contract. There was that too.

She toyed with his hair a moment, her mouth achingly close to a sensitive spot below his ear.

He released the hammer gently with his thumb, reasoning that sometimes it was better not to shoot. 'Why don't we call it a draw?'

'Oh, don't be a misery guts.' She slapped his arm softly. 'You can't give in at the last second like that. My father always said, "When you commit to something, you should always follow through." Although it was mostly with regard to war.'

'If you say so.' William stretched his arm and fired, scoring a game-winning bullseye. He couldn't avoid his soaring arrogance and self-appreciation. Goldin would have been so proud.

'Devil.' Kupela prowled around him in an impatient circle. 'It's getting late.'

William realised then that the thin coverage of cloud was beginning to turn pink. Collecting his guns, they walked arm in arm across the courtyard. Swifts and swallows wheeled through the air as the sun dipped lower, their eventide hunting enthralling Kupela.

'If I don't get home soon my keepers will slit each other's throats.' Her chuckle was light, her eyes glittering as they found his. 'They never have been good sports when it comes to cards.'

She went ahead. Pausing in an archway, she set a hand on the stonework and glanced over her shoulder at William. 'Say, do skinny things like you even eat?'

'When I get the chance.'

'You can buy me supper then.' She lifted one heel, the motion drawing his gaze briefly to her hips. 'Does tomorrow night sound good to you?'

'Yes,' he said a little too eagerly, though in that moment any trace of the contract was absent from his mind.

'Find me here at dusk then,' she called as she disappeared between two poplars and was lost behind a long hedge.

William looked about for someone to share a smile with. There was no one, so he grinned to himself. He stood there for a good few minutes unsure of what to do with himself. Eventually, he holstered his pistol, pulled his jacket tight against the cooling air, and set off for home. There was an undeniable bounce in his step that night.

The following day William went out and spent the last of his gold, which had been intended for supplies, on a fine pair of trousers and an even finer shirt. He told himself it was money well spent, getting closer to Kupela was all in aid of the contract after all, but he didn't mention to Gwyneth or Goldin exactly how much the garments cost either. Fortunately, the pair of them were far too preoccupied with their own scheme for killing the senator. He didn't think they even noticed his outfit.

He headed out early, choosing to walk to the forum rather than endure another journey with the scornful coachman. It was refreshing to walk the streets in the crisp air of dusk, and he liked to think that it would prepare him for the evening to come. Not that he could think about Kupela without getting terribly excited and anxious all at once. As a result, most of the walk was spent studying shop frontages and passers-by to distract his mind from the impending social engagement.

For all the good the distractions did, when he arrived at the forum and saw Kupela waiting outside for him, his stomach instantly knotted. She was swaddled in a fur coat with a thick collar that pushed up her curls, which bounced playfully as she bounded down the forum steps to greet him. To his surprise, she had come without her guard. To his even greater surprise, she grabbed him and pulled him into an embrace.

'You came.' She squeezed.

'Why wouldn't I?' He shut his eyes, holding her maybe a little too long. He had spent so long alone, and was only just getting accustomed to having friends, let alone navigating the labyrinth of a potential romance.

'Exactly.' She tossed her head with a giggle, then grabbed his hand. 'Come, I've reserved us a table at a little eatery just down the road. They have this dish, *peposo,* it's absolutely terrific.'

'Is Silvio not joining us?' William's eyes darted in case the old warrior was lurking in a lofty shadow somewhere.

'They're playing cards; I told them we were shooting again.' She flashed a wicked smile. 'Unless you need a chaperone?'

'No. It's fine.' William bit his lip.

The eatery seemed too small and nowhere near grand enough to be frequented by a senator's daughter, but it wasn't too surprising given Kupela's preference for the roughest of taverns. This place, however, was the antithesis of rough. There were beautifully knotted ribbons and miniature ornaments displayed behind each pane in the segmented windows and the door was propped open by a wooden sculpture of an apron-wearing nonna. William had to duck to get through the low door.

An old Vitulan with grey hair scraped across a bald pate greeted the pair and ushered them to a small round table in a dim corner. He took an order for drinks, lit the table's beeswax candle with a taper, and left them with each other. Kupela decided that they would be drinking only the finest and richest of red wines, and that she would have the carbonara followed by a lemon sorbet. William opted for the aforementioned peposo and joined her in choosing the sorbet, which he later found out to be as eye-wateringly expensive as it was sour. It couldn't be a cheap business transporting blocks of ice from the nearest peak.

Conversation continued easily and flirtatiously until just after the main courses had arrived. Somewhere amidst a conversation about Kupela's duties at the senate and forums, she interrupted the flow with a pointed question. 'What are you, really?'

William almost choked on his peppered beef when she said it, and had to force it down. It felt as though he had been ambushed. He worried that she had lured him to this little restaurant just to confront him, and perhaps Silvio would be waiting outside. Until he knew for certain, he made his best effort to stay cool. 'What do you mean?'

'In fact, I'm certain of it.' She twirled the fork artfully in her pasta. 'You're no circus sharpshooter.'

'Why not?' William tried to act casual; he took another mouthful of beef, dripping in red wine gravy. The food had lost all flavour, but masticating helped him focus his fraught mind.

Her fork was still twisting in the pasta. 'You lack a certain zest.'

'Thanks.' He snorted a laugh, feeling the pressure relax a little. 'What else could I be with shooting skills like this? An assassin?'

She laughed.

'You're too sweet for anything like that.' Her fork raised, a tight wrap of spaghetti about the tines, but she didn't take a bite. Her mouth worked subtly as she cogitated. 'But I'm still not convinced you work in a circus.'

Perhaps circus sharpshooter wasn't so convincing after all, especially with no circus visiting the city. William's "seeing the world" excuse had been rather weak, he supposed. 'I *have* worked at a circus, but it's not my profession. I escort carriages mostly, that's what brought me to the city. I'd have normally gone with another coach by now, but I found a reason to stay.'

Damn, he was charming when he wanted to be. There was also a ring of truth to it. If he was a coach guard, he definitely wouldn't have left the city after meeting Kupela.

She smirked, finally depositing the pasta into her mouth. She toyed with her fork as she chewed and washed it all down with a healthy sip of wine, then added, 'Not so exciting after all.'

'You've obviously never met a highwayman.'

'And I never intend to.' She raised her glass and took a second swallow. William joined her, feeling the warmth in his gut already.

After the lemon sorbet, when the pair were nearing the bottom of their second or third bottle of wine, Kupela moved her chair around the table so that they could talk more intimately. As a natural result of their proximity, with wheels greased by liquor, and without much fanfare, they started to kiss. Kupela instigated it, as she had done with every advancement in the relationship so far, but William was a willing participant.

He was nervous at first, and worried that he wasn't doing it quite right – life as a killer left little room to practice such things, especially for someone disinterested in paying for company – but his worries soon drifted away and he became lost in the moment. Time passed quickly in a sleepy, drunken haze, with the pair kissing and pulling one another close. It was nothing like the whirlwind romances in dog eared old books; there was no urgency to it, just a comfortable intimacy.

'Say.' Kupela pulled back, her eyes fixed hungrily on William. One of her hands was bunched in his fine shirt. 'Where are you staying in the city? I'd love to see your rooms.'

It was a thinly veiled proposition, so thinly veiled that it might as well not have been veiled at all. William's heart jumped; not only was Kupela one of the most beautiful girls he had ever met, *she* liked *him*. Nobody liked him. And the prospect of spending the night with someone who actually wanted to spend it with him was –

He didn't have anywhere to take her.

He was suddenly set on edge, reminded that they weren't just two young lovers sharing a nice evening, but that he was a covert assassin with intentions upon killing her father. There was that pang of guilt again; he pushed it away. More pressing in his mind in that moment, was how he might fulfil Kupela's request. He couldn't likely take her back to the Finchley hotel room where Goldin and Gwyneth were plotting, and the nautically themed tavern had no rooms left to rent. The thought of walking the city in search of somewhere to stay crossed his mind, but it felt sordid in a way.

'I… my rooms.' He faltered. 'They're not really all that suitable.'

'I don't mind if you don't live in a palace.' She kissed him again, this time nipping his lip with her teeth.

'I would take you, but…' He tried to think of somewhere, *anywhere,* they could go. Or failing that, a suitable excuse, although that was a significantly less appealing prospect. 'It's complicated?'

He chided himself; was that all he could come up with? Perhaps he wasn't as suave under pressure as he'd thought.

'Those are feeble excuses.' She fixed him with a hard stare, a stare that drilled right to the heart of him. 'But I suppose you're right. It is a little soon.'

She collapsed against him, her cheek on his shoulder and her head against his. Her arms were around his stomach, loose, save for a few sporadic squeezes. When she spoke again, it was soft, wine drowsy, with the latter half little more than a mumble. 'Perhaps you are a keeper after all. A veritable gentleman.'

He wasn't sure if she drifted to sleep or if she simply cuddled him for a time, but they sat together until the waiter returned to take their empty glasses and plates. At that point, with Kupela now certainly sleeping against him, William offered to settle up which consumed all he had to his name but two silvers and three coppers. Kupela stirred not long after, when the waiter clinked away with the crockery and it was time for the eatery to close.

'Sorry.' She sat up, her eyes still hazy. She had a William-shaped dent in her hair where she had rested against him.

'Don't be. I had fun.' He wasn't sure what to do with himself. He wanted to kiss her again, but wasn't comfortable being the instigator. What if she had sobered up somewhat and no longer had any interest? 'This place is closing.'

Unsteadily, they prepared to leave. William did the gentlemanly thing and helped Kupela into her fur-trimmed coat before they stumbled outside, arm in arm. The night air was bracing, sobering, but not sobering enough to counter the entirety of the wine they had consumed. They walked to the end of the street, until the forum could be seen. Silvio and his companions were sat on the steps outside awaiting Kupela's return. It became obvious that the pair should go their separate ways.

'I enjoyed tonight.' Kupela squeezed him one last time.

'When can we meet again?' William felt his mouth dry, but somehow Kupela suddenly looked more nervous than he was.

'I– um…' She paused. 'I'd like you to accompany me at the parade – a young woman needs a companion to such events… I'd like it to be you.'

'I'd love to,' he agreed without even considering that at the parade he had prior plans to be atop a roof with a rifle, should it come to that.

'There is one small thing.' Her foot scuffed on a cobble. 'My father is speaking at the event in the square and I'd rather not throw him off by turning up with a man he doesn't know. It's an important day for him.'

William saw Silvio stand. He didn't move to collect Kupela, but his observation was keen. One foot tapped on the paving slabs, impatiently.

'I know it's a little soon.' Kupela slipped her arms around William; he felt the eyes of the old warrior needling into him. 'Would you visit me at home… and meet my father?'

# 1679
## KUPELA FALADE

'What's this boy's name again?' The handmaid pulled on the drawstrings of the corset.

'Not so tight.' Kupela had become quite enamoured with the fine Garlish dresses and had taken to wearing them regularly. It was rather fun dressing up and making oneself look pretty, though she didn't agree that the drawstrings had to be quite so tight and would often have them slackened by a scullery maid once the handmaid was done. Corsetry could be rather comfortable when fitted right.

'His name's Richter,' she said on an expulsion of breath. Even just saying it brought a smile to her lips.

'Richter?' the handmaid mused. 'Is he Galman?'

'Yes, but I think he was brought up here. He's never mentioned Galmany.' She pictured him. 'Though he does have their tuneful lilt.'

The pair had been inseparable since their tryst in the solarium; they must have met almost daily. Today, he would take her back to the observatory. It was said that Pride would be visible through the apparatus that evening and the attendants were having another invitational to drum up some donations. It hadn't been lost on Kupela that it had been six months to the day since their last visit, and she was certain that Richter had something planned.

'How's that?' The handmaid finished knotting the ties and stepped back.

Kupela swayed from side to side, letting the skirts twist about her.

'It's still a little tight, but it looks well.'

'That's all that matters, dear.' The handmaid beamed, her red face even more rosy than usual. 'You'll make marriage material yet. It is a shame there's no more suitable bachelors out there, though.

You're far too glamourous to be courting a surgeon's boy. Though I suppose the surgeon general outranks even your father in some debates. If D'Elia had fathered a son you might have made a fine empress one day.'

Kupela was about to make a scathing comment when the handmaid continued.

'Ever since I was a little girl, I've dreamed of being part of an imperial wedding party.' The handmaid stared out of the window with twinkling eyes. 'All the pomp and ceremony of it.'

Kupela smiled to herself at the thought of denying the handmaid her wish; she wouldn't be choosing a wedding party any time soon. Even when she did, she wouldn't select her handmaid for a bridesmaid; she despised the woman. If it was up to her the handmaid would have been sent packing months ago, but she was under the employ of Kupela's father, so had to be put up with for as long as she lived here, and only that long.

'May I return to my other duties?' The handmaid curtseyed.

Kupela wasn't exactly sure what her handmaid's duties were other than sitting on her rump in the steamy linen room or finishing the latest raunchy novels, but she had little use for her other than tying corsets. 'You're excused.'

The handmaid paused at the door, and said, 'I do hope you don't think I was casting any aspersions on our emperor's loins? He might have taken no wife, but I'm sure he's got many a bastard.'

Kupela waved the woman away, not seeing fit to turn away from her mirror and the intricacies of applying her powders. It wasn't her concern that the emperor's loins lacked any potency. Though it was said that he had turned his curse to his own advantage, and had bedded more than half of the young women and wives in the senate. That was only one of the many reasons Kupela stayed clear when the greasy old man visited the house on imperial business.

With a harrumph the handmaid bustled away, adding distantly, 'Many a bastard, indeed.'

After a few minutes touching up her hair and powder, Kupela followed out of her chambers. It was only late afternoon so she passed the time waiting for Richter by reading.

Choosing a book was a task in itself. She could read something historical, but she didn't like the way people like herself were often portrayed. Many of the texts in her father's library were old and imperial, written before Numin ceded to the Vitulan Empire. As such, her countrymen were often depicted in the worst light; either caricatured or viciously stereotyped as somehow lesser. She could read something else educational, perhaps botanical. She had always fancied herself tending to a flower patch. Perhaps she and Richter might own one together some day, but she was getting ahead of herself.

There were a few of the handmaid's books stowed amongst the others. Kupela found The Milliner's Boon, but decided against it. She didn't want to be reminded of societal pressures to marry, and was glad that at least the handmaid had quietened down about the whole thing since she had met Richter. Gods she hoped he wasn't about to propose to her yet. It was a silly notion and she was glad she had made her feelings clear on their first evening in the solarium.

She ended up selecting an autobiography of an old explorer. The story pertained to his efforts to climb the tallest mountain in Stark, but it was a thick tome and most of the stories she managed to get through were of his visits with the locals.

She was reading in the study, and occasionally glanced out of the window to determine the time. There was no grandfather clock in the room as her father found the ticking and chimes too distracting. Once the sky went from blue to orange she worried that Richter was running late. When the sky progressed to dark grey, she feared he had forgotten their plans entirely.

She forced herself to read on, pushing her way through the following chapter that saw the adventurer straying into Marjore. The change of scenery was refreshing, but she couldn't help but be distracted with thoughts of Richter.

Once the sky outside was black, she put the book away. She found it a strain to read by oil lamp, and her chest was filled with too much worry for Richter. He should have arrived to collect her by now. She didn't know what to do then. Occasionally in her free time she would paint, but it seemed pointless to start when Richter might still arrive at any moment. She started to pace about the house, wondering whether she was meant to meet him at the observatory. They had agreed he would collect her from home, but what if he had forgotten?

Her pacing became a stroll about the house and grounds. Going out through the empty hall, she made two laps about a small wooded area beyond the formal garden, before deciding to come back. She feared that an inattentive footman would leave the door unanswered and Richter might come and go without her knowing. Besides, the sky was threatening rain.

When she stepped into the hall, Kupela found her father sat on one of four couches arranged in a square. It was strange as he usually only waited there when anticipating guests. There was a pile of scrolls on a central table and he was reading though one he had unfurled in his hands, no doubt reviewing potential new legislation.

'Evening, Kupela,' he called to her as she entered. 'Have you been out without a cloak?'

'I wasn't out long.'

'It gets cold in these northern climes.' He turned back to his parchments, adding, 'I don't want you getting stricken with anything.'

'I think I'm used to the Vitulan evenings, father.' She could barely remember what it was like in Rocca. They had left before she turned seven. 'Did anyone call while I was out?'

'No.' He rolled up the scroll and tossed it onto the heap, selecting another. 'Are you expecting anyone?'

'Perhaps.' She was reluctant to mention Richter to her father. She was certain that he knew of their courtship, but he hadn't passed comment. There was a chance he didn't approve. 'Are you?'

'Perhaps,' he replied, a hint of amusement in his voice.

She padded across the room to look out of the window and toyed with a curtain tassel. It was raining now, making the flagstones slick and streaked with light from oil and gas lamps.

'You're not waiting for that boy of yours, are you?'

Kupela's hand clenched on the tassel. This was the first time her father had taken an interest in her affairs in months, and his tone didn't sound quite as approving as she'd have hoped.

'I might be.' The words came out clipped.

'And he's keeping you waiting?' Sepo tutted like a disapproving old maid.

A carriage pulled up at the far side of the road. Kupela leant forward and cupped one hand to the glass to see better in the dark. Through the pouring rain, she made out the driver as he got down from his bench and opened the cab door. A passenger, who was wrapped and hooded in a dark cloak, unfurled himself from inside. Tall and lithe, his movements were purposeful like a dancer's, and his silhouette was far to stretched to be Richter's. He prowled to the rear of the cab to unload a trunk.

'Perhaps he will not show at all,' her father commented.

Kupela frowned, then turned to see him sternly observing her. 'What do you know?'

'Little. Which is why I must read.' He turned back to his parchments.

'What do you know about Richter?' she pressed.

'Little.' He shrugged and tossed down the parchment roll. 'But he did come to visit me a few days ago. I thought it wise not to mention it.'

'Why did he come to see you?' She feared she knew the answer already.

'To inform me of his intentions.'

'But I'm not ready to marry,' Kupela found herself saying.

'Exactly.' He picked up another scroll, apparently considering this conversation to have little more gravitas than one on the weather. 'I told him in no uncertain terms that the pair of you would not be wed.'

He worked his mouth. It looked like he was suppressing a snarl of rage. 'You are too young for marriage, just yet. I hear from your handmaid that you desire for it, but I must draw a line.'

Kupela's mouth was agape. A knot tightened in her chest.

'That's why he's not here tonight,' she snapped. 'You scared him away!'

Her eyes became glossy, threatening tears. She had to blink to clear her vision.

'No matter.' Her father shrugged, not even looking up from his scroll. 'Not only are you far too young to be entertaining the thought of coupling, but the loss of a weak man is nothing to weep over.'

The doorbell chimed.

'Is it your guest or mine?' Sepo offered, wryly.

Kupela swept across the room, knowing the answer before she turned the handle. As the door swung open, the cold wind pushed it inwards and she stumbled back. Outside, cases in hand, was the black-cloaked man. He towered over her, slender, sunken features made gaunt by the shade of his hood. Only a waxed, grey moustache was easily identifiable.

'Ah, welcome.' Sepo stood. 'Kupela, this is Silvio De Santis, I've employed him to protect you and keep you out of trouble for the time being.'

Kupela balked at the man. As far as she could tell, her father had not only scared off the only boy she'd ever liked, he had employed a man to stop her from meeting another. In that moment she was overcome with sorrow. Her eyes followed through on their threats and tears spilled forth, trailing down her cheeks. She barged past the tall fighter and ran into the street.

'Stop her then,' she heard her father shout.

'I'm afraid we haven't discussed terms yet,' Silvio replied. 'I'll retrieve her when you agree a satisfactory price.'

Kupela ran for the observatory, wanting nothing more than to apologise and explain to Richter before the towering brute came to drag her home. Her shoes weren't suited to running so she kicked them off at the first opportunity. They were immensely expensive, but it didn't occur to her in the moment, nor did the cold, wet flagstones and pebbles underfoot.

It took fifteen minutes to reach the observatory. She was unaccustomed to running, and though her limbs were nigh on frozen by the time she arrived, her chest was hot with the friction of heavy breathing. Her makeup too had been smirched by the rain and her hair flattened.

The door to the observatory had been left open and light spilled from within. A table had been set up outside, scattered with canapes and earthenware cups of exotic juices. Ink was bleeding on a cloth sign that read: "Welcome, future investors!" All of it had been forgotten in the downpour. Kupela dashed straight by. Inside, the marble floor was slippery under bare feet, and she skidded as she stopped to get her bearings.

'Are you alright?' One of the attendants looked shocked at the sight of her. They might have thought she'd been kicked by a horse or set upon by vagabonds in the street. Everyone else here was so impeccably dressed.

'Have you seen Richter?' she asked. 'I need to speak with him.'

'I don't think I have.'

Kupela mounted the stairs, hurtling up to the gantry for a better view of the room. Everyone was watching her, and she couldn't see Richter amongst them. She pressed on. The crossed iron banding of the walkway hurt underfoot, but it didn't slow her. She barrelled out of the door to the small courtyard and made for the solarium. If Richter was anywhere, he was in there.

'Richter?' Kupela made her way inside and closed the door behind her. 'Are you in here?'

She heard something from the far side of the solarium, deep in the exotic brush. It didn't sound quite right, but she thought it could be him. Perhaps some venomous beast had gotten to him in here and that was the reason he hadn't showed.

'I'm coming,' she shouted.

There was a reply, but she couldn't make it out properly over the chirping of insects and colourful birds, let alone the drumming of rain on the glass roof. She followed the path, ducked under vines and broad leaves, dripping with condensation. It was hot in here despite the chill outside, and the uneven paving was dirty underfoot. Something whooped in one ear, but when she turned to see there was nothing there. More distantly, Kupela spied the beady-eyed mammal chewing on greenery and watching her.

A small stream cut across the path in front of her, she couldn't remember seeing it last time so must have taken a wrong turn. Still, she was going in roughly the right direction to reach Richter. She gauged the gap; the stones at the sides were wet and spotted with fallen leaves. Leaping across, she landed on a slick patch of algae. Her whole body slipped from under her. She reached out for something to halt her fall, a vine, but it pulled loose from a branch and fell with her.

She toppled into the shallow stream, cracking her back and the side of her head. Pain rattled through her chilled body. She called out for Richter, her voice hoarse. Water washed over her skirts, made them heavy. Her arm had become entangled in the vines. She tried to scramble free, but her weight had pulled the strands tight.

'Richter!' she called again, before spotting someone in the corner of her blurred vision.

A man was stood on the pathway ahead, just where it swerved around a fat tree. He wore a long white coat over a brown and green knitted jumper that had more than a few threadbare holes. A long finger pushed up a pair of round spectacles. He appraised her coldly.

'It's not Richter, girl.' He sniffed. His hard features and widow's peak swam into focus as he drew closer. 'It's *Richtus*. What are you doing in my solarium?'

Kupela breathed a sigh of relief. Though the man looked strange and had an incredibly off-putting demeanour, he was Richter's father and the emperor's surgeon general.

'I came to find Richter. I need to speak with him, is he here?' She wriggled. 'My arm's stuck.'

'Ah.' Richtus pouted and tapped his lips with a finger. 'So you're Sepo's girl, the one who's been distracting my boy from his studies.'

'Yes.' She shuffled in an attempt to relieve some of the tension from her arm. 'He's my–'

'He's your *nothing* after this evening, my dear.' Richtus pulled a silver object from a leather protector in his coat pocket. It was shaped like a dip pen, but at one end had a little triangular blade. As he moved closer with it, Kupela could see that it was flawlessly sharp.

'What do you mean?' She tried to push herself away, but her bare feet kept slipping on the wet stones.

Richtus came ever closer, set his boots either side of her legs. Her skirts had bunched up and there was entirely too much skin on display. He squatted down and peered at her, his eyes piggy and small through his lenses.

'I don't blame the boy.' Richtus sniffed again sharply. 'You're quite irresistible for a young suiter, at least in his eyes.'

He flicked the little knife, severing the vine. It loosened, and Kupela tugged at the loops where they had coiled about her wrist. She got her footing then, pushed herself up and out of the shallow stream, and got out from under the surgeon general.

'Where is Richter?' She feared the worst. 'What have you done with him?'

'I had to punish him for falling behind with his duties.' Richtus shrugged, the motion made the little blade gleam terribly. 'To that end, I've sent him to live with my brother. He'll have no more distractions and can more easily focus on his work. One day, I'm certain he will thank me. You should thank your father, too.'

He smiled, his teeth were somehow too straight and too forward and too white. He added, 'You're too young to be wed.'

Kupela felt like screaming at him that his exact sentiment had been her own from the start, but someone unknown called into the solarium before she had the chance. 'Kupela, are you in there?'

The voice was syrupy yet stern. Kupela didn't recognise it, but imagined it was Silvio De Santis here to drag her home. Richtus retreated, depositing the miniature blade into the leather sleeve in his pocket.

'Your father sent me to find you.' The voice confirmed Kupela's suspicions.

'She's in here.' Richtus tossed over his shoulder as he disappeared behind the fat tree. 'Please remove her, and close the door on your way out. My work requires few distractions.'

# 1683
## WILLIAM OF FAIRSHORE

'Are you wearing that nice shirt again?' Gwyneth called from the living room; there was a mocking tone to her voice.

'You know I am, it's the only one I have that's any good,' William shouted back, neatening his collar and flattening a stray lock of hair. It was getting quite long and he had to sweep it back to prevent it from going in his eyes. He would have cut it himself, but he wanted to look presentable for Kupela and didn't have the coin left to pay a barber. Asking Gwyneth for a loan was out of the question; he didn't want her to know how much he had spent on his "nice" shirt.

'She'll think you only have two outfits,' was Gwyneth's unhelpful reply.

'I'm not going to wear my assassin's blacks to meet her father, am I?' William applied a second helping of aftershave that came complimentary with the room. 'And if I'm to impress him, I need to look my best.'

'You don't need to impress him.' Her tone had a melodic humour to it now. 'Only kill him.'

'I know that.' He marched to the bathroom door to give her his best glare, but she laughed and rolled her eyes. He plainly wasn't so intimidating in only a shirt, underwear, and socks. 'I won't get close enough to kill him if he doesn't trust me, will I?'

'I suppose not. You're not taking your pistol then?' She looked back down at some blueprints spread across the coffee table between her and Goldin.

'Kupela has four guards, all with pistols.' William returned to the bathroom to pull on his trousers and secure his belt, sans holster. 'Sepo will have countless more, I can't likely shoot him and get away, can I? And would you show up for a date with a gun?'

'I would,' Goldin interjected. He was also looking over the blueprints, although less intently than Gwyneth given that a trolley stocked with sandwiches and cakes had arrived only minutes before.

'Of course *you* would, but a non-assassin wouldn't, and that's precisely what I need to look like.' William re-emerged from the bathroom ready, save for his boots. 'How do I look?'

'With your eyes,' Goldin muffled around an iced bun.

Gwyneth laughed. It seemed the pair of them had been reduced to snickering schoolgirls the second they had joined forces and William had taken on the job of wooing Kupela. It didn't matter that he was doing rather a good job, they found endless enjoyment teasing him either way.

'You look very handsome,' Gwyneth confirmed once she had composed herself. Paying him little other heed she turned back to the plans and pointed something out to Goldin. 'We could go in through there and cut across?'

'That sounds good.' Goldin spoke around another mouthful, this time a cucumber and fish sandwich. 'But I still think the sewer is a better option, we can go straight through that annexe then.'

'But we'll stink.' Gwyneth wrinkled her nose.

Goldin looked at William, presumably in search of support.

'Don't ask me, I haven't looked at the plans.' He threw on his jacket. 'But I imagine even a simple guardsman would get suspicious if the three of us traipsed by stinking to the high heavens.'

'You don't need to worry about that.' Gwyneth's pearly teeth flashed. 'There's an old bylaw keeping guards out of the New Gods' Cathedral. They shouldn't be a problem unless a monk raises the alarm.'

'You want to shoot Sepo from the cathedral roof?' William shook his head. 'Is your plan an exact copy of Lord Beechworth's? Don't you think the imperials will have tightened security a little, given the previous shooting?'

'What can they do? No guards are allowed in.' Goldin joined Gwyneth in grinning, specks of finely-chopped herbs caught between his teeth. 'Yes, they can patrol the perimeter, but if we come out of the sewer *inside* the perimeter, I don't see what can go wrong.'

'That's all well and good,' William grumbled, 'but do you need to go over the backup plan while I'm here? I still have a week to kill Falade. Have a little more faith in my skills, would you?'

'It's just a backup.' Goldin shrugged. 'And I hope you do kill him, tonight if anything. This gunman on the roof thing is boggling my brain, there's too much to think about.'

'Which is precisely why we need to work on it now.' Gwyneth picked up a book of records from the floor and thumped it onto the coffee table. 'We need to be ready *should* we need it.'

'Well, I'm making good progress.' William ran his hand through his hair again.

'So are we.' Gwyneth smiled. 'The Guild has better records than I thought. They're awfully obsessed with you in the outpost though. You certain you're not worried about this Hunt?'

William pulled on his boots, combining the motion with a shrug. 'I met their damned leader, knocked him out, and still nobody recognised me. I think I'll be alright.'

'And you've got everything?'

'Yes.' William rolled his eyes, exasperated. 'A knife in my boot and a garrotte in my trouser pocket.'

'And that poison I bought?'

He patted his jacket pocket, feeling the shape of the small, brown vial within. He nodded to her as he left.

It was slightly further to Kupela's house than it was to the forum, so William had arranged for Gwyneth's coachman, Dunstan, to take him. Stepping into the fresh air outside the hotel, he was relieved to see the coach already waiting. After a brief greeting and rough directions, the reins snapped and they were away, bouncing and rumbling across the cobbles.

'He's doing well, your prisoner,' Dunstan said after some time.

William's brow furrowed, the man so rarely deigned to speak with him, and he had almost forgotten they had taken a prisoner. The vivid memory of the wretch being beaten momentarily overrode his worries about the upcoming introduction to Sepo Falade.

'Good. I'm glad,' William lied. He didn't care to dwell on the matter.

'We've been talking.' Dunstan steered them onto a fine road lined with tall and prominent manor houses – it couldn't be too much further now. 'I've never spoken to him much before. He's quite nice really; got some tremendous stories.'

'Why are you telling me this?' William didn't mean to be rude, but didn't have the patience for hearing about the prisoner's idle chatter. He was nervous enough without the added worry of a Badger Sett interloper and he didn't need to fuss over the man's health.

'I just wanted to remind you that I'll be sticking to my word.' The coach slowed and stopped. 'Once the festival starts, I'll be letting him go. We're here.'

'I wouldn't expect anything less.' William allowed himself out. 'We'll be done here by then.'

William's mind lingered on the Badger Sett a moment. He wasn't sure exactly what it was that they wanted, but Gwyneth had made it clear that they didn't want to see Sepo Falade killed. To that end, it would make sense that a few members would be watching the building. It was probably best to not have Dunstan call back for him, lest he be identified.

'You don't need to wait, I'll make my own way back.'

'Superb,' Dunstan remarked wryly as the horses began to move. 'Have fun.'

William was about to respond that this wasn't supposed to be fun, it was supposed to be an assassination, but discretion prevailed as the coach drew away.

The houses on this street were giant, all white blocks and columns. Each was set back from the road by a little garden and black-iron fence. William found the one Kupela had told him of, with a black door and silver thirty-two. It was one of the grandest in the row, and he suspected that many of the buildings here were occupied by senators. He allowed himself through the gate and closed it behind him gently. There were quite a few guards patrolling the area and he didn't want to draw their attention with any loud noises.

He was still irked by the strange conversation with Dunstan, but pushed it away as he knocked on the glossy door. It was opened quickly by a maid who greeted him with expectantly raised eyebrows.

'I'm here to see Kupela?' He thought for a moment that he had arrived at the wrong house, or that perhaps the brusque woman would turn him away.

He could see inside to the hall; four couches in the centre were arranged around a square table of heavy marble. There was a lit hearth too, and white busts of famous imperials, along with aged oil paintings and vibrant tapestries. The room was tall, high up into the second and third floors, with each forming balconies around the perimeter. He could make out the tattooed guard and his portly companion looking down from the second floor. He was at the right address.

'You're expected.' The maid curtseyed, allowing him to enter. 'May I take your jacket?'

William hesitated a moment, remembering that the vial of poison had been stowed in the pocket. He didn't want to be without it, but knew it would be odd to refuse the maid's request. He was forced to accept. It wasn't taken far; the maid hung it on a stand in the corner of the room before leaving through a door hidden in the wood panelling of the wall. He was about to retrieve the vial when a subtle movement in a shadowy recess caught his eye. Silvio was watching him.

'Hello.' William waved with a smile.

'Good evening,' Silvio remarked, leaning casually against the wall.

William found the guards' observation hugely intimidating, but it was only because of his subterfuge. In fairness to the three men watching him, they were trying to keep out of the way. It didn't help that shaded corners were the natural habitat for subtle guardsmen and plotting killers both.

'William, you're here.' Kupela bounded to the foot of the stairs and across the herringbone floor. She planted a kiss on his lips, unafraid and unabashed under the watchful eyes around them. Wrapping her hands around the small of his back, she pulled him in close; her attention was soft and pleasantly familiar.

William was somewhat taken aback. Yes, the pair had been kissing most of the previous night, but they had been drunk then and somehow he thought it wouldn't happen so easily again.

'You look nice,' he commented.

'Only nice?' She pouted theatrically.

'I mean, you look beautiful.' The word sounded silly coming out of his own mouth and he flushed. It was a word he didn't think he had ever said out loud before. It was a powerful word, and while he meant every letter of it, he couldn't help but feel exposed by saying it.

'That's more like it.' She kissed him again then nipped his cheek with her finger and thumb playfully, like she was congratulating a child who was only beginning to grasp the basics of human interaction. 'Would you like to join me in the study for a drink?'

'Lead the way.'

'I don't really have anything planned for us tonight.' She took his hand. 'If my father doesn't approve of you we may have to head out for the evening. If he does, well, we might be better off going out either way.'

'We'll see where the night takes us.' Although William was dazzled by the woman on his arm, it was impossible to forget that he was here for a darker purpose. As she led him across the hall, he studied each doorway and concealed servants' passage, memorising the layout as best he could.

They reached the top of the stairs and turned right, taking another flight to the next floor.

'I couldn't send word ahead to reserve us a table anywhere because I'm not certain what time my father will be ready. I didn't have chance to tell him I'd invited you tonight, he went straight to the baths after finishing in the senate.'

'You don't know what time he'll be home?'

'Oh, he's home. There are hot springs all over Vitale and this house just happens to be built right on top of one. We have our own baths right here, there's a large swimming area, a room with hot coals for steaming. I could show you if my father goes out.' She winked as she pulled him into the study.

'Sit there.' She directed him to yet another couch. 'I'll prepare some drinks, what do you like?'

'Whiskey and orange?' He tore his eyes away from Kupela, keeping aware of his surroundings.

The study was fairly standard, only everything was larger. The desk could be used for a dining table, the bookshelves rivalled that of some libraries, the liquor cabinet that of some taverns. There were big windows fringed on the other side with ivy. William made a note of them as a potential escape route should he need it. With at least four pistol-toting guards in the building, he would need to kill Sepo quietly and escape before he was found. He couldn't risk a gunfight, especially as he had only brought a knife.

'Are you sure you don't want a hand?'

'I'm quite alright.' Kupela grinned from the liquor cabinet. She was crushing orange wedges into the bottoms of two stout glasses with a muddler. 'I'm going to join you in one of these actually.'

'So, do you–' William stopped as he heard footsteps approaching on the landing outside, then the door shushed open across the study's plum carpet.

'Kupela, I–' It was Sepo Falade.

He was dressed in fine woven threads of green and blue. It was reminiscent of a Vitulan robe, but the shoulders were larger and more rigid. Though he was indoors, he had a round, flat-topped hat on top of his bald pate, woven similarly in green. He scowled as he saw William sat on the couch, looking vulnerably up at him.

'Who is this?' He stroked a tightly-curled beard that hung down from his chin.

'Father, you were quick in the baths.' Kupela stepped away from the drinks cabinet, walked towards her father until her path was obstructed by the vast desk, and stopped. William was still halfway between the pair of them, awkwardly turning his head back and forth.

'I didn't use the steam room and Giovanna said we had guests.' He surveyed William, his eyes big and hard, brows curling down cruelly. 'Who is this?'

'This is–'

'William.' He stood up and offered a hand to shake.

'We've been courting,' Kupela added for context.

'I see.' Sepo's frown deepened as he stepped closer. It took all William had to not flinch for his knife. 'This is excellent news!'

The man clutched William's hand in his own, half crushing it, and shook it enthusiastically.

'Really?' Kupela faltered. 'You're not... angry?'

'Why should I be?' Sepo was still enthusiastically shaking William's hand. 'You're a young woman now, it's about time you found yourself a good man.'

Kupela breathed a sigh and set a hand on her chest.

'Whether this one is good, however, remains to be seen.' Sepo raised an eyebrow and leant down to intimidate William a second before releasing his grip. 'So, how long have the two of you been courting?'

'A few weeks now,' Kupela lied before William could respond.

It was probably wise to not let on that they had only recently met. William certainly felt like he had known her weeks rather than days. Things had gone awfully fast, but it hadn't felt awfully fast, not when it was just him and Kupela. It had all seemed right. Now that Sepo was here, and William was staring the target of his contract straight in the face, he couldn't help but feel a little rushed.

Sepo mused a moment. 'You will join us for supper.'

Kupela's knowing smirk was meant only for William as she turned back to the liquor cabinet. It seemed her father was so used to his orders being followed, it didn't occur to him they might have refused or had other plans.

'Would you like a drink, Father? We're having whiskey and orange.'

'That sounds delightful.' Sepo flashed a proud smile, any anger in him entirely gone. 'Take me one down to the dining hall, would you? I'll have the cooks set to work right away.'

He left the study and William could hear him bounding down the stairs in the hall.

'That went well,' he offered.

'I know.' Kupela returned to slowly muddling the drinks. She appeared to be in a state of mild shock. 'I always thought him so controlling, disapproving. Perhaps I had it wrong.'

'Are you alright?' William moved to her and set a hand on her shoulder.

'Yes, it couldn't have gone any better.' She leant into his embrace. The muddler was still in her hands and left a damp patch against the back of his shirt.

William swallowed. He wanted to savour their intimacy, but a knot of anticipation twisted in his gut. He was closer than ever to the assassination.

'Why don't you go down? The dining hall is on the ground floor, first left at the bottom of the stairs.' Kupela set the muddler down and removed the stopper from a decanter. Her eyes were glassy. 'I'll finish these, I need a moment alone anyway.'

'You're sure?' William hesitated, unwilling to leave her when she was upset.

'I'm sure.'

He left the study, following her directions. A few bustling servants crossed his path, but the guardsmen were conspicuously absent. William wondered if they had retired for a game of cards, having done their duty of intimidating him upon arrival.

If he was eating with Sepo, it made sense to retrieve the poison from his jacket. It was only across the hall, but the hall was enormous. He checked for on-looking servants or guards, then broke into a half-walk-half-jog to get to the coat stand. It was quiet and quick enough, but looked tremendously suspicious.

He reached into his pocket for the vial, but it was gone. His heart leapt into his throat. Surely Silvio had come to check his pockets and found the vial of poison. Even now he could be sharing his discovery with the other guards. William patted the jacket in desperation, and to his astonishment, found the shape of the vial in the fabric.

He checked the pocket again with a muttered curse, this time finding a hole in the seam – the vial had fallen through into the lining of the jacket. Forcing his hand through, he ripped a few stitches and rooted around for the vial. It juggled away from his fingertips and he had to manoeuvre the jacket hem to roll it back to his palm. He produced the vial between finger and thumb, inspecting it in case his luck had truly soured and he had somehow found a different vial in the lining. It looked to be right.

Exhaling heavily, he turned for the dining hall and found Kupela watching him from halfway down the stairs.

'What's that?' She had three glasses held precariously in her hands.

William held up the vial as if it was nothing to be ashamed of.

'This? It's a tincture. Some foods give me stomach cramps.' Though this lie didn't exactly aid in William's wooing of Kupela, he congratulated himself that it was a rather good cover for his true intentions. 'Not that I expect the food here will disturb my equilibriums. It's better to be safe than sorry.'

'Oh, I shouldn't pry.' She smiled lightly and moved down the stairs a way. 'Take one of these would you?'

William slipped the vial into his trouser pocket and dashed over, quick to oblige. Hopefully, Kupela would forget all about it; discussing one's ailments – even falsified ones – at dinner was hardly polite conversation.

The dining hall was true to its name. The table was made out of the longest single piece of wood William had ever seen, and had chairs enough for two scores of men. He couldn't imagine the size of the tree it had been cut from. The hall was exceptionally narrow and long for the purpose of housing the table, and the walls were decorated with the heads of wild animals on plaques. At the head of the room was a great oil painting of Sepo wrestling with some grey, tusked beast. At the other end, there was another, depicting him in senators' attire, with a scroll and stone tablet.

Kupela placed her glasses on the table to the left and right of the top chair.

'Set that one over there, would you?' She indicated to the head of the table. 'My father likes to sit there. I'll get the silverware.'

William watched as Kupela strolled to a sideboard and started searching through drawers for the right implements. It was clearly a job usually left to the servants. However, it occurred to him that he was as good as alone with Gwyneth's vial of poison and the target's drink. Everything was falling so effortlessly into place. To William, the wrong roads always seemed to have the slipperiest slopes, making it all the harder to turn back.

Producing the vial from his pocket, he held it carefully between his second finger and thumb. His index finger was ready to flick off the little cork and deposit the contents subtly into the senator's glass.

Poised there, on the verge of what might be his final ever kill, he recalled the terrible night he had completed his first proper contract. He was to kill a boy, an innocent whose only crime was inheriting a great sum of money. William hadn't felt ready to kill then, but the world or the gods had other ideas. That night, everything had fallen into place as easily as today, and he stood over the sleeping boy with a bottle of ether in much the same way. In the end, the boy had burned. It was a horrible, painful death and William had regretted it ever since.

Just as subtly as he had produced the vial, he slipped it back into his pocket, unopened.

Kupela returned with a handful of silverware, and the pair of them worked together to lay the table. Before long, Sepo arrived.

'The cooks are at work,' he announced. 'I've had them prepare a cold appetiser, so we shouldn't be waiting.'

He rounded the table and sat while William and Kupela were still arranging embroidered table squares for the dishes to sit on.

'Sit, sit.' He waved them down. 'I want to get to know your William, but first let's try this whiskey and orange!'

He picked up his glass and took a long sniff. 'Smells good.'

William was glad in that instant that he hadn't spiked the man's drink with a deadly poison. For all he knew, the substance in the vial had a terrible odour that would alert the senator to its presence. And no doubt senators were more diligent than most when it came to having their food checked for tampering.

'Do you know, William? Not only have I never shared a drink with one of Kupela's young men before–'

Kupela kicked her father's leg under the table.

'–but, I've never had a whiskey before.' He inspected the amber liquid. 'I never liked the smell of the stuff, but the orange sets it off nicely. Tonight will be a night of firsts.'

He raised his drink, then tossed it back. William and Kupela clinked their glasses and followed with more measured sips.

'Delicious.' Sepo squeezed his daughter's shoulder affectionately. 'I have no idea how it's supposed to taste, but you've done yourself proud.'

William internalised a groan of frustration. In this instance, he had wholly missed his opportunity to complete the contract. His mind began to drift on what Gwyneth might say, should she find out. He obviously wouldn't tell her, but he didn't want to let her down either. That, and he had agreed to partake in her plan to shoot the man from a rooftop should he fail, and he most certainly didn't want to do that.

'So, William, where are you from?' Sepo leant forwards on his elbows.

'F-Fall Bridge.' William lingered entirely too long on the "F" as he mentally pivoted away from Fairshore. *William of Fairshore* was entirely too infamous of an assassin for William's alias to be just another William *from* Fairshore. 'It's a little village in the north of Garland.'

'What brings you to Vitale? Save for my beautiful daughter?'

'The same thing that brought you from Djurundi, I imagine: my job.'

'The imperial heart calls to many.' Sepo nodded sagely.

'I was only escorting a trade caravan.' William shrugged.

'Yes, but you didn't leave on another, did you? This city has a way of keeping you.'

'I didn't stay for the city, I met Kupela.' William smiled across at her. She seemed pleased that the pair of them were getting on well enough. 'I didn't want to leave after that.'

What William said was true. He didn't want to leave Kupela, but if he killed her father, or reneged on his deal with the Finchleys, no doubt he would be forced to run. Perhaps poison was the right way to go. Sepo would die, William would be rich – although that suddenly mattered very little. What did matter was ensuring the death would not be traced back to him or his vial. Potentially, he could stay with Kupela.

'Would anyone like another drink?' William offered. 'I'll make them. I have whiskey and orange regularly, though I can't promise it will taste quite the same as the way Kupela made it. I'll do my best.'

'Don't trouble yourself.' Sepo clapped twice and a servant appeared from behand another hidden doorway; it was the maid who had greeted William at the front door. 'Three whiskey and oranges please, Giovanna.'

The maid disappeared into the wall again, the door clicking shut behind her.

The meal passed nicely over drinks and stories of their pasts. William's were all lies, but Sepo's and Kupela's seemed to be true enough. That was, until the senator recounted the tale of how he bested beasts in unarmed combat of course.

'Don't lie, Father, it's unbecoming.' Kupela rolled her eyes at William, leaning back to allow a servant to clear away her emptied dinner plate.

'There's a picture of it up there.' He pointed behind him to the majestic oil on canvas. 'That's proof enough, isn't it?'

'Is that a rhinoceros?' William asked.

'Have you seen one?' Sepo was momentarily excited.

'Only in a book.'

'To tell you the truth, me too,' Sepo chortled. 'Some of the Vitulans, senators included, they take me, and other foreign-born imperials, for savages. When they come here and see that painting, they know their worst fears to be true. It helps me slip past their defences when it comes to debates in the senate.'

He shrugged, adding morosely, 'Maybe one day they will see the benefits of assimilating Djurundi.'

'Are you ready for the last course, senator?' One of the butlers stepped through a hidden door.

'Oh. Yes, I think we are.' Sepo perked up, the liquor making his moods quickly changeable. 'And another round of whiskey and orange, why not?'

William hoped to keep him in a good mood, at least for the time being. If they all got drunk enough, it might become easier to slip the poison into his drink. The doctors might even become convinced the man had died through complications arising from too much alcohol.

The butler emerged with a silver tray on a small wheeled trolley. He stopped it beside the table and deposited a plate each before the diners. 'Creamed peanut and banana cake.'

'That sounds lovely.' Kupela shared a grin with William. 'I'm anticipating seconds already.'

Sepo continued iterating his plans for how he might bring the Empire's prosperity to his homeland while they ate their desert. William played a good audience and remained attentive despite being distracted by one of Kupela's feet under the table. She had plainly heard her father's plans countless times and had no patience to hear them again.

'This cake is quite exquisite,' she commented, interrupting her father's political ramblings.

William had to agree, it tasted quite unlike anything he had ever eaten. It was sweet, but the creamed peanut gave it a pleasant earthiness that he had never experienced before. He liked it so much that he must have been eating it with too much enthusiasm; a piece got stuck in his throat on the way down. He coughed to clear it, but even though he managed to dislodge the blockage and subtly swallow it, his breathing still seemed harder than normal. He took a swig of whiskey to wash away any remnants of the cake. When he took a breath again after, he could barely draw it in.

He looked about and realised that Kupela and Sepo were staring at him, bemused. He tried to tell them what was happening, but the words came out as a meaningless wheeze. Terror gripped him as he realised he was unable to take another breath. He leapt up, his hands about his throat. It was as though he had been poisoned. Had Sepo anticipated his intended attack, or had Silvio discovered his vial after all and switched it with another? He staggered backwards.

Kupela was on her feet then. Sepo still sat in muted astonishment.

'I don't think he can breathe!' Kupela gasped, hastening around the table to William. 'We should send for a doctor.'

William staggered about in a feeble search for anything that could help. His shoe caught on the edge of the rug and he toppled down. Kupela was atop him moments later, trying to get her hand in one of his pockets. Was she trying to rob him now her father's guards had poisoned him?

'Where's your medicine?' she asked.

William's eyes bulged at the thought of being administered his own poison on top of whatever he was ailed with already. He delved his hand into his pocket and retrieved the vial. Before Kupela could take it from him, he flicked the cork out and let the liquid drain onto the rug. He hoped it looked accidental amidst his convulsions, but he hoped more that something would alleviate the pressure in his throat.

'Someone send for a doctor!' Kupela shouted this time.

William rolled over and clawed the carpet with his fingers. He was trying to get somewhere, he wasn't sure where, but he was trying to get there with all the energy he had left. Everything was turning to a blur. Shortly afterwards, the world went black.

'Ah, he's awake.' A man leered over William. He had little round glasses and a devilishly sharp point to his widow's peak. 'I'm Surgeon General Richtus Finchley.'

He reached over and shook William's limp hand, despite him not fully being aware of his surroundings yet. William groaned and squinted against light bleeding in through open curtains. Vials of liquids in a wooden stand on the windowsill cast colourful lines across his bedsheets.

'I feel awful,' William croaked weakly.

'You're lucky I was available.' The surgeon's chair creaked as he reclined. 'Anyone else and you would surely be dead.'

He started to scribble some notes on a parchment he had rested on a board across his lap. William listened to the scratching for a while as he came back to his senses. He couldn't quite remember why he was here. He had visited Kupela, he recalled, but had he tried to poison her father? Perhaps that was why he was here. Did he get caught? No. He had choked on something. His memories were made all the harder to recall by a constant throbbing behind his eyes and in the front of his scalp.

'Was I–' He hesitated for fear that he might give himself away, then decided it was a reasonable question from anyone waking in such a situation. 'Was I poisoned?'

'No,' the surgeon replied curtly. William thought the man wouldn't explain further, but after a little more word scratching, the dip pen came to a stop with a definitive tap. 'You were bested by a simple peanut. It's a fairly rare reaction, especially as the little *legumes* are prohibitively expensive. However, my cousin Wilfred just so happens to be similarly afflicted. I always keep the requisite tinctures on hand.

'I filled you with restoratives to aid your healing. Your little friend said you had a limp; it should help with that too.'

'*Little* friend?' William grimaced. Damn, his head hurt. 'Was Goldin here?'

'No, it was a *girl*-friend.' He set the note board to the side and eyed a clock on the wall that was subtly twanging as its gears ratcheted. 'She should be here shortly as a matter of fact. She's been visiting three times daily.'

'Gwyneth then?' William screwed his eyes shut. The light from the window was making his head pound all the worse, or was it that damned medicinal scent that he had come to hate? He realised then that the surgeon was chuckling. 'What is it?'

'I didn't realise that you were here with my niece. That explains the vial of toxin Kupela brought here with you. I had the dregs tested, but one whiff and I knew it was no antidote.'

William tried to sit up in the bed, frightened that if he didn't get out quickly he might be sentenced to hang. He had been found out.

'Calm down. I'll keep your secret.' Richtus waved his hand. 'I don't partake in the games, but I do enjoy seeing how things all play out. I won't interfere.'

'Games? What?' William managed to push himself up to sitting. His back ached from too long in one position. 'Dunstan said that too.'

'Oh, you must know. Don't you?' Richtus punched his thigh dramatically. 'Damn, damn. I've gone and interfered now, haven't I?'

'Are you saying this is a game? Killing Senator Falade is part of a game?' It sounded like a sick joke, and William expected the surgeon would burst out laughing any moment. He didn't.

'I shouldn't say, but… well, not strictly. Your girl Kupela is the subject. Killing her father merely helps to raise her station, she'll be senator then.' There was a knock at the door. 'Oh, hush, hush. That'll be her now. Come in dear, he's awake.'

Kupela was dressed more casually than William had ever seen her. Her dress was still silk, but lacked the corset, long sleeves, and intricate embroidery. She still looked as beautiful as ever, and upon seeing William awake, her face lit up.

'William! I thought you might die.' She rushed in, leapt upon him in the bed, crushing his stomach under her elbow before kissing him and wrapping him tightly in her arms. It was so tight, the experience could easily be compared to that of eating a peanut. 'I'm so glad you're well.'

Behind Kupela, Richtus looked to be delighting in the schadenfreude of it.

'But damn, why did you have to make it today and not yesterday?' She released him from her grip, then punched him playfully on the arm. In his weakened state it hurt quite a lot.

'What's happening today? What do you mean today?' William wondered how long he had been unconscious.

'Nothing is happening *today*, exactly,' Kupela replied. 'It's the festival tomorrow, all hands are on deck making preparations. I have my own duties to attend and not nearly enough time to do them in. I only popped in for two minutes to check on you. I'm late leaving already.'

Slow to process the information, it dawned on William that he must have been out for nearly a whole week.

'It's good, really,' Richtus interjected. 'William needs time to rest, and we can't have you distracting him from his mending.'

Kupela looked over at the surgeon general scornfully, but added, 'If it's best *for William,* then I'll go. Will he be out of bed by the festival?'

'It's hard to say at this early stage.' Richtus' eyes made brief contact with William's, implying that he was lying on his behalf. 'I will need to run more tests.'

'Very well.' Kupela turned back to William, her smile making smooth bunches of her cheeks. 'I should go then.'

She planted another kiss on his lips, squeezed him again – eliciting a groan – and left, looking back only once as she closed the door.

'I thought she'd never leave.' Richtus tutted. 'Always interrupting scientific endeavours, that one.'

'Are you starting the tests then?' William mentally prepared himself for all manner of prods and probes. 'I'm keen to be back on my feet. I imagine Gwyneth must think I'm dead, she won't have heard from me for so long. I need to get word back to her that I'm not.'

'You can go whenever you like.' Richtus shrugged. 'But, if you want to stay in the land of the living, you should avoid peanuts.'

William scowled. He hadn't expected to be dismissed so simply. For a moment, he considered hurrying after Kupela; he was fairly certain he could catch up with her. It was a wonder what the right restoratives could do, and he imagined, if the mood took him, he could run a mile straight out of bed. His other duties – namely checking in with Gwyneth and Goldin – took precedence, however.

'If you're groggy from the elixirs, it should walk off. Just make sure that you do something entertaining *and* dramatic. It's no use just killing Sepo, it's not a game if you don't make a show of it.' Richtus slapped himself on the leg, playfully. 'Look at me, *naughty,* interfering like this.'

# 1683
## KUPELA FALADE

Kupela was back in her fine corsetry again. She hadn't had the energy for the pomp of it while William had been comatose, and although he was still too unwell to accompany her to the festival, she was happy that he would be recovered soon enough. Of course, when attending the festival, the finest dresses were compulsory no matter how she was feeling. Duty to her father would always come first.

She had made arrangements for a show at the forum that morning and had taken a carriage back home to collect her father for the speeches at the senate. Unfortunately, she would miss the majority of the parade weaving its way around the city. At some time around two, it would arrive in the square, along with thousands of onlookers ready to see the emperor and senators speak. Naturally, they would be imbibing copious quantities of alcohol along the way.

Impatiently, she toyed with the rings on her fingers. She was sat in the back of her carriage, waiting for her father to emerge from their home. The driver had knocked on the door and informed a maid that the carriage was ready for the senator, but Sepo still hadn't shown some fifteen minutes later. Kupela began to think they would be late, and was about to get up and drag her father out by his ear, when he finally emerged. No doubt he had been fussing with his decadent ensemble.

Sepo was out to impress, more so than ever. Cloth-of-gold senator's robes glittered beneath a black silk smock with expansive bands of embroidery. His tightly curled beard was oiled and styled, ornamented with elegant beads, while his bald pate was topped with an excessively tall hat. It looked almost like those worn by the industrialists – only it had no brim.

He paused, closing the front door himself rather than leaving it to the maid. Kupela watched his shoulders sag when he sighed, then snap straight as he strode to the carriage. His smile was bright, but she could tell there was trepidation in him.

'I read over your speech,' she said as he removed his hat, stooped inside, and sat opposite. She tapped the side of the cab to set the driver to work. 'It's good, great even, and I know today's going to go smoothly.'

'Thank you.' He looked out of the window, apparently trying to relax himself with the passing festivities.

Shops, houses, and public buildings alike had been festooned with streamers and handmade chains of coloured parchment and card. A few were strewn with crafty bunting. One had even gone to the trouble of embroidering a different icon or scene on each linen triangle. It must have taken weeks of preparation, but the coach passed too quickly for it to be appreciated fully.

'Is that young man not joining us?' Sepo's nose twitched. A bead of sweat was rolling down his brow. 'Is he alright?'

Kupela couldn't tell if he was distracting himself from the upcoming event or if this was genuine fatherly concern.

'He's resting, but he's awake and doing well.' She looked him over, but his attention was drawn out of the window again. He fidgeted subtly with his hat in his lap, picking at the seam with a fingernail. 'You seemed to enjoy his company the other night, do you really like him?'

'I do. I think it will be good for you to find yourself a man and he does seem like a good one.' Sepo swallowed. 'Apologise to him for me, will you? I feel terrible about what happened to him in our home.'

'You've changed,' Kupela remarked. 'I really expected you might set Silvio or one of the others on him.'

'I haven't changed at all. You have.'

'It seems like a big change to me.' Kupela found herself sneering, remembering Richter's forced departure. 'To send one away and welcome another with open arms.'

'You were just a girl then, and you said it yourself, you didn't want to get married.' He was sneering himself now. 'And I didn't send him away, I just paid Richtus the common curtesy of informing him his son was about to propose at fifteen.'

'It was still your fault,' she snapped.

'What does it matter? It was a young fling, it would have been done by now anyway, and you've found this William.' He pinched his temple with a forefinger and thumb. 'Don't test me today.'

Kupela sniffed; she could feel her eyes welling up. 'Just because I'm happy now, it doesn't remedy prior upset.'

Her father closed his eyes and breathed slowly out of his nose. She could tell he was trying to master his temper. Finally, he said, 'For what it's worth. I'm sorry. I didn't mean to part you from Richter. Well, maybe I did, but not so decisively.'

'You hired Silvio and the others to keep me from him.' A tear spilled from Kupela's eye and rolled down her cheek.

'They were to protect you, not police you.' His hands clenched, creasing his hat. 'Do you think I really don't know you've been frequenting these dives? I didn't have them stop you, did I? I just wanted to keep you safe and give you guidance.'

He shrugged. 'When it comes to talking I'm better in fierce debate. I can't coddle you as your mother did. Even your guards are better fathers than me.'

Kupela felt that the right thing to do would be to disagree and tell her father that he did the best he could, given his responsibilities to the senate. She couldn't do it; Silvio *had* been a better father to her than him. But at least now she knew his heart had been in the right place. She leant across and hugged him. He put an arm around her and pulled her close.

'I do love you. You know that, don't you? Even if I'm no good at saying it?'

The carriage stopped. It was gloomy outside the windows; they had arrived in the stables beneath the senate already.

'You've said it now.' She released him with a final reassuring squeeze. 'You should go upstairs. I'll follow you up once I've fixed my powder.'

He alighted the carriage, thanked the driver, and made his way up into the senate proper. After a few minutes with a hand-held looking glass and a pad, she followed him, looking as perfect and fresh as she had that morning. As she made the top of the steps, arriving in the senate foyer, she felt strangely optimistic. It was the first time she and her father had cleared the air, well, ever.

When she found him, he was talking in a group of other senators, going over the running order of events. She opted to leave him to it and instead headed out to the front of the building.

Bleachers had been set up between the great columns for the senators and their significant others. As her father had no wife, Kupela would be sitting alongside him. She moved out from behind the bleachers to find her seat – that would be marked with her name on parchment – and saw the amassed crowd for the first time.

Though the parade hadn't yet arrived, some had come to the square early with plans of getting a better position. The crowd was already colossal. People stretched to the buildings on all four sides and teemed in the park at the centre. From the emperor's abode to the Giordano Archive and the New Gods' Cathedral, the square was an ocean of bodies. The sight of it sent Kupela's heart aflutter.

She turned away and sidled down the bleachers, keeping her head low to look for her seat. If she didn't face the crowd it wasn't quite so intimidating. She smiled and nodded to a few of the senators and their partners as she passed, but when she was finally seated, it was impossible to avoid the collected mass.

Waves began in the sea of bodies, shuffling and undulating as the parade arrived. Giant cloth-and-wood-frame floats pulled by brightly decorated horses crammed their way into the square. Performers in garish costumes, jugglers, acrobats, and musicians of every discipline spread through the crowd. With the influx of people and confusion as the guards tried to clear space, it was like observing a particularly tame battle. Hordes pushed one way and another. A group of revellers managed to get around the parade's flank to secure a prominent position near an ale vendor. Others were pushed back into adjoining streets.

Senators filled the bleachers according to the strict seating plan and, even before the carnage in the crowd was fully settled, it was time for the first to speak. The primo for Embor was a commanding woman with a special talent for being heard. Her voice sang over the melee like a clarion call.

There was no more jostling for position. Bulky floats were left where they stood, with people clambering on top for a better view. Kupela spotted one man, with an oversized carnival head, had been separated from the thrust of the parade. He made no further attempt to re-join them, now watching amongst the revellers he had found himself with.

The detail of the primo's enthralling address was lost on Kupela; she was too distracted by her father's fidgeting. As it was the celebration of the end of the war with Numin, her father had been given the honour of being last to speak before the emperor. She set a hand on his knee and whispered for him to stay calm, reiterating that everything would be fine. It seemed to do the trick, and by the time it was his turn to speak, he had mastered his emotions.

Kupela watched tentatively as her father strode out to the front of the stage, but saw his confidence bolstered by the roar of the crowd. There was a flare of music that reminded her of warmer climes, a deep chant from gathered Numinians that spoke of home.

Sepo spread his arms as if he was embracing the whole crowd; they were soon settled to silence. Kupela mouthed the words of his speech along with him. She had read it so many times that she knew it as well as he did. All in all, it went very well. He returned to the bleachers with a sigh, having imparted his vision for a Nok and Numin united under the Empire's banner. He paused to give Kupela a hug before sitting.

'See.' She grinned. 'I told you there was nothing to worry about.'

'I should have known you were right.' He squeezed her hand. 'You always are.'

Kupela heard the trotting of hooves first, then came the thrum of the crowd. From around the bleachers, the emperor emerged. He was atop a robust, white horse, with a ceremonial flintlock in one hand and a golden-hilted sabre in the other. In his youth, he had often orated from horseback, but hadn't taken to the senate stage in such a way in over thirty years. It was a tremendous display of strength and ceremony, and quite a feat considering the man was in his waning years. And though he had certainly not gotten up on the horse without a considerable amount of effort, he was commanding it well, and looked stronger than any man his age ever had.

The horse trotted past Kupela. She cheered for the emperor as he went. Her father stood up, hooting and clapping to show his appreciation. Other senators were up on their feet too, applauding the arrival of their first.

Distantly, there was a clap of gunfire. Kupela's stomach knotted, her heart leaping to her throat. Something sprayed blood. With a hand to his chest and a violent gasp, her father collapsed onto his seat.

# 1683
## WILLIAM OF FAIRSHORE

'I'm not going.' William parked himself obstinately on a chaise.

'But we need you!' Gwyneth knelt before him in desperation, trying her best to sound calm and reasonable. 'You're the only one who can take the shot.'

'I'm not that good.' He sneered. 'I'm sure you can manage without me. In fact, you'll have to manage without me, because I'm not bloody going.'

'It's one last job. Then you won't have to kill anyone ever again. That's what you want, isn't it?' Begging didn't suit her; she didn't have the right teeth in for it. 'Please, just do it for me? Or Goldin?'

'I'm not killing anyone for *a game.*' William shifted his arse to point himself away from Gwyneth. He stared into the flames in the hearth. He felt too hot, and started to get angry that some idiot had lit the damned thing. 'Do you not take life as sacred? It's not something to be toyed with, or used as gambling chips.'

'That's rich coming from an assassin.' Gwyneth crawled around the coffee table, trying to get in his eyeline.

'If I'm that rich, I don't need your blood money.' He folded his arms. His irritation was making him churlish and he knew it. 'Do me a favour and douse that fire before you head out.'

'We're not going anywhere without you.' She slumped back against the opposite couch, still on the floor, and flicked the blueprints on the table with a finger. They were covered in plans and notes. 'It won't work without you.'

'Come on, lad.' Goldin sat on the couch beside Gwyneth, his knees adjacent to her head. 'What do the reasons matter? We're assassins and reasons shouldn't be part of it. As far as we're concerned, Senator Falade is just a contract that needs to be completed.'

'I don't want to.'

'I knew this would happen.' Goldin heaved a dramatic sigh and rolled his eyes. 'You've fallen for that Kupela.'

'So what if I have? Gwyneth wants Sepo killed *for a game*. My opinion of Kupela has nothing to do with it.'

'Doesn't it?' Goldin scoffed. It was a fairly compelling retort – they both knew that it did.

'William.' Gwyneth moved forwards onto her knees, and set her elbows on the blueprints. 'I know you're not fond of this game. I'm not particularly fond of it either. It has its charms, but – like with being an assassin – it's a double-edged sword. I profit from others suffering, there's no plainer way of saying it, but I'm no more reprehensible than you… or Goldin.'

William harrumphed. He definitely didn't have the moral high ground he purported to have, but equally, he couldn't go along with their plans either. Not anymore.

'However,' Gwyneth continued, 'as part of this game, my team are tasked with elevating and protecting the subject, Kupela. You would like to protect her, wouldn't you? See her status raised?'

'Yes, but not by killing her father.'

'Such is the rub.' Gwyneth pushed herself up and sat on the couch beside Goldin. 'As it is, that's Alwyn's plan, and that is what I have to adhere to.'

William crossed his legs. He had his shoes on the chaise, something he had scolded Goldin for less than two weeks prior.

'If we kill him from the rooftop and we're not seen…' Goldin shrugged. 'It sounds to me like you have a decent alibi in that Richtus fellow. You'd have to try and forget about what you'd done, obviously, but I don't see any reason why you couldn't continue to pursue this girl.'

'I would need someone to protect her even after we make her a senator.' Gwyneth offered. 'The Badger Sett will still have until the end of the year to disgrace her, or worse. As her partner, you could keep her safe. She might even have you move in without her father in the house.'

Everything inside William was telling him this was wrong, but he supposed it was better to protect Kupela than betray the Finchleys and be forced to flee. It did help sway him a little, that in the future painted by his companions, he would be the wealthy partner of a senator. It was a chance to not only never need to kill again, but to change the course of his life entirely. He would have few worries, or at least less than he had now, and worries of what shirt to wear to a masquerade weren't true worries at all.

'Fine,' he relented. 'I'll shoot Sepo. Kupela told me he was an absolute shit once, so perhaps she won't be so upset.'

He flinched as Gwyneth and Goldin leapt into action. Blueprints were gathered into neat little bundles, equipment checked, outer clothes donned. They hauled him from his seat, refusing to give him an inch of calm where he could reconsider.

William tried to steady himself. 'So, what exactly is the plan?'

'Don't worry. Gwyneth has it sewn up.' Goldin tapped his nose with a conspiratorial wink.

Gwyneth opened the door with a flourish. 'It's a wonder what a family fortune can do.'

'It bloody stinks down here.' Goldin grimaced.

'This was your part of the plan.' Gwyneth had the foresight to bring herself a rag to tie about her face, but she had failed to warn either of the others.

'Yes, but I had no idea a posh imperial sewer would smell just like a village shit ditch,' he grumbled.

'It essentially is a shit ditch, just an underground one.' Gwyneth pressed on. 'I'm just glad they put these walkways in.'

She crossed over a small stone bridge that spanned the gutter of slowly drifting water and waste.

'I've heard the sewers in Valiance are just big pipes.' She shuddered. 'When they get a blockage, men have to go down in a rowboat. We would have had to swim here.'

William felt his stomach turning, and not for the first time since they had entered the sewer. He crossed the little bridge, his footsteps disturbing a rat that scampered from under an old metal dish. It crossed over his boot, but that was about the least disgusting thing that had happened to him since their arrival. He still balked at the moment he had put his hand against the wall to steady himself and it had come away black and slick.

'It should be up here.' Gwyneth halted at a ladder and peered up. She pulled a hand-drawn map from a bag she had slung over her shoulder and checked it. 'It's definitely up here. Remember, Goldin and I will do all the talking.'

'What if someone asks me about this?' William hefted the long slender case slung over his shoulder. It held the rifle he had bought, stocked with a dozen of its requisite brass bullets.

'Tell them it's a big brush for cleaning sewers, I don't know.' She set her hand on the first rung, which was an iron loop jutting out of the wall. 'Use your imagination, but don't speak if you don't have to.'

William waited as Gwyneth clambered up the ladder, followed closely by Goldin. He went last, forced to climb after the rungs had been marred by two pairs of soiled boots. He almost climbed into Goldin's feet and only missed getting his head daubed with excrement by inches. Gwyneth had stopped to lift up the manhole cover. Moments later, light bled down the shaft and they were moving upwards again.

Emerging into a modest walled garden on the surface, William almost cried out. He had expected to come across someone on route, but he hadn't expected there to be a man waiting for them.

'Thank you so much, again.' Gwyneth said to the man, who by the look of his attire, appeared to be a monk. 'If it weren't for you we would have missed the festivities.'

'It really is no problem. Anything for donors to the New Gods' Order.'

The monk was being obsequious, but was also gagging and gurning at the smell given off by the three assassins in his garden. In fact, now that William looked around, he realised it was a walled cemetery adjoined to the rectory at the rear of the cathedral.

'It's a thankless task keeping the city's sewers clear, but somebody's got to do it. I'm just glad there's kind souls like you out there.' Goldin grinned. 'Let me shake your hand.'

He stuck out his grubby palm to the monk, who visibly recoiled.

'It's alright.' Gwyneth swatted Goldin's hand away. 'You don't need to do that. Hence the baths required.'

'Ah, the baths.' The monk flicked a finger.

They followed him at a jaunty jog up an external staircase that led straight into the second floor of the rectory, then down a corridor to a room that housed five tin baths. Three were filled with steaming, soapy water, giving off a delicate floral scent.

'You can get cleaned up in here, then head straight out through the cathedral.' The monk planted his hands on his hips proudly. 'Should be ready in time for the speeches.'

'Thank you.' Gwyneth moved close to the monk, making his nose twitch. She produced a bottle of something alcoholic and expensive from her bag. 'I wouldn't have missed them for the world.'

'And the further donation?' the monk asked in a hushed voice, slipping the bottle into his robe.

'It's on its way.' She winked.

'Never has a member of the clergy been so kind and accommodating to us lowly municipal workers.' Goldin bowed theatrically. 'If you'd leave us to wash?'

'Certainly.' The monk turned to leave than paused, frowning at the rifle case on William's back. 'Say, what's in there?'

'Big toilet brush?' William shrugged.

'Ah. Most enlightening.' The monk tipped his head back wisely as he vacated the room and closed the door.

'We're really going to have a bath? Right now?' William scowled and averted his gaze as the others started to undress. 'And what if that monk identifies us?'

'He's sufficiently bought off.' Gwyneth wriggled out of her trousers. 'And the bottle's poisoned. Better safe than sorry.'

Goldin was completely naked and boldly clambered into a tub, his genitals swinging in the corner of William's eye.

'If we need to blend into a crowd, do you really want to be doing it smelling like a midden?' The little man flopped backwards into the soapy water, sending a wave out on all sides, soddening the floorboards.

'Fair point.' William kicked off his boots.

William emerged from the bathroom first, having been appraised of the plan while they washed. It was fairly simple, and the hard part had been done already. All they had to do now was cross the cathedral and climb the stairs for the bell tower. Once they were almost to the top, they could exit a door that allowed them onto the roof and a maze of scaffolding around the countless spires in varying arrays of disrepair.

The trio were dressed in brown monks' robes, and while they were comfortably warm the wool was uncomfortably scratchy. Gwyneth piled their soiled clothes in one of the spare tin baths, doused them with a bottle of ether from her bag, and set them aflame. It didn't take long before they were reduced to ashes. A little splash of bathwater ensured there wouldn't be any untimely fires while they were up on the roof.

Following Gwyneth's instructions, William led them out of the rectory onto a mezzanine for the choir. Thankfully, there was nobody up there, and anybody downstairs was huddled around the front door peering out to the festivities. There were a few guards just outside, but they didn't seem to be too attentive, and given the old bylaw, they might be the only ones close enough to cause any problems.

William skirted down one of the pews that followed the curve of the wall as quickly and quietly as he could. At the far end, he reached a door that led into a tower at the edge of the building. He lowered the handle softly and slipped through.

The room inside was small and round, merely a floor for the door to open onto between two spiral staircases, one each leading up and down. There were a few chests crowded under the steps coiling upwards, and a row of green and gold choir gowns were hung on hooks. William set foot on the first step and stopped dead; boards creaked overhead.

'It sounds like someone's coming down,' he whispered.

William scuttled back, unsure of what to do. They could try and talk their way past the descending monk, but even if they let the man continue he would still be a witness. If William was identified, he'd have to flee the city. They could hide, but there wasn't much room for it. Their best bet would have been to hurry back onto the balcony, but it would be hard to coordinate so quickly and quietly with the others. William didn't like it, but perhaps his best option would be to silently kill the holy man.

'Get under those coats,' Goldin hissed, shoving William towards the choir robes. It seemed the little man had taken William's desire to stay in the city after the assassination seriously, and would help him stay hidden even at the cost of his own anonymity.

William quickly did what he was told, ducking and pulling the gowns over himself in an attempt to hide. It quickly became apparent that the rifle case atop his back wouldn't tuck under the material neatly, but he could hear the monk's feet thundering down the steps right overhead now. The man really was in a hurry. In a last ditch attempt to obscure himself, William tossed the rifle case to Gwyneth who caught it and slung it onto her shoulder just as she came into view of the monk.

William held his breath. To any cursory inspection his presence there would have been obvious, but if Goldin and Gwyneth could keep the monk talking or move him along quickly, he might just stay hidden.

'What are you doing here?' The monk's footsteps stopped.

'We're on cleaning duty?' Goldin blurted.

'Cleaning duty?' The monk descended a few steps, slower now. 'On festival day?'

'It's less of an official duty and more a moral obligation.' Gwyneth smiled with her perfect pearls.

'Well, I don't recognise you.' The monk took another step down. William could see his sandals now and the grubby hem of his robe.

'And nobody's allowed up on the roof today. What is it you have there?'

He eyed the rifle case on Gwyneth's back.

'It's a big brush...' Gwyneth paused for a fraction of a second. 'It's for cleaning bells... and *I* don't recognise *you* as a matter of fact.'

'There's no bells up there. Only roof access, and you've no reason to be going up.'

'I had a vision.' Goldin puffed out his chest. 'I was to clean the golden bust of Lady Luck, the one sat atop this very cathedral, and when one of our gods sends me a commandment, I don't let anything or *anyone* stand in my way. And what were you doing on the roof anyway, you self-righteous, old thumb?'

William could only assume the monk was thickly set and bald.

'Pardon my friend here.' Gwyneth kicked Goldin's leg, forcibly. 'He will make reparation for that, I'm sure.'

Goldin drew a holy symbol on his chest. 'I've been a very naughty boy, but the question remains, what were you doing up there?'

'I was...' The monk moved down the last steps into the room proper.

William could see the side of his face through a gap in the gowns – if the monk turned his head it would surely be over – but he could also see the man was cradling something subtly behind his back. He squinted to make it out. It was a pouch, quite a large one with trailing drawstrings, but whether it held powder or grana, William couldn't be certain. The pouch leather was good quality and very thick; it didn't betray the shape of the contents. What was clear from the way the monk obfuscated it from the others, was that he had been up to no good with what was inside.

'I was up on the roof inspecting the tiles.' The monk nodded his head once, smartly. 'Wouldn't want one slipping free and killing a reveller, would we? As we all know, this roof is in a woeful state. It might not be wise for you to go up; you could loosen one of the tiles I was so diligently monitoring.'

'Look.' Goldin squared his shoulders. 'I'm going up there now, and if you don't toddle off down those stairs there's going to be trouble.'

'I'd like to see you try.' The monk sneered. It was an expression totally irreconcilable with the piety required to live one's life monastically, and it made him look more like a man dressed as a monk. He squared his shoulders too, straightened himself up. His fists started to bunch.

Before William could ambush the monk, Goldin threw a punch. It was deadly fast, and incredibly strong. The fact that the monk was roughly twice Goldin's height worked in his favour also, as his fist impacted directly into the monk's crotch.

If there was any doubt as to whether the man was a monk, he was certainly no eunuch. He doubled over with a low grunt, losing control of the leather pouch. It flung across the room towards William, landing on the floor with the familiar clink of little coins. It was so stuffed full that it didn't just sag and stop, it rolled over the lip of the floor and fell onto the downward-spiralling staircase. Its departure was noted with diminishing plops as it descended.

The questionable monk collapsed onto his knees, then rolled onto his side, huffing and wheezing. He didn't have much chance to feel the pain of it as Gwyneth clambered on top of him, waving a small bottle of potent ether under his nose. He struggled at first, making the liquid splash onto his face and into his mouth. There was little resistance after that, and he was soon comatose on the floor.

William emerged from beneath the gowns. 'Sorry I didn't help out much there, well, at all really.'

'Don't worry about it.' Gwyneth stoppered the ether bottle and put it back in her bag. 'If you want to stay in the city, I'll help you do it. If that means keeping you hidden, so be it.'

'We can handle ourselves.' Goldin gave a smug grin, standing over the fallen monk.

'I can see that.'

'Besides.' Gwyneth tucked a strand of hair behind her ear. 'Once we get on the roof and in position, then it's all you.'

William hoped he could make the shot. He hadn't practiced nearly as much with rifles as he had with pistols, and if the three shooter was anything to go by, this particular rifle might not be the most accurate.

Gwyneth peered downstairs. 'It seems nobody heard that little tussle, but we should retrieve that pouch he dropped. If anyone comes across it, they could come looking.'

'No, we've been delayed enough.' William hoped he was making the right decision. 'And once I fire, everyone will be alerted anyway. We should just get it done.'

They shared a nod and William led the way up the stairs. He was hurrying at first, but Gwyneth hissed a warning that other monks might be ahead and he continued more cautiously. He didn't want to be taken unawares.

When he reached the top floor, William eased the door open. As Gwyneth had predicted, there was a monk right outside. He was sat in a chair positioned to view anyone coming onto the roof and, if he had been awake, he would have spotted William straight away. As it was, his head lolled to one side and there was an empty bottle on the floor just beyond his limp fingertips. Whatever was inside had been consumed.

'Is he drunk?' Goldin whispered. 'Maybe that monk was up here bringing him supplies.'

'He couldn't have gotten drunk in that time.' Gwyneth crept to the fore, tiptoeing towards the chair. 'It could be ether. If he huffed too much he might have put himself to sleep? The inside of the bottle certainly looks oily enough.'

'We're lucky if he did.' Goldin followed her out, not bothering to crouch. 'But that doesn't mean there isn't anyone else up here still awake.'

William peered around the roof. Visibility was poor; with so many spires craning upwards it was like being stood in the centre of a dense forest. It didn't help that some were crooked or drooping over at dangerous angles as the frames inside perished. There was wooden scaffolding between and around most of the spires, all hastily thrown up to prevent total collapse. Walkways had been erected too, to allow access for workmen to undertake more long-term repairs. Multiple layers wound over and under each other and they ranged from well-built paths with hand rails to simple planks spanning gaps between scaffolds. Some walkways curled up like springs around the spires, giving access to the heavy sculptures perched precariously on top.

'There's no point just waiting here. We should find a good position quickly. Just keep an eye out.' William's hand retreated into his robes, drawing the three shooter. He had opted to bring it over his silver flintlock, reasoning that against a crowd of guards that would come running after a senator was killed, the increased rate of fire would be more beneficial than pinpoint accuracy. It was perhaps one of the few situations he could envision where quantity outstripped quality.

He selected a walkway that stretched to the front of the building and hurriedly crept along it. After a short way it twisted off to the right and he had to clamber up onto another to continue. There were two more similar twists and turns where he had to drop onto lower paths, and one stretch when he had to balance across a single plank to get to the next walkway. None of it lent itself towards a swift getaway, but if they stuck to Gwyneth's plan they wouldn't need to go far. She had brought a rope and grapple, the idea being that they would climb down the rear of the building and be right back in the sewer, free to flee.

William hopped down from the last walkway into a small, stone parapet with chipped gargoyles on the corners. It was as good a place as any to set up and take aim. Thankfully, it seemed they were alone up here. He stayed quiet nonetheless. Moving to the edge, he peered over the wall.

'We're later than I thought, Senator Falade is already speaking,' Gwyneth grumbled as she dropped into the parapet beside him.

'I need the rifle, quickly.'

'Don't rush yourself.' She knelt down and rested the case across her knee, taking care to ensure the clasps didn't click too loudly when she opened it. Inside, was the rifle and a few handfuls of spare ammunition.

Taking Gwyneth's advice, William took a moment to stock the pockets of his robe with bullets he might need for their escape. Once he was ready, he took up the rifle and loaded it. He moved slowly back to the edge and looked through the scope. Sepo had finished speaking and was returning to the bleachers. 'Damn it. He's going back to Kupela.'

'Don't worry about it.' Gwyneth's voice was soft, but William could tell from the haste of her breath that she was as nervous as he was. 'You can still shoot him when he sits down. Just don't shoot Kupela.'

'Do you think I want to?' William glared back at her.

'I can't think of anything worse for either of us.' She let out a wavering breath. 'Just take your time and only shoot when you're ready.'

There was a soft thud that made them both jump. It was Goldin joining them in the parapet. He added some whispered encouragement. 'You can do this. You're the best shot I know.'

William sighted up the rifle again, grumbling, 'With pistols maybe.'

'Don't doubt yourself.' Goldin patted his shoulder before moving to the far side of the parapet.

William wondered what he doubted more: his own ability, or the reliability of the rifle.

'And don't linger too long. The longer you sit there looking, the more chance the imperial sharpshooters have of spotting you,' Gwyneth added before joining Goldin. While her advice was always useful, it didn't exactly give William the confidence boost he required.

He took his aim, glad that Sepo wasn't large enough in the scope to have too many discernible features. The man had been nice to him and that made it all the harder, but this was surely William's best option. He almost pulled the trigger, but Sepo stood up, throwing his aim off. The man was clapping now. William saw the old emperor parading across the stage on horseback. Seconds later, he would pass in front of Sepo, obscuring any shot. William chose to wait, risking discovery with every second.

The horse trotted by. William spied Kupela in the periphery of his scope and though he longed to see her, he daren't put her into the focal point. He had told her himself not to point a gun at something you didn't want a bullet in. He swallowed, sniffed, and let out a subtle cough. His nose always seemed to get stuffy when he was nervous. Deciding not to torture himself anymore with the sight of Kupela and Sepo together, he readied himself to shoot.

The emperor passed by, there was a clear line of sight on Sepo again. William held his breath, adjusted his aim to accommodate for the distance and minimal wind. His finger tensed on the trigger, then relaxed. He watched as Sepo sat back down and leant to exchange a few words with Kupela. Even at this distance, he could see them chuckling together.

Suddenly, it all felt very wrong. Shooting Sepo hadn't felt right to begin with, but it had been a bearable guilt, one William was used to swallowing. Now, in seeing even the merest connection between him and Kupela, William saw Sepo as more than just a target, as more than a stepping stone to an easy life. He couldn't do it. He wouldn't do it.

As he finally came to terms with his decision, the muscles in his shoulders and back loosened. It was like he had been administered an antidote to a poison that had gripped him for years. He lowered the rifle by degrees.

'Is everything alright?' Gwyneth asked, tentatively.

There was a slight tightening of muscles again as William realised he would have to explain himself. Perhaps he wouldn't have to tell her the whole truth.

'I can't do it,' he voiced, and before anyone had the chance to suspect the truth, he followed it up with a lie. 'This rifle isn't trustworthy enough. Sepo's sat too near Kupela; he's sat too near the other senators. If I shoot him and miss… we might never get the chance to kill him later.'

Gwyneth opened her mouth to speak, but William felt compelled to continue. He didn't let her get a word out.

'Actually… there's more to it than that.' Now that he had broached the idea of not shooting Sepo, it seemed all the easier to admit that he didn't want to continue with the contract at all. Though William had only known Kupela a short time, he liked her. She liked him too. It might have been the fantasy of a young fool, but with her, he could see the path to a more normal future. A future where he could put all this darkness behind him and be happy. For that, it was worth risking all he had. 'I'm calling it off. I'm calling off the whole–'

Just then, there was a gunshot from nearby. William cast about, expecting to see a guard or armed monk that had followed them onto the roof. What he found instead, high up on a walkway, was another gunman. He was tall, with cropped blonde hair, and a heavily scarred face. He definitely wasn't an imperial guard; he was dressed too casually in mustard, cable-knit woollens. Smoke was trailing from the barrel of a rifle in his grip, and his sight was still trained on the senate.

With horror, William realised this gunman could be working as a backup for Gwyneth, or worse, for the Badger Sett with the express purpose killing Kupela. In that moment, he wanted to raise his rifle and shoot the gunner dead, but he wanted something else more. He needed to know if Kupela was hurt.

William turned his rifle on the scene outside the senate. Thank the gods, Kupela looked uninjured. Her father was clutching his chest in shock, blood was spattered across him, but it was spattered across many others too. It wasn't his own.

Just a short distance away, the Emperor roared. His huge white horse had been shot. Blood sprayed from its hind quarters as it kicked, brayed, and bucked. The emperor was being thrown around like a rag doll, but he wasn't unseated. It looked like he had been lashed to the beast's back to stop him from falling.

Guards shied back and forth on the stage, each too nervous to shoot at the beast lest they kill their emperor, and too wary to grab the reins and be trampled under massive hooves. The horse reared and bolted, galloping at full speed to get away from the encircling men. It launched itself from the high stage, blood misting from it. The drop was easily as far as the height of a town house, and horse and rider spiralled together. The fall was stopped abruptly, not by the ground, but by a wrought iron fence that had been erected for the purposes of preventing intruders and keeping the emperor safe. Now, both emperor and horse were impaled on it, bodies drooping, and entrails with them.

One of the gargoyles near William exploded into dust and rubble. The guardsmen below had seen him. He backed away, his stomach rolling. He could hear the rival gunman laughing then, not a sinisterly victorious chuckle, but the full maniacal laughter of delight. William rounded with his rifle, incensed by the joy that could be taken in the suffering of others. He took aim at the man, who was still unaware of his presence, and fired.

The gun clapped, spitting out smoke and a bullet. In very much the same way as the three shooter had, the bullet flew wide, striking a crooked spire and sending out chips of terracotta. William surmised, if he had decided to shoot Sepo, that his bullet would have flown just wide enough to kill Kupela.

The scarred gunman reeled around, realising the shot that had missed him had come from his very own roof. He spied William and readied his rifle. It seemed a considerably more expensive gun than William's, not only because it had been accurate, but because he had already fired one shot and wasn't stopping to reload.

There was another hail of gunfire from the guards in the square; they had now seen the emperor's real killer. Bullets cracked against the spire behind the scarred assassin. A few tiles fell loose. One slipped down the sloped edge, caught on a protruding nail and kicked into the air. It struck the gunman across the back before he had chance to sight on William. A bullet flew far wide, going somewhere into the crowds below.

'Run!' William yelled.

Gwyneth and Goldin had already been scrambling for cover, but as William turned to flee they quickly did the same. The little man was tossed up onto the nearest walkway by the combined efforts of William and Gwyneth; she followed second, climbing up using William's cupped palms. He went after, tossing the rifle away and hauling up with both arms. The three ran, using the countless spires for protection. William pulled out his three shooter and sent a couple of bullets in the direction of the gunman. He didn't think any hit, but they might have bought him extra time.

Gwyneth's bag of supplies had been left on the parapet, leaving no option for scaling the rear of the building. She directed them towards the door for the little tower. It was now the only way down. As Goldin crossed the narrow plank, he stumbled and fell forwards, gaining the opposite walkway by inches. Gwyneth scooped him up as she made it across, a bullet narrowly missing her as she bent. A spire sheltered the pair while they took a breath.

Glancing across and seeing no sign of the scarred gunman, William sprinted to join them. He reached the pair without incident, and looked back as the gunman emerged from behind another spire, closer than before. William fired the last of the bullets loaded in his three shooter. It missed. The scarred gunman's rifle retorted with an impotent click; empty. He had clearly forgotten to count in his zeal. With a curse the man concealed himself again to reload.

'Go,' William shouted, turning to run.

Gwyneth burst through the door into the tower. William was in moments after, slamming it shut behind Goldin.

'Who the bloody hell was that?' the little man wheezed, bent double.

'No idea.' Gwyneth took the stairs.

'Not a cousin of yours?' William asked, ushering Goldin ahead and following down.

'No he was not.'

'Well, I haven't got a clue then. Maybe an assassin here for the Hunt got bored and decided to make a scene.'

'It is a fallow year after all,' Goldin puffed. 'No better time for big scenes.'

'Yeah but, killing the emperor? That's not even blacklist material, that's a price on your head until death.'

'He killed the emperor?' Gwyneth stopped on the floor with the unconscious monk. 'And what about Sepo?'

'Still alive, I think.' William took a moment to reload. 'He was clutching his chest, but...'

Boots were stamping on the spiral stairs far below. Armed guards were heading up to kill the emperor's assassin, or any other assassins who happened to be up there.

'We can only hope that Sepo's heart was giving out from the shock of it.' Gwyneth pushed open the door to the choir balcony and peered out. 'If he survives this he'll hire more guards, like you said. It'll be nearly impossible to kill him.'

'You still want him dead?' Goldin pulled a knife from his boot for all the good it would do against countless pistol-toting guardsmen.

'That's the deal, isn't it?' Gwyneth looked at William. 'Are you ready?'

He flicked the loaded cylinder back into place and cocked the three shooter. Deciding to keep his wish to abandon the contract to himself for the time being, he nodded and said, 'Ready as I'll ever be.'

Footsteps from above joined the thundering footsteps from below. Not only were the guards still coming, so was the gunman.

Gwyneth thrust the door open and William raced onto the balcony. He checked downstairs for guards. People had crowded into the building after the emperor was shot, and though guards were fighting to get in, the press was so tight they were struggling to pass through the archway from the street. William dashed towards the rectory door, craning to look back every few yards in case anyone followed from the tower. Gwyneth was at his heels, but Goldin was lagging. William waited by the door to cover the little man and make sure he made it in one piece.

Just as Goldin was approaching, the door from the tower burst open and guards spilled out onto the choir balcony. William fired one shot, hitting a man in the leg. He tumbled over the edge and fell into the crowd below. Another guard, who was aiming a rifle, was shot in the chest by William's second bullet. He had been aiming for the man's head, but the kill was just as decisive nonetheless.

Goldin panted into the rectory just as the sound of gunshots erupted in the tower. The gunman was clashing with the remaining guards. One guardsman, who had just come out onto the balcony to see his two companions cut down by William, fired on the fleeing assassins. He missed, and was shot in the back by the pursuing gunman.

William disappeared into the rectory. He didn't even stop to reload, he still had the one shot and they were almost at the sewers. Pounding along the corridor and out onto the veranda, they hastened down the steps. Goldin was swift between the gravestones and got to the manhole cover first. He heaved it aside, the metal plate rolling onto the grass like a big coin, landing downside up.

Gwyneth went into safety first, slipping over the filthy rungs two at a time. William made Goldin go next; the little man only had a knife so couldn't be left in the garden alone.

William almost threw himself into the hole when he heard the door to the rectory open, but he couldn't for fear of being shot in the back. The gunman had caught up with him and needed to be dealt with. He rounded on his pursuer.

The scarred man glowered at him, a wicked smile spreading across his face, his rifle ready and aimed. *William of Fairshore.* I knew it was you, even from such a distance.'

'I don't know you.' William's hand twitched eagerly, the gun hidden in the folds of his robes, hungry. 'We have no quarrel, there's no need to fight. You need to get out of here as much as I do.'

He could hear Gwyneth shouting up to him from the bottom of the ladder, but couldn't tell what she was saying.

'I'll take my leave as soon as I've settled this.' The gunman cocked his rifle, plainly taking enjoyment in his advantageous position.

William thought about raising his pistol and firing it fast, like at a noon standoff, but he knew in such situations one needed to rely on their firearm. He didn't even trust his to make its mark at four paces, let alone the distance between him and the gunman. There was nothing to do but concede defeat; he wouldn't be winning this shootout.

Instead of taking his aim he took a step back, pulled his arms tight to his body and allowed himself to fall through the yawning manhole.

The world went from bright to black. He tried to claw for the rungs on his way down. His foot caught one and twisted up at an agonising angle, but he fell by so quickly it flicked free again without breaking. His fingers struck iron rungs, unable to find purchase. If he had, his arms might have been pulled from their sockets. Thankfully, his chin didn't catch a rung either. What did catch, was his robe on an outstretched barb of metal. It scraped his back nastily and pulled the fabric up over his head, fortunately not garrotting him as it did so, before ripping a great hole in the wool and releasing him. It was an agonising wound, but slowed his momentum enough that nothing was broken when he landed.

He hit the sewer floor, crumpled and groaning. He wouldn't have been able to pick himself up for another twenty minutes probably. It would have been more than enough time for the gunman to follow him down and execute him, but Goldin and Gwyneth had other ideas. They hauled him away, despite his protests. Goldin even managed to find a long, mucky staff, which was presumably the handle of some big toilet brush used for cleaning the sewers. He wedged it under William's arm for a crutch. Gwyneth supported him on the other side.

William was mostly dragged away from the base of the ladder, but once his friends had gotten him upright, he had just about enough energy to stagger with their support.

Gwyneth took him on a convoluted route through the sewers. He assumed that even she didn't know where they were going at this point; all her blueprints and maps had been left behind. It didn't matter so much that they were lost, but that they lost the gunman. If he had pursued them into the sewers, he certainly never found them.

When the three finally emerged at street level, they were in the worst of slums. They had made it to the far outreaches of the sewer, where the roads became the sort with open gutters of faeces. It was a fortunate turn of events, as the three of them were not the only ones looking worse for wear and covered in excrement. Though William didn't spot any other than himself with gaping wounds.

Bleeding and exhausted, he knew there was still a long way to go before they were safe. Or rather, as safe as they could be. With another stint under Richtus' care as his only meagre reward, William grit his teeth, and let Gwyneth lead him back into the city.

# 1683
## KUPELA FALADE

Kupela had been nothing but worried for days. As such, her duties, which were even more pressing than normal, were falling by the wayside. Her father had asked her to employ more guards for the house and arrange for messengers to be on hand at all times. She had done none of it. It was hard to concentrate on anything when there was something dark lurking in the back of her mind, doubly so when there were two things playing on her anxieties. She hoped that today, at least one would be put to bed.

When the emperor had been killed, her father had been gripped with a tightness in his chest. Richtus' cursory examination had drawn no conclusions. When she had later sought him out for further information, he told her William had taken a turn for the worse. As Richtus had been too busy attending other senators injured in the confusion and panic, she had no further news on either of her men.

That morning, she received word that Richtus would visit her father again. The glimmer of hope that came with it spurred her into action. She responded to numerous notes from well-wishers, arranged for a shipment of her father's favourite Djurundi fruits to be sent for, and went to the senate to petition for more messengers and guards to be stationed at the house. As imperial clerks took an age to do anything, even in less tumultuous times, she also had job advertisements put up in three of the city's forums. With any luck, she would be able to secure contractors to work under Silvio in addition to the city guard.

When she returned, Richtus had arrived. Her intention had been to head to her father's room and discover the prognosis, but the surgeon general had left strict instructions with the butler that he wasn't to be disturbed. She was forced to wait impatiently in the foyer for any news.

She fretted and paced, wringing her hands for a time, desperate for the news to be good. Even if it was bad, it was better to know it than be left wondering. The standing clock in the hall tolled as an hour passed, then two. A servant brought her a whiskey and orange, but her stomach roiled and she couldn't drink it. The longer Richtus was cloistered away examining her father, the worse she assumed his prospects.

By five o'clock, she'd had enough. She set down her glass, which she had been carefully cradling as she paced, and headed up the stairs to her father's bedchamber. She crossed paths with Silvio on the way – he was patrolling the middle floor – but didn't stop to speak with him as she normally might.

Arriving at her father's bedchamber, she knocked forcefully.

'What is it?' Richtus snapped from within. 'I cannot be interrupted!'

'Richtus, it's Kupela. How's my father faring?' She set her hand on the door handle. 'Is he decent? May I enter?'

'No you may not.' There was a lot of indistinguishable ranting, then suddenly the door thrust open. Richtus slipped out, but he closed it behind him swiftly, obscuring Kupela's view. 'I am very busy. Unlike my son, I do not appreciate interruptions.'

'I just want to know how my father is.' She squared up to Richtus. She couldn't quite believe that Richter had been his progeny. He was so kind, and handsome too – tall, with a warm smile, and eyes that had sparkled in her company – nothing at all like the crooked little surgeon. 'I want to see him.'

'You can't, girl. This is very important business I am up to.' He squared himself as well, which looked like it took substantial effort given his usual hunch. For a second she thought he might strike her, but he deflated with a heavy breath. 'Look, your father is fine and dandy. His episode at the senate was very much related to the stress of it; his heart is fine. I am here on other business and it is too important for you to interrupt. Understand?'

'I understand.' She was relieved, but taken aback by the surgeon's outburst. 'I just…'

'You just nothing. Now leave us be.' He lowered the door handle ready to retreat inside the bedchamber, then paused a moment. 'If it makes any difference, your little *friend* William will be out of my care within the week. Why not write him a poem or something you fawning girls are wont to do?'

The door slammed in her face. Kupela was furious with the vile surgeon, but her anger was tempered greatly by two bouts of good news. A smile pushed to her lips for the first time in days and she supposed that she'd better get back to work. She didn't want to be stuck hiring mercenaries and guards when she could be spending her time with William. It was better to get it all out of the way now.

'Love you, Father!' She called through the panelling then hurried off to her tasks.

The next morning, as Kupela ate a light breakfast of honeyed toast and figs, the butler came to her with a salver stacked with envelopes. Most were the usual missives from court attendees: invitations to balls, brunches, and backgammon. There were also a few tardy letters wishing her father a speedy recovery. What was less expected, however, were the three letters responding to her adverts in the forums. She admired punctuality, and these applications had been incredibly prompt. Wasting no time, she made special dispensation to interview the prospective protectors that afternoon.

Silvio and Bolek accompanied her to the Via Principale Forum, and – once she had commandeered a room – sat in the rear corners to inspect the applicants. The former had his legs crossed casually, his rapier laid across his knees. The latter had his tattooed arms folded, cord-like muscles defined beneath the ink. She sat between them at a little desk.

'So, what experience do you have?' Kupela asked the first candidate with a bright smile.

'I don't have much experience in guarding, but I'm strong like an ox and have transferrable skills from past professions.'

The applicant had a strong accent and was huge, both in height and width. He was surely strong, but his bulk was mostly tallow. He had great rolls of fat around his neck and the back of his bald head making him look half melted. His silhouette put Kupela in mind of a centrepiece she had seen at a court dinner. While it was certain that Antoine Devall's explorations were an asset to the Empire, it had been a mistake to create a likeness using the medium of soft cheese. Pushing the image – and the smell – from her mind, she continued, 'Why don't you tell me about these past professions?'

'I was a shepherd for a while; I can get people where I want them. Then a poacher, so good experience with guns. I killed a bear once.' He cracked his knuckles. They were tattooed in similar shades of blue and green to those worn by Bolek, but they weren't as fine and looked as though they had been self-inflicted.

One hand said *debt* across his four fingers, only it was almost illegible. Kupela assumed it had been scrawled with his non-dominant hand. In contrast, the letters on the fingers of his other hand were quite well formed. The only problem was that he didn't have enough fingers to properly spell *collector*. Most fingers had two letters each and even then his thumb had to be included.

'Let's say my family was in danger, perhaps an assassin enters the house. Could you shoot him if needed?'

'I have no problem inflicting pain.' He stared at the blank wall as if recalling some memory. 'One time, I broke all the bones in a woman's arm: the big upper bone, two in the lower arm – skinny ones. There were lots of tiny bones in the hand and wrist; I used a hammer to get them.'

'Excellent.' Kupela smiled nervously, glad that her existing guards had accompanied her to the meeting. 'This is all tremendous. We're going to consider your application thoroughly… and we'll be in touch.'

'Thank you for the opportunity.' The man stood, gave a little dip of his head to the two guards, and left.

The chair he had been sat on wasn't the same shape as it had been before. Its joints had all slipped and one cross member had pulled out completely. The legs were splayed in four directions, moments away from utter collapse.

'Not quite what I was expecting.' Kupela rubbed at her head. 'I hope the others aren't so… colourful. Bolek, could you exchange that chair and send in the next applicant?'

She looked down at the parchment where she had expected to write a few notes – she hadn't. There was little to review either way and she put a cross next to the man's name.

Bolek rolled up his sleeves even further and picked up the chair. One of the legs fell off, clattering to the floor noisily. He kicked it into the far corner then followed over to dump the chair in a heap. He retrieved another and set it opposite Kupela before opening the door for the second applicant.

'Next, please,' he called through.

Both remaining applicants came to the door.

'I need to see you one at a time,' Kupela said, 'it doesn't matter which one's first, I'll treat you both on your merits.'

'We come as a pair, actually.' One of the applicants, a young woman about the same age as Kupela, grinned. Her teeth were perfect and her face unmarred by scars. She didn't look like she had been in a fight in all her life. 'If that's alright? We're partners.'

'Not romantically,' the other, a diminutive man, added. 'We're just business partners, I suppose. I've nothing against her, but I like my women with a bit more meat on them.'

Kupela frowned; it was positively comical that the little man thought they could be mistaken for lovers. One was a slim, short young woman, with a pretty face and fine attire. The other was dishevelled, with messy near-black hair that betrayed a thinning patch on top terribly. His lip was cleft and she could see a tooth poking through the gap. He might have been quite a looker back in a Garland hamlet-slum, but in Vitale even the beggars weren't so unfortunate.

'You can interview us together.' The young woman strode in, and her short associate followed before any arguments could be made.

'I suppose so.' Kupela shrugged. They couldn't be any worse than her first applicant, and the whole process would be much quicker this way. 'Bolek, would you fetch another chair?'

'It's quite alright, boss.' The little man detoured. 'I'll use this one.'

He dragged the crooked chair back to the middle of the room then retrieved the fourth leg from the corner. Dropping to the floor so that he could see under the seat, he wedged the leg back into the hole it had fallen from. Then, he picked up the chair and slammed it onto the floor three times to hammer in all the legs as securely as possible. When he was satisfied, he hopped on. The thing sagged to one side but somehow held.

'Sorry about him.' The young woman giggled at his antics. 'He's a little—'

'Colourful,' Kupela commented, though this man was an entirely different kind of colourful to the last. 'Why don't you tell me how you met and what experience you have and we'll take it from there?'

She checked her parchment for the young woman's name. 'Gwyneth, why don't you start us off? I see here you're a Finchley, any relation to the senator? I've met him a few times, he's a *colourful* gentleman too.'

'Yes, I am, though only distantly,' Gwyneth replied, flashing a perfect, pearly smile. 'I used to work for one of his businesses. Finchley and Finchley, have you heard of it?'

'Is that the law firm?' Kupela tapped her lip with a finger.

'No, that's Finchley, Finchley, and Finchley. I'm talking about Finchley and Finchley Estates and Lettings. Anyway, I had to supervise a transfer of capital from Lothagia to Kumaine. We could have taken the mountains, or gone around through Vitulus, but time was of the essence. Grod was the swiftest choice.'

'That's where I come in.' The little man grinned. 'She needed a guard, so me and a bunch of pals got our guns and joined them on their travels.'

'As it turns out, toting a gun is a lot more enjoyable than balancing a book,' Gwyneth added. 'When we got to Kumaine, I tendered my resignation and have been a coach guard ever since. We both have experience with pistols, though my friend here favours a blunderbuss, and I am terribly good at sticking to the shadows and working with a knife.'

Kupela put her hand to her mouth and stroked under her chin with her thumb as she thought, tracing a thin scratch on her neck.

Everyone had a few bumps and bruises from the chaos after the emperor's death; this one wasn't far from healed.

'It's not so exciting guarding a Vitale manor house,' she said. 'If all goes to plan there aren't any exciting gunfights to be had. Are you sure it's the job for you?'

'Book balancing is bland, but did come with its comforts.' Gwyneth shrugged. 'Coach guarding can be exciting at times, but there's still a lot of boredom, and very little in the way of comfort. We're after a happy medium, and posting up in a fine townhouse suits us grand.'

'At least you're honest.' Kupela scratched a line next to Gwyneth's name; it could still be turned into either a tick or a cross. 'What would you say if I offered you a job but declined your associate?'

'I wouldn't take it.' Gwyneth's reply was resolute.

'Hang on a minute,' the little man protested, turning to Gwyneth. 'Just because I'm not good enough doesn't mean you should miss out.'

Kupela noted the loyalty in both, and though she still had questions to ask, decided they would both be getting a job. She and her father needed loyal people more than anything. In times such as these, when the emperor had left a void of power, it was better to have a faithful eccentric than a treacherous expert.

# 1683
## WILLIAM OF FAIRSHORE

William had walked, albeit slowly, from Richtus' surgery all the way to Kupela's front door. The day was a little too cool for it, but he was filled with so many elixirs he could barely feel the cobbles underfoot. All in all, he was fighting fit, and if he didn't twist his torso he could just about forget his part-healed wounds. The nausea that came with a cocktail of medicines had all but subsided too, leaving only the gentle fluttering of butterflies as he reached up and knocked.

'William!' Kupela beamed as she recognised him, throwing the door open and rushing out. 'I'm so glad you're alright!'

She wrapped her arms around him tightly. Pain surged from his back, forcing out a little squeal.

'What's wrong?' She relaxed her grip.

'I have a cut on my back. Richtus had to take a tissue sample to synthesise better medicines and went a little overboard with that scalpel of his. I have stitches up half of my back.' He stretched his arms out, rolling his shoulders. 'I'm full of restoratives. They've worked wonders for everything else, I'm sure my back will be well soon enough.'

'I'm glad.' She kissed him, squeezing him again, but softer this time. 'What's this?'

She patted his front.

'My flintlock.' He opened the flap of his jacket to show the silver barrel gleaming. He had the underarm holster modified to fit it after the three shooter had been lost in the sewer. 'I can get rid of it if you want me to. I just thought – given what's happened – the extra protection might help.'

'It's a good idea.' She pushed his jacket closed, her hand on the back of his. 'I feel safer with it here, and with you.'

'We should go in.' William shivered, though he felt warmer just for being in her company. 'There's no point lingering on the step and catching our deaths.'

Kupela's face fell, her expression pinched with worry. 'Be it from the cold or this unknown assassin.'

He meshed their fingers together, offering a reassuring smile. Kupela didn't need to know that he had come face to face with the very man, nor that the assassin in question had recognised him. William was armed, alert, and knew that Kupela's guards would likely do as much as he would to protect her.

'It is awfully frightening this business with the emperor. Nobody knows who did it – the Assassins' Guild are claiming it wasn't one of their own. That's what my father says anyway,' she explained, drawing him into the house. 'Oh, he wanted me to apologise for what happened to you.'

'What do you mean?' William had momentarily forgot in the madness of the last few days, and thought she meant his sliced back.

'Your reaction to the dessert.' She rolled her eyes. 'You don't have to act tough. We both know it's been awful for you. I'm certain he'd apologise himself, but he's working late at the senate tonight.'

She stopped in the wide entrance hall at the centre of the four couches. 'Does this cocktail of elixirs you've been taking prohibit a cocktail of a more alcoholic variety?'

'I think I can manage a whiskey and orange.' William winked. That wasn't at all like him, but somehow it felt right with her.

The past week had been a complete haze. Gwyneth had pulled a few strings and managed to get William back under Richtus' care. The cut on his back was healing well and the fresh limp he had gained had been killed with countless tinctures and elixirs. All it had cost was a significant quantity of gold from Gwyneth's personal coffers, and a full week of feeling like death. Only now was William's stomach becoming stable enough for food and drink, and damn was he ready for it.

'I couldn't trouble you for something to eat as well, could I? Richtus is fairly conservative when it comes to patient rationing. I fear I'll be asleep in minutes if just have a whiskey.'

'I'll see the cook.' Kupela trailed light fingers over his chest as she moved away. 'You go straight up to the study. Maybe you could start the whiskeys? I'd like to try one of yours.'

William watched her departure, swaying subtly in her dress. She looked back at him as she slipped through one of the hidden doors in the wall, teasing her bottom lip with her teeth. The click of the latch broke his reverie, and a little dumbly, he headed up the stairs. Once he was on the first floor, he could hear people talking above – likely Silvio and one of the other guards. Taking the next flight, he noticed that one of the voices was female. The closer he got, the more familiar it became.

He reached the head of the stairs and peered down a corridor that cut off to the left. What he saw there made his heart drop. It was Gwyneth and Goldin.

'What in all the hells are you two doing here?' he hissed, lunging forwards and grabbing them both by their jackets. He dragged them into an alcove that housed a bust of the late Emperor D'Elia; it was almost knocked over with his elbow, teetering on its plinth.

'Us? What are you doing here?' Gwyneth pulled her sleeve free from William's grip – he noticed then that it was starched and new. 'You're supposed to be resting up.'

'Richtus discharged me.' William puffed out his chest, though his back felt tight.

Inside, he was panicking. His first port of call, when he had felt well enough, was to come and visit Kupela, and it had nothing to do with the Finchleys' assassination. When he had decided not to shoot on the rooftop, he had considered the contract broken. It was over; he wouldn't make another attempt on Sepo's life. This might be his only chance at happiness. It didn't matter that it might enrage the Finchleys.

Of course, his fellow killers didn't know that he planned to retire so imminently. On the cathedral roof, he had danced around the issue for too long and had missed the opportunity to reveal his intentions. It was something that had played on his mind terribly while he had been confined to a sick bed, and he was determined to set things right. He couldn't tell the truth just yet, however. Gwyneth wouldn't react well, and it wasn't a good idea to have a row about a man's assassination in his very own house.

Deciding it would be best to keep the charade alive for now, William slipped effortlessly into the role of diligent assassin. 'I came here to finish the job.'

'And you didn't think it was worth coming back to the hotel to see us beforehand?' Gwyneth shook her head and started to pace. Her shiny black boots were brand new too, and the neat trousers. 'What if our whole plan had changed?'

'Has it?'

'No, but you shouldn't have come here without warning me. What if we'd rigged the place with explosives?'

'Did you?'

'No,' she hissed.

'Then what are you doing here?' William jabbed out a finger. 'You could have ruined *my* plans'– they had –'you're the ones coming here unannounced.' They were.

'An opportunity arose.' Gwyneth stopped pacing.

'We work here.' Goldin spread his arms, showing off his attire that matched Gwyneth's. William noticed then that the pair of them carried flintlocks at their hips.

'What? *Goldin…*' William breathed, exasperated. 'Kupela will be up here any minute. You need to tell me what's going on, and then you need to get out.'

'It's not Goldin.' Goldin grinned. 'Our new-new aliases arrived the other day. I'm Che Long, for the time being.'

'Che?' William shook his head. 'And what are you?'

'Just Gwyneth, I thought my name would help me more than any alias. It did.' She pulled an envelope out of her pocket. 'I have yours here, actually. I suspected this might be our first chance to see you. You're here more often than you are at the hotel.'

'That's because I'm working on the contract… and you two are jeopardising it.' William snatched the envelope and stuffed it into his trouser pocket.

'We're just here to help.' Goldin leant back and peered down the corridor. 'Things are getting a little hairy; we thought you might appreciate it.'

'Dunstan's been true to his word and released your– our– *my* uncle, *our* prisoner. He'll be back with the Badger Sett now, and they'll know what we're up to.' Gwyneth peered over her shoulder and lowered her voice further. 'So, we need to get this job done quickly. We were going to snoop around, see what we can find, and help coordinate another plan. You're still in charge of the operation.'

'Unless Sepo drops into our laps, that is.' Goldin sniffed and wiped his nose with the back of his hand. 'If he asks me to tickle his chest hairs with a sabre, I'm not going to pass it up. Until then, I'm going to scout out the baths downstairs. I hear there's a hot-coal steam room and I'm hoping to try it out. Perhaps I'll lay low in a soapy spring.'

'Pretend you don't know us for now.' Gwyneth smiled; she had her best teeth in. 'We're here to help you, and I'm sorry we didn't get a message to you first. It all just happened.'

'I should go. Kupela won't be long.' William emerged from the alcove, feeling queasy. He enjoyed being William the Circus-Sharpshooter-come-Coach-Guard far more than he had enjoyed being William of Fairshore. And there was something about his two lives clashing that felt entirely wrong. One had to win out, and he didn't like the way the scales were tipping.

He came out of the corridor to the landing and hurried through the door into the study. Once inside, he hurried to the drinks cabinet and rapidly sliced some oranges. Kupela came in just as he deposited the first segments into the glasses.

'Where's your whiskey? I can't find it.' William muddled the juice from the fruit roughly.

Kupela padded over, reached by his shoulder and plucked a liquor-filled decanter from the shelf right in front of him.

'Sorry, I'm just tired.' He crushed the orange even harder, sharing what he hoped was an affable smile. 'From the elixirs.'

'We don't need a drink, just yet.' She stopped his muddling with a gentle touch. Coaxing his hand away from the bar, she wound it around the small of her back. 'That's better. Let's just sit a while.'

She backed away, pulling him to the couches. Her eyes were fixed on his, impossibly large and brown and beautiful. William felt his breath heightening, felt that excited tightness in his chest. She overbalanced him easily and they fell onto the sofa together. The heat of her body pushed against him and her hands pressed on his shoulders, pinning him to the cushions. She bit the air playfully, ferociously, and then stole a kiss, one that he was more than happy to lose.

Buoyed by her escalating hail of kisses, he pulled her astride him. She squeaked at the force and excitement of it. Her hands caressed down his sides, nails scratching down him, hungrily. Kissing his neck, breath hot across his throat, she fumbled with his shirt buttons.

William traced the curve of her bodice, hands ghosting over the swell of a breast. She pulled back a little, leaving his shirt half buttoned, her eyes locking with his. For a moment he thought he had gone too far, but her nose and mouth twitched into another lustful growl. She tore his jacket back and undid the clasp on his holster, letting his pistol hang to the side. Her hands gripped his shirt collar, ready to tear it open and to hell with the buttons.

The moment was interrupted by footsteps drumming up the stairs.

'Kupela!' It was her father shouting.

Suddenly, all the heat in the air was gone. William and Kupela pushed each other away, wriggled to sit up straight. William neatened his hair and shifted to the far end of the sofa, hastily buttoning his shirt. Kupela sat squarely and quickly wafted creases from her skirts. Her father burst into the study then.

'Kupela, I–' He paused, taking in the two young adults sat so conspicuously next to one another on the couch, still panting from previous excitement and fresh embarrassment. 'I'm sorry.'

Sepo turned and almost left the room. He clearly didn't know what to do with himself.

'It's alright father, we're just talking.' Kupela offered a bright smile. It was an obvious lie, but it dispelled some of the tension. 'What did you want?'

'I have the most tremendous news.' Sepo's breathing was even more heightened than William's. He swept into the room, and passed the couch for the liquor cabinet. He topped up one of the pre-muddled glasses with whiskey and knocked back a drink. 'But first, William, I'm so glad you're well.'

Sepo put a hand to his chest and slumped against the cabinet with a sigh.

'Father, are you alright?' Kupela stood. 'You should sit down.'

'Yes, yes. I'm quite alright, and I'm fine standing.' Sepo grinned and giggled. He slapped the side of the liquor cabinet. 'This thing is sturdy enough to keep me up despite my fawn's legs. I just can't quite believe it.'

'Believe what? What happened?' Kupela looked as worried as Sepo was excited.

'It was finally determined that the rumours about D'Elia were true. He had no heirs; not even a bastard. We voted today on his successor.' Sepo moved forwards and leant on the side of the desk, panting between words. 'The announcement has gone out to the news-sheets already and there will be an official address tomorrow.'

'What is it?' Kupela prompted.

'They voted for me.' Sepo finally got his words out, a long satisfied sigh following them. 'I'm the one they've chosen. I'm the emperor.'

Kupela almost fell from the shock of it. William caught her and guided her back to the couch. They collapsed onto the seat together. Her hands were fidgeting around her mouth, her breaths coming out as desperate laughter. Finally, she said, 'We must celebrate. We must find the finest wine and get the cook to make the most extravagant banquet.'

'We shall, we shall.' Sepo licked his lips, nodding frantically. 'But I need to calm down, this is all hitting me too quickly. I should rest up for an hour or so, let it all sink in. By the gods, my nerves! I'm sweating. I should clean myself up before we dine. Why don't we reconvene at ten? We can celebrate long into the night.'

'Alright.' Kupela was still giggling. 'Does that sound good to you, Will?'

'Yes,' he whispered.

While William's external reaction was akin to Kupela and Sepo's, his feeling was more of relief than exhilaration. Sepo had been elected emperor, no doubt under the influence of Alwyn's Finchleys. It meant Kupela had been elevated to a whole new station without the need for her father's death. It surely made the contract null and void. While William would never earn the heaps of gold he had been promised, he could stay here with Kupela and find a more honest profession. There would surely be more opportunities for the partner of the emperor's daughter.

'I'll see you two later.' Sepo clapped his hands and swaggered out of the room. He left the door open absently and could be heard singing imperial songs as he trotted down the stairs.

Kupela thrust herself back to her feet and started pacing. She ran her hands through her curls, and couldn't stop giggling. William watched her, a mad grin on his face.

'I can't believe it,' she stuttered out. 'My father is... Ha! He'll finally be able to bring imperial peace to his homeland. I'm so happy for him. And... and...'

She stopped pacing and looked at William, still laughing. 'Do you know what this means, Will?'

He didn't even have the chance to say anything; he was so overwhelmed by her excitement.

'I'm a princess!' The last word came out like a cross between a furious roar and a girlish squeal. She turned to him then, planted her feet as if she might be about to punch him, then leapt onto the couch. She landed on her knees, one either side of William, straddling him. The force of it almost knocked the wind from him. There was no hesitation then. She gripped his shirt and tore it open. Buttons cascaded onto the wooden floor, rolled up to the edge of the hearth.

'Take me,' she breathed.

It didn't take any more convincing than that. William gripped the back of her bodice and tugged. The two flaps of material pulled apart a fraction, but the string held firm. Kupela gasped from the force of it. He tugged again; it didn't work. Changing tactic, he reached under her skirts. His fingers traced up her thighs; they were plump, more so than those of anyone who lived their life on the road. He liked it, clenched his hand on her skin. She mewled, biting at his neck. He found lacy undergarments and gripped, pulling them down. Her fingers found the buckle on his belt at about the same time. She yanked on the leather, pulling it painfully tight for a moment before loosening. It whipped free of the loops on his trousers and she tossed it away.

Kupela pressed on his shoulders again, pinning him to the couch. As she slithered down him to pull off his trousers, William was faced with the frowning expression of Sepo in an oil painting on the wall. He tried to look away; something was happening in his briefs and he didn't want anything to stop it. Kupela had his trousers around his knees now and was teasing her fingers around the linen drawstring on his underwear. He focused on the sensation of it, but his eyes were drawn back to Sepo in the painting. Did his damned subconscious hate him so much as to spoil this moment for him? He forced himself to look away, tried to surrender to her attention. Something drew him back.

The painting of Sepo was boasting of his athletic prowess. He was stripped to the waist, muscles on show. Was this why William was drawn to it? He had never thought himself that way inclined before, but why couldn't he look away? He shook his head, why was he thinking such things? Why wouldn't his mind let him get lost in the here and now? He had been waiting for this moment for too long. Perhaps he was distracted because he had been about to kill the man only days before and now he was about to bed his daughter. But no, even that wasn't it.

William realised then, where Sepo was in the painting. He was waist deep in a steaming pool. It could have been one of his own baths underneath the house – where he had gone to recuperate from the shock of becoming emperor. It was the exact same place Goldin and Gwyneth were.

Suddenly, the blood drained from, well, everything.

'I'm sorry,' William blurted, rolling Kupela off him and onto the couch cushion. He stood up, trousers around his ankles and shirt hanging open. 'I just need a moment.'

'What's wrong?' Kupela pouted, pushing herself up on the couch. 'I don't mind if you've–'

Her eyes flicked to his crotch. That was terribly nice of her, but he was in no danger of finishing early. He had quite the opposite problem, in fact. 'I just need to… freshen up? Give me a minute.'

William dragged his trousers up to his waist, holding them together at the front to stop them slipping back down. When his holster had been undone, his gun had slipped from it and had somehow found its way into his gusset while his trousers were around his ankles. The thing bounced uncomfortably between his legs as he dashed out of the room.

He could feel his heart thumping like a great war drum in his chest and head and ears. Sprinting down the landing, he passed the portly guard who simply scowled at him, confused.

One of William's shoes was off; he didn't remember losing it and nearly slipped on the carpet. Doubling back on himself, he took the next flight of stairs. His shirt fluttered behind him, his trousers sagged at the back, exposing his arse. He snatched the flintlock from the gusset to stop it falling out and clattering down the stairs. When he reached the ground floor, he cast about breathlessly. A maid was spying on him from a service door.

'Where are the baths?' he shouted. She didn't respond. He raised the silver flintlock and aimed it at her. 'Where are they?'

'Through there.' She pointed to a far door before disappearing into the wall.

William turned and ran, keeping his pistol in hand. He barged through a large wooden door to find himself in a tunnel carved in rock. It was lit by delicate sconces embedded in the walls and descended along a great wavering staircase. At the bottom, light danced from the room ahead as if reflected by water. He was in the right place.

Hurrying down the stairs, he began to fear how he might explain his wild actions to Sepo and Kupela. He had threatened their damned maid in his panic. Perhaps he could blame his actions on Richtus' cocktail of restoratives. Either way, he needed to warn Gwyneth of the development with Sepo before she attempted something drastic. He skidded on his one soft leather sole into a steamy cavern.

The baths were a reasonable size, equal in square footage to that of the main hall. The roof was domed and there were several lanterns up high on hoists. The floor was mosaic, a beautiful tableau of imperial diversity, from Numin to Scold, and all across the continent. Further ahead, there were two square pools recessed into the floor, filled with spring water made milky by scents and soaps. At the far end of the nearer pool, the waters were swirled pink.

William watched in horror as blood trailed from channels in the mosaic, drooling into the water. Gwyneth and Goldin were stood there, panting. Between them, on his knees, knife hilt protruding from his neck, was Emperor Falade.

'We did it, William.' Gwyneth gasped, her excitement mirroring that of Kupela's upstairs. 'We did it quietly, now we just need to slip away.'

She scowled, apparently taking in his appearance for the first time. 'What are you doing down here?'

'I came to stop you.' He swallowed phlegm. 'Sepo was made emperor today. I thought it might change things.'

Gwyneth released her grip on Sepo's robe, letting his neck slip free of the blade. He slumped forwards, his face and body striking the tiles with all the finality of dead meat. His hand was outstretched over the pool's rim, limp. Blood trailed down his finger, making a gentle *drip, drip* that echoed around the cavern. William approached slowly, following the edge of the pool, not quite believing it to be true.

'We should leave.' Goldin's head was down and he was sucking pensively on his protruding tooth. 'Will, you go back upstairs, pretend you saw none of this. I didn't mean for–'

There was a distant commotion. Feet could be heard through the stairway passage. William had made enough of a scene to raise the alarm already. He clenched his teeth, wished he could be anywhere else – wished he could be *anyone* else. Why did he always make the wrong choices?

The footsteps arrived in the cavern and stopped. For a second there was no sound, then a small faltering gasp. Kupela's scream was like nothing William had ever heard; it tore right to the heart of him. Not for the first time in his life did he think the world might be better off without him in it. Slowly, he turned to see her. Perhaps he was torturing himself for his wrong doings; perhaps he was taking one last look at the life he could have had.

She was on her knees by the time he forced his eyes to her, hands clutched about her mouth. She was wailing and gasping the worst guttural sounds of grief. Her eyes were locked with those of her father, lifeless and glassy. Words came through her whimpering then. 'William, do something.'

She still thought he wasn't a part of it, but once the shock passed there could be no explanation other than the truth.

More footsteps came down the stairs. It was one of her guards, the big one with the breastplate like a beaten cauldron. William had no reason to think this man was anything other than a true gentleman, but he still had to kill him.

Just as when William had been cast from a bridge and found himself apprenticed under Ojo, the luxury of morality was lost to him. His only choice was to survive. Reluctantly, he raised his pistol and fired.

# PART 8

## 1682
### CLAUDE BEECHWORTH

The chamber at the top of the clock tower fell quiet. Only moments before, the room had been a battleground, with countless cultists bearing in. Now, the Sacrificial Lambs were all dead, killed in a hail of fire. Resolutely, the clock mechanism continued its ratcheting overhead as if nothing had happened.

Claude limped out of the shadows. A bullet had grazed his thigh, and his dampening shirt implied one had cut through his shoulder as well. It didn't hurt; that was a bad sign. He found William of Fairshore in the gloom and levelled his rifle at him. During the battle, they had been allies. He should have known better than to trust an assassin on the blacklist.

'You killed my grandmother.' Claude tried to deliver the accusation plainly, but the words came out wavering and weak. He couldn't quite believe that the soft little sod had done it. William had strapped Claude's grandmother to a wheelchair with a box of ammunition, then doused her in ether and sent her towards the invading cultists. How anyone could use another human being as a rolling bomb, Claude didn't know. William had ignited her before the spray of bullets started; it was most certainly not a pleasant end for dear old Nanny. Her blazing body had toppled down the tower stairway and was gone.

'She was going to die anyway,' William scoffed. 'It was what she wanted.'

'That's not your place to say.' Claude jutted his jaw and sniffed the air; it was sulphurous, tinged with the richness of smouldering wood. He listened for any movement in the shaded corners of the room, but his pulse was too loud in his ears. 'But, as it seems your sponsor is dead, it doesn't really matter what your say is.'

The young assassin fiddled with his gun; Claude was sure it was unloaded. William had shot a sacrificial lamb only moments before, while he had been dragging himself out from under a fallen timber.

He wondered if killing the boy was the right thing to do. He had only killed once for revenge and it hadn't made him feel much better. Still, he had failed to kill the emperor all those years ago, and that was a mistake he deeply regretted.

'Goodbye, William.' He raised his rifle, butting it against his shoulder. 'At least you were bested by a man-butcher, not many can say that. You might be famous in hell.'

He chuckled.

'You… no Ma-an-Butcher.' The words came out slurred, came from the shadows somewhere at Claude's right. 'Beet-worth a liar and chee-eat.'

Claude turned to see the slave shambling into the light, in very much the same way he had done himself. His rifle drooped a little as he recognised the half-face for the first time.

Terrowin.

'I see you now.' Claude's smile closed. It was two against one, but he remained in a powerful position. He was the only one with a loaded weapon. 'Barber always had a penchant for bringing back man-butchers. I thought Karin was the first, but I'm not always right. Perhaps he'll bring me back when I'm gone, but that won't be for many a year yet.'

Claude raised his rifle. This time, Terrowin would stay dead.

'It pains me to do this again, it really does.' He pulled the trigger.

A bullet drilled into Terrowin's guts. Instead of crumpling, the crooked slave roared from the pain and charged forwards. A windmill of ropey muscle and bleeding flesh approached, deadly fast. He took another bullet like it was nothing.

Claude recoiled when Terrowin reached him, fists beating him, elbows jabbing him. Hands clutched around his head. A thumb went into his eye, hard. He screamed as he was forced back. His rifle was torn from his grip.

'Wait–' he cried.

A fist struck him in the face. Then, he was hit in the stomach with a force akin to that of a bullet wound. Terrowin wrapped his arms around him and charged. The pair staggered together. Claude reached out for something to hold, but there was nothing. He felt air under his shoe as he stepped back. Terrowin thrust his legs and they toppled over the edge of the stairway. They came untangled as they fell. There wasn't time to think, or contemplate one's death; fear and confusion was all encompassing.

Then, nothing.

'Good morning, I'm Dr Barber. How are you doing on this fine day?' The doctor's voice drifted in softly. 'The sun is shining, the larks are *larking about,* there are children playing in the streets. What a time to be alive.'

There was the sound of clinking porcelain and a long, protracted sip.

'Now, before you get up, would you mind answering a few questions?' He paused momentarily to munch on a biscuit. 'You're tired, I know, but this is an important part of the process. So, let us begin. The first one is easy.'

Barber leant close, one eye peering through a magnifying glass suspended from a leather headband. 'Could you please tell me your name?'

'I'm–' Words were hard to conjure through a mouth so dry, especially when one couldn't grasp the answer. 'I'm–'

'I'll give you a clue.' There was a soft clunk of wood on wood followed by a rustling of parchments, then another sip of tea from the porcelain cup. 'You were, let's say, *injured* in this year's Man-Butcher Prize. You've competed before, back in the day. Is that too many clues? I don't want to influence you too much, there's still a possibility that your brain is just useless jelly. It was rather damaged.'

'I'm…' It was terribly hard to recall a name. There were flashes of a clock tower brawl, various assassinations, a duelling bout, and blood – lots of blood.

'I managed to salvage the lion's share of his brain.' It was plain that Barber was talking to someone else now. 'Though I had to replace a portion with some bobs and bits I had lying around. I'd hoped it would work, but it's not looking too good.'

'I'm…' Teeth gritted with the effort of stirring a dormant mind into action. 'I'm Claude…'

The name didn't sound quite right coming from his mouth, his voice lacked the gravitas of his advanced years. Rolling the unfamiliar tongue, he tried again. 'I'm Claude Beechworth.'

'Ha-ha-ha! He's alive!' Claude recognised that voice: Walter Perrin.

'There's no need to get so worked up about it.' Barber dismissed the excitement. 'He was dead and now he's alive; it's as simple as waking up. Just because you don't know how to do it, doesn't mean it's all that impressive. Well, maybe it is.'

Walter leant in close with Barber. Claude's vision was still blurry, but he could make out the shapes of them against the backdrop of the whitewashed ceiling.

'He still doesn't look all there,' Walter remarked.

'Oh, it's not good enough for you now?' Barber chuckled. 'He's alive, isn't he? It doesn't mean he comes back in the best of health. It's not magic, *it's science.* He will need to mend for a while yet.'

'How does it work?' Perrin poked Claude like he was some kind of specimen and not entirely aware of their conversation.

'It's too complicated to go through with the likes of you,' Barber scoffed. 'Just know that life is a property of all matter. A rock is no less alive than a tree, or a cat, or a man. We just express ourselves better. And when the mechanics of our bodies fail, making us as inert as a rock, or a twig, or a shoe, we call that death. As you can see, with the right ingredients, anything can be reversed.'

'I think you're right, it is too complicated for me.' The mayor prodded again. 'How are you feeling, Claude?'

'Worse than death,' he wheezed.

'Ha-ha,' Barber chortled. 'There's that Garlish humour we all know and love!'

Claude crushed a dry biscuit between his finger and thumb, grinding it to dust. He couldn't bring himself to eat. The only things he would force down his gullet were Dr Barber's tinctures, though they did little to alleviate the pain in his head. It seemed to come and go whenever it pleased. Gods, he hoped that this time the pain would be brief. He screwed his eyes shut and found an unopened bottle of numbing agent on the table by touch alone – it was quite a challenge amidst the countless other little vials he had already consumed.

He flicked off the cork and tipped the oily liquid back. Moments later, the headache started to fade. It wasn't a result of the medicine; it didn't work that fast. It was just coincidental timing on the part of the fluxing pains in his skull. With a sigh, he opened his eyes. His vision was a blur, but that would pass too, in time.

Though the shapes in the room were hard to make out, he could tell the committee were staring at him. Dr Barber had made his underlings drag him from his bed, deposit him into a spare wheelchair and cart him to the town hall to take part in the Man-Butcher Prize planning committee. He didn't feel ready for it; only three weeks ago he had been dead.

'Barber, are you certain I'm in a fit state for this?' He stumbled on his words, still unaccustomed to his new, more youthful tongue. 'These aches keep coming stronger and stronger.'

'You are filled with so much numbing agent, I could pull off your arm and you wouldn't notice. These pains you are feeling, they are in your head.'

'I know they're in my head,' Claude hissed, feeling another spike of pain. 'That's precisely the problem.'

'Don't be facetious, you know what I mean. The pain can only be imaginary.' Barber whistled through his teeth and one of his underlings swooped forwards to mop Claude's brow. 'It's a hell of a traumatic experience, death, but trust me you've come out one of the better ones. You'll be right as rain clouds in no time.'

Claude swallowed with a wince. All he could keep thinking about was the fact that his own brain had been damaged so badly Dr Barber had been forced to splice in sections from other people. Perhaps that was why he had great gaps in his memory; perhaps that was why his head hurt so much. Or his body could be rejecting his mind the way skin pushed out a splinter. He hadn't seen himself in a mirror yet, but could see his hands, and had caught glimpses in reflective surfaces. He didn't belong in this form. He was living inside another man's body, perhaps a man who had been killed for the express purpose of his own revival.

'I don't think I'm well enough to be here.' He bit his lip, or was it another man's lip? Did he really bite it? They weren't his teeth.

'Nonsense, of course you are,' Barber scoffed. 'Returning to normality is your best cure. You're thirty years younger! Live a life, forget about your death and the pains will be left behind.'

The room faded back into focus. All the committee members, who at one point feared Claude more than any other, were staring right at him. Some hid their emotions well; others displayed their scorn or pity openly.

'Shall we… continue?' The mayor drummed his fingers on the table nervously.

Claude cradled his head. 'Don't mind me, Walter. Let's get to planning.'

He couldn't think of anything he wanted to do less. If there was anything to be said for the positives of dying, it certainly put one's life into perspective. Claude had wasted his in this privy of a town when he had the fortune and estates to retire in comfort. When he died, all he had amassed had been skimmed off by the Guild, and the rest bequeathed to a distant cousin. In this new life he had nothing, except for his faux friends who had only brought him back to re-establish an uncomfortable balance, and stop them from killing each other.

Claude had no desire to partake in their little committee any longer. Perhaps once he was well, he would visit his distant cousin and take back some of what was rightfully his.

'So, I think we're now all aware that this year's Prize was a tad ill-conceived.' Walter interwove his fingers and leant his chin on them. 'Cheating was rife. It was somewhat confusing for our assassins establishing whether sponsors were alive. Obviously, it led to that debacle with William of Fairshore, and our *new champion.*'

The mayor said the last two words with more than a hint of scorn.

'Why don't we just take it back to the classic rules?' Klava suggested. 'One big free-for-all, then when there's twenty left we regroup them in the square and start again?'

'It's a little…' Tobias, the weaponsmith, shrugged. 'Dull?'

There were a few nods around the table.

'Granted, I do love the regrouping at the end,' Tobias continued. 'Especially when we give the competitors access to my armouries. That was tremendous, what Ottilie did with that bomb slinger. I'd love to see something like that again.'

'Look, nobody's arguing that we should get rid of that bit.' Walter shifted his hands forwards and extended his fingers, resting them on his lips as he thought. 'I like the close quarters endings. When there's twenty men roaming the whole city it doesn't half drag it out. We have set a precedent, however, for a bit of a gimmick. If we don't have one in eighty four, we might not get the record numbers of this year again.'

'What about caches of ammunition and weapons stowed throughout the town?' The man-butcher, William Cholmondeley, was in the doorway, his high voice like a knife through Claude's brain.

'Can you stop interrupting these meetings?' Walter purpled with an instant rage; it was quite unlike the usually soft mayor.

From what Claude could tell, the boy's suggestion wasn't all that bad. The caches could be used to reward brave competitors with Tobias' armaments. It didn't matter that William's suggestion was good, he wasn't a committee member, and from his boyish swagger Claude could tell he wasn't fit for it.

'William, you need to leave.' Walter's voice was struggling to remain calm. It was plain that he hated the new man-butcher, though not wholly evident why. Given the man's friendships with the worst the Guild had to offer, clearly this boy was a rotter. 'This is a committee meeting, and it's for committee members only. You may be a man-butcher, but you still need to respect the Guild's rules.'

'Make me one, then.' William took a couple of steps into the room. He was walking like an old gunslinger, one thumb hooked over his belt, just beside his golden flintlock. 'I'm sure you could use a man-butcher on the committee.'

'No, thank you,' Baradus Brindle grunted.

Claude considered the man. They had never been friends, but they had never been enemies either. Baradus wasn't the type to scheme like Klava or Tobias. He was a thug, plain and simple; a thug with thug's ethics. Claude had often considered that if "thugfully" had been a word, it could have been used to describe everything the man did. From the way he grunted and spat, to the way he intimidated and spat.

'We don't need no little snot like you,' Baradus spat. 'We have Claude, he's a man-butcher.'

William tossed his head with a laugh, almost too casual.

'Beechworth.' He sneered.

The boy would have never treated Claude with such disrespect in his past life, when he had held himself with a menacing dignity. As he was now, shrivelled with pain, looking like the weakest foetus in one of Barber's jars, anyone might step on him as they would a cockroach. His head started to hurt again.

'Look at him. He's a has-been, quite literally. And he might have won the Prize decades ago, but he lost this year. I won.' The young boy strode further into the room. 'If that doesn't prove I'm more suited to be on the committee than him, I don't know what does.'

Any one of the committee members could kill the insolent man-butcher at any moment, but his title protected him. After Ojo had been thought killed, it had taken years for attendance in the Prize to recover; what was the point of competing if the winner didn't thrive afterwards? Claude knew the Guild needed money, it always did, damned pit in the ground that it was. The fate of the committee was now tied to the fate of this upstart child.

'What if we have a duel?' William posited. 'Would that prove I'm good enough? Or what if I send him back where he belongs, right now?'

William snatched out his golden pistol and trained it on Claude. An almighty stab of pain in Claude's head accompanied the motion. He recoiled from it, but it must have looked like fear as the boy started to laugh.

'See? He's nothing anymore, and the sooner you realise that, the sooner you can get me on this committee.'

Claude found it comical that the boy was so eager to rise to the top of the Guild, that he was willing to take part in the most mundane meeting in the known world. He would have happily traded places, but could easily appreciate the spite the boy engendered, and wasn't about to give him what he wanted. A giggle came out as a weak cough.

'Maybe I should just put him out of his misery.' Young William strode up to Claude.

'Don't shoot him!' Walter thrust to his feet, holding out his hands for calm. 'He was *very* expensive.'

So, that was all Claude was to his best friend: an expensive convenience, a necessary commodity, perhaps just a bargaining chip. He wondered if, now the Guild had financed his new life, he would be considered their property. His head throbbed at that, his knee twitching with pent up frustration.

Claude considered what might take away his pain. Barber had said he should live a life, and this life of committee meetings was not one that particularly captivated him. What he wanted to do right now was put William Cholmondeley in his place. If he did, however, he would surely be killed a second time, and that wasn't something he was in a rush to repeat.

'Put the gun down.' The Amarian Swordmistress laid the tip of her sword gently against the young man-butcher's neck. She had been late to the meeting and had somehow managed to glide into the room and end up right beside Claude without him even noticing.

It was plain William hadn't noticed either, as his eyes bulged ludicrously.

'I—' the young man-butcher stammered.

'Hand it to Claude,' she instructed. 'He'll unload it and give it back to you.'

The golden pistol was dropped into Claude's cupped palms. He looked down at it, something still throbbing in the back of his head as he took in the engraved flowers. A sudden compulsion took him. In one smooth motion, he cocked the gun and fired a ball of lead into the man-butcher's thigh. The boy screamed. Claude half-expected a slash from the Swordmistress, but she was too shocked to take action. As the boy crumpled to the floor, Claude struggled to his feet. The pain in his head was waning already.

'What the fuck are you doing?' the mayor cried.

'I'm not entirely sure.' While Claude was more than happy to take a life, he always decided upon it beforehand. It was always a conscious choice. This time, he had acted so fast it was almost as if he had pulled the trigger before he even realised what he was doing. He supposed it was a result of the youthful body that housed his old brain. As he spoke again, Claude found himself chuckling. 'I suppose I'm doing whatever I feel like.'

He staggered towards the door, almost fell, but caught his weight on the table. 'I can't stay here. I can't subject myself to these damned meetings – or your arrogant boy – any longer. It turns out, life is for living, scores are for settling, and meetings are not for me anymore.'

He shuffled to the doorway.

'Claude, where do you think you're going?' The mayor scowled.

'I think I might have a jaunt to Vitale, actually.' Claude turned back, leaning on the doorframe. 'There's an emperor there, played a part in my father's murder. I just up and forgot to kill him in my last life. I might give it a good old college try this time. What do you reckon?'

'I think you should calm down. Stay here.' Walter rounded the conference table. 'We need you. I need you. You're a good man to have on the committee.'

The mayor stepped over the writhing boy.

'We need someone we can trust, and we've always been able to trust in you.'

'You can't trust in me.' Claude was giggling again. 'I'm the one who killed *your* father. Now that was a bit of business I'm proud of. He killed *my* father on the behest of the soon to be deceased Emperor D'Elia. So, I'd just like to tie it all up in a little bow before I pop my clogs again.'

'Claude, this isn't you. You've had too much of those serums. You need to calm down.' Walter came closer still, wheedling. 'And do you think I don't know you killed him? I'm not stupid, Claude. You killed him, and that's why I can trust you. You owe me a life debt.'

'Maybe I owed you the last one.' Claude shrugged. 'This one's my own.'

He tossed the golden pistol to Walter. 'Give that back to your dog, would you? Maybe if you stop him bleeding out you can convince him he owes you a life debt too. Maybe he won't be such a little cad then.'

On trembling legs, he limped down the corridor, filled with fresh determination. 'Good luck to the lot of you, and goodbye.'

# 1683
## WILLIAM OF FAIRSHORE

William crested the rough stone steps from the baths. He was out of breath already, though it was more likely a result of lingering shock than anything else. He would have plenty of time to lament his decisions later. For now, he had to survive.

The door to the hall had swung closed on oiled hinges and was resting on the latch; William kicked it open, pistol ready. It struck the wall with a crunch and bounced back. He stepped through, putting his shoulder to the wood to keep it from closing. He couldn't see any guards in the immediate vicinity, but there was no doubt they would be coming. He waved Gwyneth and Goldin by. They dashed out and hid behind columns that supported the first floor mezzanine. When they were in position, he moved to a third.

Across the hall, the four couches at the centre of the room were unoccupied and there didn't appear to be anyone skulking between them. It was a considerable distance to the front door, and aside from the low furniture, there was little to take cover behind. Even the couches would be useless against shooters from the balconies above.

'We should follow these columns around the edge to the front,' he instructed. 'Keep under cover.'

Gwyneth moved first, then Goldin, darting from one column to the next. William braced himself, his pistol ready as he watched the upper floors for any assailants. When they were both obscured a few columns ahead, he followed. The pair of them covered him then, using the pistols supplied by the Falade household.

Feet thundered down the steps from the first floor. William held his fire just in time; it was a saucer-eyed handmaid. A heartbeat later

– his reactions dulled by age, or the quantity of drugs consumed in his youth – Goldin punctured the woman's chest with a bullet.

'Sorry,' he grunted. 'Didn't mean to…'

He started fumbling for another round in his pocket, but in his urgency to reload he hadn't concealed himself properly behind his cover. William cast about the room desperately. The dead maid slid down the stairs, the fire crackled in the hearth, and Silvio emerged from the shadows on the first floor balcony.

'Goldin, get back!' William yelped.

Silvio prowled to the edge of the landing, levelling his slender three shooter at Goldin. William fired first, but in his haste, missed his mark and struck the bannister instead. The shower of splinters forced Silvio to recoil, his shot narrowly missing Goldin as he ran. A second bullet punctured a portrait of Sepo between the eyes as the little man squashed next to Gwyneth behind her pillar.

William reloaded as fast as he could, swearing as Silvio leapt over the balcony. The cartridge slipped into place as the old fighter rolled behind the couches, absorbing the impact of his fall. Then, before William had the chance to ready his flintlock, the old fighter was up, cold iron pistol and icy glare trained on him.

William jerked behind a column. As he twisted, Silvio's shot tore a hole through his flapping shirt and shattered a marble bust recessed in the wall. For a moment, William was immobilised, then he realised the old fighter's three shooter was empty.

'Run!' he bellowed. 'He needs to reload.'

They sprinted ahead, brass-clad bullets tinkling to the floor as Goldin abandoned reloading. Gwyneth faltered as she reached the end of the cover provided by the mezzanine and pressed her back against a column. Goldin and William did the same, each separated by eight feet of floor. There would be a short, unprotected rush for the door. Gods, William prayed it was unlocked.

He peered out for Silvio. The man was still reloading amidst the couches, or perhaps he was waiting for Gwyneth to make her move. It was an impossible choice: whether they should go now or wait until Silvio had reloaded and spent three more shots. William found his mouth dry of any further instructions. Gwyneth was closest to the door, but it was too much of a risk to have her leave cover. It would be another matter if it was his life on the line.

Goldin was fumbling again with a bullet. William almost sprinted over there and reloaded the damned thing for him, but a mechanical click made his heart skip a beat. There was no doubt now that Silvio was watching their positions with a fully loaded pistol.

A wall panel burst open and the large ginger guard leapt out. He swung a fist at Gwyneth, but she ducked and darted around his side. He was quicker than he looked, however, and his other arm snatched her around the midriff. He hauled her from the floor and hugged her to his chest with both arms, blocking any shot William might make.

'Put down your weapons or I'll break her neck,' he roared.

One arm cinched around Gwyneth's throat while the other crushed her chest. William could hear Silvio's footsteps approaching cautiously. There was a possibility the man was outside the cover of the couches now, but William couldn't take a shot for him in case the burly man followed through on his threat.

'Goldin, toss down your weapon,' William instructed. 'We're better off facing a fair trial than getting killed here.'

They both knew that at this point a trial would be a formality, and if either of them got caught, their hangings would be quite the event. It was a good way of letting the little man know he had a plan in mind.

Goldin dropped his pistol. William wasn't sure if it had been loaded yet or not. He couldn't be certain, so didn't factor it into his plan. A bell started chiming from somewhere high in the building, not a deep toll like that of a chapel, but not the high peal of a hand bell either. He imagined it was an alarm that would be used to summon guards from the local outpost.

'I'm putting mine down,' William said calmly.

Instead of tossing his pistol to the floor, he slowly lowered it. His finger remained on the trigger so he could fire at any moment, but if he did shoot the ginger guard, Silvio would be on him in a heartbeat. The old fighter's boots padded ever closer on the other side of the column.

'You just let her go and we'll come peacefully, alright?'

He set his pistol on the floor, hand still on it. One by one, he delicately released his fingers from the grip as if the thing had been booby trapped and sudden movements would result in a fiery death. The ginger guard's eyes were so focused on the gun, he didn't spy William's other hand pulling a knife from a small sheath in his boot.

William launched the blade at the guard and snatched up his pistol. There was a scream as the knife impacted in flesh, but it was wholly girlish and not at all the sort of exclamation the big guard might make. He had hit Gwyneth by accident.

She fought like a feral cat, writhing, kicking, and punching at any part of the guard she could find. One of his huge arms had been grazed by the blade and struggled to find purchase on the wild woman's body. The grip on her throat was merciless, however. Even now she was turning purple.

Though William had expected to incapacitate the guard with the blade and use his only bullet on Silvio, he couldn't just abandon her to her fate. He raised his pistol, took a moment to aim, and pulled the trigger. The bullet hit the guard square in the forehead. He toppled backwards, bringing Gwyneth to the floor with him. She screamed as the knife in her shoulder twisted from the impact, and was left gasping and coughing in a heap, one leg trapped beneath the dead man's weight.

William peered around the column as he frantically tried to reload. He couldn't see Silvio anywhere. Goldin had snatched up his pistol and was trying to reload it again, muttering darkly about the failings of new technology.

There was a click at William's back then. A pistol pressed into his spine.

'Drop it,' Silvio instructed.

William did as he was told this time, releasing the gun and cartridge instantly, rather than trying anything clever. His last plan hadn't worked out particularly well and he was in a far worse position now. Resigned, Goldin threw his gun and ammunition to the floor.

'I swear to the gods if you've hurt Kupela your throat will be slit before the city guard arrives,' Silvio hissed in William's ear.

'I haven't hurt her. I would never. I—' William left it at that; it seemed ridiculous to plead his innocence now. 'She's in the baths, unhurt.'

'Why don't we head over to the couches?' Silvio jabbed the pistol into the base of his spine. 'Now you're all unarmed, we can establish exactly what you *have* done. Stolen from her jewellery box, perhaps? You first, little one.'

Goldin sneered, but obeyed, striding out from the shadow of the mezzanine. William followed, pistol still pressed into his back.

'The beacon's lit! Guards are on their way.' A shout came from high above. It was the tattooed guard leaning over the third floor balcony. 'Do you need assistance down there?'

'Better safe than sorry. Fetch a weapon and join us, post haste.' Silvio pushed William towards a couch. 'Now, explain yourself.'

'We killed your master,' Gwyneth announced. 'I slit Sepo's throat myself.'

The pressure of the pistol was relieved from William's spine as Silvio turned to face a fresh threat. Gwyneth had one arm supporting the other; the hilt of William's knife was visible between her bloody fingers, protruding from her shoulder. A pistol was held sloppily in her other hand. If she and Silvio were to have a standoff, it was clear who the winner would be.

Taking the opportunity, William snatched Silvio's wrist and pushed it upwards. The shock of it made him fire into the air, shattering crystals on a chandelier. After that, Silvio tried to shake him off, tried to force his pistol back to its target. William snarled, the combined force of both his arms barely enough to keep the pistol high, but the longer he kept it there, the more chance Gwyneth had to take a shot.

Silvio's free hand gripped William's throat and squeezed. William tried to call out for Gwyneth to shoot, but the word came out as a gurgle. He imagined she didn't want to hit him as he had done with her. A lot more damage could be done with a pistol after all, and the cost of her inaccuracy could be his death.

William's windpipe was being crushed. Even now, he was failing to keep the old fighter's pistol off target. It was only a matter of time before Silvio would overpower him and shoot Gwyneth dead. Then,

William spied a hint of gold and delicately crafted basketwork: Silvio's side sword. Steeling himself, he released one hand from the fighter's wrist. Silvio's arm forced downwards, the aim drawing closer to Gwyneth. William wasn't strong enough to counter the old fighter with one hand, but only had to endure a moment longer. With his free hand, he grasped the hilt of the sword and loosed it from the scabbard. The blade gleamed perfect silver for a moment, and then William plunged it back.

There was little resistance from the man's fine shirt and somehow even less from his skin. The blade was thin and razor sharp. It had clearly never been used in anger before; not a blemish marred the fine craftsmanship. The tip emerged from Silvio's back, just beside his spine, and the basket butted up to his stomach. As he staggered backwards, William let go of the blade. Silvio dropped his pistol to attend his wound, not realising it was too late, even as he slumped weakly to the floor.

'No!' the tattooed guard roared, now at the top of the stairs. He had a scattergun that could take off a limb within the bounds of the entrance hall. 'You—'

He didn't have time to finish. Gwyneth fired at him, missing, but causing him to dive behind the bannister. William took Silvio's pistol and fired twice to keep him subdued while Goldin helped Gwyneth out of the front door. When they were safely outside, William sprinted after.

He shoved the slender pistol into his holster and reloaded his silver flintlock, looking desperately up and down the street for approaching guardsmen.

'Where to now?' he panted, half-expecting Gwyneth to suggest the sewer.

'Dunstan's around the corner, down the road a way. He can get us out of the city.' She was gasping and sweating. The blade was still in her shoulder, plugging the wound for now, but she was still in a state of shock. 'Follow me.'

She set off at a painfully slow jog. William quickly reloaded Goldin's pistol for him as they went.

'Why do they have to be so fiddly?' Goldin grumbled, hurrying alongside. 'What was wrong with paper cartridges? I didn't mind powder pouches and ram rods.'

Now wasn't the time for an in depth discussion on such things. William tossed the loaded pistol to Goldin and hurried forwards. He slipped his hand under Gwyneth's good arm and helped to support her weight.

'I'm sorry for sticking you.' He eyed the blade.

'I had you stuck with a crossbow bolt.' She grimaced and grunted. 'Why don't we call it even? There's Dunstan.'

William spied the coach; it wasn't really all that good for a getaway – the open top being far less protective than the enclosed cab of a carriage – but it was all they had. He stuck two fingers in his mouth and whistled, alerting the coachman to their arrival.

Dunstan lifted his gaze from a wrinkled news-sheet and, upon seeing them, tossed it to the street. He hurried into place while William helped Gwyneth and Goldin into the coach. The horses were oriented in such a way they'd be forced onto the main road, there being little time and room on this side street to turn around. William ducked low and readied himself for a fight.

The horses brayed and lurched as Dunstan snapped the reins. In seconds, they were at a trot and once they rounded the corner onto the wide thoroughfare, they were already at a gallop. William leant on the rear bench and aimed his flintlock for anyone who might pursue them.

Lanterns and movement could be seen far down the street. He assumed it was the city guard heading in. More immediately, the tattooed guard emerged from the front of Kupela's house, scattergun in hand. He fired at the coach, but they were already too far away and the pellets didn't even scratch the paintwork.

William held his fire. He took a breath; the city guard were a long way behind. Even if they had men on horseback – which were faster than the coach – they would struggle to catch up across such a distance. He lowered his pistol and turned around, sitting on the bench.

'Do you want me to pull it out?' Goldin was perched over Gwyneth. There was an open medical bag between them that had been stowed under one of the benches. 'It's in there quite deep.'

'I don't know.' Gwyneth bit her lip. 'I want it out, but I don't want to bleed to death while you're wrestling bandages around me. It won't be easy once we get off these smooth slabs and onto the cobbled streets.'

'Here.' William moved across, grabbing a bottle he recognised from his time with Richtus. 'It kills pain. We'll splash a bit on now, then save the rest for later, when we have time to take the knife out properly.'

As he positioned himself beside Gwyneth, he knelt on the seat to better assess her wound. As he did so, he caught a glimpse of lights down the street ahead. It appeared more city guards were on the way to the Falade household from a different outpost. They were directly in the path of the coach and getting ever closer.

'What are you doing?' he barked at Dunstan, fearing momentarily that the scornful coachman was taking them right to the city guard.

'Don't worry yourself, I've seen them.' Dunstan pulled hard on the reins, swinging them down another street. 'I can't just take any road that presents itself. You don't want us to get stuck in a ditch or wind up in a dead end, do you?'

'No, but...'

'Then trust me to get us out of the city.' Dunstan lashed the reins. 'There's a bridge to the north, it's narrow and should slow the city guard, there's too many to pass all at once.'

Just then, guards on horseback followed from the main street in their wake. They were barely one hundred yards behind now. Other alarm bells started ringing in the vicinity as the fleeing coach was spotted from a guard tower. Nobody could know what they had done yet, but William imagined that most outposts would have seen the beacon lit in the senators' district. The guard response would be accordingly fierce. He readied himself for a fight.

As the pursuing horsemen neared, they drew pistols, steering their horses with reins in one hand. From the back of a galloping mount, they would have a much harder time hitting William than he would them. It was little solace when there were so many bearing down on him. He took his first shot, clipping a man's neck. Two guards fired back. One bullet passed overhead and the other thumped into the coach siding.

Goldin arrived next to William and fired. He hit the flank of a horse, making it collapse – its rider left in the gutter. William reloaded and shot the last guardsman in the shoulder. The man recoiled, pulling on his reins even as the horse bucked furiously beneath him.

More guards were spilling into the street now, but they were on carriages and jailer's carts, and wouldn't be able to catch up to the coach so easily. As William reloaded, he saw a rider on horseback break free of the carriages and gallop towards him. A breath later, it became apparent that William's own coach was slowing down.

He turned to shout at Dunstan for going easy on the horses, but the coachman was limp. His body lolled to one side and the top of his head was missing. Dead. With the reins loosely hanging on his lifeless fingers the horses had lost the urgency to gallop.

William quickly composed himself, though he could feel the blood draining from his face. It wasn't just that a man had been so gruesomely killed, but that his own imprisonment and execution was all the closer for it.

'Someone needs to drive!' William shouted. While he was the most competent driver, he was also the best shot amongst them. With Gwyneth incapacitated, the choice was obvious. 'Goldin, you do it.'

'But, the horses!' The little man's eyes widened in horror.

'Damn the horses.' William manhandled Goldin, shoving him towards the front of the coach. 'What do you fear more, a horse's kick or the hangman's noose?'

Goldin grumbled, clambering over the front of the cab to the driver's bench. He shoved Dunstan's body to the side and it landed on the road with a crunch. The wheels of the slowly advancing coach lumbered over it, the whole cab rolling to one side. It thumped back to the ground with a squeal of protesting springs.

William met Gwyneth's eyes then; they were bright – a good sign for her health – but he'd never seen her so afraid. He turned again to see the lone rider almost upon them. The man had arms tattooed like fish and was levelling a scattergun for the three of them.

Wrapping one arm around Gwyneth, William dragged her from the seat. She screamed as the knife in her shoulder was pressed in tighter, and both of them tumbled into the footwell. Buckshot scattered over their heads.

William pushed himself up, panting and sweating. He should have just turned and shot the advancing guard, but he needed to know that Goldin had survived. Fortunately, the little man had been scrambling for the reins when the scattergun was fired and the shot had gone over his head.

There was a thump at the rear of the coach and the whole thing dipped back on its banded iron suspension. William was horrified to see that the tattooed guard had leapt from his horse and was clambering up the back of the coach, thick arms searching for hand holds amidst the fitted cushions.

Just then, Goldin snapped the reins and the coach lurched to full speed. William's footing moved from under him and he toppled onto the bench. His face came inches from that of the tattooed guard. The man's one green and one blue eye were contorted in exertion and spite. He snarled and grabbed a fist of William's shirt. His other hand looped around a strap on the shoulder holster. All of a sudden the man's entire weight was dragging on William, hauling him over the back of the coach.

William slid across the seat. There was nothing to grip; his arms were cramped underneath him. One was reluctant to release his pistol so the other had to hold him alone. His fingers slithered uselessly against smooth leather.

'You're coming with me.' The tattooed guard tugged sharply.

William lurched up. It wouldn't take much for him to overbalance and be dragged from the coach entirely. He felt Gwyneth clawing for his boot with her one good hand; it was all she could do in the situation and it wasn't enough. If he fell, she didn't have the strength to hold him.

As William slipped another few inches, his arms came out from under him and he thumped onto the bench upright, forcing the air from his chest. At that, the tattooed guard lifted his legs and pressed them onto the rear of the coach, improving his leverage. William was dragged even further out of the cab, but jammed his knee against the wooden lip, halting his progress momentarily. It was only then he realised that one of his now freely dangling arms was still gripping his pistol. He pressed it into the gut of the tattooed guard.

'I'm sorry,' he hissed through clenched teeth as he pulled the trigger.

A ball of lead drove into the guard's belly. His grip tightened a moment, then released. He fell away, heterochromatic eyes bulging. The swiftly passing road struck him hard and he started to roll. Momentum kept him moving for a good few yards before he came to a stop in a ditch. Seconds later, the pursuing horses and carriages rumbled over him, crushing his body.

William panted as he slithered back into the coach. Gwyneth was still alive; that was a good thing. Goldin was still driving, which was a good thing too. At least William still had two positives to cling to while his life fell to pieces around him yet again.

'How far until we get to the edge of the city?' he shouted to Goldin.

'I've no idea. I'm just going in a straight line until I find fields.'

William looked back; the carriages were gaining on them still. They surely had better bred or better rested horses. He knew he couldn't fight them all off. Some of the carriages had three or four men on their roofs, all ready with not only pistols and rifles, but brutal maces as well. William liked the thought of being crunched by one of them even less than he did being shot.

'William, it hurts,' Gwyneth gagged. The knife wound was even nastier now he had dragged her to the safety of the floor. The handle had probably caught on something and worked the blade inside her. 'Can I have more of that pain killer?'

He grimaced. It was foolish to use it now when they would need it later for removing the blade. He crouched down beside her and started searching through the leather medical bag. Finding a bottle of ether and a rag, he decided that his best course of action was to make her sleep through the pain. She could do little to help now, and if they all got caught she was more likely to be taken prisoner than killed this way. He doused the rag and without warning pressed it to her mouth.

She resisted briefly, but was soon unconscious. He corked the bottle and turned back to more pressing matters. The carriages were still approaching, and those with rifles atop were readying to fire. William considered taking a dose of the ether himself; it was preferable to die in ones sleep after all.

'We're coming up on that bridge Dunstan mentioned,' Goldin called back to him. 'I don't think it's meant for coaches, but I'll see if I can squeeze us through.'

William had an idea then. He sank low to keep himself out of sight of the riflemen. Once down, crammed in the footwell with the softly wheezing Gwyneth, he uncorked the ether bottle and wedged it between his knees. With both hands, he took the soaked rag and twisted the corner to a point; it fed into the mouth of the bottle easily enough.

'Tell me when we're crossing!' He prayed Goldin was up to the task. If he wasn't, the coach would end up in a ditch or swept downriver.

'You'll know when we're crossing. It's coming up!'

William opened the breach on his flintlock and set the sodden rag across its jaw. He pulled the trigger, showering sparks from the flint. A flame bloomed from the trailing cloth, scorching his leg. He dropped the flintlock with a gasp and readied himself.

There was a crash as one of the coach lanterns was smashed off, then a terrible grating as the paintwork rubbed against stone. The coach lurched left and the lantern on the other side was knocked off too; it ricocheted between walls that sided the narrow bridge. William leapt up and tossed the bottle of ether in the coach's wake. Glass smashed and the liquid spilled out, pushing a rim of fire the whole width of the bridge. Flames drew back inwards erupting up in a ball of flame. If any of the city guard were caught in the blaze William couldn't know, but none pursued through.

When he finally looked around, the coach was hurtling through the outskirts of the city. He collapsed onto one of the benches and prayed the flaming bridge would cause a long detour for the guard.

# 1683
## CLAUDE BEECHWORTH

It had all happened so easily. First, Claude paid a visit to his dear cousin. While she had been well on her way to spending the entirety of her tremendous windfall, there was still plenty left for Claude to reclaim. She had given it willingly too, at least she had once he had clouted her son with his rifle butt and pressed the barrel to his chest.

Second, and quite fortunately, he had found a group of monks travelling to the New Gods' Cathedral. It hadn't taken long to find one who lamented his life of servitude to the gods. A little bribe passed between them and here he was, perched on rooftop scaffolding, waiting to assassinate the emperor for the second time.

His head ached dully as he carefully checked over his rifle and loaded it.

'Soon,' he whispered to himself.

He had taken to voicing his thoughts when his head started to pound, it was easier to hear them that way, and it helped him focus. Sometimes, it would also help the aching wane. Now, however, it did not. He was too eager to kill the emperor.

The way he saw it, now he had been revived, he and his body had different opinions. While he saw this as a second chance to be spent doing the things he should have done in his prior life, his body would do anything to avoid returning to the dormant state of death. To that end, it loathed inaction. Life was for doing, it was for excitement and adventure, and nothing at all sedentary. Stillness was a form of torture and his body let him know with these terrible headaches.

'Almost ready,' he hissed between clenched teeth. As he slid the bolt on his rifle forward and latched it in place, his headache started to fade.

Peering through the scope, he watched proceedings. He had chosen a spot between a marble statue and a gold bust, and hoped that glints from his scope would be misconstrued as bright metal. He had further disguised himself by setting up planks against the scaffolding edge and had brought over a small workmen's bench to crouch behind. It was unlikely he'd be spotted by any imperial marksman – anyone worth their salt was making real money in the Guild.

The Numinian primo finished his speech to a rousing cheer and returned to his seat. Claude knew from the running order that the emperor was next to speak. The pain in his head began to hum in anticipation. The fingers on his left hand started to fidget. He hissed a quiet rebuke to his unruly body.

As the emperor emerged, Claude let out a breathy chuckle. D'Elia was still up to his pompous antics, even in his waning years. He was atop a horse, a flintlock in one hand and a sword in the other. It was a symbol of strength meant to inspire awe and admiration in his subjects, but he would die just the same.

'Do it now.' A voice from behind Claude made him jump, but when he rounded with his rifle there was no one there. He swallowed and put it down to the wind between the spires and his heightened nerves. As he turned his attention back to the emperor, he reasoned that the sooner he moved on from the strange interruption, the more likely it was that it never happened to begin with.

Claude sighted on D'Elia again and watched as the man shifted on the horse's back. His arms were sagging with aging skin; his legs were liver spotted. Despite the display, through the magnification of the scope, he looked very old and very weak. Claude spotted thin ropes then, coiled around the emperor's ankles, tethering him to the stirrups. There would be others hidden beneath his robe, binding him to the saddle. The emperor was so old that he barely had the strength to keep himself upright. It was made pathetic by his reluctance to accept his aging gracefully. Speeches from horseback were a young man's game, and ideally only on the battlefield. This was a pantomime.

A compulsion came over Claude. It would be far more entertaining to humiliate the emperor and *then* kill him, rather than simply end his life. He shifted his sights to the hind quarters of the horse, a feral grin pulling his scarred cheeks. With a tremulous exhale, he pulled the trigger.

The horse reared and stamped, dancing around the stage in fear and pain. All the while, the emperor was thrown from side to side on its back. The flintlock and sword were lost, both flying out of his grip. The sword actually impaled an approaching guard through the shin – that had to hurt. Other guards moved in hesitantly, but they were too late. The horse surged forwards. Claude had only clipped its flank, so its speed wasn't hampered any. Its judgement certainly was.

Claude had prepared to fire another bullet and finish off the emperor once he had been tossed around a little while, but he didn't need to. The horse leapt from the stage, D'Elia screaming on top. Both mount and rider met a foul end on the spiked iron railing below. The sight of it was gruesome, but Claude couldn't help but laugh. Though he had never found death amusing before, living beyond a spell of it had given him an entirely different perspective.

A bullet struck the spire over his head, showering him with terracotta chips. He ducked and looked around. It didn't take long for him to realise that the shot had not come from the street. He scanned the roof of the cathedral and found three people in the very same parapet he had shot from all those years ago. What was more amazing, was that he recognised two of them. One was a dwarf whose name he couldn't quite remember and the other was William of Fairshore.

Claude couldn't believe his luck. He had just killed the man responsible for the contract on his father, and here was the man who had killed his grandmother, just stood there begging to be shot. Claude wasn't about to leave him wanting. He took his aim, ready to kill the young man and have his second helping of revenge in as many minutes.

A hail of gunfire thumped into the spire overhead. It was the imperial sharpshooters, but they were at such an angle they couldn't get a shot on him when he ducked low. As it turned out, they didn't need to. A full terracotta tile fell on him, cracking across the back of his head and shoulder. He squeezed a bullet from his rifle, but missed the murdering bastard. By the time he was ready to fire again, William and his companions were on the run.

Claude set off at a run, stopping to fire where he could. His aim was hampered by the quantity of spires and as soon as he caught a glimpse of William he was gone. Claude spent a full clip of ammunition on bad shots, and when he paused to reload, it allowed the trio to slip from his grasp. They fled into the tower and disappeared.

Though it was awkward balancing over wobbling and uneven scaffolding, he crossed the rooftop in good time. Hopping down, he burst through the door to the stairwell. Fortunately, William of Fairshore wasn't in there waiting for him with a loaded gun. Unfortunately, from the gunshots below, it seemed William was quite far ahead of him, clashing with the city guard. Claude couldn't let a nameless guardsman steal his kill.

As he came to a small chamber halfway down the spiralling stairway, he encountered guards coming up. None of them had seen him, they were all piling out through a narrow doorway to a mezzanine for the choir. He fired three shots in quick succession, and dashed forwards to collect a pistol from the grip of a dying man before he dropped it. He used that to send a bullet through the face of another guard, panting up the stairs. Quickly, he loaded another clip and was out onto the choir balcony.

A guard was ahead of him, moving for a door at the far side. Claude dispatched him quickly, then sent another shot into the crowd in the cathedral below. The civilians had come inside to get out of the chaos, but once one of the heads in the press was blown apart in a shower of gore, a fresh chaos was made. With any luck, the fearful stampede to get out would prevent the entry of any more guards.

Claude shouldered through the next door into a hallway. A door at the far end was flapping open in the breeze. He ran for it, barging through that one too, and found himself outside in a small walled cemetery. He was atop a wooden staircase leading from the rectory to the rows of neat graves. Some idiotic town planner had put an access way to the sewers right at the centre of it; the cover was off and two of the rooftop shooters had fled down it already. One of them remained.

'*William of Fairshore.*' Claude smirked, levelling his rifle. 'I knew it was you, even from such a distance.'

'I don't know you.' William looked nervous. 'We have no quarrel, there's no need to fight. You need to get out of here as much as I do.'

'I will, as soon as I've settled this.' Claude raised his rifle to fire.

Before he could shoot, William raised his hands in the air and threw himself down the manhole. He could be heard scraping down the sides before he hit the bottom with a thump. Claude was taken aback by the young man's recklessness, but he wouldn't be denied his revenge. He rushed down the steps and across the graveyard, and peered into the hole. Just as he looked, William's body was dragged out of the dim light below. Claude could see the painful twitching of his legs. William was still alive.

Hearing more guards approaching through the rectory, Claude tossed his rifle over his shoulder on a strap and opted to follow. The trio could be waiting for him, but that was a risk he was willing to take. As he neared the bottom, he hopped off the rungs to fall the last few feet. He landed in a crouch and spun around, readying his rifle. There was nobody there.

Claude stalked through the sewers, using the low light that bled down through drains to see. After a short while, it became apparent that William and his companions had gotten away. Giving up on the pursuit for now, Claude's focus shifted to his escape, and he put as much distance as he could between himself and the square.

Once he had covered enough ground, he removed his woollen over shirt and tossed it into a channel of faeces. His rifle was similarly discarded. He could always buy another. Finding a ladder, he made his way out of the sewer and into the early evening breeze.

The area of the city he found himself in was quiet enough, and he wasn't seen pulling himself out of the sewer. His priority then was to find himself some accommodation and get washed. He undoubtedly smelled horrendous, and the guard would be looking for men who had fled through the sewers. Hunching his shoulders, he kept his head down as he passed depressed revellers flooding the smaller streets. He didn't see any trouble, and found himself at a rundown saloon in no time. It was the sort of place that would ask few questions; perfect for him.

Before heading inside, a small notice caught his eye. Below a poster boasting of that month's specials – including roast shimmerfin and garlic soup – was a dog-eared square of parchment sporting a crude drawing and the words "False Butcher." Claude thumbed the edge flat and read it.

While the drawing looked more like an aged cutthroat than the fresh faced William of Fairshore, the writing read, "Join the Hunt today! William of Fairshore, blacklisted assassin, has disgraced our beloved Prize and must pay. Meetings daily at the local outpost. Attendance three coppers. Beverages provided."

Claude stroked his chin with a wry smile, noticing for the first time in days that his head didn't hurt at all. Perhaps he had found his purpose in this new life?

Claude found the outpost a few days later. It was disguised, as many others were, as a hellish little dive. What was strange, however, was that rather than being hidden away in cellars or back rooms, the assassins had spilled into the street. There were so many here that a sort of festival had sprung up between three dingy taverns. People were stumbling about, or sharing laughter and drinks. A few benches that had been stolen from a local park had been arranged in the road; any carriages were diverted down alleyways or turned back.

Claude approached cautiously, finding a group towards the centre who didn't appear too rowdy. He waited for a natural pause in their conversation before interjecting, 'Excuse me. What's going on here, exactly?'

'A celebration. What does it look like?' One of the younger men with a scuffed and dirty shirt cheered his glass enthusiastically.

Claude scowled and was about to ask why when one of the others answered his question pre-emptively.

'The outpost was raided after the emperor was killed. We were all taken in for questioning, but as none of us matched the descriptions of those seen fleeing the New Gods' Cathedral we were all released.' This one was more smartly dressed than his counterpart. His shirt was tucked in for a start, and he wore a waistcoat that fit tightly to his slender frame. He wouldn't have looked like an assassin at all if it hadn't been for the bruising and stitches around his nose and one eye. 'It seems the imperials have bigger fish to fry than a few low-rent killers. William of Fairshore for one.'

One of the others, a broad gentleman with a bald, rutted head, spat to the cobbles.

'William of Fairshore?' Claude mused. 'You think he had something to do with the emperor's killing?'

'No doubt.' The assassin in the waistcoat took a sip of his ale, looping a thumb into his pocket. 'When I was interrogated by the guard I managed to get a little information out of them myself: three men and one woman were seen in that cathedral. One was too short with dark hair. Two were blonde, one tall and scarred – like yourself…'

He trailed off, the atmosphere turning a little frosty. 'That wasn't you was it, allied with the False Butcher?'

'It wasn't me *allied* with the False Butcher, no.' Claude smirked. 'But it was me trying to kill the boy, almost got him too. Tossed himself into the sewer to get away. I imagine he broke something, but his allies dragged him away quickly enough. I lost him.'

The youngest and drunkest of the three looked on in awe and admiration. The waistcoat wearer simply showed respect, holding out a hand to shake.

'Yves Kaplan.' He smiled and then winced at the pain of tugged stitches. 'And you are?'

'Claude…' He thought back to the surnames of his college chums. The memories were foggy now, but he still managed to pull a name from the mists. 'Claude Montgomery.'

'Well, it's a pleasure to meet you.' Yves gripped his hand and shook it firmly. 'So, if you were there, you can confirm this third man: average height, blonde. It was William of Fairshore?'

Claude nodded.

'I knew it.' Yves snatched a fist in the air enthusiastically. 'I knew he was in the city, and I'm now certain it was him who gave me these wounds.'

He gestured to his face.

In his past life, Claude would have dismissed the man as a terrible failure for getting bested by one such as William of Fairshore, but he had been killed after challenging the boy. Granted, it wasn't William who had killed him, but he was still a force to be reckoned with.

'Well then, gentlemen...' Claude pulled the crumpled poster from his pocket and smoothed it out. 'This is the right place to find out about *the Hunt?*'

'You've definitely come to the right place for that.' The younger, more excitable man grinned.

The broad one clapped Claude on the back. 'What say I fetch you a drink?'

'Yes, you must drink with us! What do you like, Claude?' Yves was mirroring the enthusiasm of his young counterpart now. 'Then we can discuss our hunt.'

'Sherry should do nicely.' Claude watched as the brute waddled away through the revellers to the nearest tavern. He cleared his throat, turning things to business before they could devolve into high spirited drinking. Assassins often had good intentions, but the worst work ethics – it was best to strike while the iron was hot. 'How do you intend to find this False Butcher? What if he's left the city already?'

'I'm certain that he is laying low.' Yves huddled in close as if they weren't surrounded by a crowd of co-conspirators. 'We have good people watching every road out of the city. As soon as he is seen, word will be sent and we will strike.'

Claude pursed his lips and surveyed the frivolities in the street. 'Seems you have a decent operation going on here, despite the informality of it all.'

'You have to keep the common killer on side somehow, and we are far more likely to kill the False Butcher as a group.' Yves smiled affably, but winced as his wound pulled taut. 'I wouldn't like to fight him one on one for a second time.'

'Is everyone here for his blood?'

'I'm sure there are some here for the joy of company, but this is a fallow year. We have to make our names somehow and killing the Guild's biggest embarrassment is a good way to do it.'

'I know I'm here to make my name,' the younger assassin agreed. 'When I put a bullet in his chest, "Elias Allen" will be on the lips of every assassin on the whitelist. I'll be as famous as any man-butcher.'

Claude decided that staying with the Hunt would be a good idea. While Yves didn't seem all that much of a fighter, he clearly had a knack for organisation and was Claude's best way of tracking his target. The others could join, but he would be the one to kill William. If anyone got in his way, ally or not, they would have to die too.

# 1683
## WILLIAM OF FAIRSHORE

Though the road was wide and flagged with good stone, it was rutted in places, and slowly being consumed by persistent weeds and spiny trees. Outcrops of granite and craggy foothills obscured the way, both behind and ahead. It meant the coach would be harder to track, but there was also a chance William would steer around a corner and be no more than two hundred yards from a guard battalion.

'I can't believe they didn't follow us out.' Gwyneth had been watching the road ever since she had awoken.

'I've been thinking about it most of the night.' William navigated the carriage around a large pothole. He and Goldin had been taking it in turns to drive and only stopped when the horses absolutely needed it. 'They didn't know what we had done initially, just that the alarm had been raised and that we were fleeing. It doesn't make sense to chase us to the corners of the map.'

'They'll know now though, won't they?' Goldin sounded worried for the first time since William had known him. 'There's no telling how far they'll chase us now. Right off the edge of the map, if possible.'

'Still, we have good aliases, and we'll be at D'Arnao in no time. Alwyn will help us, of that I'm certain.' The fact that Gwyneth had to declare her certainty was not a good indication of its validity. 'It's a wonder what money and status can do.'

She shifted on the coach cushion and hissed with pain.

'Try not to move your arm too much,' Goldin grumbled, fussing over the bloodied bindings.

'Sorry,' William said. 'I really didn't mean to stab you.'

'Let it go, Will.' Gwyneth grunted as Goldin tugged on the bandage. 'If you hadn't stuck me with that blade we might all be dead. Then again, if you'd hit your mark we wouldn't be having this conversation. Regardless, I didn't hire you for your knife throwing skills.'

William slowed the horses, steering carefully around a carriage that was stopped at the side of the road. Two men were sat at a campfire, a pair of glossy mares cropping rough grass just beyond. A kettle, sat amidst the flames, started to whistle as they passed.

'How do?' One of the men tipped his hat in greeting as he lifted the kettle from the fire. His companion looked on with a flinty gaze.

'Morning.' William nodded, encouraging the horses with the reins. He didn't like coming across folk on the road. Any one of them could be an informant for the pursuing imperials. Then again, the imperials had likely sent pigeons to every major settlement warning of their crimes. The three of them didn't exactly blend easily into a crowd.

'Did you see they had birds in the back of that carriage?' Goldin whispered.

'I did,' William lied. Somehow, he thought that if he pretended he knew, it might make it less of a terrifying revelation. 'They might just be hunters or messengers.'

'Hunters or messengers for the imperials,' Goldin posited. 'What if they report our position back to Vitale?'

'Perhaps we should go back and kill them... or at least tie them up.' Gwyneth was joining in now, betraying her true fears.

'We can't just kill or subdue everyone we see.' William had to be the voice of reason. He didn't want to be, but it seemed nobody else was volunteering. 'It'll make a trail that will lead the imperial guard right to us.'

He spied the tall hotels of D'Arnao clinging to the mountainside ahead as the coach came out of light tree cover. In less than an hour, they would be in the town and under the protection of possibly the most powerful family in the Empire. If anyone could push an assassinated emperor under the rug it was them.

'We're almost at the rendezvous, like you said. Alwyn will help us.' Gods, William hoped that was true.

He hadn't quite contemplated what the life of a senator killer might be like, let alone a killer of the new emperor. Now he was staring such a life in the face, it was impossible to think of anything else. His prospects didn't look good. A life of hiding from imperial guards was made all the worse when one was blacklisted and had a price on their head. He wouldn't even have the refuge of guild outposts to keep him sane.

'You're right.' Gwyneth sat straight in her chair, turning away from the road behind. 'We made it out; there's no need to worry now. What's the likelihood of the imperials even finding us? Vitulus is a big country. The Empire even bigger.'

She paused a moment, then said, 'I suppose, once we meet with Alwyn, we'll be going our separate ways. It'll be even harder for the guard to identify us then.'

William inclined his head. It was the first time he had really considered it. He had gotten used to travelling as a trio, and having two friends was certainly better than only having one. He was still annoyed that Gwyneth had killed Sepo, but could he really blame her for it? That mess was entirely too tangled and upsetting to unpick now, and he knew that if there was anyone to blame, it was himself. He pushed Kupela to the back of his mind, where she might find good company in the restless spirit of Vesta, and tried his hardest to think of something else.

'Where do you think you'll go?' Gwyneth asked. 'Are you staying together? Or going your separate ways?'

'I'd like to think we're travelling together,' Goldin grumbled as though the prospect of splitting up hadn't occurred to him either. 'But, we do stand out as a pair, I suppose. If the imperials are coming…'

'I don't want to go back to travelling alone,' William stated, the words coming out stiff and awkward.

'I'm just trying to think of what's best for you.' Gwyneth shrugged the shoulder that was still capable of flexing. 'I don't want the pair of you getting caught as soon as I leave with Uncle Alwyn. Kupela will have reported our appearances to the guard, and you'll look far less conspicuous apart.'

'She might be right, Will.'

William tensed as Goldin said it.

'We're better off alive apart than dead together.' The little man mused a second. 'Perhaps we should part ways at D'Arnao, but have a destination in mind – somewhere safe, outside the Empire.'

'Where?' William didn't want to entertain the notion, but knew it would be far easier for civilians to relate them to wanted posters if they were together. It only took one do-gooder to bring the Empire down on their heads.

'Somewhere in Kirgh?' Goldin shrugged. 'Once we're across the border we can meet up again. Nobody will care who we are there. We can live high on the hog with all this gold we've earned.'

William wanted to say no. He wanted to say that they would be better suited fighting any trouble together, but conflicts avoided were better than conflicts won.

'Kirgh then,' he agreed. 'We'll find a map in D'Arnao and pick a nice place. Once we're paid, we'll leave town separately and reunite there.'

Minutes earlier, D'Arnao had looked like a bastion of hope clinging to the mountainside, all colourful render and gleaming windows. It now looked ominous; it was the end of something good and the start of something a whole lot worse, and it was getting closer an awful lot faster than William liked.

The carriage trundled up the hill, the road winding around rocks like a snake. A gust of smoke wafted across the route, heavy with the stink of pork fat and charcoal, dimming the blue sky above. The outskirts of the town were quiet, but William took comfort in it. Fewer people meant less chances to be identified. But, as the coach neared the square, it became apparent that something was wrong.

'Where is everybody?' Goldin voiced.

'No idea.' William peered down each street and alleyway as they passed. Since they had crossed paths with the two men at the side of the road, they hadn't seen anyone. There were no travellers or townsfolk, and not a single stray dog, horse, or twitching curtain to be seen.

'Maybe we should turn back.' Goldin's worry was palpable now. 'What if the imperials knew we were headed here? They could be waiting for us.'

'Nonsense.' Gwyneth dismissed him. 'Alwyn would have gotten word to us if they had.'

'Are you certain?' William considered turning back, but as they crested a rise and the town square came into view, he realised it was too late. There was a whole caravan of coaches and carriages waiting for them. William prayed it was the Finchleys, but something in his gut told him they were not. He hoped it was just his nerves.

'Of course I'm certain.' Gwyneth stood to get a better view ahead. 'See, here's my uncle's caravan now.'

She didn't sound too convincing, but William managed to restrain himself from asking if she was certain yet again. Tensions were high and he didn't want to cause a rift before a potential ambush.

'Have your weapons ready, either way.'

'One step ahead of you.' Goldin pulled back the hammer on the pistol he still couldn't reliably reload. He had the thing cradled in two hands, concealed between his knees.

'Mine always are, but we won't need them. Look.' Gwyneth pointed as a man came forward from the circle of carriages. He was tall and slender, his lofty body bent diagonal from halfway up his spine. There was no doubting it was Alwyn. He moved to a table that had been dragged into the centre of the square from one of the eateries and sat. Three empty chairs awaited.

William directed the coach to the edge of the square and brought the horses to a rest. Gwyneth hopped down to the cobbles first, her fears apparently gone now she was back in the safety of her family unit.

William couldn't match her cool; it all seemed so ominous. He shared a glance with Goldin. The little man holstered his pistol but kept the hammer back, ready to fire if needed. William had his guns too – the silver flintlock at his hip and Silvio's three shooter inside his jacket. He comforted himself with the fact that both were loaded and ready as he alighted the carriage.

Gwyneth dashed to Alwyn and wrapped him in her arms. He cringed away as she planted a kiss on his sallow cheek.

'I've missed you, Uncle.' She squeezed him tight, his face gurning in disgust, then released him to address the others. 'I've missed you all.'

Alwyn retrieved a handkerchief from his pocket and wiped his face where she had kissed him, then neatly folded it and tossed it over his shoulder. The monogramed square landed in a dirty puddle. 'We've... missed you too.'

William approached the table and chairs cautiously, aware of all the Finchley eyes on him; there could be a hundred all in all, shared between about sixty onlookers. There was the one whose wife and children had been killed by him and Goldin on the road, looking on with scorn. There was the lazy-eyed boy, who seemed unaware of much. The surgeon who had healed William's punctured foot was there too. Nearby, was the one who had fired the crossbow, sticking the foot in the first place. Gwyneth waved to him and he smiled back.

Another was waving at them too; a beautiful young woman with blonde hair and blue eyes, though most notably half her face was engulfed in scars. She looked to have been burned.

'Hello, Gwyneth,' she called over. 'Hello, Will.'

Her voice was high-born, with a slight lisp, and altogether too cheery. Given the circumstances, William found her more than a little unsettling.

'First of all'– Alwyn drew attention by snapping his fingers –'I'd like to preface this little debriefing by saying a rousing *well done* to the three of you.'

He paused to let William and Goldin sit.

'Never, in all my years, have I seen a game called early in favour of the elevators. I didn't think it possible, but here we are. We've won, and we get to enjoy the remainder of the year spending our victory bonus.' He clasped his hands. 'I can't wait.'

'And our payment?' Goldin was as blunt as ever.

'All sorted and secured. Though, there is *one* little caveat.' Alwyn held his finger and thumb a thousandth of an inch apart. 'The money's ready for you in the bank, but I've had to have the accounts listed under an alias. I plumped for William's – the new one, as the former was somehow compromised. Do you still have your papers?'

'I think so.' William patted his pocket; the envelope Gwyneth had given him at Kupela's house was still inside.

'All it means is that William will have to draw the money out and share it. I assume you trust each other.' He smiled.

'That's fine with me.' Goldin sniffed and nodded.

'Good. There is something–'

'Why is the town deserted?' William interrupted. 'We've not seen anyone since we got here.'

'Oh!' Alwyn chuckled. 'I imagine it was quite strange rolling into the place like that. Don't worry, we had D'Arnao cleared on the pretence of plague. We didn't want to be seen with the three most highly sought criminals in the Empire. I'm sure you understand.'

'But you can fix that, can't you?' Unease had crept into Gwyneth's voice.

'Normally, yes. There are a few wrinkles, however.' Alwyn inclined his head, or relaxed himself to his natural crooked posture. 'You didn't use an alias, so your true name is out there. That goes for Gwyneth *and* William. It didn't take long for them to figure out Aler Goldin either. There are prices on your names and heads, and the empress is determined to collect.'

'Empress?' William frowned, something in his chest sinking.

'Haven't you heard?' Alwyn chuckled. 'Why else would the game be called in our favour? You managed to get the subject to the highest station in the Empire.'

He shrugged with a frown, taking the trio's stunned silence for misunderstanding.

'Once Sepo Falade was chosen for emperor, the new line was set. You had him killed and the title fell to his daughter.' Alwyn held up his hands. 'It's quite simple, really–'

'Yes,' William interrupted again. 'We understand.'

He stared into the middle distance. He couldn't quite comprehend it; the thought hadn't crossed his mind since they had escaped. Not only was the Empire after him, but *the empress* would have a personal vendetta against him. It meant a life of hiding, and sooner or later, discovery and death.

'But you can fix it?' Gwyneth pressed. 'New aliases? Pay off the right people?'

'For you, Gwyneth, I would love to. You truly are the best of us when it comes to plotting and playing these games. It has been an honour to compete with you at my side.' He twisted his head in the opposite direction, then rolled his shoulders. There was a rattle of clicks from his spine. 'This brings me to our main issue: Uncle Freddy.'

Gwyneth's head dipped.

'Word has spread quickly. We know you kept him as a prisoner. We know you beat him. And we know why.' He pursed his lips. 'I didn't realise that you were so uncomfortable with our practices when it comes to those with bad blood. Personally, I thought you were too young to be subjected to that display you saw as a child. Perhaps if you weren't introduced in such a way, you would have a different opinion. The fact remains: we do not harm Finchleys with pure blood, and we do not tolerate those who are spoiled.'

William's hand slid casually across his leg to find his flintlock. The atmosphere had soured and he had a feeling he would be needing it.

'I'm sure Freddy will be mobilising the Badgers now,' Alwyn continued, fixing his gaze on Gwyneth. 'They will be on the hunt for bad blood soon enough. In addition, orders have come from the Patriarch himself. You are to be made an example of. As far as the family is concerned, you're bad blood too. By rights, we should kill you here and now.'

William's hand tightened around his pistol. He could feel all the eyes on him, though thankfully his hand was concealed by the table rim. If he shot Alwyn, however, there would be twenty or more pistols to retort.

'I don't want to do that.' Alwyn shrugged. 'I can't kill our best; it's madness. But all the same, you can't come with us. To that end, there is money enough for all three of you in William's account.'

There was a shout from the top of one of the hotels. William looked up to see a Finchley with a long dress and trailing beard leaning out from a balcony.

'Alwyn!' they called. 'Carriages on the horizon, tens of them!'

Alwyn sighed. 'It sounds like the imperials have tracked you down. I'm sorry we had to part this way.'

He stood, twirling a finger in the air. The coachmen took it as their signal to leave and began stirring their horses.

'Alwyn, wait.' Gwyneth was on her feet now. 'You've got to take me with you. You said it yourself, the family missed me. Maybe I could talk to the Patriarch, or the Matriarch. I can explain myself. I didn't beat him that badly. He'll recover fine.'

'It's not that you beat him, Gwyn.' Alwyn rounded on her. 'It's *why* you beat him. It shows your values aren't in line with those of the family at large. It means you can't be trusted. There's nothing I can do for you.'

'Please. You can't leave me alone.' She grabbed him by the lapels of his jacket. 'We're family.'

'I can and must.' He pushed her forcibly and she fell backwards onto the cobbles.

William was on his feet, his hand on his pistol, but he didn't know what to do with it. Alwyn had done right by him. He had completed a job and been paid for it. As far as a balance book was concerned, everything was right with the world. A deal had been done, actions had been taken, and consequences were always inevitable. But a balance book didn't feel that subtle drag of guilt, or see the heartbreak in Gwyneth.

The carriages started to move in a circular path around the statue at the centre of the square. Alwyn clambered into his coach, calling instructions to the others. The first of the Finchleys turned onto the north road, and slowly the procession followed.

'I've done all I can for you, but our business arrangements are done.' Alwyn was addressing William now. 'Don't follow us. If you bring the imperials our way, we *will* kill you. Please, look after my niece.'

As the last of the carriages rumbled away, it became apparent that one had been left behind – horseless and driverless beside the statue. The door was open but the interior was dark, and though William squinted, he couldn't tell what was inside.

'What are we going to do?' Goldin sucked pensively on his protruding tooth.

'I'm not sure.' William moved to the abandoned carriage and clambered atop. From there he could see through a gap between the buildings to the southern road. There were a lot of carriages and they were approaching fast. 'The horses still look fresh, they'll be faster than ours.'

'We can't help that, but we can still get a head start on them. If they don't see where we go they might just pass us by.' Goldin helped Gwyneth up off the cobbles.

She wasn't sobbing, but her face was a picture of despair and tears rolled silently down her cheeks. William couldn't comprehend her pain. He was used to having no one, and had lost his family so long ago he couldn't remember what the severing of that bond felt like.

'We can't follow the north road.' Gwyneth sniffed, trying to compose herself as she stood. 'We need to abide by Alwyn, even now.'

'I agree.' William hopped down from the carriage. 'South's out too, as that's where the imperials are coming from.'

'So… the way I see it.' Goldin craned his neck up. 'We can climb through the mountains and try to lose them there, or take a boat across the lake.'

'We'll be too visible on the water.' William dismissed the idea, peering into the abandoned carriage. 'And we'd never survive the wilds, even if we evaded the imperials.'

'At least I'm coming up with some ideas, what do you suggest?' Goldin started to pace. 'We can't just stay here.'

'Can't we?'

William stepped into the carriage. It was filled with armaments, sacks, and boxes. There were a few rifles along with a blunderbuss and some powder grenades. Ether bottles jangled in a crate as William's leg brushed by. He picked up one of the sacks and weighed it in his hand. It was heavy, and from the black crumbs that came through the weave, he could tell it was the best gunpowder. It appeared the Finchleys had already come to the same conclusion that he had.

'We should ambush the imperials here,' he decided.

'What, like a last stand?' Goldin balked. 'They'll wipe us out.'

'Not a last stand, no – I'd like to see the other side of it – but a stand nonetheless.' William tossed the black powder to Goldin. 'If we get ourselves in a strategic position and surprise the imperials, we might just wipe *them* out.'

The imperials moved into the town through the narrow roads and, as they drew closer, became obscured by the high buildings. William had no doubt that they would eventually find their way to the square. There was only one main road that ran through D'Arnao and it cut right through the centre from south to north. The imperials would know something was wrong by the time they got there, but would, gods willing, still be surprised by the ambush.

William had hauled a supply of weapons and ammunition to the top of a hotel and had taken position on a balcony. From here, he could rain down enough lead on his pursuers to force them to turn back. It had worked in Blackbile, when he and Beechworth had fought off countless Sacrificial Lambs, and he prayed it would work here too.

Goldin and Gwyneth were in similar positions at different hotels bordering the square. The idea was that they could be less easily cornered and trick the imperials into thinking there was more than just the three of them. It would be hard for anyone in the square to take stock when being fired upon from multiple angles.

They had of course made provisions for escape should each of their hotels be breached. Gwyneth and Goldin's were adjacent to one another. With the aid of a little black powder, a hole big enough to crawl through had been made between the two. If one of their buildings was breached, one could fall back to the other. From there, Gwyneth was in possession of a crossbow from the Finchley stash which could be used to fire a rope to an adjacent building. The pair would be safe, relatively speaking, which wasn't saying much given the situation.

William's hotel was across the square from theirs, but they had used black powder in one of the rooms and had blown a hole positioned so that he could leap down to a lower building. From there, he could make his way around the square and down the high street across the rooftops to get out. It wasn't ideal, but it would have to do.

While it was comforting to have a plan to fall back on, William knew that by the end of the day they would likely all be captured or dead. As it wasn't the most constructive notion, he ignored it for the time being, and ensured all his weapons were correctly loaded and arranged. He could see Goldin and Gwyneth preparing similarly in their own vantages.

Most of the Finchley weapons used the new bullets with brass casings, and William had an ample supply. He was, however, far more comfortable and accurate with his silver flintlock. He spent his last moments of preparation folding and filling paper cartridges. By the time he heard the rumble of cartwheels on stone, he had made himself in excess of twenty. He loaded one into his flintlock and slipped it back into his holster, opting instead to start the battle with a three-shot rifle. Accuracy didn't matter so much when firing into a crowd.

Keeping low, he moved to the edge of the balcony and peered down. The balustrade around the edge was stone, supported by thick columns. Between them, through trailing ivy, William could see into the square below and keep hidden. He waited a while, listening to the approaching carriages, his chest tightening as if a leather belt had been pulled around it and buckled. He didn't want this fight, but what other choice did he have?

After what felt like minutes, the first horse appeared in the mouth of the main street. It pulled a carriage to the right and moved some way into the square to allow room for others. Though the thing flew an imperial banner from a pole strapped to one of the corners, the men riding on top hardly seemed regimented. As William watched them aim about cautiously with firearms of every sort, he realised they were not dressed in uniform at all.

More supposed imperials spilled into the square, sticking to the edges to avoid the Finchleys' abandoned carriage in the centre. William was already working out who had followed him, when a particularly fine carriage rolled into view and confirmed his suspicions. It was red sided with gold trim and was pulled by four horses. One of the men sat on the bench was easily recognised. Yves

Kaplan, the assassin William had thumped in Vitale. He was barking orders.

William knew then that this was the Hunt, come to kill him. It was worrying, though they weren't quite as terrifying as the Vitulans. These men at least had finite resources and no chance of reinforcements. He wanted to breathe a sigh of relief, but knew it was still too soon for such things. What he couldn't stop, however, was the almost pleasant realisation that it might be possible to live through this whole ordeal. If the pressure in his chest had been from a tightening belt, it loosened a few notches.

Shifting to get a better look at the crowd of assassins curling into the space beneath, he assessed their threat more objectively. While they would be well versed in killing, a few of the firearms seemed to be of fairly low quality. One man didn't even have a weapon and was merely cracking his knuckles in preparation. The assassins also seemed unable to work together as a whole, forming instead into smaller bands. Most paid little heed to what Yves was shouting. William hoped, because of that, their numbers would prove meaningless.

There was a larger group of assassins closer to the gold trimmed carriage who seemed to be more organised, however. At first, William thought that they were obeying Yves' commands, but they appeared to be looking to another for direction. Then he spied the true leader, sat atop a thoroughbred steed. The man had cropped, blonde hair, and his face was a patchwork of red scars. William's heart sank; it was the gunman who had killed the emperor and had come a hair's breadth from killing him too. Perhaps this fight wouldn't be so easy after all.

The gunman scrutinised the square. He was the only one who looked anywhere other than the ominously waiting carriage, and he seemed to linger on prime vantages – among them, Goldin and Gwyneth's balconies. For a heartbeat, William thought the man had spotted him as his own balcony was assessed, but the steely glare passed by all the same. Moments later, the gunman slipped from the horse's back, pulled a rifle from a holster affixed to the saddle, and disappeared between the carriages.

# 1683
## CLAUDE BEECHWORTH

'When I kill the False Butcher...' The young, enthusiastic Elias was sat atop a case strapped to a carriage roof, polishing an undersized pistol. 'I'm going to use my name and status to get bigger and better contracts. Maybe contracts so dangerous it'll take a band of men to complete them. We could continue the Hunt then.'

The Hunt had been travelling for a few days now, and had been together weeks before Claude joined. It hadn't taken long for them to become closely knit. Being an assassin was a lonely life for the most part and it seemed half of them would be content to track William forever. Elias, however, was as keen for the kill as Claude.

'That's not a bad idea.' Yves tossed the words over his shoulder and gently steered around a bend in the road. 'It would be nice to work together still, once our target is dead, but you're forgetting one thing. I'm the one who's going to end that cheater's life.'

'My arse.' It was the brutish one's turn now. He was in the back of a nearby coach that was crammed with surly or sleeping assassins. Only a few paid heed to the conversation; most found Elias too wearisome. 'Look how scrawny you are, Yves. You're a good leader, I'll give you that, but you're not fit for fighting the False Butcher.'

Claude tended to agree. Yves had proven quite the ally. Not only had his band of hunters managed to spot the False Butcher leaving Vitale, scouts were able to keep track of his coach for miles. It was through a combination of riding ahead to possible destinations, pursuing off-road through trees, and spying on the coaches' progression from distant vantages. These scouts had been instrumental, and without them and their messages, William would have been lost.

'When we find him, I'm going to run up to him and nut him so hard his eyes'll pop and his head'll fall off his neck.' The brute snorted a laugh. 'Even so, I'll let you bask in my reflected glory. I imagine it'll have been quite the honour to have travelled the road with me, the Butcher-Butcher... or is that the Butcher Butcherer?'

As the brute confused himself further, Claude turned his attention back to the road, barely resisting the urge to roll his eyes. While most of the hunters were travelling in comfort on coaches and carriages, he had opted to ride in the saddle. It would enable him to break free of the pack more easily and give chase if needed. He had to reach William first, and he simply had to be the one to kill him.

'I wouldn't worry about your new title, anyway.' Elias interrupted the brute's musings. 'By the time you get to him, I'll have already put a bullet in his chest. I'll be the Butcher Slayer, and the new leader of this sorry little band of killers. Sorry, Yves.'

Yves chuckled.

'With that thing?' the brute scoffed, nodding at the eager young man's modest pistol. 'What does it shoot, dried peas?'

Claude had to admit that while the brute was, well, brutish, he was awfully perceptive and his brash remarks were often close to the bone. Claude found himself agreeing with the man a lot, though he wouldn't have admitted it. With regards to Elias' pistol, Claude had spotted the boy's mistake early, though had opted to keep quiet. It was a circus sharpshooter's pistol. The thing was built for close range accuracy and not for killing, and as such, the calibre of bullets it took was incredibly small. He had no doubt it could still blow a hole through a man at close range, but at any distance over twenty feet he imagined William of Fairshore might brush the bullets right off. Still, it was one less man to compete with for the kill.

'Jests aside.' Elias rolled his shoulders manfully. 'I've been practicing my target shooting and I think I've a good chance of besting the False Butcher.'

Elias cast about like a meerkat atop a rock, assumedly expecting some doubt in his companions. As his gaze passed Claude, he paused and cocked an eyebrow. Claude hadn't voiced any disagreement, he had been keeping quiet purposely, but his thoughts must have been painted in his expression. It was much harder to conceal one's emotions when unaccustomed to a new face.

'You don't think I will?' Elias postured. 'I suppose you think you'll kill him.'

'Every assassin here thinks they will be the one to do it.' It was a kind of non-answer, and it suited Claude perfectly. 'Maybe you'll succeed. Maybe not.'

He appreciated the work the hunters had put into tracking William, but he wouldn't let any of them take his revenge from him. While he might let them bask in *his* reflected glory once he had killed their target, if one of the hunters came close to killing William before he had the chance, he would certainly end them. He was here for one reason only, and that was revenge taken by his own hand. No one would stop him, friend or foe.

As D'Arnao came into view, a sense of anticipation came over him. This was the place scouts had spotted William arriving at only hours before. If he wasn't still in the town, he would certainly not be far beyond it, but no message had come from scouts to the north. Claude had the feeling he would be getting his revenge before the day was out; it sent a shiver through him. All the loose ends from his previous life would be tied in the neatest of bows, and everything he had left undone would be finished.

Death had been so terribly inconvenient for Claude. His life had been cut short and the world had carried on without him; everything he had been working towards had been forgotten. The feeling was akin to that of losing a favourite book, half read. There were still stories and plots to be concluded, but no way of seeing them to fruition. His second chance was like discovering that same book years later and being able to finish it at last. It didn't feel the same as it had before, the conclusions to his arcs less impactful for the intermission, but he was compelled to put an end to things for completion's sake. His only fear: what would happen then?

He had been stirred to action by his headaches. The pain wouldn't let him sit still for five minutes, his body needing the constant stimulation of lifetime activities to remind it that it wasn't still dead. Once William was killed, and his goals were achieved, would his body allow him to retire to the coast, to live out his days in comfort and peace? He dreaded the headaches coming back.

'You made it then?' A woman on horseback, one of the scouts, had ridden up to the convoy while Claude had been deep in thought.

'That we did.' Yves crossed the reins over in his lap and sat back more comfortably to peer up at the town clinging to the cliffs. 'Is he still there?'

'I believe so.' The scout rounded her horse and joined the slow progress of the carriages. 'A caravan left only hours ago, we didn't see him among them. We would have ventured into the town, but the place is deserted. It started to feel like an ambush, so I turned back.'

'An ambush, eh? It matters not. William has two allies, we have'– Yves cast an eye over his travelling companions –'enough. I doubt they can cause us much bother.'

Claude was reminded of the time he and William held off countless Lambs in the Blackbile clock tower. With the right vantage and equipment, it was possible for so little to beat so many. If William had remained in the town, he had no doubt fortified his position by now. But Yves was right – the False Butcher's efforts would amount to nought in the end. He could slaughter as many of the hunters as he wanted, they would provide a superb distraction while Claude set to work.

The convoy moved from steep fields into the town's outskirts and the atmosphere became more muted. The scout had been right, even from her cautionary sortie. There wasn't a single soul left in D'Arnao.

'How can someone clear a whole town?' Elias spoke in a hushed tone. Even so, it carried over the quiet.

Nobody replied for a while, each contemplating on the implications this had. It could mean the False Butcher had a greater force than expected. After all, three people couldn't evacuate so many.

'I think the locals had gone before William arrived,' the scout offered as comfort. 'It may have been the caravan's doing. They're well down the northern road now and not looking back; they shouldn't be a problem.'

'We can only hope,' Yves remarked.

It was slow going up the winding road through D'Arnao. As they went, passing open doors and abandoned houses, a few assassins posited that William could be lurking in any one of them. Claude didn't think so. While William might have a better chance of evading discovery by skulking in a side street shack, he would strike a better blow to the Hunt if they were all collected together. Something like that could only be done in the square, which was exactly where the road took them.

'That doesn't look too welcoming.' Yves was the first to remark on the abandoned carriage as the square came into view. He pulled on the reins to slow his carriage; others followed suit. 'Perhaps we should head around.'

'Are you having a laugh?' The brute stood up in the back of his coach and jostled the shoulders of a few of his dozing companions. 'This is that ambush you've been fearing. That means the False Butcher's here, and I say we ride into that square and draw him out.'

'I'm not certain it's a good idea: to charge knowingly into an ambush.'

'Onward!' The brute reached over and clapped the driver of his coach on the shoulder. 'Fortune favours the bold, not the meek.'

The coach of assassins started moving again, as did most others. Claude lingered a moment, wondering whether now would be the best time to part from the hunters. They were most certainly posturing their way towards a foolish death. He would rather be flanking the False Butcher while they did so, but he needed the worm to reveal himself. With a click, he encouraged his horse forwards for the square. Yves reluctantly followed.

Once in the square proper, the carriages circled around the edge to keep clear of a mysteriously abandoned carriage. Claude peered up at the vacant hotels, each one colourfully rendered with numerous ivy-draped balconies. There were tens of vantages where riflemen could be hiding, and no sign of William.

As the flow of the carriages stopped, Claude dismounted, taking his rifle with him. He tucked himself between two carriages for protection. When the ambushers leapt up and rained down lead, he didn't want to be the first to catch a bullet.

'Someone should check that carriage,' he called out. The thing was obviously central to the False Butcher's plot and whoever went would surely end up dead. Still, the loss of life would be worthwhile if William showed his face as a result.

'I'll do it.' The brute hopped down from the coach. The other assassins were all still fussing with their gear, but he apparently needed none. He rolled up his sleeves, clenched his fists, and strode up to the carriage like he might kill the False Butcher with a single thump.

Claude watched with baited breath as the brute reached the carriage, turned back smugly, and lowered the handle on the door. He braced for an explosion or some other rigged trap. There was none. The brute opened the carriage door, evoking the image of a tripwire drawing the pin from a self-fusing grenade. As the brute stepped up and peered into the gloom, there was still no violent retort. Claude found himself a little disappointed.

'It's empty.' The brutish assassin stuck his head out of the carriage, dumb confusion weighing his prominent brow.

Claude realised something was wrong. While it had been obvious this was an ambush, it wasn't as predictable as he had thought. He searched for a hint of the False Butcher's true plan, half-expecting to find a group of killers approaching the Hunt from the rear. There was no one. For the briefest of moments, he started to think that maybe William had moved on and there was no ambush at all.

Then he heard glass smashing.

He whipped around to see ether spilling across the floor of one of the square-side eateries. Fire was pushing to its edges. With a sinking sensation in his gut, Claude realised that the abandoned carriage had merely been a trick of intimidation, forcing the assassins to huddle at the edges of the square. That was where the real danger lay. His gaze followed the path of fire to a stack of sacks and crates hidden in the recess of the eatery.

'Black powder!' he bellowed, sprinting from cover to get away from the eatery.

There was an almighty explosion behind him. The whole square lit up with flames, the heat of it licking the back of his neck. Wood, glass, and nails sprayed out. A chunk of brick narrowly missed his head and cracked into the statue at the centre of the square. An orb flew over his head, but it was going a different direction to the shrapnel. He spun and focused on it, identifying the orb as a spark powder grenade. It clinked on the floor and rolled under a hunter's carriage, towards the shaded opening of a second eatery.

Claude caught the blast face first. While he was too far away for his skin to be scorched, the silhouettes of five carriages were etched into his vision as the grenade exploded in a flare of purest white. It was the kind of glow given off by a god, the type that could burn a man to a pillar of salt. He tried to cover his eyes, but it was too late. His rifle dropped to the ground and he cradled his face. Not only were his eyes streaming, but his nose was too. Blinded, and deafened by the ringing of his ears, he ran for cover.

He stumbled and gasped, smoke acrid in his mouth. He tripped, scrambled along the ground. His lungs forced out a phlegmy cough. The wooden siding of the abandoned carriage clipped his shoulder as he hurried blindly for cover; he gripped it and hauled himself upright. His eyelids were fluttering to clear his sight as he made his way to the door, the same silhouette still bold in his vision. He fell inside, colliding with someone. Whoever it was pushed him away, and he slumped onto one of the leather benches.

'Who is it?' he hissed between breaths, unable to see in the gloom of the carriage.

'It's me.' The brutish assassin hocked and spat.

'What's happening out there?' Claude wiped his eyes and face, made fists of his hands and pushed them into his sockets. Colours bloomed across his retinas.

'There's a lot of fire,' the brute grunted. 'Dead men too. Though it looks like our lads are just getting their bearings, they're firing up at the hotels.'

'Aren't you going to help them?' Claude's vision was drifting back to him now. That was the benefit of young eyes he supposed – quick to recover.

'I don't think so.' The brute ducked to try and get an angle on the high balconies. 'I'm more of a pugilist than a gunslinger, I won't be much use until we breach the hotels… and there could be tens of them up there. As soon as I step out of this carriage I might be killed.'

'Coward.' Claude sneered and shoved himself to his feet. He grabbed the brute's shoulder and tore him aside, thrusting out into the square in one motion.

There was still the shadow of the explosion faintly in Claude's eyes, but his surroundings were bright enough with fire. He ducked and collected up his rifle, dashing for the next nearest cover – Yves' fine red carriage. The thing was smouldering and Yves was nowhere to be seen. He skidded behind it, his back thumping into the painted wood. All around, men were shooting up and reloading, every now and then an explosion would sound as more grenades were tossed from on high. Claude spied Elias cowering behind a wagon-less wheel, his enthusiasm as absent in the midst of battle as the brute's bravado.

He realised then that the only assassins willing to join a hunt like this and share the spoils, were those not suited for going it alone. In other words: the weak, meek, and pathetic. He hoped he could not count himself amongst them and, as if to challenge the very thought of it, pushed himself brazenly out of cover.

He spotted William's little friend first, tossing another combustible down to the carriages. Not too far from him was the girl he had seen on the New Gods' Cathedral. He took aim for her, and though she had not seen him doing so, she ducked out of sight to reload.

A shot echoed from across the square. Claude spun on his heel and found the target of his ire. William had a pistol in each hand. He fired one shot with one and three with the other, the bullets raining indiscriminately onto the crowd of bumbling assassins. With Yves nowhere to be seen, the group had become uncoordinated and had lost maybe half their number.

'Breach that hotel,' Claude bellowed, pointing for the doors to the building where the little man was stowed away. 'There's only three of them, get in there and put them down!'

At the first signs of a bit of leadership, a few assassins started to see sense. A group of about ten broke off from those gathered amongst the smouldering carriages and charged for the hotel. Claude went the other way, for the one that housed William.

The entrance was conveniently recessed and sheltered by marble columns which helped to protect Claude while he tried to get in. Unfortunately, the door was locked. Gritting his teeth, he shouldered it. Pangs of pain rattled through his torso but the door didn't shift an inch. He cursed.

There was an explosion some way behind and splinters of wood cracked against the columns surrounding the door. Claude looked back, seeing the abandoned carriage was now nothing more than a flaming shell atop a broken axle. He shouldered the door again, but it hurt more and seemed to make even less of an impact. He feared that soon bombs and bottles of flaming ether would be dropped straight down to kill anyone trying break in.

He stepped back and tried kicking the door. While this new body was stronger and much more youthful than his last, the door was a worthy opponent.

'Out of the way.' A hand gripped Claude and hauled him aside. The brutish assassin barged the wood with his brawny mass. The door shifted an inch, splintering and cracking in protest.

Claude tucked himself to the back of one of the columns and watched the brute work. His clothes were blackened with soot, but he looked uninjured, assumedly finding his courage and purpose moments before the abandoned carriage had been destroyed. All in all, it took him only three attempts to break the wood around the lock. The big door shunted inwards, stopping against a barricade on the inside. Claude moved out from shelter to help push. He likely didn't add much to the brute's efforts, but the door was shoved open by their combined labour nonetheless, a bureau inside humming as its feet scraped against wooden boards.

The brute stepped inside first. Then, before Claude could follow, another man slipped through the doorway.

'This is more like it.' Elias rounded in the foyer, beaming. 'That massacre out there isn't assassins' work, but this is more like it. The three of us against him, that's a fair fight.'

Claude followed inside, doing his best to hide his irritation. He didn't want this pair stealing his kill. Yet again, the brute had certain uses.

'We should split up.' He decided on a course of action. 'We'll sweep each floor and check every room. That way the False Butcher can't slip from our grasp. Elias, you take the ground floor.'

He pointed to the big brute, realising that he had never bothered to commit his name to memory. 'You take the first. I'll head up to the second. Once your floors are clear, head up to the third and fourth in turn. Alright?'

'Alright.' The brute cracked his knuckles.

'If you see the False Butcher, shout and we'll all come running.' Claude headed for the stairs with the brute at his side while Elias kicked through a door behind the reception desk. The pair moved up the stairs quickly and separated at the first floor. Claude offered a parting, 'Good luck.'

The brute would certainly need it if he hoped to be first to the kill. Claude hurried up the stairs and paused when he reached the second floor. He cast a cursory glance down the corridor, spying another staircase at the far end. He had only to hope William wouldn't be fleeing down that one while he still climbed up.

Considering the second floor cleared, he continued upwards. He knew William was right at the top of the building and he would be heading straight to him. For the most part, his floor clearing plan had been for the purpose of delaying the other two and keeping William for himself.

He made the third floor and stopped to take a breath while he peered down the long corridor. He wasn't going to waste any time searching all the rooms, but it was prudent to at least glance down the corridor for traps or opened doors. William would have an escape route somewhere.

Just as he was about to turn and make his way up to the fourth floor, the brute appeared on the staircase at the far end. It seemed, despite his thick skull, he had seen through Claude's ruse. Either that, or simply decided to betray the terms off his own back. The brute paused upon seeing Claude, his expression like that of a young boy caught stealing sugared biscuits from his grandmother's pantry.

'I think he's on the top floor,' the brute grunted, awkwardly. 'We should head up, get him together.'

Claude nodded and mounted the stairs. He had been somewhat shocked that the assassin had disobeyed him like that, though he supposed the brute knew him only as Claude Montgomery and not Lord Beechworth. He didn't command the same respect that he used to, and that would take some acclimation.

As his feet thumped from step to step, Claude considered that maybe he should have just killed the brute then and there. It wouldn't do to have competition and he could definitely take William out alone. He stopped as he reached the fourth floor and readied his rifle. He would shoot the brute to ensure no further interference, but as he sighted up, he spied the man's legs disappearing up the stairs to the fifth floor.

'Hells' fire,' Claude cursed. The brute was damned fast; at this rate he would reach William far sooner.

Claude slung the rifle strap over his shoulder and doubled his efforts, taking the stairs two at a time, and not pausing to peer down the fifth floor corridor. The sixth and seventh floors passed in a blur, though Claude did have to pause as he passed the eighth. One of the doors in the corridor was open, light spilling in. That had to be William's escape route. He considered detouring that way, but if William was still above, Claude couldn't leave him to be killed by the brute.

Rushing to the top floor, he found the corridor was empty, but a few doors had been kicked in at the far end. He advanced on them, readying his rifle. There was a gunshot from one of the rooms then, and William and the brute staggered into the corridor.

The brute pinned William against the wall and punched, but William managed to shimmy downwards and the fist cracked into plaster. The brute roared like a beast and delved his hand into a rear pocket. He produced a small folding knife and rotated the blade out with his thumb. He raised it high, ready to cut the fight short with a downward strike on William's neck. The False Butcher was similarly scrabbling for a pistol at his hip, hoping to end the tussle in his favour.

Claude raised his rifle to finish William before the brute got the chance, but a flare of pain in his head screwed his eyes shut and made him stagger against the wall. He gagged on the sudden agony of it and when he opened his eyes, his vision was grey and murky. He could swear he heard distant voices, but reassured himself it was blood rushing in his ears.

There was a shot as William found the trigger of his pistol. The brute gasped and staggered back, splitting in two as Claude's vision worsened. Claude suddenly felt very sick and off balance, like he had stepped onto the deck of a storm-faring galley. He pressed his hand to the wall and retched.

'Why?' He found himself gasping out. Was this because he was about to lose out on killing William?

If the ache in his head stopped and his vision returned to normal, he could just take the shot and be done with it. Another pain needled at his frontal lobes as the brute recovered from the gunshot; it appeared the bullet had only grazed his thigh. Both his dancing images shuffled towards William's split visage, brandishing the knife.

Claude raised his rifle again and squinted to focus. He had to kill William before the brute. This revenge had to be his own.

He could hear someone shouting distantly. It was perhaps Elias or one of the others advancing up the stairwell. He didn't want to compete with yet more assassins.

Then the words came clear.

*You shouldn't be doing this,* a voice hissed though him, the same one that had disturbed him on the cathedral roof, only this time he didn't hear it with his ears. The voice came from within, like an unwanted thought bubbling to the surface.

This had to end right now. Gritting his teeth against the pain, Claude followed the swimming silhouette of the False Butcher. He pulled the trigger.

# 1683
## WILLIAM OF FAIRSHORE

'Yes!' William hissed the exclamation under his breath, clenching his fist in celebration.

It had been a stroke of genius on Gwyneth's part to transport all their spare powder from the abandoned carriage, and though he had argued against it at first, it had clearly been the right decision. While William had thought his pursuers might have encircled the carriage, it had proven too intimidating, so had pushed the arriving assassins right to the edges of the square to avoid it. It had been this that Gwyneth had anticipated, so she had William and Goldin hide the powder accordingly.

Goldin's first thrown bomb had landed on the threshold of an eatery, not only igniting itself, but the spare powder too. The subsequent explosion had torn through a good third of the assassins' forces and the rest were disorientated and disorganised. William had taken a particular pleasure in seeing the body of Yves Kaplan fly across the square like a child's discarded doll. It wasn't often that William enjoyed the killing of another, but this man had brought a small army to his door.

As Goldin and Gwyneth fired into the bewildered assassins below, William's thoughts turned back to his own survival. He quickly used his flintlock to strike sparks over the rag in a pre-prepared bottle of ether and tossed it down to the street. He had a three shot rifle and his two pistols, which meant he could take out seven men without reloading if perfectly accurate. He pushed up, leant on the balcony wall, and started firing.

He killed or maimed at least five with his first volley. It took far too long to reload all three weapons at once, and he started to fear that if he didn't keep the pressure on the assassins below, they might gain their bearings and start advancing on his hotel. He paused before sliding another cartridge into his silver flintlock and lit a rag trailing from an ether bottle. He threw it over his shoulder, trusting it would land somewhere useful in the chaos below and buy him more time.

Once he was ready, he holstered his flintlocks and continued with the rifle alone. Granted he could only take three shots each time, but reloading would be significantly faster. He killed eight assassins in such a way, dipping in and out of cover. As he ducked to reload the third time, a bullet struck the façade to his left, kicking out dust and chips of coloured render – the assassins had recovered from the initial ambush and were fighting back.

William used the hammer on his rifle to ignite the fuse on his final grenade. He tossed it over the balcony and watched through the ivy as it landed and rolled under the abandoned carriage, exploding it in a shower of smoke and splinters. As far as he could tell, nobody was killed. He cursed and reloaded his rifle.

By the time he peered out of his cover again, he could see men barging into the door of Goldin's hotel. He shot a couple, but there were still more kicking and beating at the wood like crazed beasts. It could only hold for so long. Throwing down the rifle, William pulled out Silvio's revolver and loosed three shots. He hit two more, and prayed that would grant him enough time to reload.

Fingers working quickly, he wondered how likely it would be that men were forcing their way into his own hotel. Perhaps he should have saved his ether bottle to cover the doors below in flame, but what was done was done. It was better to not risk staying much longer. He would finish those trying to break into Goldin's hotel, then flee from his own vantage. Hopefully, a great enough blow had been struck against the assassins already that when they finally got in here to find him gone, they would give up chase in favour of tending their wounded.

When he raised to shoot, another two men had joined those breaking down Goldin's door. William killed one and ducked back to avoid any retort. Once he popped up again, he thought he heard something behind him: footsteps thumping down the hallway.

Just as the men below broke through the door into Goldin's hotel, William turned away from the balcony. There was nothing he could do now. Hurrying into the suite, its scent of rose petal perfumes still detectable above the acrid smoke, he could definitely hear footsteps. The Hunt had broken into his hotel. If they were coming in force, he was certainly dead.

He had put up a good fight in the end, and those who came to kill him would definitely have a story to tell of how hard it had been to finish William of Fairshore. It was a fallow year after all, and it was tradition to go a little over the top. At least he would be remembered, even if the light shone on him wasn't so favourable.

Dashing for the door, he was about to charge into the corridor and take the advancing assassins head-on when someone else burst in. It was an enormous assassin, who roared and lunged with thick, meaty arms. William tried to raise his rifle, but the brute was on him so fast he couldn't extend it between them. The shock of the collision made him squeeze the trigger. A bullet smashed into an unlit oil lamp.

The brute wrangled William around and tried to get an arm about his neck. He was so unbelievably strong that William was powerless to stop him. He kicked out and swung uselessly with the butt of his rifle. While he didn't cause any actual damage, it enraged the brute. The man released him to tear the rifle from his grip and hurled it out of the window.

William took this brief opportunity outside the brute's grip to run for the door. He barely made it three yards before the man was upon him again. They burst into the corridor together, the brute smashing him against the far wall. He was winded and left gagging, but still had enough sense to duck a fist. The assassin's knuckles collided with the wall and he brought them away bloody. William could only think what damage it might have done had he not gotten out of the way.

The brute scrambled to unfold a flick knife and William fought with the catch on his holster. It was usually so easy, but in staring down his own death, his fingers became numb. In the end, he managed to slip the pistol free and fire a heartbeat before the brute could plunge the blade into his neck. His haste had cost him though, and the shot hadn't been the decisive victory he had hoped for. It barely grazed the man's thigh.

As the brute swallowed his pain, William searched frantically for an escape. While he had expected countless men to be advancing on him from all sides, he only found one. It was somehow more intimidating than a crowd of faceless killers – this one he knew.

The gunman from the New Gods' Cathedral, who had seemed so set on killing him, was stood watching his bout with the brute. He was shaking with rage. His eyes were bloodshot, veins stood prominent on his temple, and his nose bled freely. From the way his teeth were gritted, it looked as though his head might burst from the pressure of it, and he was aiming a rifle right at William.

The brute lunged, William ducked, and the gunman swayed and shot. With the intervention of some benevolent god, or perhaps his very own guardian angel, in the next moment William didn't find himself dead. The brute's head exploded as the long-range rifle punched a hole in it from only paces away.

William panted, locking eyes with the bloodshot gunman. He looked almost as surprised as William, and staggered, leaning against the wall for support. He started speaking through breathy exhalations, but it didn't seem to be directed at William. All he kept repeating was: 'Why, *why?*'

William fled, hurtling for the far stairs. Only two flights and he could be out through the hole blasted in the side of the building and away across the rooftops. He hoped Goldin and Gwyneth's escapes were going more smoothly than his own. He didn't imagine that, despite their initial success, they would be defeating the hunters that day.

Rounding to take the next flight, he could see the bloodshot gunman had rallied and was pursuing him like a devil, rifle ready. William leapt to get himself out of the firing line, landing at the bottom of the next staircase and sprawling onto all fours. He picked himself up quickly and sprinted down the corridor, following his planned escape route.

He shouldered through a half-open door; the handle punched a hole in the plastered wall. The room was nicely kept, with twin beds, and an airy, bright aesthetic, especially now that half the wall had been blasted away. William shut the door and put his back to it. He shoved a paper cartridge into his silver flintlock and considered waiting for the bloodshot killer to follow him in. As his last hotel room brawl hadn't gone too well, he decided a swift escape would be the better option.

He dashed across the room and leapt out of the powder-blasted hole. There was a small gap between the hotel and the adjacent roof, but he cleared that easily, landing on the apex. As his feet hit the tiles, one kinked over, sending a jolt of pain through him. He collapsed onto his knees to take the weight and prevent any further damage. His chest thumped onto the ridge and as the pressure was alleviated from his ankle, the flintlock slipped from his grip. It skittered down the terracotta and was caught in a lead gutter.

He spat a curse and looked back.

The bloodshot assassin was in the blackened hole in the side of the hotel, toying with his rifle. William wouldn't have time to retrieve his pistol. He scrambled along the roof, thanking the gods that he had managed to save his ankle from being lamed.

'There's nowhere left to run.' The bloodshot assassin cackled.

William reached the end of the apex and flopped onto a lower flat roof. He was followed by a shower of terracotta shards; a shot from his pursuer's rifle must have missed him by inches, but he was still alive. His landing, however, wasn't particularly elegant, and his shoulder struck a small tin chimney protruding from the roof.

He gritted his teeth through the pain and righted himself, desperate for somewhere to hide. It seemed that the bloodshot assassin had been right – from here there was nowhere to go. He couldn't likely flee across the rooftops with the rifleman watching him from a vantage, and a drop to the street from this height would be far too perilous. There was nothing between him and the cobbles except six storeys of smoky air. He swallowed, realising his fate was sealed.

'Hands up.'

William raised his palms slowly, turning to see the bloodshot assassin stood on the tiled roof above; he was wielding William's silver flintlock.

'Move over there.' The man gestured to the far side of the flat roof. 'I want to savour this.'

William did as he was told, shuffled away, but kept his eyes on the strange assassin. The man hopped down onto the flat roof and landed with a grunt; for a moment he came off balance and raised one hand to pinch at his eyes. Blood was still streaming from his nose, and was now trailing from his ears. But before William had the chance to capitalise, the man raised the flintlock, unseeing, and waved it in his direction.

'Don't even try it.' The gunman grimaced, smearing the blood from his nose and forcing his eyes open. He took two steps closer, the silver flintlock waving about madly. He spoke in a whisper then, but it didn't seem as though he was addressing William. 'This is what you want.'

Spittle hissed between his teeth. Blood flowed from his nose, across his scarred lip, and turned pink as it spread over clenched teeth. 'This is what *I* want. Let me be done with it.'

William considered charging at the gunman, or perhaps taking the time to leap from the roof while he was distracted in his madness. With that flintlock at such close proximity, he knew it would be certain death. Perhaps, however, he could talk his way out.

'I–' William started to speak, but he was cut off by the bloodshot assassin lunging forwards.

'Let me be done with it!' the man screamed, pressing the barrel under William's chin.

William staggered backwards, fell against the low wall around the flat roof. His head dangled over the edge. The mad gunman's weight was on top of him. He could see yet more assassins arriving in the blown-out mouth of the tall hotel. A few made the leap for the vaulted roof. William knew that he was finished, but he couldn't bear it being drawn out. It was better for it to be over.

'Do it, then!' he snarled at the rabid assassin atop him. 'Don't just taunt me. Fucking kill me!'

The bloodshot gunman pressed the pistol harder into William's throat. The muzzle was quivering against his windpipe. William felt the man's hand tremble as if it took pounds of pressure to pull back the trigger.

'I can't.' The bloodshot assassin let out a strangled breath as the pressure eased from William. 'I want to, but I simply can't. He won't let me.'

William struggled to get away, but the man had him pinned well.

Blood-swirled spittle sprayed out as the mad assassin snarled and pressed the barrel again to William's forehead. His finger tensed on the trigger. The pistol was degrees from firing, but the gunman's finger seemed unable to edge back quite far enough.

'Obey me,' the gunman growled, body shuddering with exertion. 'Let me kill this boy; it's what we both want.'

William saw the other assassins arrive at the edge of the slanted roof. Four of them in all, and all seemed far more determined and sound of mind than their companion. They watched the agonising struggle. Moments later, as William still hadn't been put out of his misery, they shared a word and decided amongst themselves to kill William and the gunman both.

'I hate to do this to a companion.' One of the assassins readied a rifle solemnly. 'But we're here to get a job done.'

'If you're not going to kill me,' William hissed, 'at least kill them. Or give my pistol back and let me do it myself.'

Tears spilled from the gunman's eyes as he strained harder.

'If you haven't the stomach to kill the False Butcher, you have to make way for those that do,' the rifle-toting assassin concluded.

'It's not *your* pistol.' Something changed in the bloodshot gunman. His pupils narrowed to pinpricks a moment, then widened once more as they regained focus. His hands stopped quivering, as if whatever ailed him had been beaten. Then he grinned, a wild, wicked grin. His bloodshot eyes and blood-smeared canines gleamed in the glow of fire from the street below. 'It's mine.'

Just then, the bloodshot gunman rolled off of William and spun with the silver flintlock. The motion provoked the rifle-toting assassin to fire, but the bullet clipped the flat roof wall by William's head. The silver flintlock retorted, blasting the smirk off the assassin and sending him tumbling from the vaulted roof. The bloodshot gunman leapt up, seeming to have more energy now than ever. He tucked the silver flintlock under his belt and pulled the rifle from the strap on his shoulder, shooting another of the remaining hunters.

William scrambled up, unsure of what to do or where to go. He couldn't tear his eyes away from his attackers and he couldn't jump for the street without looking. With little other option, he delved for brass bullets in his pockets, found two, and slipped them into Silvio's revolver.

The bloodshot gunman started cackling and surged forwards with the fluidity of a drunken boxer, tossing his rifle up and catching it again by the barrel. The third assassin had been torn between shooting his mad companion and ending William, and by the time he had realised who posed the greater threat, it was too late. The bloodshot gunman swung his rifle like a bat, cracking the stock into the assassin's shin and snapping it clean in two. The leg buckled and the assassin dropped to the tiles, slid down, and fell to the street shortly after.

William snapped Silvio's pistol closed, caught in a similar predicament to the assassin whose leg was just smashed. His only advantage was having one bullet for each assailant. The last assassin caught a bullet first, having raised a pistol to secure the kill of his target. William watched him slump backwards, dead, before he turned his final shot for the bloodshot gunman.

'That was brilliant!' The gunman rounded on William, arms spread like he was greeting an old friend. He dropped his empty rifle and came closer. William would have killed him then and there if it hadn't been for the man's wholly different, almost cheery demeanour.

The gunman offered a hand to shake.

William didn't understand, but his gut told him not to shoot the man who had been trying to kill him only moments before. He swapped Silvio's revolver to his off hand, keeping it close just in case, and shook the bloodshot gunman's hand.

'I'm... William. And you are?'

'I'm not completely certain, but, for now, call me... Terrowin.' He grinned. 'We should get out of here.'

Without another word, the bloodshot gunman shoved William towards the wall and crouched to offer him a boost back up. The only way to safety was back through the hotel.

William scowled. This man was perhaps the most deranged he had ever met, but for the time being they were allies, and he could do with as many as he could get right now. Setting his boot on Terrowin's palm, William clambered onto the roof and helped his strange new ally up.

Across the square, he was heartened to see that Goldin and Gwyneth had done well. The pair had managed to keep their hotels from being breached by dropping flaming ether bombs as he had failed to do himself, and though the buildings were now burned, he could see the rope strung across the square that they had used to escape. Below, only a handful of assassins were left alive and most were injured or dazed. Whatever enthusiasm there had been for battle was all but gone. Most were slumped in the wreckage, staring blankly from the horror of it all.

Returning cautiously through the hotel, picking off a few would-be hunters as they went, William and Terrowin made their way through the kitchens and into a quiet alleyway. As they returned to the square, the last of the assassins had either been killed from on-high by Goldin and Gwyneth – posted up in a new vantage – or had taken their chance to flee. A handful could be seen shuffling away down the main road.

'That was exciting, wasn't it?' Terrowin tucked the silver flintlock under his belt and dusted off his hands.

'I'm not sure exciting is the word I would use to describe the last hour.' William rubbed his forehead, trying to clear the ghostly feeling of the pistol muzzle and his brush with death. 'Harrowing or terrifying, maybe.'

'Oh, lighten up.' Terrowin smirked. 'That bit when I had you pinned down was good though, wasn't it? Thought I was going to kill you for a second there. Claude nearly cried when I stopped him.'

William cleared his throat, wondering whether it would be prudent to shoot this madman before he became a problem again. He decided not to, opting instead to sit himself on a piece of rubble near the centre of the square.

'You catch your breath.' Terrowin scowled down the road. 'I'll make sure the survivors aren't regrouping.'

William didn't think they would, the Hunt had suffered enough losses for one day, but he supposed it was better to be certain. He, however, didn't have the energy. He thanked Terrowin and watched as the man strolled off.

When he was alone, William took a breath. He had survived almost certain death; it was a strangely calming experience. Ever since he had fallen into the estuary in Fairshore he had felt like he was treading water, merely fighting for his life. First, it was the slavery. Then, it was being forced to kill by Ojo. After that, it had been loneliness and desperation. He had entered the Man-Butcher Prize and never truly expected to live through it. More recently, it was the shock of losing Vesta, followed swiftly by the Finchley onslaught. Obviously the Falade contract had been a mistake. But here he was, on the other side of it all.

He had money, which meant he had the power to fight the tide that kept dragging him back down. And for the first time, he felt like he had a chance to breathe. The Hunt was defeated and the imperials could be miles away. Granted, he had his fair share of emotional baggage, but he could haul that across the border, and start again in Scold or maybe the Far East. He and Gwyneth and Goldin could take their money, buy a modest house, and maybe take up work doing something more fulfilling. He might even do some good.

'William!' Gwyneth shouted down from her vantage. 'To the south! The imperials are coming.'

William's heart sank. He had dragged himself out of the ocean, only to find himself on a barren island. The gods didn't see fit to allow him any respite just yet.

'There're bloody thousands of them,' Goldin echoed. 'There won't be any fighting these. We need to get away. Now!'

William was about to ask for more details, but they had already disappeared inside to hurry back to the street. Terrowin was returning to the square too, and William called out to him. 'See if you can find a living horse in this mess.'

'Aye.' Terrowin gave a cheeky salute and scaled a smouldering carriage for a better view.

Though William knew his only course of action was to run, he had to see the advancing army for himself. Information like their exact number, or a precise measure of how far from the town they were could prove vital in a successful escape. He moved towards the closest hotel; if he went back to his balcony, he could get all the information he needed and not lose much time.

As he neared the smashed-in door, a young man stepped out from the shadows, and before William had the chance to react, raised a slender flintlock. There was a puff of smoke and William felt a thump in his chest. That was it, a thump. At first, William didn't think he had been all that badly hurt, but as he staggered backwards, his hand came away bloody and his legs buckled.

He heard Terrowin approach, though he was certain it was too late.

'Claude.' The young man addressed Terrowin, and looked down at his pistol, awed. 'I did it. I killed the False Butcher.'

'Elias, you fucking idiot.' Terrowin's boots skidded on the slabs next to William. 'What did you do that for?'

'I— what do you mean?' Elias stuttered. 'It's what we came here for.'

Terrowin's only reply was a gunshot. A body hit the ground.

William gasped like a fish, beached on his barren island. His hand clutched at his chest. He heard Gwyneth call out, more footsteps approaching. Then Terrowin tore open his shirt and started prodding at the coldly numb area.

'Is he—?' Gwyneth arrived at his side.

'Not yet.' Terrowin reached around William's back. 'But he'll bleed out soon enough. The bullet went straight through, good news if we had a field surgeon... as we don't...'

'My uncle has a field surgeon.' Gwyneth shifted around so that William could see her. 'We'll get you to him and he'll make it right.'

'Gwyneth.' It was Goldin. 'They'll be long gone by now and they're only getting further away. I'm afraid there's not much we can do, gods be damned.'

Something smashed nearby. William thought he heard Goldin start to sob, but the little man moved out of earshot as more things began to break and shatter.

'Claude has an idea,' Terrowin commented calmly. 'He must be coming around to my way of thinking.'

'Who's Claude?' Gwyneth started to ask, but clearly thought it unimportant. 'What can we do?'

'Well…' Terrowin swallowed. 'There's a whole army of imperials coming this way. They'll be wanting to take William alive for hanging, and they'll definitely have a decent surgeon or two.'

As William drifted from consciousness, he wondered if he could hear the rhythmic tramping of imperial troops drawing closer, or if it was simply his heart pounding in his ears, pushing blood out of his weeping wounds. The last thing he heard was an exchange between Gwyneth and the strange gunman.

'You want us to leave him for the imperials?'

'No.' Terrowin let out a breathy giggle. 'I want to take him right to them.'

# EPILOGUE

## 1683
### WALTER PERRIN

'I think Baradus was on to something before.' Walter felt like the committee was finally getting somewhere after far too long spent planning nothing. 'These powder-free zones might provide just the kick next year's Prize requires. It's been too long since we saw a good sword fight.'

'I agree, but I have a little something to add.' The Amarian Swordmistress leant forward on her elbows. 'I've been thinking about the logistics of it for a while, but I never found the solution. That is, until Baradus suggested his powder-free zones.'

'The logistics of what?' Barber smirked. Walter knew the pair often shared lunch, so this was no doubt a leading question.

'Well, we only advertise the Prize within the Vitulan Empire. Strange, I would say, given that we are unaffiliated.' She shrugged. 'What if we sent fliers to Nok, Stark, Marjore, and of course The Amaris Isles? We might see attendance ten times that of last year. And with these powder-free zones, sword principals from the east might be more inclined to compete.'

Walter stroked his chin. This was quite possibly the most ambitious idea anyone had posited yet; he liked it. From the faces around the table, he could see all the other committee members were in favour too. All except one, that was.

'I want another drink.' William Cholmondeley tossed his ale glass onto the long table. It spun on its edge a way, but ultimately stopped upright. 'And one of your tonics, Barber. My leg is awfully pained today.'

Walter pursed his lips and exhaled slowly from his nose. He hadn't a clue what had come over him when he had allowed the brat of a man-butcher to join the prize committee. No, it was worse than that. He did know why he'd done it. It was for pity, because the boy had been shot in the thigh by Beechworth. Now, after countless meetings with the little snot, he didn't think he'd be able to sum up an ounce of pity even if the boy was being burned at the stake.

'Someone get him a drink,' Walter sighed, hoping to get proceedings back on track without further upset. He spied one of his clerks passing the door and flagged him down, praying a little liquor might placate the boy for a while. 'A large one, please, Cyril.'

'Not a large one,' William harrumphed. 'It goes stale too quickly. I'll just have a half pint and whoever it is can make an extra trip when I'm done.'

'Very well; a half.' Walter waved off the clerk. 'Now, as I was saying.'

'And the tonic,' William interrupted again. 'Barber, are you going to send off for one?'

Barber looked at Walter. He plainly wanted to say no.

There wasn't a man or woman in the chamber who wouldn't delight in seeing the little upstart in pain, but they each knew the value he held. He had to be nurtured, he had to recover, he had to be trained, and he had to be made a success. Man-butchers were supposed to be the best assassins there were. If this one simply faded into obscurity, or was killed before he could complete any high-profile contracts, it would discourage others from competing for future prizes. The Guild's funds would surely wane as a result.

'I'll send someone, presently.' Barber nodded to one of his dead-eyed assistants, who was lurking in the corner of the room. Though the looming shell seemed mostly vacant, it must have gotten the salient point, as it sloped out of the room without remark.

'Happy?' Walter raised a brow at the young Butcher.

'I wouldn't go that far.' It was William's turn to sigh this time, though it was more theatrically laboured as was the custom with adolescents.

'Good.' Walter rapped his knuckles on the table, ready to restart proceedings.

'Sir?' It was another interruption, this time from Walter's assistant in the doorway. 'There is an imperial envoy here to see you. He says it's most urgent.'

'Send him in then,' William Cholmondeley replied before Walter drew a breath to speak. 'We'll hear him out and if I don't like what he has to say, I'll put a hole in his head.'

The young man-butcher smirked, adjusting his belt so that the golden pistol at his hip was raised by degrees, glinting.

'No.' Walter tried to be stern, but he wasn't the one with a flintlock at his hip. The most violent thing he had on his person was a glass dip pen in a leather sleeve, and while it might be mightier than the sword, it was no match for a pistol. He certainly would like to jab it in the boy's neck though. 'This is the *prize committee,* and a visit from the imperial envoy is a matter for the mayor and his advisor only.'

He turned to his assistant.

'I'll meet with him in my office, presently.' Walter cringed at himself. He didn't think he had ever said "presently" before in his life, and echoing it so closely after Barber made him sound foolish. He corrected himself. 'Shortly – in my office…'

That made it worse.

'Barber, are you coming?' Walter stood and made his way to the door.

'Presently.' The shrivelled little doctor smirked as his wheeled chair was pulled across the room by a second of his addled beasts.

'Why does he get to go with you?' William Cholmondeley's whine gritted Walter's teeth.

'Because Barber is my trusted advisor and you are… hurt.' With that, Walter about turned and strode down the corridor for his office. Once inside, he quickly tidied his desk of walnut shells and stray papers, then sat. Barber was pushed in moments after, and by the time he had been taken to the corner of the room, the imperials had arrived.

The envoy was accompanied by two imposing guards. Each had a pistol and side sword, along with a set of thick iron manacles affixed to their belts. They moved into the room with the envoy and took up positions at either side of the door. Walter might have thought it threatening, but he had an entire population of killers against this man's two.

'Drink?' Walter offered.

'No. Thank you. I'm strictly here on business.' The envoy was fairly old for a man in his profession and his cheeks were gaunt. He wore a sneer openly. 'If it's all the same to you, I'd like to relay my missive and be gone.'

'Very well.' Walter gestured for the chair opposite. 'Read on.'

The envoy strode to the chair, but didn't sit down in it. He pulled a scroll of parchment from a leather tube on his belt and made a display of cracking off a wax seal with his thumbnail. Everything the man did seemed so measured and dower; Walter was now certain that whatever news the man had brought was bad. He unfurled the scroll and cleared his throat.

' *"Walter Perrin."* ' The envoy paused, smoothing down the edge of the scroll. ' *"I hope my envoy finds you well."* '

Walter inclined his head.

' *"As you are well aware, the Vitulan Empire has recently been the subject of a spate of assassinations. Namely our Emperors D'elia and Sepo Falade. We thank you for your letters, clarifying your guild's involvement in these killings—"* '

'We weren't involved,' Walter blurted. The interruption made the envoy twitch.

' *"While we believe your claims that the Guild wasn't involved in the organisation of these killings,"* ' the envoy continued, ' *"we do believe it is your members who are to blame. Failure to manage these assassins is what brings the Empire to your doorstep."* '

Walter wondered if it was too late to get a stiff drink for himself.

' *"The Empire understands both our position and yours. While you claim to simply be mayor of a town and the leader of a guild, all parties are aware that you rule the lands of Grod with the force of a monarch. As such, we will extend our generosity as though we are dealing with another legitimate nation."* ' The edge of the envoy's lip curled up. ' *"Our new empress has no desire for war at this turbulent time, though if you fail to pay reparations, you will be crushed."* '

'Reparations?' Walter swallowed, his mouth was as dry of saliva as the guild coffers were of coin.

'The reparations are lenient, something that you're no doubt pleased to hear.' The envoy shimmied the parchment in his fingers. ' *"All crimes on the part of guild management will be pardoned and a swift justice upon your guild will be avoided, all you need to do is satisfy the solitary demand of our good empress."* '

'Spit it out already.' Barber rolled his eyes.

'Hand over to my custody, with immediate effect, Emperor Falade's killer: the one known only as William.' The envoy rolled the parchment tightly and slipped it back into the leather cylinder. 'Should you fulfil this request, I will return to Vitale and take my five hundred foot soldiers with me.'

Walter smiled as if there was no problem at all. Inside he was a wreck. 'Could you give us a moment to discuss your proposal?'

'Be my guest.'

The envoy didn't move, and it didn't appear he was going to either. Walter considered sending the man out, but didn't want to push his luck. Instead, he waved Barber over, and once the doctor's chair was pushed close enough, started whispering frantically in his ear.

'What in all the hells are we going to do?'

'I like William of Fairshore, but he is on the blacklist and assassinating members of the senate is strictly off limits.' Barber was far more cool and collected; he made a good advisor. 'While it pains me to say it, we have a simple choice between a blacklisted man and the fate of the entire guild. The answer seems obvious to me.'

'That's all well and good, but this envoy wants William now. I don't even know where he is.'

'We'll just play for time.' Barber shrugged.

'And how do you suggest we do that?'

Just then, William Cholmondeley limped into the room. It appeared to have taken some effort for him to get down the corridor as he was wincing, panting, and had a hand pressed to his thigh.

'I would appreciate…' he hissed sullenly, 'if, in future, you don't omit me from such meetings.'

'Ah!' Barber's face lit up. 'Please, let me introduce you – I'm sorry my good sir, what is your name again?'

'Alberto.' The envoy nodded his head.

'Well, *Alberto.*' Barber had to pause a second to stifle a cough or perhaps a giggle. 'This is William.'

'Pleased to meet you.' William Cholmondeley offered a hand to shake.

The envoy looked at his guards, then to the Mayor of Blackbile. All it took was the slightest dip of Walter's head and the men were upon William in an instant. He was disarmed and thumped and shackled and gagged in record time. One of the strikes must have hit his wound as he crumpled and had to be hoisted up by one of the guards, mewling and crying.

'Well… that was relatively painless.' The envoy looked at Walter, his eyebrows raised. 'I'd thought you killer types would have been somewhat difficult. Regardless, it was tolerable doing business with you.'

'We can be quite accommodating when we want to be.' Barber offered a cheery wave with his three-fingered hand. 'Until next time.'

Walter watched in stunned silence as the envoy and his guards departed with his young man-butcher in tow. Once the door clicked shut, and he was certain the imperials were out of earshot, he rounded on Barber, even more frantic than before. 'What in the hells are we going to do *now?*'

'Continue the plan?' Barber seemed unperturbed. 'The way I see it, we have bought ourselves a little time. We have until the imperials realise they have the wrong William. Plenty of time to find the right one. And if William Cholmondeley gets killed in the process, no matter, we will spin a story of his greatness. It shouldn't be too hard if he dies at the hands of this new empress.'

'Right.' Walter stood and found he was a little wobbly on his feet from the shock of it all. He stumbled to his liquor shelf and took a healthy measure of whiskey straight from the decanter. 'We should send men out to find William of Fairshore then; the best we have. The fate of the Guild is resting on it now.'

Barber offered a wicked little grin. 'I'll send someone, presently.'

Thank you very much for reading, I hope you enjoyed *Crooked Empires: Vol 2 The Butcher in the Night.*

It can be very hard for self-published authors to find their audience, as such I would greatly appreciate it if you could leave a review online and share with friends and family.

William's story will conclude in

# CROOKED EMPIRES: VOL 3